EAST OF THE GIANTS

East of the Giants

A Novel

By George R. Stewart

THE BOOK CLUB

111 CHARING CROSS ROAD
LONDON W.C.2

This edition 1939

Copyright. All rights reserved

TO
THEODOSIA

ALTHOUGH incidental references are made to various historical personages, the actual characters of this novel are imaginary. Accent-marks have been used with Spanish personal names, but, in accordance with American usage, have been omitted from Californian place-names. As a reminder of the pronunciation the accent-mark has, however, been retained for San José.

PART ONE
1837–1838

CHAPTER I . . . . . APRIL 1837

WHITENESS AND STRENGTH "—the words popped into Mr Melton's mind again as he looked forward and saw Judith Hingham come on deck. Yet it was a poor way of expressing what he felt—" a vile phrase," as Polonius said. Strange, he thought, that a man like himself could spend so much of his time reading and enjoying poetry, and yet when he came to making up a poetic phrase the best he could do was " whiteness and strength." ' Strength ' was a good enough word, but ' whiteness ' was wishy-washy. Yet those were the very words which had come to him when he first saw her standing on the deck of the *Spanish Belle* in Boston harbour, as the brig at the last moment was taking on its powder-kegs, and in all the five months and some odd days of the voyage to California he had not been able to do better.

The phrase suited her too. If you looked at her hair carefully you might discover that it was yellow, but at an ordinary glance you would certainly think of it as a great mass of white. He kept wondering what impression a girl with hair like that was going to make in California. The people there might have seen that kind of hair on a man before, some Swedish or German sailor, but he would wager they had never seen such hair on a girl. It was whiter even than you expected in New England.

Apart from the hair, he would grant that she was not really pretty ; that was where the ' strength ' part of it came in—eyes grey-blue and not distinguished ; nose large, and cheek-bones a little high ; mouth and chin firm. She carried herself with a sort of ramrod stiffness, and her shoulders stuck out broad and square from the base of her neck. They were shoulders for a military cadet to be proud of. She was tall enough for a cadet too—about five feet nine, he would say.

Yes, 'strength' was her word as well as 'whiteness,' and that was a strange coupling. Black and brown and red seemed to go with strength; you thought of white along with soft things like snow, and foam, and apple-blossoms. Yet you could see strength even in her ease of movement. But it was not exactly a woman's kind of grace; it reminded him of the grace of a young sailor swinging himself aloft or of a vaquero sitting a skittish horse.

She stood some yards forward from him on the brig's deck. As she moved her head about, trying to get a glimpse of something through the thin fog-bank which lay ahead, he had a good chance to watch her, pretending at the same time that he, like her, was merely trying to catch sight of the Californian coast. He had not got tired of watching her, even in five months. Yes, she would certainly make an impression among the Californians. At the thought he felt a quick pang of bitterness.

She was wearing her bottle-green dress again, the same that she had worn when they left Boston. As a man who dealt in ladies' dress-goods, along with a hundred other commodities, Mr Melton had an eye for such things. The colour was right, for it set off her white hair magnificently. But the dressmaker should have done something to break the line of those grenadier shoulders. Anybody knew that a lady's neck-line should curve gracefully down from ear-lobe to shoulder-point.

As he looked the sunlight faded from her hair. It went, not all at once as you might blow out a candle, but deliberately and ominously, while you might count one-two, as if some one were turning down a whale-oil lamp. The brig was entering the fog-bank.

Mr Melton felt nervous. They had had a landfall at Cape Branco and another in the Strait of Le Maire, but for the last three months they had known their position only from Captain Hingham's reckonings. Mr Melton had sailed with the captain before, and had the greatest confidence in him, but still the captain's observations seemed very little evidence on which to be sure in a fog that you were sailing into Monterey Bay instead of piling up on the cliffs of the Santa Lucias. A moment later the look-out called something; orders were shouted, and the *Spanish Belle* changed course slightly. Mr Melton felt a little more nervous.

He and Judith Hingham both moved towards the larboard rail and looked forward to see what it was. In a minute, moving steadily with a light breeze, they ran by a great tree floating low in the water. It was two hundred feet long, Mr Melton estimated—twice the length of the brig. It was like an island. Surf broke upon it, and driftwood floated against it. It must have been afloat a long time, for the smaller branches were rotted off and there was barnacle growth. Gulls perched on the trunk, and flew up surprised as the brig neared them. Mr Melton felt himself shivery as he looked. That tree would have been a nice place for the brig to pile up on in the fog! Yet it seemed all of a piece. To get to California you voyaged five months and rounded Cape Horn in the storms and crossed the equator twice; then at the end the coast hid itself from you behind a fog, and where no rocks were charted a great tree lurked, waiting.

Instinctively seeking human companionship, he had moved along the rail towards the girl.

" It's the kind of tree the Californians call ' *palo colorado* '—that is, ' red tree,' " he said. " It grows along the coast close to the ocean. '*Palo*' means stick in good Spanish, but out here they use it for ' tree.' "

He stopped, disgusted at himself for his pedantry. A young girl wouldn't be interested in that. And, to tell the truth, he wasn't at all sure that the tree, now falling astern into the fog, really was of that particular variety. The words interested him, the dialect, not the tree itself.

" Do you think we'll get into the harbour to-day? " That was her only answer. Youth, he thought—she's looking ahead, while I'm wondering what would have happened if we had hit the tree. He could see by her face that she was not nervous as he was. It might be ignorance, or greater confidence in her father's seamanship, but he knew also that it was natural strength and courage. He had seen the same thing when they fought the gales off the Horn; he had huddled in corners, sea-sick and fearful and miserable, while she had gone about untroubled.

Trying to retrieve himself, he looked at his watch deliberately. It was three o'clock. Yes, he said, they might get in that evening—

provided, of course, the fog didn't get any worse. And more likely it would thin out; these fog-banks often lay off the coast, but closer in you would run into sunshine.

"I didn't think any place," she said, "could possibly be so far away from every other place as California is. I wonder if I can find anything to read in Monterey?"

"I'm afraid not; it's not a literary town. Don Enrique Godoy might have a copy of *Don Quixote*, but it would be in Spanish. My own books are all at Santa Barbara."

"That was a crazy way for mother to do, thinking that I had strained my eyes and not letting me bring anything along to read all this voyage. My eyes were as good as anyone's, but I didn't want to fight too much about it because I was putting everything into the big fight, which was to come along at all. I'm sure she did it just to get her own back on me for having us come."

She had never spoken so openly before, and Mr Melton hurriedly introduced a new subject. He did not like family fights, and between two such women as Mrs Hingham and her daughter he felt that he might well be torn to pieces.

"It was bad luck for you too," he said, "that I was bringing nothing but French books along this voyage so as to improve my French. I've picked up a little Swedish from that sailor too."

He stopped short, realizing that he was letting his hobby carry him away into being pedantic again. In the silence the brig stole on through the fog. Then came the call of a woman's voice from below:

"*Ju-u-dith!*"

Mr Melton saw his companion's face stiffen.

"Mother's calling me," she said.

As she left he noticed a gesture which he had seen her make before. She gave a quick shake of her head, so that you suddenly became conscious of her hair. Mr Melton thought of a white plume and a knight going into battle.

He felt sorry that she had had to go. He was sorry that the voyage was ended, in spite of what had happened a week ago. Perhaps he would see her once or twice while the *Spanish Belle* was trading along the coast.

The fog was still around them, but it was not very thick, and he no longer felt nervous—or, in a way, he was nervous about something else; he hoped Judith Hingham and her mother were not arguing. The *Spanish Belle* was only a hundred-foot brig, and the partitions were thin; so he knew rather more than he liked about the Hinghams' family relations. It was an old story, he supposed—mother and daughter too much alike, and both strong-minded. By Jove, there was something like that in Byron, wasn't there? How did it go? . . .

> Her father's blood before her father's face,
> Blazed up and proved her of his race.

Only here it should be 'mother,' for old Captain Peleg Hingham was a rather easy-going man—more easy-going and gentle than you would expect of a shipmaster. It was easy to imagine that what he thought of his two womenfolks coming to California didn't count for much; the argument would have been between the two women themselves.

Well, he himself had had quite a surprise when he went out to the brig in Boston harbour and found the two women already on her. He couldn't understand it then, but now he knew Judith Hingham better, and he understood. A girl like that, vigorous and eager-minded and romantic—she wouldn't want to spend all her life in a New England village. And she liked to read books about adventure and knight-errantry—Scott and the *Morte d'Arthur* and Froissart; if they had wanted her to be contented in the village they shouldn't have taught her to read. And probably the boys there would fall in love with the simpering pretty faces, and wouldn't appreciate a girl like Judith, who would be almost plain except for her hair. They would be afraid of her because she read so many books. Well, probably they themselves were just yokels who wouldn't interest an intelligent girl like Judith.

Then Mr Melton was suddenly disturbed. He, as he recollected, hadn't interested her either. By an association of ideas he turned and looked across towards a point on the starboard rail forward. That was the place where he had proposed to Judith, one evening a week ago. She had been very good about it. Later he had realized how foolish he had been. It wasn't likely that a middle-aged fellow like himself, turned thirty-seven, would attract a fine young girl like Judith, who could hardly have passed twenty-one.

Mr Melton, leaning against the rail, became keenly conscious of his own lengthy, loose-jointed, and rather ungainly body and limbs. He had no illusions that there was much romantic about either his appearance or his personality. Humbly, he really thought the more of Judith for having refused him. He would have been happy if she had said yes, but he was afraid he would not have been the husband for her.

He did not feel ashamed of himself either—successful enough as an agent in the hide-and-tallow trade, beginning to have a little money of his own to venture with now and then. And yet sometimes he felt out of place too—a man who liked to read poetry and think and dream a little—being in California, where most people couldn't even read or write their own names, and where hardly anyone but himself read a book between years' ends. It was simply, he reflected, as he gazed uselessly into the fog, that he had been out of work in Boston in '29 and a little panicky, and had been offered this California place because, thanks to his hobby of languages, he knew a little Spanish. Most changes of work merely meant, so to speak, that you were in an office in Fifth Street instead of in Eighth, but this one had taken him around Cape Horn. He liked it too—the long riding from ranch to ranch, the courteous, easy-going Californians, and the great, open country. It was a hard, primitive land, but not unfriendly. He had his books, and he did not mind the lack of other things which men called civilization. He felt oppressed now when he was back in Boston. There he had to wear a tall beaver hat, and he preferred a sombrero. In Boston you had constables and doctors; he liked the feeling of freedom which came with carrying your own pistols and your own calomel.

How long he mused he did not know. Shouts brought him to himself. There was excitement. Judith Hingham, her young face flushed with eagerness, had run up on deck and stood at the starboard rail. The *Spanish Belle* was breaking from the fog; well off to the south he saw breakers spouting about a rocky headland.

Behind it rose dark pine-covered hills which he knew for Monterey Peninsula. Old Captain Hingham had squarely hit the broad entrance to the bay. Mr Melton went to congratulate him.

In the late afternoon the breeze sank to a mere breath, and they were a weary time working down towards the town and the anchorage. They were all eager for land after five months at sea. Mr Melton stood beside Judith. She was hardly able to keep her feet still in anticipation of getting ashore. She was disappointed in the country, for as the brig came towards Point Pinos all that could be seen were the dark woods inland, the yellow strip of rock and sand along the shore, and the blue waters of the bay breaking into the white of surf.

Mr Melton explained :

"The town is around on the inside of the point. Here you must be seeing just about what the first explorers saw." He began to tell something about the early voyagers, until he saw in a moment that she was too eager with thoughts of the present to listen to him.

First of all they saw the top of the flag-pole, with a Mexican flag flying. It was a very dingy and faded flag, and the red stripe was half frayed out. Next came a little squat fort with a few cannon. Then they made out the low church-tower. But by the time the brig had worked around into sight of the town twilight had fallen and they could not see much.

A single vessel lay in the harbour—a brig of about their own size. Mr Melton recognized her.

"She's Peruvian," he said. "They run up to collect tallow; they use it for candles in the mines."

Captain Hingham brought the *Spanish Belle* to within hailing distance of the other brig, let go his anchor, and brought the five months' voyage to an end.

CHAPTER II . . . . . APRIL 1837

THAT NIGHT Judith Hingham lay in her bunk listening curiously
to a familiar sound, which she realized she had not heard for
months—the barking of dogs. They sounded just like any dogs,
but it was funny to think that if you spoke to them you would
have to talk Spanish.

But mostly as she lay awaiting sleep she thought of the day to
come. Her father would be busy with the customs, but Mr Melton
had invited her. They would go riding. He had been very polite
and formal in inviting her mother as well. But Mrs Hingham had
declined flatly. She was past getting on a horse, and she had not
much desire, in any case, to set foot on this country, which was
heathen, or Catholic at best. Next day the Mexicans would come
swarming aboard to look over the cargo, and they would un-
doubtedly steal everything that wasn't nailed down unless she was
there to watch them.

Her mother's refusal had seemed to embarrass Mr Melton, and
he had suggested that he might be able to get some Californian
lady to accompany the two of them. But this suggestion had
merely aroused her mother to the point at which Mr Melton was
cowed. What, demanded Mrs Hingham forcefully, had the world
come to when an American gentleman couldn't take care of an
American lady, whether they were married or not, without the aid
of a Roman Catholic? And Mrs Hingham, with her usual take-it-
or-leave-it manner, strode away. Mr Melton's embarrassment was
so great that Judith really felt that she should withdraw; but, as she
now admitted, she was simply too selfish to do so. Another day
on the brig was more than she could stand. It might be all right
for her mother, but after so many weeks at sea her own young
body cried out physically for firm land. Besides, there was nothing
in the world which she enjoyed more than riding; she was very
proud of having learned to ride so well, for not many New Eng-

16

land girls could; she would like to show herself off on a horse. The tongues of Monterey might waggle at her going alone—she was sure that that was what Mr Melton was afraid of—but she would go, anyway. She might see some people worth seeing too. She was tired of middle-aged Mr Melton, agreeable as he was. Perhaps it wasn't just right to be letting him take her ashore so that she might see some man who interested her more—but if she was doing wrong it couldn't be helped. Certainly she must explore this new land to which she had come. She wanted to know its smell, its texture, its height, and its depth, not merely from the deck to look at it as a flat picture, a panorama of painted canvas. She wanted to know its men and women—yes, she thought, drifting off to sleep . . . that was right . . . its men. . . .

She went on deck the first thing next morning. Shreds of the night fog still hung about, but she could see the town pretty well —not that there was much of it. It was only a village, even though it was the capital of California. Some of the houses were whitewashed and stood out cleanly; a few were two-storied, and looked spacious and comfortable; but most of them were little mud-coloured huts, roofed with what seemed to be some kind of branches. It was disappointing.

After breakfast she went on deck again, and found the customs officials just scrambling aboard. They were dressed as Mr Melton had told her all Californian gentlemen dressed—in big-brimmed hats and long cloaks of black or dark blue. Even though they had just come out in a boat, most of them had long iron spurs which clanked as they walked about the deck.

There seemed to be no hurry about business. First Mr Melton greeted them all round very formally; then he introduced Captain Hingham to three of them whom the captain had not met before. Then the captain summoned Mrs Hingham and Judith and introduced them all round. The men bowed very low and gracefully. One of them, who strangely enough was called Captain McPherson, said, "Honoured to make your acquaintance, madam," and "Honoured to make your acquaintance, miss." Judith could hardly keep from laughing, for his speech sounded just exactly what you would expect of a Scotsman who had talked Spanish so

B

long that he had almost forgotten English. The Californian gentle-men said things also when they were introduced, but Judith could not understand them. She did not even understand very well the way in which they acted. First they looked at her hair as if they did not believe it was true; next they took a long, sweeping look which began at her neck and finished at her toes. Judith had been looked over before; in Boston, or even in Appleby, men did that. But they did it when you weren't watching them, and when you turned unexpectedly and saw them at it they looked away hastily, and you could see a sort of vanishing leer on their faces. But these Californians looked you over calmly, respectfully, it seemed, and even as a matter of duty. She didn't know whether to like or to dislike it.

And she was sure the things that they said were about her; Mr Melton's being embarrassed showed that. But then her father was grinning; so the things that they were saying must be polite and complimentary. She was ill at ease, anyway, and was glad to draw off.

Her father had wine brought up, and everybody had a glass. Then Mr Melton passed a box of cigars round, and some of the gentlemen took two and some took more than two. That perhaps was not strange, Judith concluded; for she could see now that some of the handsome-looking cloaks were really very threadbare. Only after they had all lighted cigars did they settle into serious con-versation.

The talk was in Spanish, but now and then her father and Captain McPherson broke into English. Judith gathered that there had just been a revolution, as a result of which a young man called Don Juan Bautista had become Governor. It seemed to have been a young men's revolution. She imagined cavalry charges with Don Juan Bautista and his friends—Don Maryano and Don Hosay, their names seemed to be—waving swords and riding as only Californians (so Mr Melton had assured her) could ride. The three must be young and handsome. Dark, of course. She liked dark men. Perhaps they would look like Lord Byron in the engravings. They were not old or middle-aged, like these customs officers; they would not smell of tobacco—at least, not more than was manly—and not at all of garlic; and they would not have bad teeth and dirt under their finger-nails the way some of these customs officers had.

But Judith understood so little of the talk that she lost interest and began looking at the view again. Except for the town everything was really very beautiful. There were bright-green meadows with pine-trees on the hills beyond them. But something was lacking, and after a moment she realized that she was missing the sight of cultivated fields. It was queer for a village not to have some farms about it. Then she remembered that California was given over to great tracts of cattle-country called 'ranchos,' where men called 'vaqueros' herded the cattle. Mr Melton had told her about these vaqueros; they were great riders, and they caught cattle in a curious and almost incredible way—by throwing a noosed rope. She would like to see it done.

Beyond the crazily scattered houses of the village the big pine-covered hills looked surprisingly like New England. To the south everything looked home-like too, for there she saw sand-dunes that might have been on Cape Cod. Northward was nothing except familiar-looking and very blue water. But to the east, far across the bay, she made out strange, yellowish cliffs along the water, with no hills behind. There, building upon what Mr Melton had told her, she felt the suggestion of open plains, wind-swept and treeless —a land of noose-throwing horsemen, mysterious and frightening to a girl who had known only the wooded hills and little fields of New England.

After a while Mr Melton came to tell her that he had arranged for the two of them to go ashore.

Judith went to her cabin and put on a close-fitting bonnet which covered up her hair almost completely; she was tired of being stared at by all and sundry. But she found herself thinking that if she saw anybody whom she really wanted to look at her she could easily find an excuse to take the bonnet off.

As soon as a horseman with two led horses appeared on the beach she and Mr Milton hurried into the boat. When the boat grounded in a foot and a half of water with little waves flopping on the beach Judith wondered for a moment how she was going

to get ashore. She stood up uncertainly. Then a big sailor called
Farn was in the water and leaning in over the gunwale. He put
one arm behind her knees and the other around her back, and
before she knew what was happening he was splashing through the
water holding her against him. Her heart flip-flopped once or
twice, for it was a strange sensation to have a man holding you
so intimately and without even so much as by your leave. He held
her very tightly, and she felt correspondingly helpless; his arm was
clear around hers, pinioning it to her body, and she could feel his
big fingers close to her right breast. For a moment she liked the
feeling; then she recollected that Farn had two front teeth broken
off down to the stubs and all the rest of his teeth stained brown
with tobacco juice. A few seconds later he set her on the beach.
She thanked him quite matter-of-factly, but she knew she was
blushing a little. Farn grinned:

"Begging your pardon, Miss Hingham, but that's the way we
carry the Spanish ladies. No offence."

Farn brought Mr Melton in pick-a-back, but just as he got to the
shore he stumbled and fell. Mr Melton made a curiously agile
spring, and came scrambling up the sand on all fours, losing all
dignity, but getting only one leg wet. The sailors in the boat haw-
hawed, and Farn got to his feet, wet and laughing. Mr Melton
came up too, spitting sand, but grinning. He threw Farn a coin,
anyway.

"A put-up job," he said to Judith, as he was wringing water
out of his trouser-leg. "But you expect anything in California."
He fussed a little about taking his death of cold just to give some
sailors a laugh.

It was good to walk the beach while Mr Melton was inspecting
the girths. Judith felt like stretching out full length on the hard
sand just to enjoy the solid, unmoving feel of it, but she knew
that that was no way for an American lady to behave, especially
when she could see a scattered ring of village urchins surveying
her from a distance.

Mounting, they swept through the town at a gallop, their
vaquero following behind. Just as they were about to pass one of
the last houses an old man ran out shouting. They pulled in their

horses, and Mr Melton began talking. In a minute he introduced the old man as Don Federico, or, he added, "Herr Volberg."

"Herr Volberg," he went on, "teaches me German, but the
point is now that he has just brewed some beer, and he says it's
good German beer and the only good beer in California. He heard
I was going riding—everybody in Monterey knows it probably—
so he watched for me. He insists that we have a glass."

Judith had seldom drunk beer, but after her months on restricted
diet aboard the brig she suddenly felt that the beer would taste
very good. They went into Don Federico's little yard, and sat at a
little iron table with iron chairs. They had no common language
for conversation, but Mr Melton explained that Don Federico had
come on a German ship years ago, and had been left behind with
an attack of smallpox. On getting well, he had liked Monterey,
and stayed there. As for the glass of beer, that proved to be a
large stein, so that the visit lengthened out, especially since the
two men had second ones. Don Federico was still more jovial by
this time, and even took a stein out to the vaquero. Finally they
left with profuse good-byes.

They were taking the road to Mission San Carlos, and were
ascending the hill. Nevertheless, the horses moved rapidly, seeming
scarcely to know any gait slower than a gallop. The road was a
mere rough way, little travelled. The scenery, the wild rhythm
of the galloping, the sense of being ashore, all worked together
to exhilarate Judith. Even Mr Melton began to appear more
romantic; she might marry him on a morning like this if he asked
her again. She was surprised at how well he rode; he was a little
ungainly in the saddle perhaps, but there was no question about
his seat.

The country was beautiful as a park. Open glades shifted into
forest and back. In every grassy space were cattle—long-horned
and wild-looking—which raised their heads to stare belligerently
or else broke into ungainly, galloping flight. Rabbits bounded
away, and quail sprang up in sudden flight. In a glade a big deer
stared momentarily with poised head, and then with long jumps
floated into cover.

Before it seemed possible Judith knew that they had topped the hill. On the down-grade the pace grew even faster. Riding in California, Judith decided, was a race, or even a steeplechase, for her horse took puddles and rocks with great leaps. But, remembering Cape Horn, she thought she could stand it as long as Mr Melton could. He had said it was only four miles.

They pulled rein at the Mission gate, with the horses sufficiently blown to stand still without their usual curveting and pawing. Everything around the Mission was in disrepair; at the courtyard one gate was off its hinges, and the other obviously soon would be. A few dirty and half-naked Indians came to look at them, and, talking Spanish, Mr Melton learned that the priest in charge had gone to Monterey, leaving the church closed. Judith had never been so close to people wearing so few clothes, and she was surprised to find that she was not embarrassed. If she had met a man in that state in Appleby she would certainly have blushed and run for shelter. But here every one took it as a matter of course, and that seemed to be the only way for her to take it too.

They did not dismount at the Mission, but rode on towards the river. The Missions, Mr Melton explained, had been having a hard time since Mexico had separated from Spain. With the recent revolution they would fare even worse, for the Californians were land-hungry.

They came upon a grassy spot marked off by bushes and less cut up by the cattle than most places they had seen. They dismounted, and the vaquero took off the saddle-bags with the lunch. All at once Judith noticed that Mr Melton had disappeared, and glancing round sharply she saw him going behind a bush. It was not a very high bush either. Judith felt herself getting angry; Mr Melton was positively disrespectful! Then she saw the vaquero; he was still holding the horses and could not seek a bush, but the position of his blanket indicated the utmost respect. At this there was nothing to do but laugh. So she laughed and went off to a bush of her own, having still enough of New England left in her to select one farther away, and larger and thicker than Mr Melton's. She remembered the beer and the general chilliness of the day.

The vaquero, having tied up the horses, ate his lunch at a distance, and then lay down to sleep. Mr Melton did the same. Judith sat leaning against a rock, her mind buzzing with reflections upon the morning.

It was certainly a strange country, California. A man took her into his arms; Scotsmen and Germans were called ' Dons '; people went naked, and departed casually behind bushes. Her friends at Appleby and Cousin Carrie in Boston would have been profoundly shocked, she felt; but for herself, she couldn't help admitting that she rather liked it all; it was an easy-going kind of freedom; lack of freedom was what made one seem suffocated at times in Appleby. Then she wondered what new experiences the afternoon would bring forth. She would not see the new Governor, for Mr Melton said he had gone south, to what was called the ' down-country.' But perhaps they would meet other people. Judith realized that she was lonely; she needed something that Mr Melton did not supply.

Mr Melton woke up, stretching and yawning. For the ride back the horses were rested. The riders flew by the Mission so quickly that the Indians had not even time to gather. They pulled rein hard at the outskirts of Monterey, for many children were playing about, and Judith was in terror of overriding one. She thus got a better impression of the town too—or really a worse impression. The children were no better clothed than the Indians at the Mission, and most of them, in fact, looked like Indians. The streets were dirty with horse-droppings and general filth; a few pigs and many chickens roamed about; in one place a dead dog lay unnoticed. Had not the clean wind been continually sweeping through the place must have smelled.

They came on to the beach, and Mr Melton signalled to the *Spanish Belle* to send out a boat. While they were waiting two men came to talk to Mr Melton about that interminable subject, the revolution. Judith walked off a little way along the beach.

She was not thinking of anything in particular when she noticed that two vaqueros were driving a steer along the beach. The animal, in spite of its long horns and wild appearance, came docilely enough; both men had their lassos in their hands. They came opposite her, not twenty feet away, and then things happened, so all at once that she could not have told which was first. But there was the steer flat on the sand with one lasso around his horns and the other around a hind foot, and the horses standing steady with the ropes taut so that the steer couldn't move, and one vaquero getting off his horse and drawing his knife. She watched, fascinated, as he leaned down and thrust the knife into the steer's throat and gave it sawing motions back and forth, while a great horrible red burst of blood came out over his wrist and arm and ran down on the sand, and the steer gave a long wheezing moan. Then Judith felt a sensation that she had never felt before. There was a sudden coldness coming from within, not without. She felt dizzy, and shook herself to overcome it. But she was sinking into a cold, but very comfortable pool, and she was getting away from the ugly sight and sound of the steer and the blood. And she was sinking, sinking. . . .

There was a sudden bang, and the comfortable sinking feeling was gone, and she was unaccountably lying on the sand with a sickness in her stomach and a headache; she was horribly cold. Mr Melton was leaning over her with a pistol in his hand. But she couldn't lie thus on the sand even in California. It was too undignified. What was the matter with her? She raised herself on her elbow, and sat up determinedly, biting her lips. Her head ached and swam horribly; she bit her lips, took a long breath, and made her head clear a little. She drew in her feet and pulled her skirts down.

" Lie down," she heard Mr Melton saying. " You've fainted."

Yes, that must be it. She had never fainted before, but she had seen others do it. She swallowed down the sick feeling and felt better. Mr Melton held a flask to her lips, and something burned her throat. The brandy lit in her stomach with a thud; it made her sicker, but stronger too. She felt ashamed of her weakness in fainting.

Now for the first time she looked around. The boat was coming in from the brig with the men bending hard to the oars as if it were a race. On the beach one of the Californian gentlemen was berating the vaqueros roundly for having so thoughtlessly killed a 'beef' in front of a lady. The two, both Indians, stood blankly, quite unable to realize what their fault had been or why anyone should behave so strangely at the sight of blood and death. The horses still held the ropes taut; the steer she did not dare look at. The pistol in Mr Melton's hand might be accounted for by his having fired it as a signal to the boat to hurry. At a little distance she could see forming the inevitable ring of half-clothed children.

Two hours later, on board the *Spanish Belle*, Judith was eating beefsteak, and enjoying it. She did not inquire whence the fresh steak had come; the answer was too obvious. But she was young, healthy, and vigorous. An hour's lying down had restored her; another hour had brought back her appetite in time for dinner.

But it was a warning. Her pride of strength had met its fall. Never again could she feel the same disdain for Mr Melton's weakness in rounding the Horn. She had come in past Point Pinos as a conqueror to subdue the land. Had the land subdued her? Here men wore knives and pistols, and used them. It seemed a man's land, not a woman's. For that evening she felt ready to wish that the voyage back had begun, and that, in the sailor's phrase, "the Boston girls had hold of the towline."

WATCHING CARGO GO OVER THE SIDE into the boat and ashore was interesting. Sometimes she could actually see the articles; otherwise she could read the labels and see the shape of the boxes and crates and bales—bolts of cotton, bleached and unbleached, coarse and fine; bolts of velveteen, fustian, cambric, and bishop's lawn; cotton and silk handkerchiefs; cotton lace; black and blue cassimere for cloaks and shawls; flannel and linen. Besides all this cloth, the little brig seemed jammed with everything conceivable—ironware, tinware, brassware, silverware, earthenware, glassware; pots, kettles, pans, griddles; needles, thread, thimbles, patterns; boots, shoes, slippers; carpet and oilcloth; soap, perfume, combs, brushes; kegs of sherry, kegs of nails, kegs of powder; finally, to top everything, a huge four-poster bed. She wondered why the Californians couldn't make some of these things for themselves.

Most of what went ashore was Mr Melton's consignment. Mr Barnes, their own agent, came aboard the second day, and soon had the sale-room working. The boat began to bring aboard Californian ladies and gentlemen. A few had cash, but most of the dealing was in a complicated system of credit involving so many hides to be turned over at such and such a time and place. Judith was not versed in the real value of hides, but she gasped at the prices demanded in silver for even the shoddiest Boston goods.

Judith met most of the people who came aboard to make purchases, for Mr Barnes said that a social point of view helped a lot in selling goods in California; Miss Hingham's hair, now, might be worth a thousand dollars of trade a day if many gentlemen came aboard. Thereupon Judith decided she didn't like that way of business, and tucked her hair up more closely than ever under her bonnet. Nevertheless, she always went to meet the Californians, for it was the chief amusement she had. (Mr Melton was still living on board, but had not asked her to go riding again; he

was much too busy—or else he didn't think she should go un-
chaperoned.) She rather liked the Californians. The children had
big brown eyes, and hid shyly. The mothers were fat, and looked
jolly, and talked a great deal. The fathers were dark and often
handsome, but they generally seemed small to h:r. Every one of
decent age was married, and some even of indecent age. Girls of
fifteen and sixteen, and boys who didn't look more than eighteen
would turn out to have a child or two. Business usually took a
long time, for first Mr Barnes would pass round glasses of port or
sherry, and next cigars for the men; and then just when Judith
usually thought they were going to leave the Californians would
start buying.

But in spite of all this Judith, after a few days, found herself
bored, with many hours when she had nothing to do but sit on the
deck knitting and looking ashore, and she found that she had
exhausted the possibilities of the view, beautiful as it was. On the
beach, in the foreground, nothing much ever seemed to happen.
So she was doubly surprised on the afternoon of the fourth day
when Mr Melton, who hadn't paid much attention to her lately,
came up and said :

" Look ashore, and I think you'll see something interesting."

She looked where he pointed, and saw three horsemen riding
a-gallop, well down around the curve of the beach. All were on
bay horses. Every one galloped in California, but she saw that
these three must have let their horses out to the full. One of the
riders was about two jumps ahead and the others were neck and
neck.

" A race? " she asked.

" No, the two behind won't ever catch up, but you'll see some
good riding."

She saw what he meant, for just ahead of the riders was a spine
of rocks running down to the water, and on this side of it a little
stream made a gully. She waited to see the riders gather in their
reins to take the obstacle, but they took it full speed. One jump up,
one down, one across the water, one out of the gully—at least, that
was all it seemed—and then they were racing down the open sand
and close to the houses. Judith gasped.

" Yes, that was riding! "

"Almost any good Californians would do that, but still you won't find better riders in California than those three."

Mr Melton looked out to where the three were splashing their horses knee-deep through the water just opposite the anchorage. "Yes," he said, "now I recognize them for sure; I thought I did even at that first distance. They're Don Juan Godoy and Miguel and Ramón. The last two are Juan's vaqueros; that's why I knew they wouldn't catch up and pass their master. He's a very good friend of mine; owns Rancho Amarillo up north of here; father and mother both dead. He's cousin or something to the new Governor; in fact, I'm surprised he isn't in the South backing him up right now."

" Would he be a good backer-up? "

"For fighting, yes. And you could count on those two half-breeds to follow him anywhere too. And three good fighting men in California are worth a lot; most of these Californians in my opinion aren't worth so much in a show-down."

" Why did you say ' for fighting '? "

"Because I'm not so sure that Juan would be worth much as a diplomat or for his brains. But he has a kind of brains too. You'll probably see him this afternoon; I imagine he'll be aboard to see what Mr Barnes is offering."

" I shan't be able to understand a word he says, of course."

"Oh, yes you will! He talks excellent English. Languages are his gift; that's what I meant when I said he had a kind of brains. I envy him. He talks pretty good French; he's learned more German than I have from Don Federico; he knows a little Russian that he picked up from the Fort Ross people. And the Lord knows how many Indian gibberishes he can handle! He does it all by ear, without any work." She could see that Mr Melton was wistfully envious. "But," he ended, "I think I can stump him on this Swedish I've been picking up."

Judith was in her cabin that afternoon when she heard the boat bump alongside and passengers coming aboard. As she started up to the deck she heard a new voice speaking English. It carried just the trace of a Spanish accent, giving it a soft, rolling tone.

Judith calculated the space of two breaths. She went back to her cabin, took off her bonnet, and freshened the look of her hair. "It's rather silly," she found herself thinking to her reflection in the little mirror. "When I see him close up he'll be sure to have a broken nose and smallpox pits. He's probably married. Still, he's young and speaks English. I think I've been waiting for some one like that; it may be some fun." She studied her face a second—no; too high cheek-bones and too strong a nose. She had to trust to her hair and her good carriage. She changed to the bottle-green dress; it gave contrast for her hair, and she could count upon the soft wool clinging to her a little and setting off her figure. She did not put the bonnet on again.

On deck she saw Mr Melton talking to a man who wore the usual big hat and long dark-blue cloak; below the cloak she saw deerskin leggings and shoes with shiny places on them where they had rubbed against the stirrups and stirrup-leathers. The man had his back to her, and she could get only about a quarter-view of his face. He looked young; he was talking English; he was taller than most Californians—a little taller than Judith herself. She noted coal-black hair, a firm-set jaw curving forward beneath a bronze cheek, and a high, thin nose. She stopped about ten feet behind him, knowing that Mr Melton would see her and that the young man, who was certainly Don Juan Godoy, would turn round. The distance was right for her hair and figure; he would get that impression as a whole. Why she was displaying all this art she hardly knew; it was certainly not a habit; it must be something in the Californian air or her not having seen any men of her own age and language for so long. She heard his voice, rich and well modulated.

"Just the old family business," he was saying to Mr Melton.

"Cattle, that is," said Mr Melton.

"Yes, and the other old family business too."

Judith was wondering what he meant, and then Mr Melton saw her, and things began to happen just as she had planned. The young man swung round suddenly and gracefully. After that nothing happened as she could have planned or even imagined.

She saw piercing black eyes, a high forehead with sleek black hair above, a smallish mouth half open, and even white teeth. She saw the jaw drop even lower. His eyes were full upon her, and did not sweep down in the lingering glance she had come to expect. Suddenly he spoke, not in English, but in quick Spanish, something that sounded like an oath, or a prayer. He took three quick steps forward, went on one knee, seized her right hand, and pressed it hard to his lips.

Judith felt that inner cold and a quick dizziness as if she were going to faint again. She knew that Mr Melton was introducing them, but she could hardly hear what he said. She felt herself panicky for a moment; she had not meant all of this. Then she felt herself prouder and happier than she had ever been; Juan Godoy had risen and was looking at her again; she wanted just to stand there and be looked at. There was nothing to say, and she said nothing; neither did Juan Godoy. Mr Melton, getting very red, said something about this being the person she had seen riding.

Then Judith felt her mother's arm upon hers, and heard her voice:

" I need Judith in the cabin. Will you excuse us? "

For a moment Judith wanted to resist, but she could not make a scene. She bowed, turned, and went below. She did not glance back. . . .

At supper she hardly knew where to look. They were always cramped at meals, anyway, the four of them. All the others must have seen what happened; there really wasn't anything to say about it; every one knew such things happened, or they ought to know it, at least. But was she in love? Well, she couldn't face that yet. She could see her mother in black, close-lipped indignation. She could see Mr Melton, apparently—gentle soul—in as much embarrassment as she herself. But on her father's lips she could make out now and then a certain ghost of a smile.

She went to her cabin as soon as possible. In the afternoon her thoughts had been merely a whirl—or, rather, she had had no real thoughts at all, only feelings. Now she faced herself.

He wasn't married; she was sure of that now. If so, her mother would certainly have said so at supper. And yet, in spite of all the tumult going on inside her, she could not help giggling for a

moment at the way her mother had unconsciously done just the
wrong thing, or, from Judith's point of view, just the right one.
Judith could not think what she could have done next if her
mother had not interposed. That had been the perfect ending.
Tableau, curtain! " There's a little of the theatre in everybody,"
thought Judith, " and I played that scene pretty well. But it took
mother to end it." Then she thought that her own dignified
handling of the exit was good enough too; that not looking back
was the right touch.

Yet, she thought, this was no play. In a play the actress dropped
her emotions when she entered the side-wings. Now she was feeling so hard and with such excitement that everything seemed
churning inside her. Was she in love? She was not really sure
what the expression meant, and she thought of it in terms of
books that she had read more than of her own experience. Certainly she had never felt so excited about Mr Melton or about any
boy at Appleby. Still, she said firmly, she wasn't. But she might
be if she ever saw that man again. And to see him again was what
she wanted more vividly than anything else she could think of.
If it wasn't for a strong, calculating sense of prudence she felt that
she would already have lost her head completely. But it was the
impracticality of the thing. It was unreal. It was like having seen
a picture or a statue. Really, now, you couldn't let yourself be
too much disturbed over the memory of a bronze forehead, a half-
opened mouth, two black eyes, the pressure of hand and lips upon
your hand, and a voice that blurted something which might be an
oath in Spanish. For all she knew this man might be without ears
and a left hand. She had no recollection of them. Could you
possibly be in love with a man you had seen for only two minutes?
What was the sense of it when you might never see the man
again? Besides it wasn't right—and this she felt firmly—for anyone
to be so much affected without being certain there was some return.
To be sure, Don Juan Godoy's actions might indicate some return.
But she wasn't sure. Was it anything more than just Spanish
courtesy, or even philandering? How long she sat there she had
no idea.

Mr Melton's knock roused her. " Come on deck," he said, " if you want to get a taste of one of the few really romantic things about California." He led her to the rail on the landward side, and motioned her to be silent. Everything was quiet on deck, with a steady breeze from land to carry sounds to them. Some one was singing, and Judith could just catch the faint accompaniment of the guitar.

"Serenade," said Mr Melton.

Everything fell into Judith's mood. The night was clear and beautiful; the starlight seemed to give just a suggestion of glitter to the water. The singer had a fine baritone, and the song took him well into his higher register; above the irrelevant jingle of the guitar she could feel the yearning of the lover's voice. Breaking her mood with a start, one of the sailors let out a cat-call.

"Stop it!" she heard the mate growl, and he came over to her. "Good voice, ain't it? Sings well too—but they all do out here. Prob'ly nothin' but a dirty half-breed singing to a kitchen wench, anyway."

But Mr Melton saved the wreckage of her dream.

"Oh, no, Mr Thompson—might just as well be a gentleman. When one of them falls in love he goes in all over, takes to sere-nading just as hard as anyone."

Judith's hands gripped the rail—"just as well be a gentleman." Why not? In heaven's name, *why not*! From the few words she had heard him speak she could not tell whether he was a baritone. She dared not ask now if Don Juan Godoy played a guitar. But this singer—wasn't he walking up and down the beach? Now and then she could just glimpse him, or thought she could. If he was serenading some girl of the town wouldn't he go and sing under her window?

The song ended; the guitar sounded on through a coda, and silence fell. Judith was tense.

"One of the old songs," said Mr Melton, breaking her golden moment. "They make up new verses for them to fit the occasion. He's so far away I could only catch a few words—'amor,' of course; 'blanca'—that means white; 'linda'—that's 'pretty.'"

"White!" came the mate's comment. "He must have been

meaning her teeth then; that's the only white thing about these Monterey girls."

Before Mr Melton could discover her confusion Judith paid her hurried excuses and fled below. It was useless to argue with herself how many occasions a song might have for using the word 'white.' Something deeper than argument associated that word with herself.

Once safely alone she was calmer. What pitiful little scraps of reasons she had! An ejaculation in surprised Spanish, of which she did not even know the meaning; a singer, perhaps walking the beach; a common adjective. If she only knew the customs of the country! . Even yet she dared not give rein to her own feelings. As she lay in her bunk finally what she treasured most was the memory of that look almost as of exaltation when he had turned and seen her; and he had looked directly at her—no calculating downward sweep. But could not a man look or even feel that way for a moment, and laugh about it an hour later? She had no experience by which to judge.

Her cabin was on the wrong side of the boat; listen as she might, she could hear no singing; she did not dare to go on deck again. She lay still, feeling she could never go to sleep. But her body was young and abundant in health; in ten minutes she was sleeping sound.

UNCLE ENRIQUE SQUIRMED IN HIS CHAIR, shivered slightly, and looked across most sympathetically towards his favourite nephew. Being of a thin, shivery nature, Uncle Enrique got up and put another stick of pine-wood into the fireplace; the action served also to give him time to think before answering the astounding speech which Juan Godoy had just made to him.

" What you have done," said Uncle Enrique, resuming his chair, and speaking carefully in his character as man of the world, " or perhaps I should say what has been done to you, is only what I should expect. I can say nothing of what you may have inherited from your mother's side, but the Godoys certainly were never men to fall in love slowly and with reservations. Your father "—Uncle Enrique here made a calculated gesture with his hands, throwing both palms upward to indicate complete revelation—" it is not fitting that I should talk to you about your father's passages with love. But even I "—he paused, letting thoughts of Mexico City and the Señorita Yáñez y Alvarado flash into his mind—" even I "—this time he raised his right hand and moved it in a circle to indicate dizziness symbolic of a grand passion—" yes, yes, I am a dried-up, little old man now, but once—if I may quote Horace to my ends— ' Non sum qualis eram bonae sub regno Cynarae.' "

" Amo, amas, amat," said Juan shortly and ironically. " That's all the Latin I know to answer you by. Why do you always talk in the only language you know that I don't? Talk Spanish! "

" You hardly speak with the reverence due by courtesy to an older kinsman—but then you never do. If I had not known that you had uttered all the Latin you knew I should have said that you summed up the situation in three epigrammatic words. What more to say! I love; you love; he, she (we may omit it) loves! In our situation the questionable case is the third person feminine— she. I could quote Horace at this point too, but it would irritate you."

He could make out Juan's handsome face glowering darkly in the pale light of the fog-covered morning; he saw that any more baiting would be dangerous. Actually he knew that he would do anything short of highway robbery to help his nephew out of what looked like a very bad fix. But at the same time he did not know what to do about it. His reputation as man of the world was high in Monterey, but it was based slenderly upon his having spent a year of his youth in Mexico City. People came to him for all sorts of advice, and that was why Uncle Enrique—rather roguishly, he considered—had come to talk of himself as an old man, although he was only forty-five. But he at least knew the value of sparring for time; so now he commenced rolling a cigarette, and passed the materials to his nephew.

Juan scowled at the cigarette paper. " What's the matter with this paper? It has dirty marks on it."

" If you had pursued your education more assiduously," said Uncle Enrique with ironic suavity, " you would see that those marks are the famous Phœnician characters known as the alphabet. In brief, there being between arrivals of ships a paper shortage, I passed over to the schoolmaster some paper, stipulating that he return it to me after use. Some other gentlemen did the same. Now, having cut the paper into suitable sizes, we smoke "—he paused, and with mock unctuousness blew a large ring—" and at the same time feel virtuous as patrons of education."

" What's the use of teaching so many people to write, anyway? " Juan was in no mood for suavity.

" Ah, there, my nephew, you seem to agree with the ancient Persians—to offer another allusion. Their gentlemen took as their education—' to ride, to tell the truth, and to shoot with the bow.' No mention of reading and writing. We Californians, being a pastoral, horse-loving people, resemble the Persians. You yourself now. You can certainly ride; I believe in your truthfulness. As for the bow—you leave that to the Indians whom you pursue. We might sum up your accomplishments : ' To ride, to tell the truth, to throw the lasso.' The list is not complete; you have also other virtues. You can, in spite of my ironic implication to the contrary, read and, after a fashion, write in Spanish and in English."

Uncle Enrique felt himself inspired by his own talking. He saw a way to approach the problem, and dropped his bantering manner sharply. He raised three fingers reflectively, as if to indicate a threefold analysis, although he had no particular three points in mind :

"Let us first, Juan, consider yourself with relation to the situation. For the first time in your life you want something you cannot —at least not immediately—get. This complete satisfaction that you have known is not the result of having had much, but of having wanted little. What have you asked of life? Horses—and you have always had more than you could ride. Food—but beef, beans, and tortillas have satisfied you. Indians to fight—and God has been gracious! A place to sleep—on a rawhide bed with a serape to cover you. Clothes and horse-trappings—but your experience was so narrow that the limits of your imagination were always well within the limits of your purse. Finally, you have wanted— I shall not say love—but something like it. You have found this when, and as——" Uncle Enrique left the topic, suddenly seeing by Juan's face that it was not the proper one for the moment. "The point is," he continued, "you must consider that what you think a great love may be only a feeling produced by a wholly unaccustomed and therefore severe failure to attain immediately what you want. In a week it may be gone." He stopped, noticing at once a heaving in Juan's chest and a little twitching of his fingers.

Juan spoke with a level voice and no suggestion of humour : "It was a good thing you stopped. I was just about to slap your face."

Uncle Enrique tut-tutted mentally. What was the family coming to? This was what two generations of a frontier ranch did. No respect for Latin, or for one's elders! Juan was certainly a barbarian, and yet a lovable one in his simplicity. Uncle Enrique was also a little ashamed of himself for what he had implied, for surely it was nothing remarkable or reprehensible that a Godoy should fall suddenly and deeply in love. It was merely embarrassing that Juan should have picked this American instead of some girl of a good Californian family. The thought of something other than such a complicated affair as marriage flitted only momentarily across his mind. No, the depth and sincerity of Juan's feelings, as well as the Señorita Hingham's position, made that doubly impossible. He returned to the problem resignedly.

"What I have said, I said partly in test; it is only honourable to your family that you should feel as you do. You may count upon me to help you. I know little—that is, not as much as I should like—of the marriage customs of Americans, but my experience of the world teaches me that a gentleman should always act as the best customs of his own country indicate. If, then, you were in love with a Californian girl I, as your only living older kinsman, would approach her parents, tactfully putting your case and asking that you be accepted as a suitor. You would continue the suit, and proving acceptable—or, at least, not inacceptable—we should go on with negotiations for a suitable dowry."

With the new direction of affairs Juan's face had lightened. His smile showed the line of his even white teeth.

"I shall ask for no dowry," he said.

"Like many young men, you are in error about the dowry. It is not a bribe to the husband. It is the daughter's just portion; without it she herself is dishonoured. But that is a later step, and does not matter now. What I purpose then is that I shall go to talk with Captain Hingham, whom I know already very pleasantly, and with his wife whom I do not know. I shall be handicapped by not knowing the English language, but I shall ask my friend Mr Melton to act as interpreter. It will be difficult "—Uncle Enrique shook his head woefully—" there will be, for instance, the matter of religion; the señorita is not a Catholic."

Juan spoke again with directness: "You may say that I shall become a heretic."

Uncle Enrique, horrified instinctively, made one motion of crossing himself, but recollected that he was anti-clerical; it had seemed as if Juan were denying his father and mother.

"But "—Uncle Enrique returned upon another angle—" it is not a question of belief—or disbelief—the civil laws are involved. It may be difficult."

"When will you go?" said Juan.

Uncle Enrique's heart warmed within him at the lover's impetuosity. " I shall go," he said, " the moment you have told me all I need to know. I can tell you now that I myself saw the señorita as she rode through town. There was some gossip about her riding unaccompanied by an older woman, but that was only the provincials—they did not realize that the ways of different people are different. Yes, I saw her." He drew himself up to his full height of five feet four, and added roguishly, " And if I had not been an old man you might have had a rival! Now tell me—have you ever talked with the señorita? "

" I said only four words to her, and those more to myself than to her." Juan's dark face took on a poetic exaltation. " As I turned round and saw the light playing about her hair I said, ' Holy mother of God! ' "

Uncle Enrique crossed himself fully. The little cynical worldly shell about his romantic heart melted completely. " Yes, yes," he said, " that is enough; I need to know no more." He was remembering what he himself had thought, yes, and said too, at that ball in Mexico City in the days of the Viceroy when he had met the Señorita Elena Yáñez y Alvarado, not knowing that she was about to be betrothed to that rich sugar-grower of Cuernavaca.

J UDITH LAY ON HER BUNK, sick with the strain of indecision. What she had been through in the last three days showed in her face a little, in heavier lines under the eyes; even her hair seemed to have lost lustre a trifle. She felt a vague sense of the injustice of destiny. Why should she in the next few minutes, upon insufficient evidence, and not even knowing for herself just what she wanted, nevertheless be forced to make a decision which in its results would carry her for years ahead and commit her into all sorts of circumstances and actions of which she had now not the slightest knowledge?

But mostly she was tense with the strain of suspense. Would she hear the bump of a boat? Or would there be a knock on her door? Or a whisper from somewhere? And what—*what* would she do?

Nevertheless, she felt all her faculties clear; she was alert with the sense of emergency. She saw the darkened outlines of her cabin furniture clear cut as at midday; she heard the lap of waves; she automatically recorded every noise on deck—few enough, now that it was past midnight. She was thinking swiftly and keenly too; the trouble was there seemed to be no answer; she merely thought round in circles.

She was dry-eyed and firm-lipped. Never during these three days, even in the solitude of her own cabin, had she shed tears or whimpered. She was proud of that; in some way she felt that California was no place for a whimpering woman.

Three days! Scarcely three. It was Tuesday morning about ten when, quite unsuspicious and incurious, she had watched little Don Enrique come aboard. Now Thursday night had just passed over into Friday morning. An analogy struck her. It was like being married : nothing much happened—only an ordinary succession of seconds; then all at once you became somebody else just as

Thursday became Friday; you could no more become again who you were before than Friday could turn back and be Thursday.

In Appleby three days meant nothing. On Tuesday perhaps you ironed, and by Thursday you had got round to cleaning upstairs. But the last three days! . . . She felt like saying conventionally that they had made an old woman of her, but she knew that really they had only served to bring out her strength. With that realization she suddenly sat upright; she reached the little port-hole in two quick steps, and leaned against it, looking out. She was fully clothed.

For the hundredth time she ran back over events, seeking more evidence for a decision. Yes, she remembered just how Don Enrique had looked at her and said a few words in halting English; she had liked him immediately. Then he had drawn Mr Melton aside and talked Spanish to him, and all at once she had seen Mr Melton turn beet-red and glance desperately around as if he were looking for something to hide under. But he had spoken to her father and mother, and all four had gone below. She thought nothing about it until they all came on deck. Then she saw Mr Melton was still red with embarrassment, and her mother was turkey-red, as she got when she was angry and indignant. But Don Enrique and her father were pale.

Judith still wondered what might have happened if her mother had been a little more subtle. But her mother had only told her bluntly that Don Enrique had presented Juan's case to her father and mother and that they had decided that they could have nothing to do with it. At the first words Judith felt as if all her insides had turned over, and for that moment at least she knew she was in love; the next moment she was flaring with anger, and she said that she would thank them to consult her about such a matter. She was old enough to know her own mind, and was an American citizen and had to be allowed to act as she wanted, and she knew that she was old enough to be out from under her parents' legal authority, and she would go ashore when she wanted and see Juan, and did her mother think that was better than letting him come to see her? But it was flint against flint. Her mother flatly contradicted her. What Judith said about parents' authority might be right in Massachusetts, but in California what parents said went for law, and, besides, Captain Hingham was master of his own ship, and no sailor would dare take her ashore contrary to orders. Then she went on the offensive about Juan, saying he was a Catholic, and was so dark he must be half-Indian, and that all these Californians were fickle and loose-livers with the Indian women (or where did the half-breeds come from?), and, besides, California was a barbarous country. The more she said the angrier Judith got. In a minute she was defending Juan; the more she said in his favour the more she cared for him and the more she thought to say for him. But somehow it made no difference to her mother, and she retorted with more and still worse things about Juan. Then Judith spoke up, and they began throwing back and forth ugly little sentences. Each gave as good as she got. Judith was afraid that they must have sounded like two hired girls fighting. But they were too much alike for either to come out ahead, and it ended by Judith's flouncing off to her own cabin, leaving matters worse even than they had been at first.

In her cabin Judith felt the reaction. There was really a lot in her mother's arguments, after all. Judith wished sometimes that she could leave off thinking and just give herself up wholly to the buoyant feeling which she had when she thought of Juan. But she had too logical a mind for that, and so her mother's arguments kept coming round. She had read a good many books which told about love, but the only one which seemed to fit her case was *Romeo and Juliet*, and that didn't help. For first she thought of the ballroom and the balcony and was all for following her feelings, and then she thought of the apothecary's shop and Juliet in the tomb, and she didn't know.

That was what had made the horrible indecision of these days —she was caught by the situation. She could think of ways in which the world might have been kinder to her. For instance, her parents might not even have told her about what Don Enrique had said, and then she would probably have forgotten all about Juan before long. And, again, if they had let Juan come aboard to see her she might not have liked him when she had really come to know him. But it was not like her mother to do either of these things. And then, finally, if Juan himself had let her alone! . . . And yet, she couldn't really wish that last.

Every afternoon Juan had ridden on the beach just as on that first afternoon. Of course, that was for her to look at. The two vaqueros followed him, and everything was just the same, except that every day they rode different-coloured horses. On that first day they had had bay horses; Tuesday they were black; Wednesday white; and to-day they had been a sort of brown-sugar colour. But there was more difference than that for Judith. On Monday she had been merely astonished and excited when the horsemen took the spine of rocks and the little gully at full speed. Now when they approached it she felt tight in the throat until the first rider was across it. But she would always remember particularly the ride on Tuesday afternoon, just a few hours after Don Enrique had left, for that showed that no matter what report he had taken back Juan had no intention of taking it as a dismissal.

Then every day had come a note from him. There was something practical about that, something which steadied her feelings about him. It meant that he had bribed a seaman, and perhaps the boatswain or the second mate. No matter what the ethics of that might be it showed practical ability. It also showed ready money, and there was something comforting in that thought. The first note had been put under her door suddenly when she was sitting in her cabin. She knew immediately what it was, and looked at it carefully before opening. It was sealed tightly with red sealing-wax. This showed he was taking no chances of any-body else reading it. The wax had been pressed down by a thumb. She could see the mark clearly, and in one place there was a little scar. With a choking sensation she knew suddenly that she had something real and personal and distinctive of Juan—even more intimately of him than a miniature. The mark was small for a man as big as she remembered him to be; it was pressed down hard. This last, she half laughed to herself, indicated Juan's character just as well as his riding did: quick, impulsive, decisive—yes, even courageous and rash. For a man who pushes down soft sealing-wax with his thumb runs his chance of being burned.

The note itself was not quite what she wanted. There were incoherent phrases about herself, her beauty and her hair, and equally incoherent protestations of love. But something—besides the misspelling and the scrawl—was wrong with it. The thumb-mark held her, but the note almost threw her back to accepting her mother's arguments.

Then there was her father. She knew that he would never say anything directly to her; when she and her mother rose up on different sides her father disappeared. He could not even wield a balance of power or cast a deciding vote. Yet she knew that he, a deep-sea captain, was a cosmopolitan, whereas her mother was a villager. He had necessarily learned to look beneath skin-colour and foreign language. She had heard him praise a Kanaka seaman and speak with real affection of two Chinese merchants, his friends in Canton.

Then, on Wednesday afternoon, she was in her cabin, but just about to go on deck, when she heard her father come down to his and her mother's cabin and in a moment emerge and stand at her door.

" Daughter," he said.

" Yes, father." . . .

" Oh, nothing, I guess. You'll be coming on deck in a minute, I suppose."

He had gone off, but she knew he had meant more than he said. She looked out, and saw his cabin door open. That was strange, for her mother was very insistent upon having it locked. She looked in, and saw her father's treasured spyglass carelessly left lying upon the bunk. The port-hole of the cabin faced the shore.

That afternoon she saw Juan as if he were almost in the room beside her. At first she had half-pleasant, half-fearful tremors that her mother would descend and find her. But she forgot them as she watched. His dark face was even more handsome than she had remembered. The firm jaw-line, the arched nose, the high fore-head, spoke of aristocracy. The steady graceful ease of movement meant confident male strength. There was openness, lack of duplicity, in the careless freedom of gesture. Although she knew that he was courting her as surely as if they had been sitting properly in the same parlour at Appleby, still she had a certain secret sense of pleasure in being, by means of the spyglass, so much closer than he could suspect.

And every night too he serenaded. (She had no doubt any longer about that first night.) Old songs of Spain came faintly over the breeze, which in friendly fashion always blew on those nights from the shore to the ship. There were other songs too which Judith herself knew, songs in English; she wondered where Juan could have learned them—*Lord Randall*, *Barbara Allen*, songs of Tom Moore and Robert Burns. Once she heard enough to know that the song was neither in Spanish nor in English. Sometimes the songs were incongruous, as when he sang the *Cherry-tree Carol* and the tinkling nursery rhyme:

> I'll give to you a paper of pins,
> If that's the way that love begins.

But Judith caught the spirit. Denied any closer access, he was offering himself through his music across the stretch of salt water. Anything that was in her language could be a tribute to her; she accepted them all as love songs.

On Wednesday afternoon she had her second note from him. This one pleased her, and she decided that the trouble with the first note was that he had thought it in Spanish, which she knew was a very flowery language, and then put it into English, which was a sober language not allowing for romantic sentiment. The second note was brief; indeed the scrawling hand and bad spelling showed again that Juan wrote with difficulty. It expressed love, but it stated also, " I am making a plan." This time a sailor had slipped the note to Judith on deck; there was a request for an answer. She had sent no answer, not knowing what to say. " A plan " at once pleased and frightened her.

Towards evening of that second day, however, she found that something new had happened to her; her intelligence had turned traitor. It was weaker than her desires; had been corrupted by them, and was now bolstering them up. It made the ' plan ' seem not only attractive, but also prudent. Marrying Juan, she would become a great lady in California, wielding power and holding position as she had always wanted. Juan was the cousin of the Governor. He owned a vast ranch; she pictured a great house backed by barns and storehouses, stretching plough lands round about; uncounted cattle and sheep on the hills beyond. Juan might become Governor; a revolution might make California independent and make Juan President. California, everybody said, was a rich and growing country. She stopped short of thinking of herself as queen, but as President's wife she got as far as taking herself to England on a frigate and enjoying a reception by royalty in London. She wished she could ask Mr Melton more about Juan, but that was impossible, doubly so now that Mr Melton in embarrassment had precipitately packed up and moved ashore.

On Wednesday evening Juan used a violin instead of a guitar. "Drink to me only with thine eyes" was his first song; it suited his high baritone perfectly. Her father, Judith could see, had tears in his eyes; her mother's face was adamant. Judith herself was for the moment ready to dive overboard and swim for shore—to Juan, Rancho Amarillo and the royal reception. Juan played dances, and other pieces which sounded like concertos—difficult of technique. He played well, but Judith felt the vision fading; it was replaced by another less fortunate one of Juan as a dog, doing all his tricks.

Next afternoon—this afternoon—the third note had come. It was the longest of all, but she took it in with one sweeping glance. The plan was complete. He would have her brought from the brig to the shore some time after midnight. He would be waiting on the beach with horses. They could be married within two hours. He protested love, honour, and respect again. With a simplicity that gave her a catch in the throat he said that if she refused he would go to Yerba Buena by land and be there when the brig arrived in San Francisco Bay.

There was a postscript. A password would be necessary. And— Judith almost laughed in spite of herself—he had chosen the words "Jesús María." But in his last sentences she saw that there was an underlying vein of shrewdness and no lack of good taste here; the choice was not as naïve as it sounded : "I hope you will not mind these words. They are not bad ones in Spanish. The J sounds like an H. They are good words for us. Even your sailors use them. If anybody hears them they will just think we are swearing." Judith could remember having heard the words.

She had fled again to her cabin, her only refuge for privacy. She was the nearest to crying that she had been. It was her mother's voice that decided her. The knock had come sharply.

"Come on deck, Judith. There are some customers to meet."

She winced at the hard nasality of her mother's accent; her shoulders set themselves against the peremptory note in the knock and the command. She thought of the clear baritone; she imagined the wide-sweeping stretches of Rancho Amarillo as contrasted with this little buying and selling.

She went on deck and met the customers. She spoke a few sentences with one old gentleman who talked a little English.

Then she went forward; she was close to the sailor who had brought her the note; she spoke quietly and firmly:

"*Haysus M'rear!*"

It was the closest her tongue could twist to the Spanish. He did not seem surprised, and answered her back in the same words and accent. She wondered if there was a leer in his look.

"The answer is 'Yes,'" she said, and walked back to exchange more politenesses with the old gentleman. . . .

That had been eight or nine hours ago, and it should have settled the indecision. But of course it hadn't. Judith remembered how it used to be with the game that they played in a neighbour's hay at Appleby when she was a little thing. You jumped from the barn-beams into the hay; no one had ever got hurt, but still it was scary when you looked a long way down. "I'm going to jump," you would say, and start climbing up to the beam. Half-way up you would say to yourself, "It's all settled; I'm going to jump." Standing on the beam, you would say it to yourself again. And yet, somehow, until you had actually leaned forward and lost your balance, you knew that you might decide not to jump. And now and then, when not too many others were looking, you did turn about and crawl back without jumping.

She had said "Yes." But that had not finished matters.

There had seemed to be a new note in Juan's voice on the beach to-night. At one moment she felt herself going out to meet that new note of ecstasy. Again it had seemed to repulse her; it sounded as if it meant possession. . . .

She left the port-hole, and lay down again. She was still alert; she had too much vitality to be really worn down physically. But she felt she could not stand this indecision much longer. She had not packed any of her things. She had again put on her bottle-green dress, however. She looked well in it; besides, it was the one Juan had seen her in; it was a practical dress, suitable for riding.

She heard no boat, but there came the slightest little scratch at the door.

"*Hay-sus M'rear!*" she whispered through the key-hole.

The same sounds came back to her.

"Just a moment," she whispered again. After the long waiting action was delightful. She thrust into a little hand-bag a variety of articles, practical and impractical—comb and brush, handkerchiefs, her tiny bottle of cologne water.

The sailor stood by her door, his finger on his mouth. They tip-toed past her parents' cabin. On deck the sailor led her quietly towards the stern. She saw no one; Juan must have spent his money well. Under the brig's side lay a boat. There was no time to hesitate.

"I can still order the men in the boat to bring me back if I want to," thought Judith, as she went down the ladder. She sat down beside the steersman.

The two oarsmen with quick, silent strokes sent the boat out from the brig's side. Those were no landlubbers' strokes. But these were not seamen from the *Spanish Belle*.

It came to her—Juan had hired a boat-crew from the Peruvian brig. Even if she asked it these men would not take her back. Without knowing it she had leaned forward too far and lost her balance. Nothing now but to make the jump. Behind her the hull of the *Spanish Belle* was already dim to the sight, but she could see the masts and rigging silhouetted plainly against the sombre midnight sky.

A T A SUDDEN JERKED-OUT EXCLAMATION from the man at the tiller the two rowers swung hard together and sent the boat's prow into the sand. One of them, bare to the knee, sprang into the water to steady the boat. Even yet as in a dream, Judith lurched forward over the thwarts towards a figure which came splashing out through the shallow water. She saw the silhouette of the big hat, and a flash of white which was the neck-cloth.

He swung her out of the boat, one arm beneath her knees, the other close around her body, just as any sailor would have carried her, and just as matter-of-factly. Only when they stood on the beach he drew her close and raised her mouth to his. Happily Judith felt her body bend to his. But the embrace was only for the passing of a second.

"*Jesús María!*" the boat-crew was calling out; they were laughing as they backed water and swung the boat around. Horses were coming down the beach; their hoofs made no sound in the sand, but their accoutrements clinked softly, and one of them nickered. There were two riders and two led horses, vague shapes in the darkness. " In the night all horses are grey," Judith felt herself thinking foolishly and inconsequentially. The riders must be the two vaqueros, of course. They swung out of their saddles and brought the horses to a stand.

She felt some one taking her little hand-bag; then hands cupped themselves beneath her foot, and she swung herself into the saddle. From somewhere reins were pressed into her hands. A sharp word, and they were off, all in silence, except that her own horse snorted and fought the bit. Some one leaned over from his saddle and seized her reins just behind the horse's mouth for a moment. Her horse settled into a steady gallop, just as they struck the hard earth of the village street with a sudden pounding of hoofs. A single dog bayed fiercely, and then the air was full of yappings and barkings from all sides. For three jumps a little white dog ran bouncing alongside, snarling viciously. Then with a sudden softening of tone the horses had left the hard-trampled earth of the street, and were drumming quietly on a country road.

The suddenness, the release, the action, had worked on Judith like strong drink. She felt herself laughing quietly, her whole body fell into the rhythm of the gallop. In what order they had ridden through the village, or whether anyone had said anything since that first sharp word on the beach, she could not have told. She had never been so wildly happy.

A few minutes' galloping sobered her. The vaqueros had fallen behind, she realized. This was Juan who rode at her left side just about his horse's nose in advance, so that he could lean over and seize her reins if necessary. He did not know how well she could ride—she would show him! She laughed happily to herself. His face was dark under the great brim of his hat, but she could still see the flash of white at his neck. She noticed—and a proud sense of conquest and possession rose within her—with what strong grace and perfect ease he sat the saddle. With a flood of weakness all over her, she remembered the moment when he had held her close on the beach. He had carried her through the wa—! *His feet!* He could not have changed—he must be wet to the knees That was terrible—he would take cold. He mustn't—then Judith laughed again to herself; here she was getting wifely already.

The prudential thought had cleared her head of hysterical excitement. Now she felt herself abnormally alert. This, she recognized, was not the road to the Mission that she had ridden with Mr Melton. No; it was skirting around the southern edge of the bay. There was no moon, but the starlight was good, except when they swept through a wisp of low-lying fog. The road wound through stretches of brush, then passed through a series of glades set with compact rounded trees. In every glade big animals, grazing, threw up their heads, then, startled into flight, broke for cover with ungainly leaps, their rumps rising ludicrously. Once the animals were smaller, and disappeared into the brush with such long, graceful bounds that you could have thought that they were flying. Now the galloping horses burst out into a narrow valley. Judith could

D

see great treeless hills hemming it in on either side; their outlines were blacker even than the sky; to her right, through the middle of the valley, a long, sinuous strip of mist marked what might be a stream. Then both the horses shied, and she fought for a moment to regain control. What mysterious scent or sound from out of the night had sent them into fright? This was wild country. Judith could not remember seeing a light, or a house, or a ploughed field, or hearing a dog bark, since they had left the village. This was not New England; this was not even that friendly country through which she had ridden with Mr Melton. For the first time Judith felt a still stab of fear. Yet even that was almost pleasant. Not for a moment could she wish herself back on the *Spanish Belle*. Better to be riding courageously and whole-heartedly towards some unknown destiny, through the darkness, with her lover.

Neither of them had said a word since starting. Judith was glad that Juan had not tried to speak. After all, what was there to say? For herself, she knew that as they stood for a moment on the beach she had spoken with her body all that was needed.

A new thought took her. What if there were no priest at the end of the ride? What if Juan should merely lay a blanket beneath one of the oak thickets and the two others should fade into the night at his word? She knew that she would not resist—no, she would yield submissively, even gladly. In the last wrench of leaving the brig, and in that moment on the beach, she knew that she had already given herself. Words spoken before other people would make no real difference. And yet, deep within and passionately, she asked that he would not demand it of her. She had left her family, she was rushing through wild, strange country on a galloping horse at midnight, but still she felt something of the New England village with its prim, white-steepled meeting-house refusing to die within her.

Then as she looked at Juan she felt that he would not ask this of her. She could see his profile dimly by the starlight. It was the firm-set outline of the face of a man who rides for a set goal. It was not the shifting look of a man looking for where he may stop, planning something other than he has said.

How long they had ridden she had no idea. She was not even yet thinking of being tired when Juan leaned over, pulled in both horses together, and swung them into a side-road. The sound of the hoof-beats lessened, for here grass grew high between the faint wheel-ruts.

"Look out for low branches," called Juan, breaking the long silence.

Twice she leaned forward, and felt leaves whisk above her. Then they came out into an open valley and halted. Juan waved his hand; the two vaqueros rode ahead. Dogs bayed. Judith heard some one shouting in Spanish—to the dogs probably. Then there was silence.

"All right; this is the place," said Juan briefly, and let the horses go forward at a walk. Judith made out the bars of a fence, and smelled a place where horses were kept. Then she saw a door-like rectangle of very dim light. They dismounted, and one of the vaqueros—she realized that she did not yet know them apart—held the horses. Juan took her arm, and, directing her ahead of him, he brought her in through a doorway so low that they almost had to stoop. Inside she saw a woman blowing at a tiny, uncertain flame burning in a little stove or brazier of some sort in the middle of the room. Then the woman got up, saying something rather sharply, and Judith saw that it was really not a woman, but a priest in a robe. Something inside her felt much better as she saw that there actually was to be a priest; she had not realized how much of a strain she was under.

The priest was not a very good specimen. What hair he had was rumpled, his face looked dirty, and there were big sleepers in the corners of his eyes. Bare ankles and feet stuck out below his robe, and his feet looked just as dirty and gnarled as a sailor's. The cord around his middle was not on straight, and it made his robe stand up higher on one side than on the other. He was the picture of a man just roused out of bed, and, as a matter of fact, there was the bed right in the corner of the room—a four-poster with the bedclothes rumpled and thrown back and the dent still in the pillow.

There was a little talk in Spanish, and then Judith realized that she was being introduced to the priest—or whatever it was that happened to you with a priest. She was extremely vague about the customs of a Catholic country. Then Juan and the priest talked a little more.

Judith sat down on a stool beside the little fire. She looked around the room. It was small. There was a rough plank floor, such as you sometimes saw in old Massachusetts farmhouses, only rougher and much dirtier. The walls were big earthen bricks which had once been whitewashed; there was no ceiling, but instead she could look right up to some kind of thatched roof. The bed was very imposing, and looked too large for the room, but the rest of the furniture consisted of only a few homemade-looking stools and chairs and an equally rough table.

Juan and the priest seemed to be having an argument. Then the priest went out by a side-door into another room. Juan came over and squatted down beside the stool, taking her hand. He was speaking in a low voice:

"The dirty——" And then there was a Spanish word. "For what I've given him he would really marry me to a heathen Indian, but he thinks he has to make a fuss to save his face or something." Then she was suddenly frightened, for she could see Juan was worried. It was a relief when he blurted out:

"Do you mind becoming a Catholic?"

"No," said Judith promptly. She had been brought up to think that a girl went to her husband's church. There was Eliza Whately who had married a Unitarian minister, and everybody in Appleby said it was too bad, but still it was a good marriage, and a wife naturally went with her husband. She had hardly ever seen a Catholic, except Paddies, before coming to California, and she had only a few very vague ideas about priests doing some terrible things and about Jesuits being particularly dangerous.

"Will I have to curse my father and my mother?" she said, after reflecting; she had a hazy idea of having heard that something of that sort was required.

"I don't know. I'll find out. You wouldn't want to do that, would you?"

"Not my father," said Judith, before she realized how funny that sounded.

"Of course not," Juan said, not seeming to see anything funny. He went into the other room. A moment later a woman and a half-grown boy and girl came in through the door. All were very poor and dirty-looking; the woman was like an Indian, but the children were whiter. All were shy, and did not speak. The children sat, or rather squatted, in a corner, and in spite of their shyness seemed fascinated by Judith's hair. The woman, who had some bed-linen over her arm, began to tear up the bed and make it up with clean sheets.

Judith closed her eyes, and saw a picture of Juan as she had just seen him in the light of the little charcoal fire. She wished now that she had put on a finer gown instead of being merely practical and wearing her bottle-green travelling dress. Juan was evidently dressed for his wedding. She could still picture his finery—the embroidered shirt, the white neck-cloth, the blue damask vest, the jacket and trousers in black velveteen, trimmed with scarlet and silver. But the bottoms of his trousers were draggled and wet; he must not do that sort of thing any more.

Juan came in again. "It's all right," he said. "I told him you were a Catholic already."

"But he doesn't believe that!"

"Oh, yes. Why not?"

She could see Juan smiling a little. She wondered how much he had had to pay to make the priest believe that. She didn't like lies, but at least it meant that Juan was taking care of things, and she liked that. As long as they could get married, what was the difference?

Then the priest came in, and they were all standing up. The woman finished making up the bed, turned down the sheets, and stood looking on with her impassive Indian face. The two children with their handsome big black eyes were beside her. Miguel and Ramón were there; Judith saw their dark faces, and the long knives in their belts.

Why, Judith realized, in a minute she was going to be married! It was different from a wedding day in Appleby, and how much better! There everything was so proper and so slow and so cold-blooded. This was as a wedding should be—all excitement and defiance, the swift drumming of hoofs through the midnight, and the swift pounding of blood in one's temples.

They were standing up before the priest now. Only then did the meaning of the bed strike Judith—*that* was to be her marriage bed! And upon the shock of that idea came yet another. Among the few articles she had thrown hurriedly into that little hand-bag something was lacking. She felt herself blushing all over, and then as suddenly grow calm. This was not Appleby; Juan was no shipping clerk or sedate young lawyer. Now she was in California. It was all of one piece this night: her husband wading through the water, the wild ride, the horses shying at the scent of danger, the dark vaqueros with their long knives, and the remembrance that from her hand-bag was missing that last vestige of civilized respectability—her nightgown. . . .

That next afternoon they rode back to Monterey. The two vaqueros still trailed them, but everything else seemed different. By tacit understanding, they held their horses in to a canter. The tension had gone out of life; they no longer had to strain forward towards some culmination. Except for a deep reflective pause now and then, they were talkative; Juan was teaching her Spanish words, and they laughed together at her errors in pronunciation. Around bends of the road, where the vaqueros could not see, he leaned across, laying his hand upon her knee.

The country too was different in the light of day—as unmysterious as a cow-pasture. The hills and trees were only hills and trees. The cattle which stared and then bolted clumsily were only stupid cattle. The strange creature leaping into the brush was only a big doe. There was no scent to scare the horses.

As they came into sight of the bay they saw the Peruvian brig far off, beating out around Point Pinos. The *Spanish Belle* still lay at anchor, and at the sight Judith had her first qualms. As they came into town every one stared at Judith, and she could see a boat rowing in from the brig. She held her head high; she had a new pride in herself as a woman who had done what a woman might do. She was Juan's wife in every way that one could become a wife; it was a thing done, and all the authority in California, parental or legal, could not make it undone.

They rode right down to the custom-house, but there was no scene. There was what might be called a wedding-reception, for a little crowd gathered, and Judith went confusedly through much gay introducing and embracing and kissing.

Then there was a sudden hush and frigidity, and Judith looked up to see her father and Mr Melton. But that was all over in a minute too. For her father merely embraced and kissed her, and then stood holding her right hand between his and saying over and over :

" Bless you, daughter, bless you."

Then he shook hands formally with Juan, wishing him happiness, while Juan, out of embarrassment on top of Spanish respect for elders, went down on one knee, as if for a blessing. Meanwhile Mr Melton had in proper form claimed his kiss from the bride, and some one (Captain McPherson or Don Enrique was Judith's guess) had hurried out glasses and brandy for toasts.

So in the end, Judith concluded, except for the absence of her mother, the wedding turned out to be just about as conventional and sentimental as it could have been in Appleby.

TWO DAYS LATER, in the grey dawn, Judith slid out of bed and stood by the window. She was just in time. The topsails took the wind, and the *Spanish Belle* moved through the water. Within a minute the brig passed out of sight, first the hull and then the masts, as the buildings nearer shore cut off the view. The *Spanish Belle* was gone.

Judith glanced around the dim room; she saw again her little clothes-chest, her carpet-bag, and the tiny hand-bag she had brought with her when leaving the brig. They were all she had left with her of that former life of Appleby and the United States, when she was Judith Hingham—those and the little purse which her father had pressed into her hand when he kissed her good-bye. There were ten gold eagles in it, and a little Spanish silver. She would rather not have taken the money, for she knew that her father was a poor man; but she knew also that his honour was tied up with the gift; he could not let his daughter pass penniless among strangers.

Her belongings had come, down to the last pin, packed neatly and firmly so that no handkerchief or small scarf would take one wrinkle more than was necessary. That was her mother. But her mother had not come to see her or sent a note. That was her mother too.

Juan stirred, and then came awake all over at once, like a child. At sight of her he broke into a roguish reminiscent smile that made her smile back and forget about the *Spanish Belle*.

"Good day, little one. How are you?" he said in Spanish, using words which he had already taught her.

The morning was still fresh when they took the road. It was the season, Juan said, to be at Rancho Amarillo; before they knew it, it would be killing-time. He had wasted three months going south with Don Juan Bautista. There was never any fighting, but everything just puffed out in talk and tobacco smoke. The down-country people, those below Santa Barbara, were a lot of ninnies.

They had left Judith's empty chest and carpet-bag behind to be brought up some time later. Now she could see her bundles of clothes bobbing about on the back of a horse galloping with the rest of the herd. There would be plenty of creases and wrinkles after that. But Judith refused to worry. She had given herself over now, she felt, to the Californian ways.

It was glorious riding at least. Ahead galloped two horses with light packs and a dozen more horses to be used as reliefs when those carrying riders grew tired. At the head of the herd was a bell mare, white, with great splotches of black. Judith noticed that all the other horses were bays, and she asked Juan how he had happened to ride a different-coloured horse every day on the beach.

" Oh," he said, " I borrowed those others—but at home I have horses of all those colours, and others too. When I came south I brought only one herd along."

The first part of the ride was along the same road that they had ridden the night of the marriage, but after the first change of horses the hills drew back suddenly. The cavalcade splashed through a wide, shallow river. Beyond it Judith all at once felt an oppressive sense of being very small. On all sides stretched a vast country for which a girlhood spent among New England hills had not prepared her. The great valley lay treeless, fenceless, houseless. To right and left she saw no bounds to it; behind, the hills had already sunk to insignificance; far, far ahead were more hills, half concealed in haze, but looking just as bare as the plain. Was this California? Was that intimate bit of pines and hills about Monterey merely a bait set to lure her to the trap? In such a country as this she would die of the sense of her own littleness.

The vaqueros still shouted and sang happily, and Juan looked just as contented as a man should who is bringing his bride home. Then as Judith got farther into the plain she saw that it really had some variety. There were little ups and downs which you failed to notice at first. There were bunches of cattle here and there eating grass. And the grass itself was tall and very green. But it was the flowers that first began to win Judith's heart a little. She was used to flowers in gardens or speckled about pastures; but here she came to great splashes of colour that covered acres—yellow, soft blue, or brilliant orange. The splashes were so lavish and gigantic that they were almost intoxicating. Judith could not imagine picking one flower from such millions. Was such gigantic beauty real beauty at all? She felt chilled again. Must not real beauty have intimacy?

Then they overtook and passed two carts with great, slow-moving, creaking wooden wheels. Half-naked Indians walked alongside with goads, but the oxen seemed to think twice between each step, anyway. The riders swept by as if the carts had not been moving at all. Coming back from Monterey after taking a load of hides down to the ships, Juan explained. In some way the carts made Judith feel better, for if those snail-like oxen could cross this plain at all, surely their galloping horses must make little of it? Besides, she reflected, Rancho Amarillo was in the hills; she would not let this plain worry her. In truth, by the time they changed horses again she could see the slopes ahead quite clearly. They were well up among the ridges when they stopped to eat their lunch by a little stream with some trees along it. All round the big hills were treeless. Judith didn't like them, and found herself looking over her shoulder occasionally. Treeless country meant meadows or plough-lands to her, and they were more or less level. But hills, especially big hills, should be covered with trees. These great bare hills looked naked and indecent. Their forms suggested gigantic unclothed people sometimes; a ridge was like the line of a hip and thigh, or a knoll stood up like a girl's breast. Bodies were more real to her than they had been a few days ago. But she hoped that the hills around Rancho Amarillo wouldn't be like this.

She enjoyed the lunch. They had chicken and turkey and beef, cold beans with peppers in them, good coarse wheat bread, and some of the little, thin cakes like pancakes, but made out of cornmeal. There were sweet cakes to end with. There was also a bottle of native red wine, but it made Judith choke and cough, and was too sour for her, anyway.

Afterwards she leaned against a tree while Juan laid his head in her lap and went to sleep. She held his head very happily for a few minutes, until suddenly he woke up again all over at once. She wondered what made him do that, for she had noticed that other grown-up people woke up stretching and yawning.

Judith was a little stiff and tired when they mounted again, but she did not say anything about it. Juan was talkative after his nap, and taught her some Spanish words. His English was amazingly good, she thought. But when she wanted to know about birds and trees and flowers he had trouble. Even when she asked him what they were in Spanish he would usually say just " little bird," or " tree," or " yellow flower."

They came down out of the hills at a mission called San Juan Bautista, but Juan said they called it Juanita because there were so many pretty half-breed girls there. He did not know what Juanita was in English, but Judith was learning a little now, and decided it was probably about the same as Jenny.

They walked about the plaza a little while the horses were being changed; Judith was stiffer, and felt as if she might be getting some saddle-burns. She had never ridden so far in her life before, but Juan never seemed to think of stopping, and she decided she was not going to be a weakling; a man must hate to have a wife holding him back.

Judith was depressed at how dirty everything was around the village. There were a number of Indians and half-breeds about, and a few people who could have passed as white. Juan introduced her to these last, and one of them, who seemed about the dirtiest person in the place, greeted her very warmly in good Yankee talk. He would have kissed her if she had not drawn away sharply. He said he was a Marblehead man, and had 'left' his ship, a whaler, when it touched at Monterey. Judith had her father's dislike of deserting sailors, and, besides, she was disgusted at having such a dirty creature claim her as a fellow-countryman.

Of course, everybody stared at her hair, although she had covered it as well as she could. The Indians and half-breeds stared most of all, and she was irritated because she knew that they were talking about her hair right in front of her. She had got her ear tuned to Spanish well enough now to make out a few words here and there, and she realized she was hearing over and over again the two words ' *señora* ' and ' *blanca*.'

When she started riding again her back hurt, but she said nothing about it, and instead asked Juan about those two words.

" *Señora* is ' lady,' and *blanca* is ' white,' " he said.

" They were talking about my hair, I suppose? "

" Yes, sometimes they were saying, ' How white the lady is! ' and sometimes, ' The lady is very white! ' and sometimes something else—but those two words kept coming in."

She thought of moments when Juan himself had showered endearing terms upon her in his native language.

" But I don't remember your calling me ' *blanca*.' "

" But I know better words. You see *blanca* isn't really the right word, but these Indians only know a little Spanish. Then I think they are so used to black hair that yours must seem really white like a cloud."

Judith thought of something which seemed to have happened years ago.

" But when you sang on the beach, that first night, you sang ' *blanca*,' and I thought you were singing of me! " The memory was so vivid that she felt a disappointment even now. She had been so sure he meant her, and yet he had only been singing about a white cloud, or a white dove. It was for a minute as if she had fallen in love under false pretences. Then she thought it was like the way you sometimes at school worked out an arithmetic problem in the wrong way but happened to get the right answer. For he had been singing to her, anyway, though that particular word was just an accident.

The afternoon was mostly a feeling of aching muscles, sudden sensations, and snatches of conversation. Impressions were coming too fast for her tired body to record them.

Some animals, big as calves, but slimmer, burst into wild flight, their rumps flashing white:

" *Cabras*—goats," said Juan.

Those are no goats, thought Judith, some kind of antelope perhaps, but it was not worth while to argue.

Cattle—cattle grazing, lying down, standing knee-deep in pools—long-horned, slim-legged, wild as deer. The land was filled with cattle.

They startled a great animal with branching antlers like a deer's, but looking large as a horse; it sniffed at the riders and then plunged out of sight into a gully. There was a burst of excited Spanish from the vaqueros. "Bull elk," said Juan. Hardly any were left in this part now, he explained; north and east there were still plenty. Sometimes he and his men went hunting them, running them on horseback and throwing lassos over the antlers. On level ground a horse could outrun them, but the elk always headed for rough country. That meant dangerous riding. It was fun; besides, the finest tallow came from elk. . . .

A sudden stench in the nostrils as they swept by a spot white with skeletons of cattle. . . .

"Last year's killing at Rancho San Felipe," was Juan's matter-of-fact reply to her querying, half-horrified look.

They passed isolated ranch-houses at long intervals, the vaqueros whooping and hallooing. Queer people these Californians to build their houses out in the blank open; treeless knolls they seemed to prefer to a beautiful grove of oaks or the nestling arms of the hills. "Why?" she asked.

"They like to look around," said Juan, smiling. His smile meant that there was something more to it, but the phrase had got into the rhythm of the riding—they *like* to look a-*round,* they *like* to look a-*round*—and she was too tired to speak. . . .

"There's Rancho San Jorge," said Juan. "You can talk with Aunt Leticia while we change horses."

Judith felt herself reeling. Change horses! She could never go farther. Then stubbornly she decided she could. She had reserves she had not yet used. But when they swung in and pulled rein her spirit ebbed. Miguel helped her down, as he or Ramón always did, but when she was on the ground she felt herself sway. She still seemed to be crouched upon the side-saddle, and could not quite straighten her back. A big fat woman was embracing Juan in the doorway, and the two of them were talking Spanish so fast that Judith could not catch a word. Then the fat woman gave a sudden little horrified shriek, and looked at Judith, and most surprisingly drew back her hand and gave Juan a full-shouldered slap on the cheek that swung him half round. Then she waddled forward to Judith, calling out what even Judith could tell were endearing and commiserating words. Sooner than there could be any explanations Judith was lying restfully upon a bed with her clothes loosened. Then Juan was leaning over, looking sheepish and saying:

"My aunt says I'm the biggest fool she ever knew for making you ride from Monterey to San Jorge in one day, and if I never have any heirs to my name this will be the cause of it."

Aunt Leticia kept Judith in bed all the next morning too. Judith did not feel that she needed such babying, but still she really enjoyed the rest after all the excitement of the past week, capped by the physical strain of the long ride. Besides, she enjoyed just lying and watching, for everything about Aunt Leticia's place gave her so much quiet amusement. First of all, there was Juan letting himself be ordered about and made into a small boy; that was the way, she supposed, a Californian was expected to act before his elders. Then there was Aunt Leticia herself, who was at once so good-humoured and so good-hearted that she would have pleased anybody. Judith learned a lot of Spanish that morning, for Aunt Leticia was always popping in and pointing to this or that and saying the word for it. She kept going through a whole panto-mime too; it included the action of riding a horse and becoming very tired, and then nursing a baby, and then gestures to show that the second would not follow the first. Judith decided that Aunt Leticia must be really worried about what Juan had said yesterday; it must be some superstition about young wives not riding horse-back just after they were married. That amused Judith too, for she thought it was just an old wives' tale, and, besides, she did not see why they were thinking so much about babies, anyway. Aunt Leticia seemed to think that a baby followed marriage as inevitably and just about as closely as the tail followed the horse. In Appleby they at least gave the bride a couple of months before they began looking at her. Here Judith had been married only a few days, and Aunt Leticia was all for having her start making ready a cradle.

Then the arrangements about the place amused Judith too. Aunt

Leticia was a lady—you could see that at a glance; but probably she was one of Juan's poor relations. The house was much like the one in which Judith had been married. The main room where Judith was in bed had a plank floor, but she could see that the one which opened out of it was floored merely with hard dirt. Aunt Leticia seemed to have plenty of servants at least, for three Indian women wandered into the room at one time or another and busied themselves in most leisurely fashion about something or other. They were barefooted, and wore (you could see) only a single garment; they seemed fairly clean except for their hair. Each of them looked at Judith's hair and smiled shyly. Besides the Indian women, every now and then a chicken wandered in through the open door, and walked around chirping and looking for food, and made itself very much at home. Then Aunt Leticia would come in and see that the chicken had been there and shout for one of the Indian women. It was a sort of endlessly revolving triangle —chicken, Aunt Leticia, Indian woman. Judith wondered why they didn't either keep the chickens out, or else just forget about trying to keep the place clean. She could not see how Aunt Leticia could be so fat when she had to work so hard keeping her servants working; Judith started giggling to herself with the thought that a Californian lady who had six servants must have to work twice as hard as Aunt Leticia who was lucky enough to have only three. And, in addition, Aunt Leticia was knitting all the time.

Besides the chickens and the Indian women, three dogs took turns wandering through the room. They were of different sizes, but otherwise were all alike. All were mongrels with a yellowish tone to their hair; all were long-legged, and all laid themselves down on the floor suddenly with a sound as if you had dropped a sack with some sticks in it. Then they scratched. . . .

Through the open door she could see a lot of other creatures which, she was relieved, didn't seem to think they belonged in the house. It was like watching a parade, except that it passed in both directions. There were any number of skinny, clumsy turkeys, and a few ducks. There were more than a few pigs, and, once or twice, a donkey. One of the pigs lay down and went to sleep where she could just see its hindquarters, not ten feet from the door.

It all amused Judith very much, especially when she remembered she was leaving it behind and going on to Rancho Amarillo in the morning. Even the living arrangements were amusing, for when Judith had started to look for the out-house there had been a sudden to-do, and one of the Indian women came in with a crude earthenware vessel. Afterwards the woman had taken it through the front door and about three steps beyond and there let it go with a big *swish*, causing a scattering of fowls. After all, thought Judith, what's the difference, if they let all those animals wander around right up to the doorstep?

She saw nothing of Juan that morning, for he and the two vaqueros had gone for a ride. And the thought of that, after yesterday, amused her too. . . .

Next morning Judith said good-bye, and, rather proudly and self-consciously, exercised her first function as mistress of Rancho Amarillo by asking Aunt Leticia to come to visit them. Aunt Leticia counted on her fingers, and then said quite soberly, yes, they could expect her about the middle of February. Juan looked puzzled, but Judith caught the point and laughed, blushing a little too, at Aunt Leticia's seriousness.

One change of horses brought them to the little town of San José; it was a good deal like Monterey, except that there weren't the few good-looking houses that there were in Monterey. Hardly any people were about, but Juan said it was washing day and they would all be down along the river if you wanted to see them. His voice implied that he could get along just as well without.

They changed horses in the plaza. While Juan talked to some old men, Judith looked around and had a curious illusion that the ball on top of the village flag-pole was a man's head Of course it wasn't. But she had to look back to be sure that it wasn't—and it was! Judith felt a little sick, but she decided that she had been through a lot since she had seen the bullock killed, and, besides, the ground in the plaza was too dirty to faint on. So she ventured a good look. The head must have been there some time, and there wasn't much left of the face, but the long black hair looked like an Indian's. Judith had read in *Scottish Chiefs* about Sir William Wallace's head being put up over London Bridge or Stirling Castle or some place, but she never thought she would be where that kind of thing was done. She didn't like it—and yet it seemed to fit in with the way life was lived in California. As they rode out of the plaza she gestured towards the head inquiringly, and Juan glanced at it and merely said:

"Oh, yes, that's Ignacio."

It was just as if he might have said, "Aunt Leticia has dropped her yarn." And who was Ignacio, anyway?

A few miles along the road they swept through Mission San José, causing a great running among the chickens and turkeys and naked brown children. They went through at full gallop because Juan said he didn't like the priest there. It was remarkable, Judith began to think, how many people Juan didn't like.

But now she felt a new lift of excitement as they branched off the main road and entered the hills. They passed two poor little ranch-houses in narrow valleys. A family named Gómez lived in the first, and one named García in the second. The Gómez place was swarming with half-naked little children, and the García place had even more children, some of them nearly grown. Juan stopped and talked briefly at each place, and seemed to inquire about something which called for gestures towards the horizon. Juan didn't dismount, and from the way he introduced the people to her she concluded they must be rather low-down families. Also the Gómez father took off his hat while he talked to Juan, and probably the García father would have done so too except that he wasn't wearing any hat, or any shoes either, for that matter. The only person in whom Juan seemed much interested was the oldest García boy, Pablo, who was about fifteen and very straight and active-looking.

When they rode on Judith asked Juan if he liked these neighbours. He made what she thought was hardly an answer, for he just shrugged his shoulders and said:

"They keep sheep."

Above the García place the road wound through a narrow valley and crossed a little stream several times. Hills rose on either hand, but not very steep or high. They had some trees and brush on them, but many stretches of grass too, and bunches of cattle were

E

grazing as usual. Miguel and Ramón kept yelling back and pointing, and Judith gathered that these cattle must belong to Rancho
Amarillo—that is, she thought proudly, they must belong to Juan,
and to her. She saw the brand-mark, which was like an X laid on
its side with a line connecting the two right-hand points.

The valley walls drew together sharply, so that the stream came
down through a narrow little gorge and the road had to swing up
over a low shoulder of the hill. At the top they reined in, and
Judith drank in her first view of Rancho Amarillo.

The little valley was like the bottom of a saucer, with the hills
rising all around it. The level space was roughly circular, and must
be, Judith guessed, about two miles across. It was bright green
with grass, except where wildflowers made splotches of yellow,
blue, and orange. She could see cattle and horses grazing.

Then she looked at the hills a little fearfully; but they were not
bad hills. They were mostly the same grass-green as the valley,
but they were marked, as if by veins, with the darker green of
trees. Even already Judith had learned that each vein was a water-
course, and that the trees were growing where there was most
water. The highest hill of all was right opposite them. It differed
from the others by going up to a peak instead of a ridge, and in
having its top covered by a scattered growth of some kind of trees
or brushes. Juan saw her looking and said something in Spanish;
then he paused a moment and said, "Brushy Peak." Judith decided that the name of the hill must be something which could be
translated by those words.

The stream which they had been following came out of the
hills just at the base of Brushy Peak, and Judith's eyes swung back
along the line of the trees which marked the stream's course right
across the middle of the valley until it broke through the hills by
the narrow passage just below where she was now standing. The
little stream came nowhere near filling its bed, and swung back and
forth between the high banks. It looked, Judith thought, like a
child trying pathetically to make use of something big enough for
a man.

Across the stream, and nearly in the middle of the valley, stood
the ranch-house. Three tall, slim trees rose up in front of it, but

she could see that there were three buildings, rather close together. She was too far away to get a more detailed impression. Almost across the stream from the houses she saw a curiously irregular-shaped field marked out by a very rough fence of brush. Part of the land within the fence looked just like the grassland outside, but about half of it had been ploughed, and was growing some crop, which might be wheat.

That was all she had time to observe. She could see Juan was fidgeting, and she herself was anxious to look at the house more closely. Below her the road led on across the valley floor, winding a little from side to side for no apparent reason, just as a path winds. The two vaqueros with the pack-horses were far ahead, nearing the stream-crossing in front of the house. They had let the horse-herd go, and behind the spotted mare the bays were cantering off at an angle from the road.

With a sudden impulse Judith took off her bonnet. The sunlight shone bright upon her hair. Her eyes were looking far ahead; she gave her head just the slightest toss. Thinking great thoughts, she rode down the little hill into her kingdom.

JUAN GODOY WAS VERY HAPPY as he rode down the little hill with his wife. He had at that moment not a need or a desire or an imagination which was unsatisfied, or which at least could not be satisfied within the near future. He watched the herd of bays streaking off behind the spotted mare; they had had a long journey and needed a good rest now; he would have the roans brought in right away. He thought of the roans because already he had spotted that a horse-herd, probably the roans, was somewhere in among the sycamores by the creek.

Before he and Judith had ridden half the distance to the stream-crossing he knew also that the blacks were in one of the side-ravines to his right. This was reassuring, and increased his pleasant inward feeling that everything was satisfactory. Having, as became a cavalier, thought first of his horses, he let his mind turn to the less interesting details of the land and the cattle. Within the three minutes which it took him to ride to the point where the road dipped to the stream-crossing he had learned that his cattle were in better than usual condition considering the time of the year, that the crop of calves was normal, and that the grass was also in a little better than usual condition, except that there seemed to be still more of that tall yellow-flowering mustard weed which had first appeared only a few years ago.

Juan was so happy that he even forgot to be in a hurry. He pulled his horse in, and took the ford at a walk. He was drinking in sensations like a dog with its nose thrown back. The *squash-squash* of hoofs in the mud was music. The stream was a foot deep; that meant good reserves of water in his hills against the summer.

As he came up the opposite bank and into sight of the house only a hundred yards away the sensations multiplied and became a torrent, too many for individual recording: they blended. Smells

—the barnyard, decaying meat, hides, wood-smoke, Indian servants. Sights—the squat lines of the house in grey adobe brick, and the hard blue sky above the line of the ridge-pole; two dark naked children scampering away, but looking back to be sure they missed seeing nothing; the horizontals of the corral bars; the verticals of the porch supports, with a contrasting diagonal where a window shutter hung from one hinge.   Sounds—dogs, chickens, turkeys, children, two heavy grunts of a hog, and from somewhere faintly the *pat-pat* of a woman making tortillas. Juan let out a little whoop like an Indian. He pulled his horse to a halt at the horse-rail. Then he looked proudly at Judith.

Something had happened. Her face looked dull and wooden. She had put on her bonnet again, and in an absent-minded sort of way was pushing stray locks of her hair up beneath it. Of course—he had been a fool again; he had ridden too long and hard in spite of what Aunt Leticia had told him. He kept forgetting how little she could stand. He helped her down from the horse; her body felt heavy.

" Are you tired? "

" Yes," she said, " I feel very tired."

But when he sent Antonia scurrying to hunt for some cleaner sheets Judith said that she did not want to go to bed and was really not so very tired. This encouraged Juan immensely and he set to work enthusiastically to show Judith both rooms of the house. First he showed her the inner room, for that was where they were, having come through the outer room in order to put Judith to bed. Juan pointed to the three windows. He was very proud that they had glass in them. Some of the panes were broken out, and a good many were cracked, and all were dirty, so that they let in only a kind of grey light. Nevertheless, they were glass windows, and could be opened and shut. Most ranches had just wooden shutters on the windows, so that you took your choice of having the room dark or having the wind blowing through. Still Juan did not like to boast; so he merely said about the three windows :

" That means lots of air, and I like lots of air. That's because I'm used to sleeping out. I don't like to sleep with closed shutters the way they do in Monterey."

Judith agreed rather quietly. Then he showed her the cot of criss-crossed rawhide thongs that he liked to sleep on better than in the big bed.

"But of course not now," he added.

"No," said Judith, but she failed to give him that quick half-bashful, half-enticing smile that he had expected.

Juan decided that perhaps he was not a very good person to show off a house, for he could not think of anything more to say about the inner room, and in some way Judith still seemed tired, even though she said she was not. He started into the outer room, and then thought of the floor

"It's a fine floor," he said, scraping the dust back with the toe of his shoe. "It was made back in my father's time, and there's a trick to making one like this that most people don't know. You see, it isn't really dirt. You level the floor first, and then when you're killing you bring up buckets of blood and mix it with the earth and tramp it all down. It comes out very hard, and it almost has a polish. We'll have Antonia sweep it out to-morrow. It's a very healthy floor too."

"It *is* very hard, isn't it?" said Judith, as they went into the outer room.

Juan could not seem to find much to say about the outer room either, especially since Judith seemed too tired. He pointed out by way of contrast its being a dark room, but that was nice in hot weather. The bed was a bed, and the two chairs were just straight wooden chairs; and there was nothing unusual about the two chests, and the bench was home-made. Some dried beef was hanging from the rafters. On the wall were two swords, and his leather jacket, the steel helmet he had inherited from his father, two guns, and a brace of pistols. They were the same things that were always there. Juan pointed them out with a wave of his hand, but he could not think of anything to say about them; it would have been just like pointing to his own face and commenting, "See, I have a mouth and two eyes, and my nose has two holes in it." Of course, he might have said something about the weapons, but Aunt Leticia had said he shouldn't on account of the baby.

But the fireplace was different. Juan was very proud of it, and liked the family story behind it. So he told Judith the story:

"Yes, my father said he was going to have a fireplace, although hardly anybody in California has fireplaces. But my father said that a gentleman's house always had one. His father's house even in Mexico had a fireplace, and *his* father's house in Mexico had a fireplace too, and *his* father's house in Spain had a fireplace. I don't know how my father really knew about his great-grandfather's fireplace. But, anyway, a priest at Santa Clara made fun once of what my father was saying, and asked, ' *Why* should a gentleman's house have a fireplace?' And my father said, ' So the gentleman can *spit* into it, and not on the floor the way a Jesuit does!' Of course my father said Jesuit, but he meant Franciscan, for the priest was a Franciscan, but my father didn't say Franciscan because the Church was very powerful then, and, besides, you should never insult a priest or a woman, because they can't fight. My father didn't like priests, and I don't either."

But Judith did not laugh much over the story, and Juan was disappointed, for he had tried very hard to amuse her. It must be that she was tired. The only other thing he could point out in the outer room was the floor; this was a plank floor, and had only two broken places in it.

"I can just remember when we put in this floor," he said. "You can see it has been used a long time, for the wood is worn down and the knots stand up."

"Yes, I can see that they do," said Judith.

Then, more rapidly, he took her down the roofed passage-way to the kitchen, and pointed out the storehouse, and the well, and beyond the well the quarters where the vaqueros and the house-servants lived. Behind the kitchen, but on this side of the storehouse, the men had just slaughtered a ' beef.' Juan knew this, because around the corner of the kitchen he could see two of the dogs sitting and looking out for whatever scraps might come their way; also Juan could sniff the familiar sour smell of the fresh blood. It was different from the staler, fetid smell which lingered from former slaughterings.

Then they went in and ate their dinner on a table placed just beside the single window of the outer room. This was convenient to the kitchen, being just at the end of the passage-way from it. Juan liked eating there, because there he could get through the window and the door almost all the familiar sights and smells and sounds which had been so delighting him since he came home. He was terrifically hungry too—hungry for good fresh beef and for Lupe's tortillas. He helped himself several times, and polished all the gravy off his plate with rolled tortillas. In fact, he was drinking his chocolate before he noticed that Judith had hardly eaten one tortilla and had left her beef almost untouched.

"I really must be very tired" was all she said when he asked her. He could not see why she seemed to go back and forth so much; when he was tired he knew it. But he persuaded her to go in and rest.

In the inner room Antonia had made up the bed with clean sheets, but Judith was not satisfied with the way it was done. In spite of being so tired, she tore the bed all to pieces, and when Juan left her—he was getting a little disgusted at the way she was behaving—she was shaking out all the bedclothes, and peering down into the corners of the mattress and bed.

It was siesta time, but Juan was overflowing with energy, and he wanted to see something more of the ranch. He found the roans already in the corral. He roped the one he wanted, and held him while Miguel saddled and bridled.

The ranch looked better the more he saw of it. There was plenty of water in the little valley called Ojuelo, and fine grass everywhere.

When he came back Judith was sitting on the veranda looking out south across the valley. She still looked tired. Juan shooed a turkey hen away, and sat down.

"How far is it to the Garcías?" Judith asked.

"About half an hour's ride."

"And the Gómez place is about the same beyond that?"

"Yes."

"And then to the Mission where we turned off the main road?"

"You can ride it in about an hour from where Gómez lives."

"Then it takes two days' hard riding to Monterey?"

"Yes." Juan did not consider it two days of *hard* riding, especially if she were counting from the Mission, but he let that pass.

"And we were nearly six months from Boston to Monterey."

Juan did not see the point of all this. When she began asking

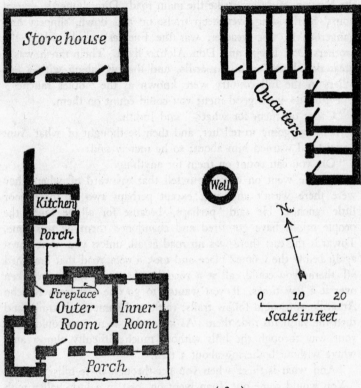

Storehouse

Quarters

Well

Kitchen

Porch

Fireplace
Outer
Room

Inner
Room

Porch

0   10   20
Scale in feet

RANCHO AMARILLO (1837)

what lay in other directions from the ranch he warmed up. He became more encouraged about Judith than he had been at any time since she arrived at the ranch. It was a good thing for a person to want to know the landmarks and understand how all the valleys, and ridges, and streams lay. So he explained eagerly. The Garcías were the nearest people, and they were south and a little west. North, you could ride over bad trails, and by bearing

off to your left, westward, could come out on the level land of the
Contra Costa, lying along San Francisco Bay. There were some
big ranches there, to which they could go visiting some time soon.
But really the easiest way to get there was to go back almost to
the Mission, and then strike the main road. Directly north, several
hours' hard riding over steep trails, up and down, slippery and
dangerous in wet weather, was the Fuentes' ranch, where the
brothers Don Diego and Don Alonzo lived. Their ranch was a
great deal like Rancho Amarillo, and the two along with a few
others in the hill country were known as the "outer ranches."
The Fuentes were good men; you could count on them.

"Count on them for what?" said Judith.

Juan was going to tell her, and then he thought of what Aunt
Leticia had warned him about; so he merely said:

"Oh, you can count on them for anything."

Then he went on quickly to tell that eastward of where they
were there wasn't anything, except perhaps two or three poor
little ranches. He said 'perhaps,' because for all he knew the
people might have got tired and abandoned them by this time.
Towards the east there was no road at all, unless you went down
again below the Gómez place and took a poor road that branched
off there; you could call it a road because carts had been taken
over it a few times. If you wanted to go due east from Rancho
Amarillo you could follow trails; cattle and game made trails, and
then the vaqueros rode them. As far as that went, you could work
your way through the hills without much difficulty almost anywhere without bothering about a trail.

"And what is there when you get through these hills?"

You would come out, Juan went on, first in a little valley with
a two-peaked mountain to the north of it. If you went on still
farther you crossed some more hills, and came into the Great
Valley, called sometimes the Valley of the Tulares because of the
big swamps in it where the tule reeds grew. The valley was so
long that nobody knew how long it was; it must be a thousand
miles long.

"Why," said Judith, "you could put all of New England into
that."

Juan took her word for it, having no idea how big New England was. But he went on warmly with his geography There were lots of elk and wild horses in the big valley, and wild Indians lived there. A big river came down through it; he supposed it was the biggest river in the world. Even in autumn you had to swim your horses. (He looked at Judith, but she didn't seem to doubt his statement.) But the Great Valley, long as it was, was not so very wide. After you crossed the river it was only half a day's ride before you came to the hills. Those hills were different from the ones here. They went up more slowly, but longer. First you came to oaks and small pines, and then you came to big pines, and at last when you stood on ridges you could look ahead and see very high mountains.

Juan paused:

"They have snow on them even in summer."

Again he looked at Judith, and again she seemed to believe him. She only asked:

"Have you been to where you could see snow?"

"Yes," he said, and added proudly, "I have been as far into those mountains as any Californian has been." Then he wished that he had not said that; for, on account of what Aunt Leticia had said, he did not want her to ask why he had been there. But she only asked:

"Has anyone ever been across the mountains? What is there beyond?"

"Sometimes trappers, Americans and Frenchmen, come across. They say there are deserts beyond the big mountains and more big mountains. Their horses after they came through all those deserts and mountains have bones sticking out all over them. I wouldn't ride such a horse. But if you can cross all those places you come to a town called—what is it?—San Luis. The trappers say it is a very big town."

"St Louis!" said Judith. "It's not a big town; it's almost Indian country; it must be a thousand miles west of Boston and New York and Philadelphia and all the big cities."

Juan did not argue. He knew about the mountains having snow on them, but as for the size of St Louis, he knew that the trappers liked to tell big stories. And as to how many miles it was from Boston, he could not see what difference it made.

That night Juan was almost embarrassed at the way Judith clung to him and the things she said. She had been acting strangely since they got to the ranch. Of course he liked to have her say she loved him, and that she would die without him, and that he was all she had left in the world. But it was a strange way of talking for his wife, who was mistress of Rancho Amarillo—as fine a four leagues of grassland as there was in California, offering everything in the way of happiness that anyone could ask.

IT WAS EARLY JUNE, and the first day of killing. For a week Judith had felt the undercurrent of excitement. This morning every man who could be mustered was at work—Juan to superintend, Miguel and Ramón as seconds in command, the eight or ten Indian vaqueros who lived in the quarters, even two little boys of ten or twelve who could help in one way or another. A few extra men had been hired from somewhere—Pablo, the oldest García boy, among them.

The men had been gone since daybreak, and the sun was still low when Judith rode out to see what was happening. The killing-ground was in a glade close to the stream, near where it flowed out of the valley; already dust was beginning to rise, for the grass was dry. Judith did not fear that the sight of the killing would bother her this time; her fainting on the beach, although it was only about five weeks past, seemed a long time back—something she had done as a foolish little girl. Besides, now she was mentally prepared.

When she got to the killing-ground she found that she had been right. The death of a dozen steers was in some way much less impressive than the death of one. She had imagined a scene of much excitement—horses galloping, steers bellowing, men shouting, lassos swinging. Actually it looked like not much excitement and a lot of hard work. Already a sufficient number of cattle for the day's killing had been penned into a corral. When a steer was needed two men would lasso one, bring it to the proper place, throw, and stick it. Then commenced the tedious process of skinning, stretching the hide to dry, taking off the tallow, melting it down in big pots, and finally running it off into hide bags. The carcass they merely had to leave to rot, or to become the food of the grizzly bears and coyotes which came out of the hills after dark. It seemed a terrible waste to Judith, but there was no market for beef.

A few minutes satisfied her curiosity, and she turned back towards the ranch-house; she had other plans for the morning. She smiled a little wistfully at the thought; it was about the first time since coming to the ranch a month ago that she had had such a definite plan of her own for a morning. Sometimes she felt that she had been in a daze all that time.

Of course, she hadn't been really. Things had happened, and she had participated. She had learned some Spanish and begun struggling with the supervision of the servants about the house. Once she and Juan had ridden thirty miles, visited another ranch overnight, and had a pleasant evening of songs and parlour games. Once Mr Williamson, a supercargo from one of the hide ships, had come to the ranch, stayed overnight, and gone away with a promise of a good share of Juan's hides; he was a professionally pleasant, chatty person, and Judith remembered their evening with him as highly entertaining.

Then she had had to spend one afternoon very busily writing a letter to her father, telling him various things, especially books, which he was to bring her back if he could find them This was in reply to his hurried letter, brought from Yerba Buena by a rider, to the effect that their agent had made a deal by which the *Spanish Belle* transferred most of her own cargo, picked up some hides and other Californian products, and made a voyage to the Sandwich Islands. Peleg wrote that he would be gone six months at least; the only way to reach him would be to get a letter to San Pedro before May 20. This idea appalled Judith, for San Pedro was four hundred miles south and there was no mail service. But Juan laughed, and next morning Miguel galloped off with the letter in his pocket. He changed horses at ranches as he went along, rode the eight hundred miles in so few days that Judith hardly believed he had delivered the letter, and was back at Rancho Amarillo as if nothing had happened.

Yet, on the whole, there had been a good deal of daze about these first weeks of marriage. She had been horribly downhearted on getting to the ranch, but she had clung to Juan, and that had so far seemed to be enough. In fact, she had been happy; somehow, the nights more than compensated for the days. She had not dared to think much about the future. She had lived with her body and her feelings. Whether she was with child or not—and in the last few days she had begun to believe that she was—she knew that her body was changing. She was conscious of a new feeling of pressure about her breasts.

She could not go on this way much longer; for ever riding about the ranch in the morning—that was already boring her. Then dinner and a siesta. Then a dull afternoon with nothing to do, vivified only by the touch of excitement as the evening came on and turned into darkness. No, she could not go on thus indefinitely. A woman, she herself at least, needed to meet life at more points than this one. She needed interests, plans, and contacts to be happy.

Perhaps this very feeling that she had so strongly this morning was another evidence of what she already thought. She had heard that a woman started planning for her child even while that child was scarcely formed.

As she rode back to the house she looked out southward. It was the same view that she had from the veranda, and already she could feel in herself an affection for it. At first it had been bright, lively green. Then one morning she had looked out and blinked once, thinking that her eyes were still full of sleep. But no—overnight it seemed that the green had lost its vigour and become darker and duller. In a week of hot, sunny days the valley and hills turned golden by acres and square miles. In another week they were brown. Judith had loathed the change. All her life she had known only a green or white landscape; brown hills seemed a betrayal of nature. It was like death. Curiously, a new point of view about it had come from Juan—her Juan, who really had no more philosophy than a jack-rabbit.

"It's not dead," he had objected. "It's ripe." Was there any difference? Certainly the cattle seemed to find none, but kept on eating the brown grass just as they had the green. That would account for Juan's feeling, and yet Judith thought that somehow Juan had been more profound than he knew. Was it death only when something was cut off incomplete? When something went its full cycle, fulfilled its purpose and went to fruition—was that ripeness, an ending not mournful?

That was the first time she had really ever thought of Juan as a person, not merely as a lover. He had few of the qualities of a civilized man; she was not even sure that he was very intelligent. But he was full of strange knowledge—the ways of grass, the ways of water in a country where water was life, the ways of cattle and horses, the ways of the Indians who were his servants. If she should study all her life she could never learn those things which Juan had by some old wisdom, deep as instinct.

Only after he had said the grass was not dead but ripe had Judith turned from loathing of the changed view, and discovered that the beauty was still there. The green of the grass, the gay colours of the wildflowers, had been mere decorative effect, a trifle garish. In the dull brown, broken only by the dark lines of the trees along the watercourses, the beauty was purer. It was a beauty of line, of structure, of architecture. She liked to let her eyes follow upward the lines of the hills building themselves up by knoll, watershed, and ravine until they culminated in the long restful skyline of the ridge. What was colour compared to that? Yes, she felt some affection for that view to the south.

But for the house—no! She tied her horse to the rail, and considered the veranda as she walked towards it. It was long, narrow, and low. It was too low! Its brick-tile floor was only three inches above the dirt with which it seemed to mingle by the breaking off of most of the tiles along the edge. Other tiles were broken, leaving holes in the floor. Five uprights, not evenly spaced, but about seven or eight feet apart, supported the roof. They were sycamore posts, taken probably from the trees along the creek, and not one of them but had at least two noticeable bends in it. (Judith thought of the straight-sawed pine posts and the square, sure carpentry of Appleby.) Every post of the porch had a little fork at the upper end, in which rested the transverse poles supporting the edge of the roof. Beneath the years' long weight of the roof of crude, locally made tile these poles had sagged. As a final irritation, Judith noticed that the bottom of every post, being very close to the ground, had rotted—not badly enough to give way, but enough to show that it was rotten.

The outer room, into which Judith entered, did not improve

her humour. It was of a good enough size, being fully twenty feet long, and nearly as broad. The room as a whole was dark, but one corner of it was particularly gloomy, and this was where the chest stood—the chest which she wished this morning to investigate. She went to it, and wondered again why anyone should have gone to the trouble of building such a curious, dark, inconvenient, and wholly useless alcove. It stuck out in all directions from the corner of the room, even spoiling the symmetry of the house's lines on the outside. One place where it jutted out formed the end of the porch; here was a very small window, a slit a few inches wide, with glass set right into the adobe—not a window you could open. Through it Judith could look all the way down the length of the porch. The opposite corner of the alcove had no window, but she knew that if there had been one it would have looked down along the wall of the house and the passage-way to the kitchen, and the kitchen itself, and along an old broken-down wall, which for some reason ran part way from the kitchen to the storehouse. This corner too was the darkest of all, for structural safety had required the main wall of the house to be carried along two feet into the alcove. The place where the chest stood was thus a dark recess, hemmed in on three sides by solid adobe walls.

There was another chest in the room too; it was unlocked and unmysterious, containing only extra sheets and blankets. But the chest in the alcove was different. It had been intriguing Judith ever since on her second day at the ranch she had tried to open it and found it locked. There was no reason why she might not have asked Juan for the key immediately, but she had cherished the chest as a kind of mystery. It was the only thing about the house which stimulated her imagination. Once she came to explore it she was afraid it would prove entirely commonplace. She imagined such remarkable and even terrible things about it that in the end she was really afraid to ask Juan for the key. Finally she had screwed up her courage that morning. Juan had merely laughed, and hunted up the big iron key; then, being busy about the slaughtering, he had hurried off without saying anything more.

The chest was not very large, and Judith easily slid it out of the alcove and over beneath the west window where she had light.

F

Then, with a fine feeling of mystery and of a kinship with Blue-beard's wife, she shut the doors to keep out the servants.

The lock was stiff and squeaky, as things that turned always were in California. She paused before throwing back the lid, feeling sure of being disappointed. The chest, she felt, had come to have for her the significance of a chest which might come floating ashore to a man marooned on a desert island. Her father could tell stories like that. The man would be living like a wild beast grubbing out roots, swallowing mussels raw, shambling about barefoot with long, shaggy hair, shivering at night beneath a covering of damp grass. In the floating chest might be flint and steel, pistols and gunpowder, knives and a hatchet, shoes and blankets, even a bottle of brandy to keep his soul alive until some ship's royal yards should break the horizon So Judith hoped that her chest might give her something to renew her contact with the life of civilization, something to reassure her that life from dawn to dusk need not merely be a matter of steaming beef with tortillas and hour-long contemplation of cattle eating grass. Concretely, the only thing she hoped definitely that the chest would contain was a set of the Waverley Novels.

She threw back the lid. Her nostrils sniffed the faint aromatic smell of some herb which a careful housewife had laid there years before to keep the moths away. Yes, she was disappointed. The chest was only half full, and the disorderly mass seemed to be mostly old dresses. But her curiosity rose again.

First she fished out of the confusion a black silk lady's costume of the Mexican or Spanish mode. Juan's mother's, she supposed. She might have laid it away neatly enough some time before she had died twenty years previously, but careless hands had pawed over it many times since, seeking things deeper down in the chest. The dress was a ruin, the silk cut in the creases. Judith smoothed it out and laid it over a chair respectfully; it had once been something fine, and she respected it as such; more practically she noted that the lace could still be salvaged. Three other dresses, in equally bad condition. . . . A ruined mantilla. . . . A shawl of fine brown wool, rumpled, but in perfect condition. . . . A fine piece of lace, some kind of head covering perhaps, still usable. . . .

Next she fished up a little casket—obviously a jewel-box. The tiny key was in the lock. Again Judith felt disappointed. There was little in the box—nothing certainly to indicate that it had ever belonged to a lady of great wealth or social station. One pair of earrings were set with what might be diamonds, but the stones were very small. Other articles had merely the native Mexican stones which Judith had seen all the Californian ladies wearing—turquoise, opal, garnet, obsidian. Some of the gold-work, especially of the rings, was heavy; the silver bracelets were even heavier. The workmanship seemed to her crudely barbaric; such as some Indian might hammer out. Judith supposed that she might have anything she wished, but nothing in the box really appealed to her.

Then came a series of scattered articles such as might be found laid away for safe keeping in any house. Six spoons of heavy plain silver, wrapped in cloth and tied, but badly tarnished nevertheless. . . . A pair of clumsy brass candlesticks. . . . A silver snuffbox. . . . A very small, handsomely ornamented pistol. . .

Next she saw a squat leather bag. Its weight and chink meant coin. Judith glanced at the doors, and for extra safety let the bag stay down in the chest while she inspected it. Inside were a lot of silver coins mixed with a few gold ones, and a smaller bag. In the smaller bag all the coins were gold. Many of these were old and worn. Some of the dates were well back in the seventeen-hundreds, and the most recent was only 1804. Most of the coins were Spanish doubloons, but she recognized French and British gold also; some coins she could not even identify by country. In the outer bag the coins seemed to be of much more recent date. The silver was mostly Spanish pieces of eight and Mexican and American dollars. She recognized some Peruvian pieces too. The gold was Spanish and American with a few British sovereigns.

She estimated the value. The gold in the inner bag might come to five hundred dollars. The silver and the little gold in the outer bag would hardly reach to that figure. Considered as capital, it seemed a pitifully small amount to represent the whole working reserve of Rancho Amarillo. Yet something about that inner bag stirred Judith's imagination. It spoke of wars, revolutions, and raids. It spoke of times when quick money might be needed—to ransom back the head of the house, or to shut a sentry's eyes. It was a bag that a woman might clutch to her breast as, to the sound of galloping, the family fled through the night and grim-faced retainers turned back with cocked pistols to hold off pursuers. Yet no coin had been put there for a generation; and the leather thong had given off brown dust as she untied it. That dust meant long years of lying undisturbed and unneeded. Nevertheless, throughout all those years no one had spent the gold; it had lain there—inviolate, against the day.

She put the money back carefully into a corner of the chest, and then looked at the two books which it contained. They were in Spanish, but she made them out to be religious manuals of some sort. They did not interest her in the slightest.

She picked out a bronze bowl, just large enough to cup in both her hands. To her surprise she recognized the work as Chinese; it was like bowls which her father had brought from Canton. This was the first article which gave her the pleasant feeling of contact with her former life; she decided not to put it back into the chest.

She unrolled and scanned two parchment documents. The circumlocutious official Spanish baffled her, but she made out one document to be an officer's commission to Esteban Godoy. That was Juan's father. The other document had to do with the granting of Rancho Amarillo. It might be very important, but at any rate she could think of no safer place for it to be.

She was down now to a scattering of oddments on the bottom of the chest. There were a good many loose letters and one diary or notebook. She hesitated about these, but they looked so old that they seemed historical rather than personal documents, and, besides, they were now her own family correspondence. She gathered them and laid them beside the Chinese bowl.

There was an old newspaper in Spanish. Doubtless some one had laid it away because he was mentioned in it; Judith let it wait until she could read Spanish better.

She looked more curiously at a silver-framed miniature—a pretty young woman, very Spanish-looking, in a very Spanish headdress. She might be Juan's mother—more likely his grandmother.

All that was left now was the collection of trifles that might lie at the bottom of a chest anywhere in the world—those curious little objects of fancied value which a person lays away and forgets. Looking at them, Judith had a sense of the kinship of all humanity, for she could remember a similar collection in a drawer at Appleby. You forgot the things, or else you forgot why you saved them, but you remembered you had thought them valuable and so didn't throw them away. Here, in the bottom of the chest, were flints, some in the form of arrowheads, some not; here was a larger rough implement, perhaps a spearhead, in dark stone. Broken leaves of the aromatic-smelling herb, a small cracked hand-mirror, thongs and strings, two or three bronze and small silver coins, little sea-shells, bright-coloured pebbles, other pieces of rock which looked like ore specimens, the rattles of a snake. There were other things, but nothing that seemed of importance.

Well, that was the chest. There was nothing there that would make much change in her life. She laid the things back, and shoved the chest into its corner again.

She took the Chinese bowl, the letters, and the diary, and went to sit on the veranda, where she could look at the view of the brown hills. Except for dinner and the siesta, she spent the rest of the day there poring over the handwriting. Her knowledge of Spanish was limited, and she had no dictionary. Now and then she went to the kitchen, pronounced a word according to the spelling, and tried to have Lupe explain what it meant. One of the letters proved to be not a real letter at all, but a document sworn before the notary of some Mexican town; several people seemed to be swearing that Esteban Godoy was of pure Spanish descent unmixed with Indian. Most of the letters were more in the nature of receipts or memoranda saved as a matter of business. The real letters were chiefly from Esteban Godoy to his wife, but some were from Jaime Godoy to his son Esteban. These latter were written from various places in Mexico. The notebook was beautifully written, and the script gave her no trouble. It was a very irregularly kept journal starting in 1761. At the front the author had written his name, " Antonio Godoy," with a great complicated flourish beneath, and then some words in Latin. Below this, in the handwriting of Jaime Godoy, there was a note in Spanish, which she translated: "born in province of Asturias, Spain, 1730." Judith made out that Antonio Godoy had been an officer in the army; he had kept the diary, as he felt like it, in garrison; some of the gaps indicated times when he had gone campaigning against the Indians.

Judith went and got one of the notes which Juan had written her. Then on a bench she laid first the journal, then a letter of Jaime Godoy's, then a letter of Esteban Godoy's, and then Juan's note. There she had four generations, from Spain through Jalisco and Sinaloa, to California. The progression was discouraging. Don Antonio had written easily and quoted his Latin, a man of the world. Don Jaime wrote well enough. Don Esteban's laboured letters showed that his hand knew the bridle-rein much better than the pen. Juan simply scrawled. At this rate the next Godoy would be making his mark.

At the thought Judith felt her back stiffen. *She* would have something to say about the next Godoy. But it was a little terrifying, just the same. The Godoys were gentlefolk, more so than her own family; but they had been going in the wrong direction for four generations. Would she be able to turn them back? When she thought of Juan down on the killing-ground that minute like one of his own Indians she was frightened. The pressure of circumstances was against her.

That same heavy pressure of circumstances weighed upon her when she thought of the dull resistance with which the servants met every effort of hers to change their methods of housekeeping. Looking at the journal, she could imagine Antonio Godoy coming to Mexico with a trim Spanish valet. But the servants had degenerated along with the handwriting until Juan Godoy was served by stolid Indians a generation from the wickiup. At Aunt Leticia's she had thought it was funny, but here things were even worse. For here it was not only that she had to face the ordinary Californian slovenliness and shiftlessness, but also the fact that, since the death of Juan's mother twenty years before, the place had been without a mistress. Juan and his father had just camped in the house until the father had died when Juan was seventeen, and since then Juan had camped alone. For a while there had been what they called a major-domo, who was a kind of steward, but something had happened to him, and Juan had never bothered to get another. Juan bought supplies, chiefly corn and beans and peppers, from San José; but if they happened to run out of anything it made little difference, for they grew enough wheat in the field across the creek, and they could always go out and kill another steer.

The house servants were Lupe, Catalina, and Antonia. They were all mostly, or perhaps wholly, Indian. Lupe was the cook, and she was the least trouble. She was more cleanly than Judith would have expected. Her meals were coarse but edible, and Judith usually had a strong appetite. The other two were a problem. Catalina and Antonia were supposed to divide the housework between them. That was just what they did, and as far as Judith could see their principle of division was that whenever anything was to be done each stood back and waited for the other to do it. Both must be somewhere in their forties, but, like most Indian women, they looked older. Catalina had a swarm of children. She seemed to have some kind of seniority over Antonia which she was always trying to enforce and never being able to. In the end Judith noticed that Catalina did most of the work. "The difference is," Judith thought, "that Antonia has some brains and Catalina hasn't; neither has Lupe. She just cooks by habit. But I'd trust either of them further than I would Antonia." This conclusion really made Judith think rather more of Antonia than of the others. She thought of her mother's proverb, "Use a knave, but don't trust him; send an honest fool on a long journey, but don't let him carry money." If she would be needing a nurse Antonia would be the best; she would have brains enough to take the baby outside if the house started to burn down.

But for the present there was really nothing to choose between Catalina and Antonia, and Judith's efforts to get anything done around the house were just like the crock beating itself against the wall. The girls just did as they always had, and if pushed too hard would always shrug their shoulders and say they couldn't understand Judith's Spanish. Judith pondered unsuccessfully on some way to get under their skins. She couldn't discharge them, for they were really more like slaves or feudal serfs than paid servants. She couldn't threaten to reduce their wages, for all they got anyway was an occasional coin which Juan gave them as a kind of tip when he happened to remember.

"I'm sure Juan would take a stick to them if I asked him to," she thought, "but I haven't quite got to being a slave-whipper yet."

So in the end it seemed easier to keep on camping in the house and putting off the real battle with the situation. Maybe tomorrow . . .

And now it was getting late afternoon; the shadows lay heavy in the ravines as she looked out from the veranda across to the hills. Juan would be coming in soon. Her heart was suddenly light.

She had been brooding over the letters for a long time. Now she gathered them up and put them back into the chest. But she kept out the Chinese bowl, and put it on the table where she could see it. There might be a story behind it—strange that a piece of Chinese bronze should turn up at a Californian ranch. Yet she knew that a durable material like bronze might pass through a hundred hands in way of trade. She looked admiringly, wistfully, at the studied curves of the dragons' tails, the delicate overlap of the scales, the minute lines of the enveloping ornament. No barbarous Indian had been that craftsman. The design spoke of great cities, and of a taste cultivated and refined through centuries. It was far beyond her—as far beyond her and her village upbringing, she thought, as she felt herself beyond Rancho Amarillo.

So from her exploration of the chest Judith kept only the little Chinese bowl. It was a symbol, a battle-flag perhaps, but it was hardly practical. For the present, the marooned seaman must continue eating his raw mussels.

Next morning Judith was sick. She lay in bed, miserable and wholly without spirit. Juan looked at her with wondering but unsympathetic eyes. Juan could not be sympathetic, she realized; he had probably never been sick. It was rather a new experience for Judith herself. She counted on her fingers, and decided that Aunt Leticia had been right about her coming up about the middle of February. It was nearly noon before Judith managed to get dressed. She certainly did not feel like starting anything with Catalina and Antonia that day.

ANTONIA WATCHED THE WALTZERS WHIRLING BY, and shook her new earrings to make them sparkle. She could not remember having been so excited for a long time. Being three-quarters Indian, Antonia let nothing show in her face, but she was feeling a certain languorousness; she was old enough to know what it meant, and young enough still to have hopes of satisfying it. Moving her tongue slightly within her mouth, seeming almost half asleep, she watched the gentlemen waltz by--the tall red-haired French lieutenant; the square-shouldered, hairy-handed Yankee mate; huge Don Ignacio (there was a man!). She hardly noticed the ladies; then she caught a flash of yellow-white hair.

"So-oo, so-oo," Antonia cooed inwardly. The mistress had got rid of that too short Frenchman, and was dancing with the big captain from Mexico City again. A good-looking pair! And how lucky that the master had been called away so suddenly this afternoon! Still looking at the captain, Antonia absently raised a hand and felt one of her earrings. She knew, she knew! Handsome captains did not give beautiful Boston earrings to not so young Indian women without reason.

Ah, he was a sly one! That was two days ago. Coming over to her in the corner of Don Francisco's patio, and laying the little package on the table so that no one would see him giving her anything:

"Antonia, you are a fine girl; here is something for you," he had said—only that; nothing that anyone could tell anyone else with leers.

"Thanks, señor," she had said, taking the cue of discreetness. But she had understood. He was a sly one! He would never get a lady into trouble with her husband. He knew the game.

At first Antonia had thought it was almost dishonest of her to take the earrings. What with so many people around all day, and what with the master close at hand every night, Antonia did not see where, even with her to help him, the captain would have any chance. But he was a sly one, and this afternoon the message had come from Don Juan Bautista, the Governor. The master had cursed, but she could see he was glad to be off. He would rather, she knew, be chasing stolen horses than cutting figures at a dance —not that, she thought loyally, he couldn't dance better than any of them. He had not told the mistress what he was off to do; he had grown very tender of her in the last few months; "business for the Governor" was what he had said. Antonia had heard him telling the mistress:

"You must go to the dance, anyway; you can go with Don Francisco and his family. Antonia can go along. With so many French officers off the frigate there won't be enough ladies to go round, so you must go to be hospitable."

The mistress had protested in her broken Spanish that she would rather not go. She had said just the right things, thought Antonia, just the right things to say to a departing husband on the eve of a great ball—not that the speaker or anyone, except possibly the husband, would believe them. Still, Antonia, remembering the gossip of the Monterey servants' quarters, knew that they were the right things to say, and was proud of her mistress, just as she was proud of her master. She was also proud of the captain whose attention the mistress had attracted.

Moreover, Antonia was proud of herself, and had been so, in fact, for several months. It was a triumph not to be any longer a mere other Catalina to work generally around the house, but to be almost a lady's maid, with the half-promise that she might later be the baby's nurse. It had been, too, a tremendous satisfaction to be brought all the way to Monterey in the ox-cart just to take care of the mistress. This was seeing the world!

"How many people are there in Monterey?" she had asked as the servants sat with their beans and tortillas in the kitchen at Don Francisco's.

"How many people?—about a million," said Margarita the cook.

"Seven hundred, I heard Don Francisco say once," said Rafael the vaquero.

A million, or perhaps even as many as seven hundred people, thought Antonia—certainly a great city!

They had good talk in the kitchen and in the patio at Don Francisco's and at other houses. Much of the talk was about love-making, with fine whispered scandals about the way ladies lived their lives in great towns. Antonia learned fast.

She had been in Monterey most of October now, and had even been out on the ships, where the mistress was purchasing all sorts of things—clothes for herself and for the coming baby, house furnishings and dishes, spending money as if it were nothing. Antonia had a feeling that life was very exciting and that she was enjoying the very centre of civilization and sophistication, where life moved at a vicious pace. She would have enjoyed a little flirtation, but there were so many young girls around that she had not had any luck.

It was a great stroke of good fortune that the French frigate had come in. Naturally there had to be a ball for the officers, and it must be very select—not a free-for-all fandango open to common people. It had merely been luck—the master's going away—that Antonia had been able to come as a kind of chaperon in addition to Don Francisco and Doña Ana. But Antonia could feel herself a lady. Other ladies, too old or too heavy to dance, were sitting just as she was on chairs near the wall. Some of them were keeping hawks' eyes upon unmarried daughters. An orchestra of no less than six pieces—fiddles, guitars, and a drum—was playing valiantly. Waltzes were in demand. The Frenchmen did not know the Mexican dances, and after several months at sea they seemed to prefer the waltz to the quadrille. The dancing was vigorous; there was excitement in the air.

Yes, Antonia felt very well pleased—partly from her thoughts, partly from the music, partly from the sight of so many well-built gentlemen, and partly from the drink of brandy which the captain had so kindly given her, surreptitiously, from his flask.

The waltz ended, and just in front of her the captain and her mistress sat down. She listened with keen Indian ears.

" It is horrible to think of you buried on that ranch—you who could be an ornament to society anywhere. Ah, Mexico, the City

—you should see the balls there, the masked balls at the theatre! "
And the captain burst forth into vivid description.

Sitting behind, Antonia listened and watched. The watching was
more important, for the talking merely covered the actions. By
fractions of inches, as if thoughtlessly under mere warmth of
conversation, Antonia could see the gold braid on the Captain's
knee nearing, touching, and beginning to press the lavender ruffles
of the skirt, and then as the lady suddenly became conscious the
captain's knee was decorously inches away, and he was leaning
over to adjust the shawl. It was nearly midnight of a foggy
October evening; in the intermission many ladies grew cold; you
could see several French officers adjusting shawls. The captain was
a big man, and big men often have clumsy hands. Antonia saw
the captain's hand pass along Judith's bare skin from the point of
her shoulder to her neck. Antonia saw her start suddenly.

Next Judith danced with a French midshipman. He was a mere
child, very tall and slim. Nothing but a pole of a man, thought
Antonia; she liked men with heavy necks and shoulders, like the
captain. He meanwhile danced with Doña Lupe Aguirre, making
love to her openly; but that, Antonia knew, was only to make his
attentions elsewhere less obvious, and perhaps to raise a little spite
of jealousy.

It was midnight, and the dance was growing even more furious.
The fiddles, guitars, and drum hardly stopped at all. Earlier, there
had been a bowl of harmless punch specially for the ladies. It was
empty now, but if a lady grew thirsty—as many did—there was
red wine, and angelica, and even brandy. Antonia began to see
new and darker faces. There was no guard at the door, and if the
uninvited half-breed girls wandering about outside felt their feet
beginning to twitch with desire for dancing nothing prevented
them from coming in. They had pretty brown faces and slender
figures, and wore no petticoats. A devil-may-care French lieutenant
seized one of them; they danced.

Don Luis Hernandez and his wife Doña Rita were the best
waltzers on the floor. Their movements were so graceful that
people kept saying he could carry a glass of water on his head
without spilling it. As such graceful waltzing required, there were

several good inches of space between the two partners. There was not so much space between the French lieutenant and the slim half-breed girl; it would have been difficult to pass a knife-blade between them; it might even have been dangerous. At the thought Antonia chuckled secretly and salaciously.

By now a dozen officers had followed the bold lieutenant's example. After three months at sea they seemed to care little about graceful waltzing. The slim bodies of the half-breed girls were clinging close to the dark uniforms. Momentarily a new spirit seemed entering in; what had a few minutes before been a formal ball was becoming something wilder.

Breathless, Judith dropped again upon the bench in front of Antonia; she was with the captain; they had been dancing vigorously. Antonia saw her mistress swaying a little, as if dizzy with the whirling of the waltz; she coughed once. It was a tiny cough, but the captain was on his feet; he was back in a moment with a glass of angelica. Judith hesitated.

"But, ah, the punch is finished." The captain seemed almost overcome with embarrassment. Judith gulped; the insidious sweet wine soothed her cough, but it did not quench her thirst. The captain brought her another glass, which she sipped more slowly.

Antonia's hopes for herself were dwindling. There were too many young girls about. Every now and then, if you watched closely, you could see a pair of dancers stop and separate as they neared the door. Then the slim form of a half-breed girl slipped out through the door followed by a sturdier form in a naval uniform. These couples did not return immediately.

Ah, it was in the air to-night. Antonia thought how lucky her mistress was. She even wondered why the captain was so badly smitten. The hair—that was remarkable, yes. But she was stiffly square-shouldered, and could not dance with half the lithe grace of the Californian ladies. And her taste in clothes was insipid— putting herself into plain lavender when she might have been in black set off with purple and red as some of the others were!

"But," Judith was saying to the captain, "I don't think I shall be in Monterey more than a few weeks more. And I don't know when I shall be back. Going up, we rode. But coming down, I came in the ox-cart, and it took a week."

She did not say, Antonia noted, why she had had to ride in the ox-cart, and from her figure the captain surely could not guess as yet. Remembering this, Antonia felt that this was a time when her mistress deserved a little fun. Antonia studied the line of her mistress's neck and shoulder; they seemed to be softening somehow. The captain was claiming the next dance.

The musicans had exhausted the brandy allotted to them. There was a blur to the music, but the rhythm was deadly. Antonia patted with her foot and swayed her shoulders a little. The captain and Judith passed; they were dancing together. Antonia wondered if she was clinging to him as closely as the half-breed girls were to the French officers, but with the kind of dress she was wearing no one could tell.

When they came back to their seats the captain brought another glass of angelica. Judith drank without protest, but this time she choked a little and coughed. The captain was all solicitude. Judith apologized.

" I'm not used to wine. Those other glasses were sweet and easy to drink. This one seems stronger."

A deep inward smile did not show on Antonia's Indian face, she was thinking of the captain's brandy-flask.

She saw the gold braid tight among the lavender ruffles now. The captain was smoking a cigarette. He pointed out to Judith that many of the ladies were smoking.

" You must try it," he said. " The trouble with you American ladies, if I may say that there is any trouble "—here the shawl seemed to need adjustment—" the trouble, I should say, is that you are too unwilling to try new things, too stiff in a certain unbending primness drawn from your own cold country."

He rolled a slim cigarette, and she smoked a few puffs before he took it from her.

" The gesture is enough; more might make you ill, and "—his eyes were slits above the black moustache and the shining white teeth of his smile—" I do not wish you ill—to-night."

They rose to dance; Antonia noticed her mistress standing

steadily, but with feet a little apart; she almost fell into the captain's arms. Antonia thought again of her mistress's luck; in all the room the captain was the finest figure of a man.

The older ladies of Monterey still sat along the walls. Their hawks' eyes followed their own unmarried daughters, but for everything else they had an easy tolerance. Their faces seemed to say that men must have their pleasures. Once a girl is married let her husband watch out for her—if he can! As for half-breed chits, they have their place, after a ship has been three months at sea.

That feeling of release, of the ship just in, seemed to spread. The captain was a big man and his eyes were growing possessive; no one else tried to dance with Judith. More times than Antonia could recollect they danced, and sat down

Each time they sat down there was another glass of angelica, and another adjustment of the shawl. Antonia watched from behind, and smiled inwardly at the way the captain's hands, after each successive dance, moved farther, more surely and more boldly. And something subtle—it could probably be noticed best from behind—was happening to her mistress's shoulders and back. They no longer showed quite those firm, square-set lines. They seemed to be sinking into curves—and curves which had a tendency to incline in the direction of the captain.

And then, finally, Don Francisco was apologizing to the captain. He pleaded for excuse his own grey hairs, and those of his wife; they must retire (it was now two o'clock) and let the young people dance through till daylight; unfortunately this required taking the Señora Godoy home. The captain was all graciousness.

"I would not be the means of keeping the señora one minute from her bed. With regret, I shall get another partner"—his eyes were upon Judith's—"for the next dance."

With decorum he kissed her hand and helped her put on her cloak. As the others were going he stood in Antonia's way, slipped a coin into her hand, and spoke softly under cover of the music:

"At the patio gate in half an hour."

Antonia felt a warmth flow into every part of her body. If she might be too old to compete with those chits who had slipped through the door and into the arms of French officers, still she was not too old to open a gate in the service of love for a man worth any two of them! That was a man! No mawkish serenading. A friendly servant in the outer court, and then a light knock on the lady's door. In half an hour she is in bed and thinking—of whom naturally? Then the knock. *Jesús Maria!* He will be discovered; some one is coming; my honour is lost! I must let him in for a moment, hide him, and send him quickly away when the coast is clear. But once in her room and she in her nightgown—it is a poor man surely . . . Antonia knew the gossip of the servants' quarters.

" We will walk," said Don Francisco outside. He said it as something notable, although his house was distant perhaps six minutes strolling. He waved away Rafael the vaquero who brought up the horses. " I have found," Don Francisco went on, evidently feeling that explanation of his vagary was necessary, " that walking in the open air, after long hours in the ballroom, clears the head of crotchets, and sends me to a sound sleep."

Antonia felt a certain uneasiness; she watched the line of Judith's shoulders, neck, and head. They were still dissolving into curves; Judith's arm clung tightly to Don Francisco's—her body seemed to incline towards him; her feet followed an abnormally straight line. But Antonia did not like this walking home; as Don Francisco said, it cleared the head. With interest Antonia watched her mistress.

Two minutes from the house Antonia saw the form in front of her straighten and take some deep breaths; the lines of the shoulders and neck became firmer; the feet moved more normally. Antonia was worried, and then in her own subtle way she had suddenly a new and entrancing idea.

When she had helped Judith get out of the lavender dress she stood a moment instead of leaving as was expected :

" Would the señora like a plate of hot frijoles? "

She saw Judith's mouth move at the thought of the steaming red beans.

" But why? And isn't it too late? "

" There are always frijoles," said Antonia, shrugging her shoulders. " Margarita left some to keep hot for me when I was coming in late."

Antonia managed also to warm up a few tortillas.

Sitting up in bed in her nightgown, and wrapped in a shawl, Judith ate the tortillas and beans. Antonia could almost see visibly the solidity and warmth and matter-of-factness which they brought back. The last vestige of a certain dizzy-headed nonchalance disappeared; the usual firm-set expression returned—or perhaps it was even firmer than usual; it was more like the look she had when she went about most unreasonably showing the servants at Rancho Amarillo that they had missed sweeping in the corners. Antonia thought of the proverb: "The deeper the stick is thrust into the water the harder it springs back."

Then Antonia talked—about Juan. She was brief and shrewd. She declared him the best of masters, and the handsomest of men, and the most affectionate of husbands. She could see Judith looking pink and very contented. Then, knowing that enough is enough, Antonia took the empty plate and said good-night. She stuck her head back in to say not to forget getting up to bolt the door.

The captain had already knocked gently at the gate before Antonia got there. She quieted the growling dogs, slipped the bar, and opened the gate just enough. The captain did not slink. (Ah, he was a man!) He strode across the patio, and Antonia pointed out the right door. She would have liked to stay within earshot, but she was really frightened at all she was attempting, and so scuttled back to the gate.

It seemed hardly a minute when she heard a muttering. No, it was louder than a muttering; it was dangerously loud. The captain was coming towards her, and he was swearing. Antonia felt an additional tremor of delight. No one but the gentleman whom she felt the captain to be could ever have cursed so fully or expressed himself so accurately upon the lowness and dishonesty of women, and a woman, and their and her ancestors. He felt for the bar at the gate, and just then Antonia pressed herself against him. He threw her off with a curse, but she was back, her hands about his loins. In the darkness he could not see her faded, homely face. Her body was still vigorous. He cursed again, but she drew him into the shadow.

BY THE BEGINNING OF THE NEW YEAR Juan could recollect that he had been sleeping on the rawhide cot for nearly a month. He was beginning to feel restless and jumpy. And yet he knew that Aunt Leticia must be right; she knew everything about such matters. He certainly did not want the baby to have a hare-lip or a club-foot or even a red splotch across the face. Besides, when he looked at Judith now, or sometimes when he thought of her, he had a feeling of embarrassment or even of distaste.

First, all summer Judith had gone about looking greenish, and being constantly sick, and having no life for anything during the morning and most of the afternoon; but during those months she had always felt better towards evening, and so their life could go on in some ways almost as usual. And one thing that he had rather enjoyed about that time was that Judith being so ill and spiritless had stopped fussing with the servants over the house-cleaning and the cooking, as she had begun to do when first she came to the ranch. That had caused a lot of trouble. And what was the use of it, anyway? Things were good enough as they had been.

About the beginning of October she had got to feeling better; then he had taken her to Monterey, and it had been a fine change. Everything had been pleasant, and he was proud of how well Judith had got along in Monterey. The only matter of that visit which still worried him a little was that business of the wild-goose chase he had been hurried off on; he had been following stolen horses when no horses had been stolen. He had tried to reckon it out, but all he could find was that the report came somehow from that big fool of a Mexican captain who had left town just afterwards. But, anyway, Judith had felt well during October and November at Monterey and had looked just about as usual.

Then a month ago, just after they had come back to the ranch—as if it might have been overnight—Judith had become heavy and

98

awkward and listless and enormously big. Even her face changed; it got coarser-looking and blotchy in colour. He had seen plenty of women carrying babies; the Indian and half-breed women about the ranch had babies as cows had calves. That was just it! You expected them to have babies just as cows had calves. But with Judith the change had something almost repulsive about it. The finer he had thought everything about her before the more horrible it began to appear now.

Then this very morning they had quarrelled. It was about fleas. Judith had had them before; newcomers to California always got bitten. Usually fleas worked in somewhere under the clothes, especially around the belt; Juan could remember a new supercargo out from Boston who was bitten all round the middle and looked so funny when he went in swimming to get rid of the fleas that all the other men stood on the bank and laughed at him. But at least his bites were decently under his clothes. This time the flea had worked over Judith's throat and left cheek. She had scratched at them before she got well awake, and that made the ugly red blotches stand out worse than ever on her white skin.

Juan had not said anything, but just tried not to look at her. And he tried so hard that she must have noticed it, for she burst out with something about having to live in a dirty old ranch like this and get bitten. He tried to explain that in California fleas were just part of the country, and even the finest houses in Monterey had them. She snorted back with something about the best houses in Monterey not being any better than dog-kennels, anyway; and nobody but dirty Californians would live in them. He bridled up worse than ever because he knew she meant that he was dirty. So it went back and forth two or three times more, each getting madder.

Juan scooped up his breakfast standing in the kitchen, as he used to do sometimes before he was married. Then, filled with eggs and tortillas and beans and coffee, he stepped outside. He still felt resentful of Judith and what she had said, and in spite of its being early morning he had a restless feeling. The good coffee and the warm food were nourishing him so fast that he could almost feel himself getting more vigorous minute by minute.

Then he saw Paquita. Of course he saw Paquita every day, just as he saw every one else around the ranch. If she passed within twenty feet of him he would say " Good morning "; and if she were farther away he might not even say that much. But this morning he *really* saw Paquita.

She passed a few yards away, carrying some washing on her head, going towards the creek with it. She was young, slim, and vigorous. She walked with the springy, even tread that her Indian blood gave her. Once she raised an arm to steady the bundle, and the sinuous lines of her breast and side sprang into relief beneath her single garment. As a little gust of wind struck her she swayed gracefully to bring her bundle back into balance. She started down the slope to the creek, and had to bend backward a little. Juan bent in sympathy; his back muscles contracted a little; his groin muscles answered with a balancing pull. Then, as at a signal, the forces dammed back through his weeks of sleeping alone on the cot broke loose within him. He no longer saw Paquita; he felt her. He felt her by memory bridging back to those last months before his marriage. He felt her by anticipation. A single garment—ah, he knew!—one swift movement, and release. From that moment he progressed from point to point merely as desire pushed him on, without thought.

Horses stood, as always, tied to the rail in front of the house. He mounted, waving back Ramón who came up to accompany him. By the creek he spoke to Paquita from the saddle, as master speaks to servant:

" Leave the washing, and come to the big sycamore."

" Yes, señor." She spoke in matter-of-fact tones, like an Indian; her expression did not change.

Juan rode on towards the big sycamore, holding his horse at a canter.

In half an hour Paquita was again at her washing.

Juan went back near enough to the house to wave to Ramón, and then the two of them rode off on one of those innumerable tours of inspection which the ranch demanded. The early rains had been heavy; the grass was again green and beginning to be tall.

By the time they were returning it was noon. Juan's senses were keen, and his judgment clear. He had made out a mountain-lion's trail which Ramón had passed by. What had happened under the sycamore loomed no larger in his mind than what he had eaten for breakfast. He had no more resentment against Judith, and such matters as her heaviness and her flea-bites had become unimportant temporary conditions. In fact, as he came into sight of the ranch-house Juan felt himself remarkably happy, and his happiness was tied up in his wife and his coming baby. He thought of Judith as the most beautiful and remarkable woman in the world. It was fine too that she had not, as Aunt Leticia had feared, become homesick because things were so different at the ranch from what she had been accustomed to. At least, as far as he could see she was not despondent. But mostly he thought happily of Judith as a sudden vision of yellow-white hair, as he had seen her first on the brig. And he had one of his very rare day-dreams.

He imagined the ranch attacked. Perhaps there was a revolution, and the down-country people—of whom he had a very low opinion—were the attackers. Then his imagination wavered. At one moment he thought himself and Miguel and Ramón rushing to Judith's defence and driving off the down-country people in confusion and blood. And again he thought of himself and his men overcome by numbers and wounded; but, nevertheless, he was carrying Judith away on horseback. As for Paquita, she did not even appear in either version, and so in the second must have been left behind to the fury of the invaders.

When he came into the house he kissed Judith most respectfully and affectionately too, although with certain reserves still on account of her condition.

That evening they sat before a fire in the outer room. Judith was on a rug with some pillows to lean against. She drew her feet up beneath her, and the lines of her dress fell so that her figure no longer looked heavy. The side of her face with the bites was away from the fire. The firelight played entrancingly with her white hair. Juan sat with his guitar on a bench at the opposite side of the hearth. He was extremely proud and happy as he thought of his child. He did not have a sense of irritation in

Judith's presence, as he had had lately. He was happy just to be with her, quietly looking at her.

He sang some English songs, and some love songs in Spanish. Then, for fun, he sang the little comic song that some one had made up about Governor Chico and his " niece." Judith did not understand the Spanish of this, and Juan did not like to translate. The Spanish of it did not seem so bad, but the only English equivalents of it he knew were the words that sailors and trappers used. So he tried to make her understand by gesture and knowing looks. She laughed, and he was relieved. From his friend Mr Melton he had always understood that American women were prudish, but Mr Melton was not married, and perhaps that made a difference.

Then Juan took his violin and played—Spanish dances, and *Money Musk*, and the few more difficult pieces that he had played to her when he was serenading. She asked him how he knew *Money Musk*, which was an American tune, and he said that he had learned it from a trapper who had come from Santa Fe. And two days later the trapper had got knifed in a fight and died. That was the way he learned his English songs, too, from trappers and sailors. If he heard a tune just once he could play it, and after singing the words two or three times he could usually remember a verse or two, and if he didn't remember exactly he filled in. The more difficult pieces he had picked out from some printed music on sheets that a lady in Monterey used to have. She had told him what the printed notes meant. The lady was dead now, and the music had been lost. It was a pity it was lost, for in a few places he was not just sure he played the notes right.

Judith said that they could easily get music sent out from Boston, whole books of it if he wanted them. This was an amazing new idea to Juan, for he had in some way assumed that all the music there was in the world was just what the lady at Monterey had had, except of course for songs and dance tunes which floated around without anybody bothering to write them.

Then Judith told him about people called Mozart and Bach and Handel. This was an amazing idea too—that people could actually spend their lives making up music which other people put down in books. Juan had always assumed that the people in the world were ranchers, trappers, and sailors, except, of course, priests and Indians and the few people who lived in towns—and they didn't count for much.

"But," said Judith, "what do you suppose the sailors do with all the hides they take away, and who makes all the things the ships bring in from Boston?"

Juan laughed at how keenly she brought out this argument, and felt again how happy he was to have such a clever and experienced wife. But he wished he could have some of those books of music. How could they go about getting some? Judith said she thought that she could manage it.

Then she told him about hearing a violin-player who stood on a platform before hundreds of people and for two hours played pieces for them.

"Did he play any better than I do?"

"Well, yes."

Juan was a little piqued, for he believed that he played better than anyone else in California. But he felt better when Judith explained that that fellow had done nothing all his life but play the violin, and that he had a violin which cost a great deal of money. Juan knew that playing a violin was quite all right for amusement, but a man who could only play it without being able to ride an unbroken horse and handle a lasso was hardly worth calling a man. But the idea of a better violin was a good one, for sometimes his own squeaked on certain notes, and one of the pegs was likely to slip at the worst possible moment. Judith thought that they might be able to order a new violin also. It was bedtime now, and Juan finished the evening with the strange feeling of two new and un-fulfilled desires, and also a vague realization that perhaps the world was a more complicated place than his twenty-one or nearly twenty-two years of experience between Rancho Amarillo and Monterey had led him to believe.

Judith went to bed in the four-poster. Juan, comfortably tired and very happy, went outside for a look around, and came back saying there might be frost. Judith was lying there with a warm flannel nightgown that came up well around her neck. They exchanged smiles. Juan's going to bed was simple. As preliminaries he wound his watch and looked to the priming of his pistol, and laid them both on a chair beside his cot. He slipped off his clothes, blew out the candle, and wrapped himself in two big serapes, a soft inner one and a heavy outer one. He lay down on the cot, and turned over once to put the serapes well about him and settle himself properly on the rawhide thongs Then in five breaths he went to sleep.

IT WAS THE END OF JANUARY when Mr Melton left the García place behind and rode up the faint road towards Rancho Amarillo. A single stolid vaquero rode behind him. To the steady throb of the hoofs Mr Melton was considering, as he did almost every day, discharging the vaquero and riding alone, and, as always, was deciding against it. The vaquero's value as either bodyguard or groom was negligible, but the dignity of Mr Melton's profession required at least one vaquero to make the proper impression when he arrived at ranches. The other agents and supercargoes, most of them, managed to arrive with even more of a flourish. And, after all, that was one of the big parts of business among these Californians, who had not the slightest idea of what one per cent. more profit might mean, but who nine times out of ten would do their business with a man they liked. Mr Melton knew he had some dangerous rivals too; the competition was getting keen. There was Daniels, for instance, with his golden-brown hair, who ogled the older ladies so charmingly without giving offence to their husbands; and there was Williamson with his cognac, who managed to get the usually abstemious ranchers to take just one drink more than they intended.

Not that he himself, Mr Melton ran on mentally, didn't have some good friends. This very year old Don Felipe had saved him the better part of his hides, though Daniels and Williamson had both been there first. And at Rancho Amarillo too, even though he had put off his visit this year and let others get in ahead, still he knew that Juan would have saved something for him. He should have been to Rancho Amarillo three months ago at least. Since he had last seen Judith Hingham at Monterey on the morning after her marriage he had ridden through Mission San José half a dozen times, and every time he had considered going up to Rancho Amarillo. He did not believe that he was nursing a broken heart, but still he flinched at a meeting. He kept hoping that he would meet her accidentally at some dance or while she was visiting another ranch. And Rancho Amarillo was certainly one place in the world where you could not arrive and say lightly, "Oh, I just happened to be passing, and dropped in." No, it was road's end, if there ever was one. But now he was in for it.

He topped the little hill, and drew rein a moment. Yes, it was beautiful. The cup of the valley among the hills! He searched his memories of Byron and Wordsworth for a quotation, but could find none. Probably they had never known anything like such a scene. Already he had been sighted from the house. A mile away through the rain-washed winter air he could see a boy scurrying, and could make out dogs barking, although the sound did not yet reach him.

Before he had even arrived at the creek-crossing Juan had sprung into the saddle, splashed through the water, and come to greet him in English. Mr Melton warmed at the show of friendship.

Juan and Mr Melton each offered courtesies as to the apparent good health of the other.

"And—Judith?" added Mr Melton. He noted that Juan's face fell a little.

"She is well. That is—but, of course, you know she is to have her baby in about a month." He hesitated and stopped.

"I hope that she is eating well, and the right things." The ladies in California discussed their pregnancies freely, and many of them thought that all Americans were to be consulted as doctors. So Mr Melton knew most of the problems, and he also knew the restricted diet on an isolated ranch in mid-winter. "See that she gets plenty of green stuff," he added.

"She does not seem really sick. But she is very heavy and slow, and does not have much interest in things, and she seems very . . ." Juan hesitated for a word as he rarely did in English, but the complicated situation seemed to exceed his simple vocabulary; perhaps it would have been too much for him even in Spanish. He took refuge in the concrete: "She cries when she thinks I am not looking."

"Greens might help, anyway," said Mr Melton, embarrassed, but clutching at the straw of his belief that the feelings of pregnant women were a matter of diet. The thought of Judith weeping by herself made him feel unutterably miserable.

"One other thing," said Juan. "Everything has been quiet lately —the old family business that we talk of. Don't say anything. Judith doesn't know of it, and Aunt Leticia says I must be careful not to tell her now. It might mark the child, thinking about blood and worrying. I hope nothing happens in the next month."

As Judith met them in front of the house Mr Melton had first a sudden feeling of shock at her appearance—lustreless hair, puffy and blotchy face, body incredibly large and heavy-looking. But as she greeted him he thought that Juan had been wrong; never had she seemed more animated. She grew flushed, and was wild with questions, which she put far too fast for answers.

But inside five minutes later he knew what Juan had meant. Juan himself, with his ever-renewing physical energy. had gone out to see about something. Judith and Mr Melton sat before the hearth; the fireplace smoked a little, and the wood spat and sizzled.

"It's wet from the rains—and green, anyway," she said. And at those words she seemed to remember something, or many things that came flooding up from somewhere deep down. It was queer the way she seemed to go all into a heap, although if you had taken a tape and measured you would probably not have found a quarter of an inch difference anywhere. Mr Melton was almost terrified; the light had gone out of her just as if you had blown out a candle. He rallied desperately to amuse her.

"Oh, I know all about how vaqueros go about bringing in wood. They lasso a dead branch, and then if they can't break it off they hack at it with knives. Then they discuss it this way and that a little, and whether it is worth working on this one or trying another. There isn't a decent axeman, except Yankees, in California."

But this description was perhaps too realistic to be funny, and Judith only continued to look dully at the drops sizzling and dropping from the wood. Mr Melton tried again:

"There's a ship just in at Monterey with some news. She's American—the *Sarah Leeds*; I know her captain—name's Browning—and what he tells ought to be straight. Anyway, there's no reason why it shouldn't be so, except that rumours always start about something like that. Browning didn't have it very direct at best. But it seems that the *Sarah Leeds* had trouble off the Horn, and ran into Valparaiso for refitting, and there they heard it along the waterfront."

Mr Melton paused to make his suspense last as long as possible, and was highly pleased when Judith raised her head. She spoke only the one monosyllable:

"What?"

But that, thought Mr Melton, meant curiosity—and curiosity meant life. He went on, still holding back his point:

"But you see it wasn't very direct, for the English ship left before Captain Browning came in. But they said in Valparaiso that the English ship—come to think of it, she was a barque, not a ship— she was out of Bristol and had a quick run, and her name . . ." This pause was pure art on Mr Melton's part, for he was quite sure that Captain Browning had not mentioned the name. "Well, some way I can't remember the name. But, anyway, the captain of the barque had told everybody that the King of England was dead. They have a Queen now. Her name's Victoria."

By God, Mr Melton thought to himself, he had got her out of it! The idea of an English Queen had forced whatever it was deep down into Judith's brain, and she was vivacious as she had been when he first came. She burst out with questions again. Mr Melton, not daring to allow her to stop and think, supplied off-hand the fullest and most picturesque answers. He felt that he was skating on thin ice, and sometimes jumping open water. He made his minute's amount of knowledge of the Royal Family spread out over a quarter of an hour; he presented a picture of the new Queen as young, beautiful, intelligent, and clever; he went so far as to predict a golden age beneath her rule. Finally he fell through into the chilling water, just at a point when the ice seemed fairly firm.

"She isn't married yet," he was saying. "Of course her husband won't become King, just some kind of consort." And then he knew that the something had come swirling up into her mind again. All she said was:

" Oh, she isn't married—yet."

But it was a comment, not a question; there was no more curiosity; the light had gone out again. He rallied desperately and glibly: " She'll have to marry royalty—can't marry for love." (Wrong, by George, now she's in deeper than ever!) Before he could think of anything more she made another comment:

" Kings have lots of—morganatic marriages."

This was a lead, for Mr Melton had always thought that the affairs of the royal dukes had a lot of comedy in them, but at that moment he couldn't unscramble Mrs Fitzwilliam from Queen Adelaide, or remember whether either or both was or were connected with the Duke of Cumberland or the Duke of Kent or King William. And then he saw that whatever it was had got hold of Judith so strongly that he might as well try another subject from scratch. He cursed himself for a dull, slow talker; Williamson would have had Judith laughing out loud by this time. But he consoled himself by thinking that perhaps what was really lacking was a good big dish of greens.

During the day they had a good deal more of conversation together, and it was always the same. Something, he could not always tell what, would get Judith excited, and she would forget whatever that other thing was, and then something else—again he could not always tell what—would bring the other thing back into her mind, and she would go down into the dumps. He went as far as to ascertain through Lupe that the señora had actually been served greens and had eaten of them. But of course there might be something else lacking.

When Judith got excited and started asking questions the questions were very intelligent. But then he had known for a long time that Judith was a very intelligent person. She asked two questions about language, and since that was Mr Melton's hobby he liked those questions particularly. The first she asked was whether ' Godoy ' really meant ' Goth,' as Juan said it did. Mr Melton considered carefully, and as usual found that in a particular etymology all his rules failed to work.

" ' *Godo* ' means Goth,' and there were Goths in Spain, but I don't know whether '*Godo* ' would ever change into ' *Godoy*.' "

"Juan says the Goths were the real aristocracy of Spain, and so his family name shows that it is very aristocratic. But I always read that the Goths were big, tall men with blue eyes and light hair. But Juan isn't much taller than I am, and he is dark with black hair and the blackest kind of eyes." (A pause.) "I think it's just one of his funny ideas." (Another pause.) "It doesn't make any difference."

Mr Melton had by now given up trying to direct the conversation, and so he considered the last two remarks in silence. "One of his funny ideas"—that showed that the wild ecstasy of the midnight elopement must have passed a little; that was a judgment in which she looked upon Juan rationally. "It doesn't make any difference" —well, as applied to ' Godoy ' meaning ' Goth,' all right, perhaps, although as a student of languages he could hardly agree even there. But from the way she had said the words he was afraid the little pronoun ' it ' might include Rancho Amarillo, her marriage to Juan, her coming baby—and, in fact, life in general. Certainly, just as she had spoken, the light had gone out again. Mr Melton could not subscribe to such a philosophy; as a deist and follower of Thomas Paine he saw the world as the purposeful creation of Divinity.

The other linguistic question had intrigued Mr Melton even more : why was the ranch called ' Amarillo '—that is, ' Yellow Ranch '? He wondered, in fact, why he had not thought of that himself. He considered carefully, and replied sententiously :

"Most Californian ranches are named after saints; they just put Rancho and then the saint's name, like Rancho San Luis. Some of them have some other noun put after the Rancho, like Rancho de los Osos, which means Ranch of the Bears. But hardly any have adjectives, like Amarillo."

"I don't care whether it's an adjective or a noun, but why would it be called ' yellow,' anyway? There's nothing particularly yellow about it."

Mr Melton swallowed, preparatory to pronouncing a quick judg- ment, but Judith went on. He could see that she must have been thinking pretty seriously about the ranch.

"I've been here well on to a year, and I haven't seen much

yellow. Of course the grass is a sort of yellow after it gets dry, but so it is everywhere else too. And the sycamores turned bright yellow with the first frosts, but they must do that everywhere else too."

This burst of information seemed almost to cover the possibilities, but Mr. Melton for his honour as a linguistic student brought out one other:

" Sometimes there was an Indian word and the Spaniards didn't understand it, or else forgot about it. It sounded like 'amarillo' maybe, and so after a few years they just took to saying 'amarillo.' It happens that way sometimes. We'll ask some of the older Indians some time."

The evening, with Juan present, and with the wood having sufficiently dried out, was pleasant enough. Juan sang, and Mr Melton taught him some new verses he had just learned for an old chanty. Juan promised some hides.

Next morning Mr Melton rode away, and was rather glad to be gone. He was so terribly worried about Judith that he felt actually sick at times, but he did not see what he could do about her. He did not know what was the matter, even. He still thought it might be lack of greens. Of course she was probably feeling pretty bad with her baby and all. Rancho Amarillo was a lonely place for a New England girl; the house was more broken down than it ought to be, and probably the servants were a worry. But then she certainly had fallen desperately in love with Juan, and Juan was a fine boy—one of the finest boys in California. Mr Melton thought of Juan affectionately and in a fatherly fashion in spite of some pangs of his own over Judith.

There was only one matter concerning Judith about which Mr Melton had a secret difficulty, and he felt that he couldn't let himself think such a thing. California was really a small place—at least, as far as people were concerned; you were likely to run across everybody who lived or came there—that is, the white people. Mr Melton vividly remembered sitting in the courtyard of a little place in Los Angeles that served meals. It was an evening about two months before, and he was eating alone. At another table three men were sitting; they had finished dinner and were drinking brandy and were a little loud. Of course they got to discussing women. Two of the men lived in Los Angeles, and Mr Melton knew them; they were respectable persons. The other man Mr Melton had never met, but he knew who he was. He was one of the men sent up from Mexico to look over the new government which had come in with the revolution last year, and to make arrangements between the central government and this new government in California. He was a captain in the Mexican army, and was wearing his uniform.

Mr Melton was paying very little attention to what the three men were saying. He did not consider himself a prude, but the calm physical way in which Spanish-speaking men were likely to talk about women always rather disgusted him. But then the talk shifted to American women. The captain, who must have drunk a good deal, was doing the talking on this subject. Mr Melton could see that the two Californians were embarrassed at having the captain talk about American women in the presence of an American, and Mr Melton was embarrassed too, for it was possible that the captain might say something publicly which Mr Melton as an American gentleman could not pretend not to hear, and which having heard he should resent. Mr Melton did not like the idea of resenting anything to the captain, who was a big fellow, certainly armed, and enough in drink to be nasty. Mr Melton tried to hurry with his supper, but the captain talked faster than anyone could eat. Mr Melton did not like to recall the exact words, but the upshot was that the captain had known American women intimately, and that they were cold and grudging and dishonest. And then Mr Melton could not forget the exact words :

"I have known one Yankee woman in particular—yes, in particular. I am thinking of her. And it was neither so very long ago or so many thousand miles away. She was a blonde, yes, very light-coloured hair " In the pause Mr Melton did not look, but he imagined the captain's smile, with a slight movement of the mouth and narrowing of the eyes. " She was everything that I have said about the Yankee women. And yet, my friends—all of you "—the captain's voice was loud enough for the whole courtyard—" you must not imagine that I speak bitterly, or from lack of opportunity to know, for——"

One of the Californians was on his feet, and both were shouting for the waiter so loudly that they drowned out the captain. They were gentlemen, and had no wish to see a fight started. But they had been slow Mr Melton felt himself cold from his waist clear down to his ankles. As if it had been a sledge-hammer, he could feel the weight of the loaded pistol in his side-pocket. He did not clutch it and stride across to the other table with his right hand in his pocket. Instead he thought with great rapidity and accuracy in a direction most comforting to the coldness in his interior. If this were Monterey there would be no question. But here in Los Angeles it was doubtful whether anyone would think of there being a reference to Judith. Did the captain even intend one? Therefore, it would be silly to take offence at a reference to abstract American womanhood. The captain was drunk, anyway, and probably known for an ass when sober Thereupon Mr Melton had risen as if not caring for any more supper—which was true enough —and walked out. The two Californians were still talking loudly, but Mr Melton heard the captain saying something about American men; he tried to believe that it had not been in reference to him, or that, if so, it had been merely casual and not derogatory.

Mr Melton could justify his actions, but he had not slept much that night. He kept thinking what Daniels or Williamson might have done. Williamson could jolly old ladies along, but still Mr Melton had seen him go white with anger and have to be held back by a man on each arm and another pushing in front. But mostly Mr Melton had a kind of picture which almost slipped into a dream at times. It was like melodramas he had seen at the theatre. A lanky trapper who had come across the deserts and mountains was sitting where Mr Melton had sat; he was one of those ruffians whom the Californians called " white Indians," and who, Mr Melton often said, gave the Americans a bad reputation in California. Yet to-night Mr Melton sometimes seemed to think of himself as being the same as the ruffianly trapper. As the captain let fall his words this Mr Melton, the trapper, rose drawing his long knife and saying very nasally:

H

"See h'yar, greaser, them ain't good words about a lady. You eat 'em or you'll run into trouble."

Thereupon the captain had gone down on his knees in funk apologizing abjectly, and praying for mercy. The trapper, or Mr Melton, had then contented himself by doing a little carving around the captain's nose, cheeks, and ears—not seriously, of course, but just enough to leave those members slightly ragged round the edges after the bandages came off in a couple of months. . . .

But that would have been what a ruffian would have done, and in the early morning light as Mr Melton rode away from Rancho Amarillo he knew that he was not a ruffian and could not have done such a thing, pleasant as it might have been in some ways. But the captain's words came back to him in spite of everything. The captain was a big, handsome fellow, no doubt of that. Those balls at Monterey could get pretty wild. What if the captain had turned Judith's head for a moment, and what if she still kept a feeling for him? Or what if the captain had been too much for her in one way or another? Was there really a sure line between seduction and violence? Then—Judith might be nursing a wildly guilty conscience. Mr Melton counted on his fingers with a feeling that he shouldn't be—no, she couldn't be worrying about the baby. It couldn't be, anyway; the whole thing was insanity. The captain was obviously a boaster and a liar, and he may never have even heard of Judith. Judith wasn't fickle enough to lose her head so easily, and she was too clever to be trapped.

Still, he wished he knew what had gone wrong with her. Something pretty serious had happened.

JUDITH woke up, and lying in bed felt very fine and happy and contented. That was while only her body was awake. In about two breaths her mind came to, just as if some one had pushed a wheel off dead centre and it had swung a quarter round and then clicked and fallen into line with other things and gone to work grinding out thoughts. And the very first thought, as every morning, was Juan and the half-breed girl. Then, as every morning, Judith felt in body and in mind so miserable and heavy that she felt she might sink right down into the bed and have the blankets and mattress come over her and smother her, and she really would not care. What with the baby being so big now she needed very painfully to get out of bed, but she could not even bring herself to that until again, as every morning, she had made a mournful round of thoughts to see whether there was anything to be done about anything. She felt sometimes as if everything had walled her spirit into a prison, and she was just the way a man might be who had been in the same cell so long that he had gone crazy and every morning would go around inch by inch to see whether he might not have been mistaken in his impression that the cell was all ugly solid stone except where it was iron bars. So every morning she made the rounds in her thoughts to see if there wasn't really an open little door somewhere through which she could walk out and be free and happy again. But there never was.

First she thought about whether it was really true—that is, about Juan. Then she remembered that she had really been sure of it— it must be for a month now; she could almost remember the day—just because she had felt that change in Juan. She had been married to him nine months now, so that she could tell even little changes in him. And this seemed a big change. She didn't see how anyone could miss how he stopped being nervous and really disagreeable, and then became as quiet as it was possible for him to be quiet and at the same time really very much pleasanter to live with. And then, about ten days ago, she had been looking out the west window—just as simply and accidentally as that—and had seen him speak to Paquita, and then they had wandered off, although not together, in the same direction. It was not much to see, but it was enough. No, there wasn't any little door for her spirit to escape through on that side.

Then she would get a little angry and wonder why she could not get angrier still and say things to Juan the way she said them to her mother sometimes. But the difference was that she really loved Juan too much. She didn't want to say things like that to him, and she was afraid that if she did she might lose him more than she had already.

The next step was to think, " Well, why not? " Why not fight it out, and then leave, baby and all? The practical difficulties were appalling, but in her anger she felt herself strong enough for them all. But what made it impossible to get out that way was again that she might lose Juan, and in spite of everything that was the one thing she couldn't face.

Then she would think of it in a different way, and for a moment she would really think she had found a little hole she could slip through, away from oppression and into happiness. That was when she suppressed her feelings and thought very hard and logically and philosophically about it. " Now look," she would think, actually putting it into words to make it seem more real. " Now look, you are in love with Juan more than you feel anything else in the world. That means you want him to be happy. The way things are now he is happy—or happier than he was for a while. And it isn't really doing you any wrong really, because—with the baby and all, anyway. . . . So—since you love Juan and want him to be happy and he is happy you are happy too." And for just a moment she would think she was. Then she would realize that her argument might be all right for Juan to use himself, or for another man, or even another woman, but not for her. For something tremendously strong came up suddenly from inside her and smashed the little chain of arguments all to pieces, and she felt just as miserable as at the beginning.

By then she had gone all the way round the circle of thoughts, and there was nothing to do but get up, wishing she could lie still and never get up again.

This particular morning—Mr Melton had been gone several days —everything was happening as usual. Juan was already up. Judith walked stiffly about the damp, chilly room Outside, she could see it was cloudy, and ready to rain. She could hear all the usual early morning sounds of the ranch—chickens clucking and scratching about and talking to one another, Lupe patting tortillas, some one pulling up a bucket of water from the well, other undefinable but familiar noises, which might be men or horses or other animals or even the wind. Then—chuck! The familiar noises stopped for just an instant and a new set of noises began. It was as if, the idea sprang into her mind, Juan playing a tune on the violin had stopped between two notes and some one else had begun on the guitar with the middle of another tune.

For just a moment she was frightened; then she knew what it was, although it had never happened quite so early in the morning before. Some rider or riders had popped up over the little hill where the road came into the valley. The moment that happened some one at the house, or maybe it might be a dog, realized it, and let people and animals around him know it, and thus the wave of excitement rolled out in all directions, getting bigger, until every one knew it. Even the less intelligent creatures like the pigs and chickens and turkeys were alarmed by the barking of the dogs and the running about of people so that they changed their usual noises for more excited ones and seemed to be perturbed by the approach of visitors.

At the rate people rode in California it was usually about a couple of minutes from the time when the noises changed until the time when whoever it was came spurring his horse up the bank from the creek-crossing. That, Judith had often thought, was the time they would have to get ready for an emergency if the emergency should ever come charging across the valley towards them. During the months she had been at the ranch a good many riders had come over the hill. Most of them had been some of their own people who had been off on some errand and were returning; in those cases the excitement began to die down by the time the rider had got half-way to the house and been recognized. The strangers who had come had come for various reasons, but there was never anything to be construed as an emergency. Since she had been there, Judith decided, life at Rancho Amarillo had been about as lacking in excitement as life at Appleby. But there was a difference—at Appleby you were sure that nothing exciting would happen ever, and in California you were not. Even Juan, she had noticed, jumped fast whenever the noises changed, and took a quick look at what was coming.

This morning Judith was not much interested and did not hurry to look out. She knew that with the heavy rains the road across the valley was so deep in soft mud that no rider could travel it to the house in much less than five minutes. She took time to wrap herself in a cloak against the chill, and peered out through the peep-hole in the front shutter.

It was only Pablo García. He was badly mud-splashed, but that was natural. He was excited and yelling something, but that was natural too, for Pablo seldom had the chance to show off by tearing into Rancho Amarillo so early in the morning. But he seemed a little more excited than that would warrant; so Judith thought that his mother, who was always going to have a baby, had suddenly set about having this one before its time, and had sent Pablo for Antonia or Catalina to help her. Pablo went tearing round the house, and disappeared; from the sounds, he must have gone into the open space between the kitchen and the well.

Judith wandered back and sat on the bed, feeling very miserable still about everything. She heard noises in the outer room, and thought that Antonia or Lupe might be coming to tell her what was happening and to ask for something to send down to the Garcías. But instead she heard some clanky noises, and the foot-sounds were like men's. That was unusual, for the vaqueros, even Miguel and Ramón, seldom came into the house.

"Well, if they want me they can come and get me," thought Judith. She supposed she ought to feel more sympathetic about the García woman who was going through what she herself would soon be going through. But she was so miserably spiritless that she just couldn't bring herself to go out and offer clean sheets or what-ever it was might be needed. But, with the sense of something happening, she combed her hair with just a few strokes; her hair was so faded-looking now that combing it wasn't much satisfaction, as it once had been. She heard sounds of horses being brought up—ten or a dozen maybe. One of them was kicking and plung-ing. Why did they need so many horses for the García woman? Judith began to feel that whether it was love for a fellow-woman or mere curiosity, she would have to go and find out what was happening. But on account of her size she was very slow in getting her stockings and boots on, and while she was working on them she heard more clanky sounds from the outer room, and more kicking noises and squealings, as if the horses were sensing excitement.

Just as she finished her boots she looked up, and there was Juan opening the door. He looked so funny and so surprising that she wanted to laugh. To be dressing up for theatricals at this time of the morning, as if he were going to act *Julius Cæsar* or *King John* or something! He had taken down the nice old ornaments that hung above the fireplace—the funny iron helmet, and the big sword, and the queer heavy leather jacket. Now that he was wear-ing them they looked more like a knight's sword and armour than ever the kind Walter Scott wrote about.

When she saw his face she did not laugh. He came across the floor to her with his quick step, but in spite of her size she jumped so quickly that she met him half-way between the bed and the door. The leather jacket made him feel strangely hard, and it hurt her breasts when he pressed her against it so tightly. With the iron brim in front of his forehead he had to twist his face round before his lips could fall into place upon hers. They stood that way a long time, it seemed. Judith's heart was jumping inside her, and the baby was jumping too. She wanted to cry, but wouldn't.

It was Juan who took his lips away.

"I've got to go. I have to chase some stolen horses. Maybe they aren't even stolen—just as it was that time at Monterey. I'll be gone all night—maybe more than to-night."

He still held her close. Judith thought of lots to say. Are you wearing this leather jacket so that the horses won't bite you? Do you use a sword to chase horses with? She could feel now that he had two pistols in his belt.

She did not say anything, and she did not cry. She remembered that she came of a seafaring family. When your man started out for Labrador ice, or China-Sea typhoons, or Straits-of-Malacca pirates, you did not cry; you smiled gaily and said that when he came back the baby would be saying " papa."

Juan spoke again :

"I'm sending that oldest brat of Catalina's down to tell Aunt Leticia to come right up and stay with you. She would have come in a few days, anyway. In this weather it will take her three days after she starts. I'll be back by then too. I'm leaving Ramón here to look after things."

Judith found her voice :

"You'll be in an awful mess of mud when you get back. I'll see that you have clean clothes ready and hot water."

He broke away, and strode out. Judith had only the wildest idea of what was happening, but she followed him, through the outer room and the passage-way to the kitchen. and into the open space about the well. Every one was there—the women and children in a scattered outer circle, the men forming a vague line and standing at their horses' heads.

Antonia was nearest, and Judith seized her. " What is it? "

"Indians," said Antonia. " Wild ones from the big valley. They got García's horses; maybe some of ours."

At the word Indians Judith felt the nausea of nightmare. Indians meant all that the tradition of a New England girlhood had made her fear—Deerfield and Lancaster laid waste, King Philip's hate, captivities and tortures. She did not think of crying now; for a moment she thought she might faint.

She rallied by making herself think whether there was anything that she, the captain's wife, could do to aid Juan. She looked along the irregular line of the eight or ten men. Every one appeared ready to mount; she wondered why they were not already galloping away. She saw it was Juan who was holding them. It was a new Juan to her, and she was prouder of him than she had ever been before. Juan the galloper, Juan the guitar-player, Juan the lover, she knew. Juan the gay swordsman or charging cavalryman she could easily imagine But here was Juan the captain. He was walking along the line of men, inspecting the equipment, testing the saddle-girths. When they started they would be able to drive through as far as their little army could be expected to go. They would not have to come straggling and limping back because in excitement they had galloped off before they were really ready.

Judith stopped being physically afraid, and was merely worried about Juan. Then she noticed that no one else seemed to be even worried. The faces in the outer circle showed no more concern than if a round-up instead of an Indian battle were in prospect. One of the women was yelling out loudly in the Indian dialect, which Judith did not understand. It must have been some fine obscene witticism, for there was a great burst of laughter, and Judith noticed several people glancing roguishly in her direction to see if she had understood. Lupe came running from the kitchen with something steaming hot in a skin bag—beans or corn meal. There was another burst of laughter at her picking out a particular man to give the bag to, some joke of the kitchen probably.

" Mount," said Juan.

He himself was still standing; Ramón, glum-faced at being left behind, held the horse. Juan's eyes swept along the little troop, and Judith's did too. Her mind was working so fast now that she felt she could give a report on every bridle strap and a description of every man's face. Juan was giving his orders :

" Juanito, warn the Mission and the town, and go on to Rancho San Jorge. You can start now."

The face of the little half-breed boy was lighted up with the excitement of his first service as a man. He swung his big roan around, struck in with his single spur, and in three jumps was out of sight around the house. Judith knew that he could stick to the horse as long as the saddle did.

" Felipe and Luis—you ride north. See Don Diego Fuente or else Don Alonzo. Tell whichever one you see that I expect him to be at the big rocks on the ridge, the place with the caves, by day-break to-morrow, with eight men. He can watch for my smoke-signals out on the flat country."

The two vaqueros—Judith noted they were the two oldest men in the company—swung their horses, and were gone. Only five men were left in line. "Juan Bautista and Bernardo, keep with Miguel. Pablo and Panchito, keep with me."

Juan gave one more thoughtful glance along the line of horseheads. He turned and strode across the muddy ground towards Judith. Again she felt the sharp but comforting pain in her breasts as his arm pressed her against the stiff leather jacket.

"I'll be back soon; nothing to worry about."

Dry-eyed and smiling, she played up to the code which she knew sea-captains' and warriors' wives must follow:

"That's fine; hurry back."

Juan struck his spurs, and the long-legged black stallion seemed to jump with all four feet at once. The six horsemen swept around the corner of the house, and for a second after they disappeared the air seemed still full of kicked-up bits of mud and drops of muddy water.

Judith paused where she was, uncertain for a moment. What was to be done next? She had a vague idea she might be expected to start rolling bandages. Then she heard Lupe the cook calling to her daughter Rita to come in here and help get the señora's breakfast ready. Well, she apparently was supposed to eat breakfast whatever happened.

She went back into the house. Then all at once it struck her that during that time of the mustering and departure she had never once thought of Paquita. Now she remembered that Paquita had been standing there, not ten feet away. But it was to his wife that Juan had returned when he was going. Judith felt her broken pride mending. Her love, humiliated, but never destroyed, rose up anew. Juan was riding to fight Indians. Beside the thoughts of danger and death all the thoughts which had made Judith miserable for a month seemed small and unimportant. If only he came back she felt now that she would thankfully share him with a dozen women.

She cried quietly for a few moments; then, still following the code for sea-captains' and warriors' wives, she dried her eyes quickly as she heard one of the servants coming.

BY THE TIME JUDITH DRIED HER EYES and Antonia came into the room Judith would have said that a long interval had passed since the horsemen rode out of the yard. Yet when she went and stood looking out of the front window so that Antonia could not see that she had been crying she was startled to see the men still in sight. They had quartered across the valley, and were now close to the place where the main stream of the creek came out of the hills. What struck Judith most of all was how slowly they were riding. It was surprising; for when Juan went on an ordinary errand he galloped as if he were riding for his life, and now when you might think he really was riding for his life he held his horse in and rode at an easy, swinging canter. As well as being surprising it was both comforting and disconcerting. It was comforting because it showed that Juan was still using his head shrewdly by not letting his horses wear themselves out in the first few miles galloping over soft ground. It was disconcerting because the steady canter seemed to predict a long chase.

The lower air was still clear, although the mist was half-way down the hills. The riders were well strung out, so as to keep as much as possible out of the way of flying mud. Judith could easily see Juan in the lead, with little Pablo García behind him; Miguel brought up the rear. She saw the colours of the horses, and the ridiculous long lance which some of the men carried. Then, turning along one of the creek-branches, they went behind a little spur of hills—one, two, three, four, five, six. They were gone, just as totally, Judith thought incongruously, as if they had passed behind the solid corner of a brick house at some Boston street-corner.

She made herself eat breakfast. While she ate she reckoned time. It was hard to remember the days of the week at the ranch, but they always kept Sunday after a fashion. It was a long time since there had been a Sunday, and Judith finally decided that this must be Friday—Friday morning. Juanito would be nearly at the Garcías already; then he would go on past the Gómez place, and on to the Mission. There he would get a fresh horse, and continue to San José; he would give the warning there, and she supposed that some men would ride out to reinforce Juan, although he had not said anything about it. Juanito would get to Aunt Leticia's place in the early afternoon—that is, if he could be counted on to ride hard and not stop too long to eat and gossip. What if he met the Indian raiders? Well, that might hold him up, but Judith did not worry much about Juanito himself. He was so much Indian that—she smiled at the idea—if he had time to take his pants off they would think he was one of the tribe. Or if he had warning he could bolt into the chaparral and hide so well, Indian fashion, that no one could find him for a week.

But even if Juanito got to Aunt Leticia's early this afternoon, by the time she had got ready, and located her men, and they had got the oxen in and made the cart ready—by that time it would be so late that they would decide to start next morning. It would take three days more for the ox-cart to cover what the horseman could do in a short day. No, Judith decided not to expect Aunt Leticia before Monday evening.

How about Juan? He had said, "All night—maybe more than to-night." But she didn't like the look of that steady canter. And, besides, he had sent north to the Fuentes to muster their men and join him; that would take time. Judith decided that she would not expect Juan back until Tuesday night. She would not start worrying till then; that is, she would not worry very much; that is, she would try not to worry very much.

Within an hour she had already worried so much that she could feel pains, and began to think that the baby was coming, although it shouldn't come for a month. She decided that she must do something, or she would be going crazy in less than the four days. It was all very well to think about being a warrior's wife and a sea-captain's daughter, but the wife and daughter had to have something to do when the man went away. She thought of her mother with more sympathy than usual. Yes, she supposed that her mother did love Peleg, although it must be in a very different way from the way she loved Juan. But what did her mother do when Peleg went away? Then she remembered that they always cleaned the house—in fact, practically tore it apart and put it together again. Her mother had always been very gruff, saying, " Well, now that that man is out of the way with his tobacco and muddy boots we can get the place back to looking like a place to live in; it looks like a pigsty now." Judith had always thought that it was harsh of her mother to speak that way, but now she wondered if it hadn't been just her way of covering up her tears.

So Judith looked to see if the house needed cleaning. It did. The superlative in Appleby had always been that a place was dusty enough to write your name on. Judith decided that she needed a stronger one. " Dirty enough to bury a penny in! " That might do.

Then Judith sat down and considered herself a minute. She was really a little appalled at seeing how dirty the place was, especially when she remembered that any time now the *Spanish Belle* might be back on the coast and her father coming up to see her. In spite of the way she liked to sneer at Appleby housekeepers spending all their time cleaning, still she had always thought that she would keep her own house at least efficiently. Now she had been well on towards a year at the ranch, and actually she counted for less in its running than did Catalina, or Lupe, or Antonia. At first thought it seemed impossible to imagine how she could have let things go that way, and then on further thought it seemed very clear. For she had been just a bride when she first came, and she had come into a house which was all arranged and running, if you could call it running. And at first she had not been able to talk Spanish. Then she had been too sick with having the baby, and then she had been away, and then when she came back she had settled down into a kind of coma of physical contentment, just letting the baby grow inside her and making clothes and things for it, and then in the last month there had been this other awful matter which had seemed to paralyse her completely. She had needed something to shake her out of it.

" And. *Jesús María*! " said Judith, putting her thoughts into words, and being glad it wasn't swearing in Spanish, "I surely got something to shake me."

She went to the back door, pitched her voice low, and called vigorously:

"*Antonia! Lupe! Catalina!*"

Antonia and Lupe actually came, almost running. "Two out of three!" thought Judith. "That's good! From the way I called they must have thought the Indians were coming."

She set them to work, and it was rather fun. Lupe got out of cleaning on the grounds that she had to cook, but Judith sent Antonia to bring in two or three more girls. There always seemed to be half a dozen or more of them living in that L-shaped low adobe building over beyond the well which was cut up into little cells and called the 'quarters.' The women were always sitting around there boiling beans in earthen pots and suckling babies, or looking as if they surely would be suckling babies within a week. Some of them were probably married to the vaqueros and some of them probably weren't; it didn't seem to make much difference somehow in California. Anyway, thought Judith, they eat our food; so we might as well get some work out of them.

Judith didn't feel that her idea had been so bright when one of the girls brought in turned out to be Paquita. First Judith felt like flying into a rage and telling Paquita to get out of the house. Then she decided that that was just what she certainly could not do. Twenty-four hours ago she could not have borne being in the same room with Paquita, and would beyond doubt have gone into the inner room, and lain upon the bed and cried. But now she was in a fighting mood, and she rather enjoyed ordering Paquita around, and making her clean out dirty corners. It was a pretty small revenge, she realized; but still she enjoyed it. Another funny thing she noticed was that Paquita and the other women who came in from the quarters seemed half frightened at being in the house, where they were usually not allowed to enter. With the graceful set of their heads and their big black eyes glancing nervously around they made Judith think of deer. She still disliked Paquita intensely, but sometimes it was difficult to realize that they were what you might call 'rivals.'

Judith went to bed early; she was very tired, but she had forgotten all about the pains which she had thought she had in the morning. "Well, the house is clean," she said to herself; and then, "What difference does that make?" and then, "It got me through the day, at least." She thought in a kind of detached fashion that she ought to worry about Juan, but she was too—tired—to—do . . . And then it was morning.

It was only the very earliest grey morning and she was very uncomfortable with the baby and had to get up. She dozed again, and then heard Ramón, who had slept in the outer room, stirring around. The sounds of the ranch began; it was a dull, drizzling morning. She supposed she ought to worry about Juan's having been out all night in the rain, but Juan was always so much the master of the world he lived in—horses, cattle, grass, and weather —that it seemed foolish to worry about a man who never even had a cold in the head. About the Indians, however, Judith had chills; she tried to steady herself by remembering that no one else, Juan included, was showing any worry. But that did not help much, and she knew that she dared not let herself think very much about what she had vaguely come to call 'it,' meaning some kind of situation which might arise between Juan and the Indians. If she thought too much of 'it' perhaps the baby would start coming before it was supposed to—and, what was worse, before Aunt Leticia came.

"I can't clean house again," she thought, putting her thoughts into sentences as if she were talking to some one. "How do you suppose I'll ever get through *this* day? Anyway, I'm not thinking much of Paquita; the bigger worry seems to drive out the little one. I wish I had something to read, even something I've read before—something in English; Spanish is such slow work that I can't really forget myself. Or maybe it's only that those two religious books, which is all I have in Spanish, are just too dull, anyway."

The imaginary confidante, as usual, remained silent.

"You're a patient listener, but your repartee really isn't brilliant," thought Judith, feeling that she was putting it rather whimsically. "Well, then. Can't read. Can't ride, on account of my condition and the Indians. Can't clean house. What is left then "—her imaginary voice became very ironic—" in the way of social pleasure and gaiety? "

But here the confidante spoke up sharply: " Why, conversation, of course! "

" And would you be good enough to say just with whom I should talk in this place? "

" With one of the girls. "

Judith shook herself. She had better get rid of this habit of silently talking with herself. It carried a distinct suggestion of going crazy. She got up.

But there was nothing crazy, she decided, in that last suggestion of deliberately making conversation with one of the girls. Which one? Lupe was a good enough cook, and clean too—but otherwise she was dull-witted. Catalina was housekeeper to the extent of making up the beds and presumably cleaning up; but she was even duller than Lupe. That left Antonia.

While she dressed Judith thought about Antonia. Antonia was no fool. There was all that incident at Monterey, for instance—the handsome and very amorous captain. The more Judith had thought about that the more she had come to feel that Antonia had figured somewhere. Judith did not like to think about that whole matter; she had sent the captain packing fast enough in the end, but she could still remember, and it gave her little shivers now, that she had liked the way the captain's hand had dragged across her shoulders when he adjusted the shawl; she blamed it on the wine, but still the wine could only let loose something that must be in her, anyway.

But she would talk with Antonia; there were a lot of things she wanted to know about the ranch. Antonia might be dishonest, but at least she was shrewd.

It worked very well to keep the day moving. Antonia knew a lot about the Indians. You couldn't tell, she said, why they came at a particular time any more than you could tell where or when they would came. But they came often. There had been many raids just before Judith came to the ranch, and, in fact, this last interval had been about as long a quiet one as Antonia had known in several years. They came from the great valley, and some of them were wild Indians, and some—the worst—were renegades who had run off from the missions and the ranches. Ignacio was one of the worst renegades. That was why after they killed him they put his head up on a pole at San José; they thought maybe it would discourage others from running away. The Indians always took horses, because they could drive horses off faster than they could drive cattle. Would they kill people? Oh, yes—and Antonia described with some detail the fate of Pedro Rojo; the Indians had tied him to a stake, shot his less vital parts full of some forty arrows, and otherwise made sport with him. But that happened rarely. (Once in a long time was too often, thought Judith.) Did they attack houses? Oh, no—but when Antonia thought about it she could recollect that the Indians had sometimes come up to houses trying to lure the people out; she didn't think they would ever attack a house. Of course, you couldn't be really sure, she added cheerfully. Judith felt a sudden warmth for the thick adobe walls, heavy shutters, and tile roof of the ranch-house; it took away that horrible picture of early New England days —the blazing house, and the women and children rushing out through the flames to meet the yelling savages and their tomahawks.

There was always just the faintest chill to Antonia's reassurances. Oh, no, the Indians didn't kill, torture, or attack—that is, not usually. Juan had chased Indians a hundred times perhaps. Might not this be the last time? Judith recollected uneasily that there was much more Indian than white blood among their own ranch-people. Might not Antonia's own nonchalance result from her being three-quarters Indian?

"Would you like being carried off and going to live with a tribe, Antonia?"

Antonia shrugged her shoulders, but apparently the question was a ridiculous one.

"No," she said. "Squaws have to work too hard."

This was a strange place and a strange life, thought Judith, to be dragged into by a treacherous madness of her own body. Yet she could not regret it. She thought of nights at Rancho Amarillo in May and June. No; she had merely followed her star, even though her star, she smiled tenderly, had black hair—a veritable dark star, which came to rest above the lonely valley among the lonelier hills.

I

Too many emotions stirred up within her. The child moved again. To escape from Antonia's prying eyes she went through the back door, and stood in the passage-way looking out through the little drizzle at the place where Juan had mustered his men.

She had the vision of them still, and realized how funny they had looked. She had always supposed that when men went fighting Indians they would at least be well equipped. Here it was getting on to the middle of the nineteenth century, with cannon and rifles, and even those new pistols she had read of that shot as much as six times in a row. But those eight horsemen had looked as if they might have come down from the time of *Kenilworth* when men were still using the old armour and spears along with awkward fire-arms. Juan with his sword and helmet and leather jacket looked just as she might have imagined Marmion, except that he also had two pistols and a short stumpy-looking gun. Miguel had a gun of the same kind, and so had one other man. There were no other fire-arms. Four men had long lances, which were just rough slim poles with iron points. Some of them had leather jackets, although with their serapes over their heads you could hardly see what they were wearing. They all had big hats, lassos, and knives. But what really amazed her most when she stopped to think was that one of the men had actually had a short bow and a quiver of arrows. Why, that wasn't any better than the Indians they were going to fight! In fact, the only things that looked efficient and first-class throughout the whole troop were the horses and bridles and saddles.

That evening when Judith went to bed she decided that Antonia had really got her through the day. It was easy to talk with Antonia in some ways, for she gossiped naturally. Judith had learned a lot about the ranch, and about the quarters especially. They were good things to know too, now that she felt she was really going to take over the running of the place just as soon as she got finished with having the baby. In other ways Antonia was hard to talk to. It was like talking to the Pope. What she knew was so, and there was no argument or possibility of variation of opinion, as in the matter of childbirth. Judith had always been a little huffed at the way every one around the place seemed to take her baby for granted. To be sure, even in Appleby babies were pretty common: yet there the

expectant wife had always been paid some little attention and
deference as being engaged in an important work, and at the lying-
in there was a distinct excitement and a running-about after doctor
and midwife. But here on the ranch most of the women seemed
to be carrying babies most of the time; every now and then a baby
was born out in the quarters and Judith would not even hear of it
till later; once a girl had died in childbirth.

Judith had to admit that most of the time lately she had felt
physically well enough, but she had resented not having more attention. Even Juan seemed to take for granted the coming of his heir.

So she had burst out to Antonia this afternoon, with heavy irony:
"Why, you people seem to think the same of having a baby as of
squatting down in the grass the way you do."

"Yes, yes," said Antonia, calmly missing the irony and quite
willing to equate the two physical processes.

"But some people die having babies; Francisca died."

"Yes, yes, and some people suffer dreadfully from piles.' Thereupon Antonia launched out upon a wholly vivid description of the
remarkable suffering from that malady of one Eusebio García some
ten years previously.

Next day was Sunday. Sunday was a holiday at the ranch. Usually
some of the people rode down to the Mission. There they heard a
short Mass and spent the rest of the day at cock-fighting, horse-
racing, and general amusement. They didn't usually manage to get
much to drink, but occasionally there was a row and one of the men
came home with some knife-carving on him. This Sunday nobody
would go on account of the men being away.

Judith wished that she could go. She would like to see somebody.
The few white people who came to the Mass usually had nothing
much in common with her for purposes of conversation, but to-day
she would have given a lot just to see one of them. About going to
church she did not care at all. They had straightened out Juan's lie
about her being already a Catholic. There had been too much Uni-
tarianism floating about Appleby, however, for Judith to have a very
set religion. Juan too made little effort to get to Mass; by some
sort of heredity he was a Catholic in feeling, but he disliked priests,
and, like most of the ranchers, he mistrusted the wealth and power

which the Missions had once had, and so was anti-clerical in politics. Judith was bored at Mass, because she had not much idea what it was all about. Confession rather appealed to her, if she could have confessed to some one for whom she really had great respect, or even to some perfectly anonymous unknown person. But when all the time she knew it was only little Father Cypriano confession seemed to her rather a farce. She felt too intelligent to believe that Father Cypriano changed much when he went into the confessional.

The morning was terrible. Judith kept thinking about Juan. She did not have any pains, but the baby kept jumping around as if there were a fiesta, and Judith could not help wondering whether that meant anything. Then about noon, in a very different sort of way, things began to happen. First of all, in came the two vaqueros who had been sent out to get Don Diego Fuente and his men. They said that they had gone with Don Diego and ten men to the big rocks, and had seen Juan's smokes next morning out on the plain. There had been different fires and puffs of smoke, and they had built a fire to show that they were there, but they had all disagreed as to what Juan was trying to say with his fires. So they had sent two men, hard riders, to reach Juan, and then to signal back—with definite instructions how—what was wanted. This next time there was such a hard wind blowing that the smokes got mixed up and still no one was sure. But Don Diego thought that the second fires were farther out on the plain than the first; so he decided that Juan must be advancing, and the only decent thing to do was to go to join him. But after they were down out of the hills and started on the plain they met their own two men coming back. Then there had been much cursing, and the two men had explained that Juan had recovered some of the horses, and that just shortly before they had overtaken him he had turned back, and that they had signalled to Don Diego to go home. Don Diego cursed them for not realizing that in a high wind they must make allowances in their signals. Then they had turned back, but darkness had come on, and they had spent an uncomfortable night on the plain with a cold wind blowing. The men said they thought Juan would not be back till Monday night, or even later, for he would scatter his men to look for horses, and then have to gather them again.

Then in the late afternoon a rider came in saying that Aunt Leticia was at the Gómez place and would stay there all night unless Judith needed her right away; in that case she would come on by horseback that night. Judith felt warm all over at having Aunt Leticia so near and so faithful, and she wanted to send back word, " No, stay where you are; have pity on the horse! " or some such foolishness. But she merely sent word that she was very well and not to hurry.

Judith watched the road all next morning, although she knew that the oxen could not make it before afternoon. Then it happened, as it would happen, that she went to sleep in her siesta, and slept through the barking of the dogs and all the familiar noises until what awoke her was the unaccustomed sound of the squeaking cart-wheels. She pulled on dressing-gown and slippers and rushed to peep through the shutters. Her half-opened eyes blinked as she saw a man getting out of the cart. She blinked again as she saw a curious roll in his walk, which could mean only sea legs. Then she screamed and rushed out just as she was across the mud to Peleg.

It was all simple enough. Peleg had come into the Gómez place late, and hearing that everything was all right with Judith, and being intolerably in pain with saddle-burns—seamen were always poor riders—he had stayed and come up in the cart.

Judith would have thought that she would have been much more happy and interested at seeing her father than Aunt Leticia. But she had forgotten that the baby was the big fact in her life now. And her father could not do anything about the baby. In fact, he did not even talk about it, and seemed embarrassed when other people did. But Aunt Leticia took Judith into the inner room, inquired about everything, and gave just the sympathy and respect which Judith had found herself wanting. Apparently an heir to the Godoys amounted to something, even if a child born in the quarters did not. Then Aunt Leticia had Judith undress; she felt over her, and looked for signs and measured with her hands, and seemed greatly pleased with the breadth of Judith's hips. Judith began to feel that she was in a civilized country, and then she doubted it again when she heard Aunt Leticia say:

" Well, I hope it holds off a little while, for the closer a baby is born to the equinox the easier time the mother has."

Then Judith, almost overcome with her new riches in company, talked with her father some more. He said that he had had fine voyages both ways. He told her—without sparing technical language—how the *Spanish Belle* had had three sails blown away in a gale, how it had happened, what he had done when it happened, and how the ship had behaved in the emergency. Then he told her that he thought Carrie and Deborah, her two Boston cousins, would be much interested in her marriage, and would be glad to buy things for her in Boston.

"That means," thought Judith, "that my mother washes her hands of me."

But she said, "That would be very good of them. I suppose you mean that they will buy dresses and women's things that you can't get for me very well."

"Yes, yes," said Peleg hastily, and went on to tell another incident of the voyage.

She could see he was dodging something, but it was almost sundown before he got to it. He had received letters in Monterey. The other owners had outvoted him; the *Spanish Belle*, they said, was too small for the long pull to California; it could not compete with bigger ships carrying more hides; the brig would be profitable in the Mediterranean trade.

Peleg sat before the fire, mourning in every line of his body. It was partly, Judith knew, that he would not see her any more; but it was more that he considered the Mediterranean trade a sissy business.

Then he got out his presents. There were curious native-made things from the Sandwich Islands, and a bolt of cloth and a shawl, which had merely come out of the brig's cargo somewhere. But what Judith really pounced upon was the package of books.

"That was luck, getting them," said Peleg. "There was one missionary who had some novels and poetry, but the other missionaries thought they were worldly and he should just read the Bible and religious books. So he traded them to me; but I could see he hated to let them go."

It was not a very large package, but Judith was breathless as she tore it open. It turned out pretty well. There were four or five of the Waverley Novels, *The Vicar of Wakefield*—she would have thought the poor missionary could have pretended that one was religious!—*The Lady of the Lake*, *Gulliver's Travels*, two volumes of a three-volume set of Shakespeare, Malory's book about King Arthur, and half a dozen volumes of novels and poetry by people she had never heard of. Few as they were, the books were a treasure; now she would have something to read during those long days when she must lie in bed after the baby came, something to stir her imagination and take her away from the dull routine of the ranch.

Juan and the men came in long after every one had gone to bed. He was a sight. Judith kissed him, anyway, and came away with mud up and down the front of her nightgown and the taste of mud on her lips. According to her promise, she had been keeping water hot for three days. Juan was not ordinarily very fond of baths, but this time even he seemed glad of one. With his knees under his chin he steamed in the tub. Modestly he kept his back turned to Peleg and Aunt Leticia. He talked in Spanish, because Peleg could understand it pretty well, while Aunt Leticia knew no English. Judith was glad he was talking Spanish, for he relieved himself by a great deal of cursing, and cursing never sounded so bad in Spanish as it did in English.

The upshot of it was that the Indians had been a very ordinary lot and the chase a merely irritating ordinary chase. They had been ambushed once, half-heartedly in a gully; one horse had got an arrow-graze on the neck. They themselves had fired a few shots, but had not hit anything, and by the time he and his men had scrambled over some big rocks the Indians had run away, as they always did. All you could see were some not quite so wet spots in the grass where the Indians had been sitting, waiting for them. Just beyond this they came to the body of a horse which the Indians had slaughtered for food. They broiled some of the horse themselves, and went on until they came to where the Indians had split into small parties, each with a few horses. Juan divided his own men into three groups, and set them to following the three Indian parties that were headed straightest east. They overtook some of the Indians and made them leave the horses and hide in the thickets. Then Juan's three parties had come together as planned, and by swinging north across the plain had spotted some more Indians and got back some more horses.

Judith said that it sounded very successful, but Juan said it was not. They had not killed any Indians, and the Indians—those that went to the south—had got off with some horses. They would think it a pretty good raid. He cursed a little, and said that it was mostly he wished the Indians would stand and fight. It was a disgraceful business, and made him ashamed of himself, to have to chase through chaparral, and sleep in the mud, and live on horse-meat and corn-meal, and then never even have a fight. He was sick of it. He was always hoping he could pin a lot of Indians against a cliff or corner them in a box-canyon, and then go in and finish them. Maybe he could if he had more men, but you couldn't split six men into more than three parties.

"Why not into six parties?" said Judith, thinking to be funny. Juan as usual missed the funny side:

"Oh, you never have more than three men you can trust. If you sent the other three men out alone they would get scared and start for home, and then say they lost their way."

Then she asked him if any men had come out from San José to help him.

"No," said Juan. "And what use would they have been if they had come? The San José men are ninnies, and soft. It takes men from the outer ranches to chase Indians."

Juan was all scratched about the face and hands from hard riding through brush and trees. He had been badly bruised on one shoulder when his horse fell in going down a muddy gully. He made nothing of these matters.

"If there's another raid," thought Judith, "he'll be off again at daybreak."

After his bath he rolled up on a cot in the outer room, and went to sleep, dog-tired, without ceremony. Peleg was on the bed in the outer room. Aunt Leticia, in spite of Judith's protests, insisted upon sleeping on the cot in the inner room. So Judith took her own bed.

As she lay waiting for sleep she could hardly remember all the changes that she had gone through both in body and in mind in the last few days. There had been all her hatred and despair about

Paquita, and then her fear for Juan, and then her fear for herself as to what might happen, and whether the baby might come while she was all by herself. Then everything had changed. She had not thought the same about Paquita, and Peleg was here. and Aunt Leticia was taking care of her, and Juan had come back safe. There was nothing to be afraid of, and she felt full of contentment. Oh, yes, and she had begun to have an interest in taking care of the house. She was happy, and wished the baby would come this very night, equinox or no equinox. Then she felt she did not wish it to happen, for if the baby came this night Juan was so tired he probably would not even wake up to look at him.

THE sun was just below the line of the hills, but the sky in the east was brilliant with light. It was April; the storms were over; there had been a week of unbroken sunshine.

Judith got out of bed quietly, for Juan was still sleeping hard. She looked down tenderly upon him; it was something of a triumph to have him sleeping as late as this. She felt how good it was to have Juan again. It had been like another wedding-night. If it had lacked that wild excitement and intoxication of strangeness it had brought in compensation a new sense of reunion and a deeper satisfaction.

The baby should have been awake already; usually Antonia brought him in to her before this. Her breasts were so full that they hurt, but it was a happy kind of hurt carrying with it the consciousness of relief in a few minutes, and of actual pleasure as the baby nuzzled into her and settled down with his vigorous tugging. It was good to have a lusty son already a month old.

The first edge of the April sun broke the line of the hills; the level rays poured in through the windows, outlining on the opposite wall the gridiron of the vertical wooden bars. Juan stirred, and then came awake suddenly all over, as he always did. " Like a child waking up," Judith had thought at first; now she knew that he broke out of sleep with the abruptness of a soldier or an Indian fighter—men who must wake quickly and completely or else may not wake at all. As he thus came suddenly to life Judith felt a quick bashfulness, as if it had really been her wedding-night. Before Juan saw her she slipped through the door into the outer room. A lusty husband and a lusty son—it made a woman's life very full, she thought happily.

Antonia was still asleep, but Luis was stirring about. Judith picked him up from his crib, and felt him. " Not even wet," she said. She cuddled him against her. She walked across to the front door, opened it, and watched for a moment how all the summits stood out brilliantly in sunlight while the sharp shadows lay along the west slopes and stretched out over the ravines and high up the east slopes. Some horses—the roans—were grazing just beyond the creek; the sun was making a little steam rise from their backs.

The baby blinked at the light; then, his wizened little face showing a curiously human satisfaction, he proceeded to wet himself. He yawned, as naturally as if he had had years of practice at it. Then he whimpered for his breakfast.

Judith nursed him as she stood at the door. She felt so strong that she did not care to sit down. She wanted to stand all alert to enjoy the baby's tugging. She wanted to watch the shadows shortening every minute. The roans were no longer steaming. Cattle had come out from the shelter of the ravines across the valley, and were starting to graze.

Judith felt that she had been waiting a long time for this morning. For a while life seemed to pause. Now it had started again. Aunt Leticia had come and stayed a month and gone, still equally full of wise advice about babies, and of foolish tales. About the middle of that time, the first day of March, the baby had been born. It had been about average for a first childbirth or a little on the easy side, even as that kind of thing was rated in California. That was to be expected, as Aunt Leticia said, seeing that the equinox was only three weeks off.

Peleg had not been there when the baby arrived, but he had come up a week later, braving saddle-burns again, to look at his grandson. He had been obviously proud, but had had little to say. " It's a fine boy, daughter," was about the limit of his remarks. He would not be back again before sailing. Perhaps he would never be back now that the *Spanish Belle* was shifted to the Mediterranean trade. Judith was glad he had been at the ranch anyway. She liked to remember him walking about the house with his bent-hip, long-armed shuffle. Every time he got on a horse it seemed that he was starting to scramble up the rigging and felt surprised when he found himself so soon at the top.

Judith's mood of complete satisfaction lasted as far as the breakfast table. There was nothing wrong with the breakfast. The broiled beef was juicy; the eggs were plentiful and good; the tortillas were just right; the beans were steaming and tastily hot with peppers; the chocolate was deep with foam. Judith ate heavily, and enjoyed everything. Yet she found herself thinking—this is the same breakfast that we have every morning. Why should it be? Why shouldn't life, even breakfast, be a little more various and subtle? Why shouldn't there be some fruit-trees so that even at this time of the year we could have preserves or dried-apple pie?

After breakfast Juan rode off with Miguel and Ramón following him. There had been no more Indian raids, except one which had struck well to the north, and the Fuentes had handled that themselves. Nevertheless, Juan kept patrolling as well as he could during the rush of the spring round-up. Judith knew now why he kept riding so much; he was looking for trails and signs. She understood also a great deal more about the ranch and its life now that Juan had broken that silence which Aunt Leticia had imposed on him. Strangely enough, the story had not made Judith fearful or nervous, but had given her a new pride and feeling of dignity.

For Rancho Amarillo, Juan kept explaining, was not an ordinary ranch. During the last few years, if you were a decent person and not on bad terms with the Governor, you could get a grant of land for the asking. But Rancho Amarillo had been granted nearly thirty years before, when the power of the Missions was still unbroken. In those days Juan's father had come up from Mexico as an officer in the army. After a long time of service he wanted some land of his own, an estate such as a gentleman should have. The Governor was friendly, but the mission priests fought such private grants. (That was one reason why Juan's father and Juan after him disliked priests.) The only way Captain Godoy could get his land was to take it far off in the hills. "That," said Juan, "was so the priests could get fat and loll around with Indian girls while my father rode himself thin. Before he could take possession of his land he had to promise to patrol the hills to the north and south of it. And also he had to chase and return Indians that ran away from the Missions. Some of them he sent back, and some got away, and a few he kept for his own ranch. Most of our people now are children of those.

"It was all wild country then. My father was betrothed, but he didn't dare marry and bring my mother here until the place was safe. He was an officer; so he planned Rancho Amarillo as a fort."

Then Juan had taken Judith to the curious dark alcove where the old chest stood, and explained why it was built. He did not know the English word, but Judith from her reading knew that it was what Massachusetts people of two hundred years before would have called a 'flanker.' The little window which looked out along the porch had once been only a loophole from which to take in the flank with musketry any attack against the front of the house. On the other corner had been loopholes which commanded all that side, as far as the storehouse. The three buildings themselves—house, storehouse and quarters—had been planned as three corners of a square with the well at the centre. High adobe walls were to have run between these three buildings and a fourth which was to have stood at the remaining angle. This last would have been a tower, commanding the whole valley, and mounting a swivel-gun.

"But," said Juan a little sadly, "my father never finished the walls or built the tower or even any more flankers. The Indians were not so bad that we really needed to. And, besides, the Mission priests did not want the ranch to be too powerful, and my father thought they kept the Governor from giving us a cannon for the tower."

The story of the ranch had made Judith feel happy ever since. It explained so much, and it stirred her imagination. "Without a dream the people perish"—she remembered a quotation like that from somewhere. She had been without dreams, and the story of the ranch brought them back. Now she knew that Juan was upholding the honour of his father's promise when, with Miguel and Ramón behind him, he rode patrol day after day—reaching out northward to watch for trails and signs until he touched hands with the Fuentes, reaching out to the south until he came to rough mountains not easily crossed. Now she knew that they lived at Rancho Amarillo not merely to have beef to eat and horses to ride, but also to maintain the honour of a generation-old promise and to hold the frontier so that civilization might grow up behind them. It gave a meaning to life.

It gave a meaning even to the construction of the house. She was no longer irked at the two-foot adobe walls, which seemed to turn the windows into mere slits and keep the house gloomy on all except the brightest days. She no longer minded the heavy shutters and stout wooden window-gratings, or felt like losing her temper when she had to shove with her shoulder to move the ponderous front door, three inches thick of oak.

As she read and re-read the books which her father had brought these too proved not a mere pastime. The Waverley Novels and the *Morte d'Arthur* brought home to her the likeness of her own life to that of the days of chivalry. Juan was no Gareth or Galahad or Perceval surely (her smile was a little wry); he was not even a courtly and self-searching Lancelot; but he might pass as a Gawain or a Lamorak—hard-fighting, unthinking, headstrong, bitterly loyal. But *The Lady of the Lake* gave her most during the weeks she lay quiet and read hour after hour. She had read it before, and seen it through the haze of romance. Now she read on and on, delighted at noting how often the poem seemed to touch her own life—the hill country, the thick copses, the stag; the rough lodge in the wilderness, with the sword hanging on the wall; Roderick Dhu, as dark as Juan and not unlike him. Then she thought of the vaqueros, more like clansmen or retainers than hired servants. Sometimes her life seemed to exceed the romance of the poem. What was a bare-kneed gillie scurrying afoot over the hills to summon the clansmen? What was that picture to compare with the two vaqueros, lassos at saddle-bows, knives in belts, horses alive with fire, spurring northward to raise the Fuentes.

There was one other old favourite which had stirred her again, very strangely. As she had read *Gulliver's Travels* her eyes had pounced upon a word which she would have said could not possibly have been there—California. It was used to locate Brobdingnag, the land of the giants, as well as Laputa, the country of the flying island. There was a map in the book. On one side of it were those mythical places and on the other were Cape Mendocino and the Bay of Sir Francis Drake, and even Monterey. She knew at once the reason. To make people believe in a land where men were sixty feet high Swift could not locate that country close to England, but must put it in the most distant place possible. And what place was more distant from every other than California? That was where she was living now—east of the giants—in a land so far removed that she might be thought to have the Brobdingnagians and a flying island for her neighbours.

All these thoughts passed through her head—not for the first time —on that morning of the first week of April 1838, when she had got up feeling so happy and become discontented by thinking of the quite unimportant matter that the breakfast was the same as always.

Juan and the two riders who followed him had disappeared into the hills by the time Judith came out through the front door. She walked a little way off from the house, and then stood looking at it. It was as unprepossessing as ever. The roof still sagged, and the rot still showed at the bases of the porch-posts. Judith remembered that terrible depression which had struck her when she first came to the ranch and realized that it was not better than Aunt Leticia's, but worse. Now she was not depressed; she was thinking not of what the house was, but of what it might become.

What had she to work with? There was Juan. He knew the ways of cattle as well as any man; he could keep off the Indians. That was enough from him as far as the ranch was concerned. Yes, she could count on Juan.

What about herself? Señora Blanca the Indians called her, and she had sometimes begun to think of herself in those words. Perhaps her hair was really the most important thing about her; probably it had done more than anything else to determine her life; it must have been chiefly the hair which, for good or bad, had got her Juan. But still, she thought doggedly, she had other qualities besides her hair. She had strength of body, ambition, determination, and intelligence. All these traits were good when it came to making real the dream which was beginning to shape itself about the dirty grey adobe bricks of the ranch-house. The shock of a new environment, the vehemence of her love, the physical strain of pregnancy—all these had temporarily made her weaker than she really was. Now she felt her strength again; no longer would she weakly let herself be shaped by circumstances; now she herself would begin to shape the world around her.

She swung on her heel and looked out over the valley. It was beautiful. One could live a beautiful life there. She knew the valley in all its moods now—tender when the first green showed after the early rains, terrible when the great rainstorms struck, lush in the foot-high grass, gorgeous with wildflowers, beautiful like a deep-breasted woman when the grass stood tall, austere in the browns of summer. Her child—her children—would know that beauty, but they must not know it as mere savages.

"Without a dream the people perish." Now she had begun again to dream.

As she turned back towards the house she noticed a little boy, one of the swarm which usually kept around the quarters. He was wandering along, making for the creek. Right in front of the house he stopped, squatted, and relieved himself as unthinkingly as an animal.

Judith felt a wild rage rising inside of her. It was not at the child: it was at the whole way of life. Why think of beauty—first, she must build latrines! Beyond the little pile which the child had left she could see the horse corral deep in dung. Between the corral and the house the grass was trampled down, broken and ugly; there the dogs and fowls wandered. With her rage flaring out through her eyes, Judith swept it all away. As in a vision she saw peach-trees blossoming in pink, gravelled paths, and a rose garden. *Jesús María!* —she would do things, if she had to spend the last hoarded gold-piece in the chest!

What she was going to do this minute she did not quite know, but she was certain that she was going to start something. She squared her shoulders; she tossed her head so that the hair flung back the light of the morning sun, as a knight's plume might have done. With quick strides she bore down upon the house. They had better come running this time, she thought grimly; worse than the Indians were upon them. She pitched her voice low, so that it would cut in beneath the chatter of the women in the kitchen. Then, with a light in her face as of the joy of battle, she called:

"*Antonia! Lupe! Catalina!*"

*A*NTONIA! Lupe! Catalina!" Judith had shouted, and all three had come running. It was scarcely more than an accident, of course, but in the years that followed she often thought of it as symbolic. She had imagined that some great struggle lay before her, but really it had been easy. Year by year, with her own abundant energy, she worked closer to the vision of her dream, and came more to love the lonely valley and the life which centred there.

This was the cycle of the year at Rancho Amarillo. By July, after killing-time, the grass was dry and brown. That was a good time to dry adobe bricks in the sun and to build, for the cattle needed little care. By August the cattle were eating the brown grass close down to the ground, and were getting thin. The creek shrank to a series of muddy water-holes. In September came hot, dazzling, sunny weather, with sweeping dry winds from the north, making the lips crack, and wearing the nerves thin too. That was a dangerous time, and there might be quarrels and knifings among the vaqueros. By now the hides were cured, and great high-loaded bullock-carts creaked slowly off towards the boat-landing on the bay shore; later they would return with the winter supplies, corn and beans, chiles and onions, from San José.

In October or November came the first good rain. The tension of the dry weather eased, and you slept better. Within two weeks afterwards you would look out one morning and see, faint and delicate, the first green of the new grass. In December and on until March came the great storms, sweeping in over the southern hills beneath immeasurable thickness of murky grey cloud, low-lying and wind-driven. The creek rose till you could hear it roaring in the night. Between the great storms came fine weeks of sunny weather, warm in the day, crisp cold at night. Once in a while you would look out in the morning to see the whole valley a-glitter like silver with frost, and the cattle standing out darkly, steaming in the newly risen sun. With the cold and the wet, and the new grass not yet having much nourishment, the cattle were still thinner.

Apart from the ploughing and planting of a few acres of wheat, there was little to be done at the ranch during the rainy season, and so it was a good time to go down to Monterey and spend a month in town with dances and much visiting among friends. The women talked gossip and babies, and the men talked politics and raced horses. Also you could go out to the Boston ships and make purchases for a year.

After that you were eager to get back to the ranch, and when you arrived the cattle were belly-deep in grass and getting fat again. In March the men were ready for the round-up. For two or three weeks everything was colour and excitement. They worked the herd in from all corners of the ranch, the vaqueros whooping behind, and the trained steers, as they had been taught to do since they were calves, cleverly leading the way and keeping the flanks in. The rodeo-ground was at the upper end of the valley, but even at the ranch-house you could hear the shouting men and bellowing bulls and lowing cows, and the calves crying as they were roped and thrown, and cut and branded

After that there was little to do for a while during April and May. It was spring and the pleasantest time of the year. Poppies and mustard and lupine set the valley alight with great splotches of orange and yellow and blue. Yet there was always some excitement too, for the vaqueros would be breaking colts, and the Indians, restless and hungry after the winter, would be pretty sure to sneak over from the great valley after horses. Then would be quick mustering of men. In a day or two or three they would be back, perhaps with the horses, perhaps not; and there might be a vaquero with an arrow-wound to be dressed.

One day in May you would look out and see, always as a surprise, a curious leaden sheen upon the tall grass. That would be the first sign of summer, and then in two weeks the hills would be more brown than green, and it was time to harvest the wheatfield.

In June the cattle were at their fattest and would yield the most tallow; so it would be killing-time. By the time the killing was over the grass was wholly dry and brown again, and you had come round the cycle of the year.

Often it seemed strange to Judith that her own cycle should be different from the year's. For she had borne Luis just at round-up time. At killing-time she was nursing him and growing stronger; and in the fall, at the dead of the year, she was light on her feet as a girl; and at Monterey she danced through every one of the nine Christmas parties. But the next year at round-up she was sick in the mornings, and at killing-time she was heavy and slow, and in the dead of the year, on September 29, with a hot wind blowing, little Peleg was born. That Christmas time at Monterey she had to go home from the dancing early to nurse him, but in the spring she was light on her feet and rode the hills with Juan.

So it went. For Leticia was born just after round-up, on April 10, 1841; and Enrique just before the first rains on October 9, 1842. The little one that never lived was born during the round-up in '44.

A child within her, and one in her arms, and another pulling at her skirts—but there was much more. There was always Juan with his handsome dark head and his hard body. And more and more there was the ranch itself—servants to be managed, and accounts to be kept, and building to be superintended. Even after she had hired Julio as major-domo she seemed to have as much to do as ever. More and more she took over the marketing of the hides and tallow. American herself, she could meet the lean-faced Yankee supercargoes on their own ground, get a better price for her hides, and shame them into a discount on the outrageous prices they demanded for their cheap Boston goods.

Especially in the summers she raged in a fury of doing things. She drove her Indian labourers like a slave-master. She planted an orchard—apples, pears, apricots, plums, peaches; from '43 onward every July saw trays of orange and purple fruit drying in the sun. She planted a vineyard on the hill behind the house. She planted a rose garden in front of the house. She gravelled the paths and paved the ford with cobbles, and cut down the three old half-dead poplars. And she built.

In '39 they started the new wing of the house. Juan had a lingering wish to complete the quadrangle, but Judith built to the south. Along the back of the addition was a dining-room and a room for Julio the major-domo. Along the front was a large room with a fireplace, which they called the office. Above this was a second-story with two sleeping chambers. The walls of the new addition were of adobe, but the windows were wide; the roof of wooden shingles instead of tile showed that an American had planned it. The old flanker was quite obscured from the outside, being now merely a passage-way into the office. So Rancho Amarillo lost something of its squat, fortress-like appearance.

Pleasantest of all was the sunny patio, shut in north and south between the walls of the new building, east by the old house, and west by an arcaded walk like a mission cloister. The patio was paved in home-made brick tiles; along the south side a stairway ran up to the new sleeping rooms, and in the centre was a fountain set with Mexican glazed tiles in yellow and blue. The sun flooded into the patio, and so the children played there, and the two house-dogs lay in the sun, and in the summer the little lizards came out and darted here and there on the adobe walls, looking as if they wanted to be friendly, but were too timid.

Also they built a new storehouse between the old storehouse and the quarters, and two latrines, one for the family and one for the servants. They built an outdoor covered washing-place convenient to the well, and a long adobe wall to separate the ranch-house from the quarters.

But in spite of the building and furnishing and the dozens of mouths to be fed, in spite of the ruinous prices of Boston goods and the drought of '40—in spite of everything, the bag in the old chest grew heavier with gold. In those years any rancher with decent sense was making money. California was experiencing its first boom.

Along a sea-coast of five hundred miles, upon the hills and in the narrow valleys, the grass grew and the cattle bred. With little attention from their masters the calves came to maturity; each year the increase of the herd was killed and flayed, and the hides hauled in huge awkward carts to the nearest boat-landing. Beyond the boat-landings lay the Boston ships, each with its trading-room outfitted like a department store, each with its supercargo ready to trade manufactured goods for hides to supply the shoe-factories of Massachusetts. It was easy supply and quick demand, and as simple as

water flowing over a dam—that is, if you were a rancher with lands
and not some poor devil of a half-breed vaquero, or a villager with
nothing but a little patch of corn and beans and chiles on the outskirts of the dirty *pueblo* of San José.

For those few years it was really almost an idyll. The brilliant

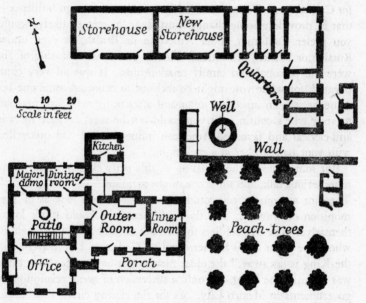

RANCHO AMARILLO (1844)

young Don Juan Bautista Alvarado, who had come in with the
revolution of '36, ruled uneventfully, and the annals of his reign are
short. In '39 came Sutter, hale fellow and a smooth talker; Alvarado
granted him eleven square leagues in the Sacramento Valley, and
lived to regret it. In '42 some new president in Mexico City remembered that there was a distant territory called California, and
sent up a governor to replace Alvarado. The new one was named
Micheltorena, and he brought along what looked to the Californians
much like an army of occupation. This battalion had been raised
largely by the simple process of emptying some gaols.

But if California did not have much history in those years it had
plenty of politics. There was the division between up-country and
down-country, according to whether you wanted Monterey or Los
Angeles to be the capital. There was the old division of clerical
and anti-clerical. There were the centralists, who supported government from Mexico City, and the separatists, who wanted California
for Californians. Then there was the question of foreign influence—
that is, providing some change must come, as seemed likely, would
you prefer California under American or British, or even under
Russian or French, protection? Finally, and most confusing of all,
were the personal and family relationships. It was all very complicated, for while you might be inclined to count on some one because he was an up-countryman and a separatist who was married
to your wife's cousin, still you could not be sure, because he was
anti-clerical and favoured American influence, and had quarrelled
with your half-brother at a cock fight.

But sometimes in the midst of all this petty chatter would come
more serious talk, and some one might mention " the closing circle."
Then for a moment you could see in some faces a look as of pre-
monition of tragedy. For those of them who could think knew
themselves to be like soldiers thrown out to hold an outpost, behind
whom the main army has retreated. " God is in His heaven, and
the King is far away," the older men might have said. Now there
was not even the King, but only a succession of weak revolutionary
governments in Mexico City. As for the closing circle, that meant
the Indians of the back-country on one side, and, on the other, the
foreigners whose warships year by year came cruising along the
coast, awaiting only the proper moment to land their marines.

To all this talk Judith paid as little attention as would be
expected of a busy wife and mother and mistress of a household.
In the winter nights at Monterey she might worry a little, but once
back at the ranch she let the peace of the hills again enfold her.
During those years she passed—one can scarcely say aged—from
her early into her late twenties. Beyond acquiring a certain maternal
fullness she hardly changed in appearance. She had always been
strong, and even the strain of child-bearing did not weaken her.
And by Californian standards her child-births did not even rate as

frequent. In the gossips at Monterey the other ladies always referred to her as comparatively unfruitful; they had their children every year, or every fifteen months at least. But Judith noted silently that most of her friends' children were in the churchyard, while four of hers were living and strong and the death of one was only the bad luck of a midwife's blunder.

In personality the mistress of Rancho Amarillo differed somewhat from the young girl who had sailed from Boston. She had lost her uncertainties; she had gained dignity and poise and force and self-confidence.

Yet in much too she remained the same—in her love of reading, in her romantic quality of seeing in dream some vision beyond the actual, in her intellectual force which made her strive onward strongly to attain the vision in reality. Every year came the boxes of books sent out from Boston by gentle Cousin Carrie. Boz's latest novel was always among them, but the staple was history and travel. Novels were amusing, but the other books gave more for her mind to feed on. All history, when you read it rightly, seemed to tie together. It was reassuring for her to think of herself not as an isolated individual on a lonely ranch, but as a definite if infinitesimal link in the process of this world. It was flattering to think that her being at Rancho Amarillo was as definitely an historical event as Waterloo and just as surely the result of historical causes. For if Charles V had not been what he was, or if Desaix had not charged at Marengo, or if any of a thousand other things had happened differently, she might not be sitting looking out over the valley with a herd of roans grazing.

And as for travel, so much of the world was just being explored. Africa, Australia, the South Seas, Arabia, the Arctic, even the interior of the great continent which lay behind her—every year some traveller was penetrating farther and coming back to write about what he had seen. These books too kept Judith contented and flattered her. They showed that the earth had places even farther removed from civilization than was Rancho Amarillo—places to which even traders from the Boston ships did not penetrate.

Sometimes also in this kind of reading she realized that not only in California were people living on lonely ranches holding a frontier until civilization could build up behind them. There was that little book about South Africa. It was dreadfully dull on the whole, a sort of missionary tract; Judith suspected even that Cousin Carrie had sent it, as she sometimes did send books at her own expense, in the hope of quickening the moral sense of her errant cousin who had turned Catholic. But among the maudlin sentiment about the Hottentots there was one passage describing a farm on the edge of the Great Karroo. The picture blurred, for the writer was interested in souls, not in things; but still there were cattle and grasslands and a lonely house with hills behind it. The life must be like her own, thought Judith. Did they have round-ups, and throw lassos, and go somewhere occasionally for dances and picnics and weddings? Why couldn't the writer tell something interesting, instead of bleating on about such a problematical question as the fate of some particular Hottentot's soul? Then in that book about Van Diemen's Land there was an engraving entitled *The Home of Richard Cleveland, Esq.* She studied the picture—grasslands and sheep in the foreground, a stone house with barns and storehouses behind it, then brush-covered hills rising up. She could see the shuttered windows and the out-buildings compactly set about the house. Like Juan's father, Mr Cleveland must have built for defence with a feeling for the doubled power of musketry when directed against the attackers' flank. Such a picture helped keep alive in Judith a dream that was necessary for her happiness—the dream that she filled a little niche somewhere in a vague scheme of all things, that she did not merely eat and drink and pass from day to day.

So usually she dreamed and was happy. But occasionally as she lay awake at night she felt that great oppression of loneliness and isolation which had paralysed her during her first months at the ranch. In those moments she felt herself isolated futilely on the last frontier of a barbarous land. She longed intensely for what she thought of as civilization and which in her mind meant people of her own kind to talk with, stores to buy in, friendly clustering houses, a theatre perhaps, and possibly one of these new railroads which seemed to be coming in so fast now.

The magazines, reviews, and recent books sent by Cousin Carrie now and then had items which showed that civilization was indeed reaching out a little towards her. Many settlers were crossing the Mississippi into Iowa. Wagons were going to New Mexico to trade. There was excitement about Oregon; she read the new books by Irving—*Astoria* and *The Rocky Mountains*. In 1841 a few Americans, immigrants, came overland to settle in California. They had to leave their wagons in the desert, and scrambled down over the mountains half-starved, living on horse-flesh. A year later Judith heard that Americans had got through to Oregon by wagon-train. Maybe so, maybe not—anyway Oregon was a long way off. Even farther off was civilization.

One thought of such things now and then—in the quiet of the siesta, or in a wakeful hour of the night when one lay and listened to a coyote howl mournfully. But most of the time one had a deep happiness. There was much to do, and every year the children seemed to grow more interesting. They were dark, all of them, like their father. Mix a pint of printer's ink and a pint of milk, and the result looks like printer's ink. And yet, thought Judith, the milk must be there somewhere.

She felt herself mostly in Luis, the eldest. At six he showed a certain sense of responsibility, an interest in books, and an inquiring intellectual curiosity—all of which she recognized as her own. Guito, the second, seemed to be just his father over again. His name was really Peleg; she had had him christened with the English form of the name over the priest's protests, but it had done no good. First the name had been shortened into Peleguito, and then he himself had further shortened it to Guito, so that only a vestigial consonant was left to remind anyone of his Yankee grandfather. Guito was interested only in riding and playing vaquero and Indian. Leticia and Enrique, the two youngest, were still babies; Judith could not yet quite think of them as having personalities.

As for Juan himself, he remained the same. He was approaching thirty, but he had not put on an extra pound of flesh. Constant riding about the ranch and an occasional Indian-chase kept him physically hard and mentally happy.

In '40 Aunt Leticia yelled at a servant for the last time, and then slumped down with heart-failure. That same year the *Spanish Belle* foundered somewhere between Boston and Fayal, and Peleg Hingham joined his many ancestors who had found their graves in salt water.

Mr Melton prospered. He was clumsy in manner, but the ranchers knew he was honest; they liked his kind-heartedness and his careful grammatical Spanish. He did not marry, although more than one rancher would have been glad to entrust him with a daughter's happiness and a few leagues of land as a dowry. But that would have meant becoming a Catholic, at least in name; and Mr Melton stood with St Thomas Paine as against St Thomas Aquinas. More important, he may not have seen a rancher's daughter who particularly appealed to him. He was turned forty now, and was greying around the temples. In these later years he was riding with two vaqueros and a dozen horses galloping behind him. Mr Melton, his long legs dangling, never could learn to sit a horse gracefully, but he could ride as far in a day as the next one.

Thus he came riding to Rancho Amarillo one evening in the summer of 1844. He came into the valley at sunset, and saw dogs barking at the ranch, and people running to look at who was coming. When he came up the little rise from the ford Judith was standing in front of the house with the sunset glinting in her hair in a way which gave him a moment's pang. With her were Juan, and Julio the major-domo, and old Don Enrique Godoy from Monterey. There too was Williamson. He and Mr Melton were rivals in the hide trade, but Williamson was such a jolly fellow that he was friendly even with his rivals. He was holding up a bottle of his French brandy in each hand.

"Come on, Dan," he yelled. "Glad you come. Goin' to have a big night at ol' Rancho Amarillo."

PART TWO
1844-1850

CHAPTER I . . . . . JUNE 1844

BY NINE O'CLOCK, having finished Williamson's bottles of French brandy, they all felt very friendly. Judith decided to try some that had been made right there on the ranch. They were getting pretty civilized, she thought, as she brought the bottle in, now that they could grow their own grapes, make their own wine, and distil it into brandy right on their own place.

Williamson took one sip, then jumped up in the air and cracked his heels together and howled like a coyote. " I'm a lost soul burning in hell," he cried, " and no one to give me a drop of water! "

After that the others sniffed gingerly and mixed in plenty of water, and joked Judith about the liquid fire she raised at Rancho Amarillo. She tried to explain that after all the brandy was only nine months old, but privately she decided that they must have let the still run too long or not long enough.

Everybody seemed to be having a good time, and Judith knew that she certainly was. It was fun being the only woman with five men. If there had been more women some of the men might have got amorous, and maybe nasty. As it was, when she had said something good and Williamson jumped up and kissed her smack on the lips, it was all in the spirit of good-fellowship and Juan laughed. Even Mr Melton and Uncle Enrique laughed, and they were men who laughed seldom. Julio was the only one who snickered, and he perhaps had already drunk more than he should.

Usually the idea of much drinking was repulsive to Judith. It meant sailors reeling in the streets of Monterey singing filthy songs, and Indians lying like pigs in the gutters. Or else it meant the wild fandangos which they went to sometimes at the various ranches.

Anybody in the district who had even a drop of white blood could go to those fandangos, and there was plenty of liquor. But the liquor there always seemed a little sinister to Judith, for it seemed to serve chiefly the purpose of getting the half-breed girls excited to the point where they would slip out into the darkness. Then towards morning two young fellows would be sure to start quarrelling over the same girl, or else some wife—and not always a half-breed—would start too serious a flirtation. Then there would be a high staccato of oaths, and a screaming of women, and knives would flash. And if the older men didn't jump quickly to intervene blood would be flowing.

But to-night Judith could understand why the old Greeks made Bacchus out to be such a fine and great god. She felt a great human love for everybody in the room except Julio, and she did not even have any great objections to him. She decided that perhaps they did not do enough drinking at the ranch; perhaps some people needed to do more drinking than they did. Juan now—he was abstemious by nature, but with more drinking he might not be broody as he was at times. And Mr Melton—he surely needed to let himself go now and then. And Uncle Enrique—more brandy might keep him from being cynical. Certainly to-night they were all jollier than she could ever remember them being, and they were saying things which were at once brilliant and profound and funny. Probably, she thought, what really was happening was that every one was saying the things which he had had in his mind for a long time and never said because he thought people might laugh at him. The brandy made all those things come bubbling up, and at the same time melted down the barriers between people's minds so that every one knew that the others would laugh with him and not at him.

Then she remembered that she had had something like that in her mind for a month and had thought that she would never dare to tell Juan. But now it would be fun. She went and got the book, and stood hunting for the place. Williamson said something about reading from Scripture, and everybody laughed, for the book was large and formidable-looking like a Bible.

"It's the gospel according to Alfred Ludleigh, M.P.," said Judith.

"That little squirt!" said Mr Melton, and you could be sure that he would never have spoken out so except for the brandy. "Has he written a book too? He must have been planning it all the time."

"*Eight Months on the North-west Coast in the Years 1840–41*," Judith held the book for them to look at. "It came out with my last batch of books from Boston. There's a section telling *all* about California, her past and present, lots about her future. Chapter Eighteen tells about coming to Rancho Amarillo, but he spells it l-y-o at the end."

"Yes," said Mr Melton, "and I'll bet he spells Vallejo V-a-l-l-e-g-o and coyote c-o-a-t-i, the way that youngster did who wrote his book a few years ago—Damon, or whatever his name was. He was a common seaman, and never got inside a decent house in California except when he got in with the rest of the seamen at Alfred Robinson's wedding fandango, and yet he put in his book that Californian ladies were generally unfaithful to their husbands."

"You must have been his authority for that, eh, Dan?" Williamson slapped Mr Melton on the knee, and they laughed again.

"But, say," he went on, "there ought to be a law against these fellows coming out and writing books about us as if we were animals in a circus. They must think we never see what they write?"

"We wouldn't, if it weren't for Judith," Uncle Enrique put in. The laugh was on Williamson there, for every one knew that he never read a book.

"It's an old habit," said Judith. "Even Swift put us near the Brobdingnagians who were giants."

"I knew a shipmaster named Swift," said Williamson. "Didn't think he ever wrote a book. I've heard that story about giants over by the big salt lake—lots of trappers tell about them; but I never believed them."

Judith could see that only Mr Melton was smiling. She began reading:

"'On August fifth I left the Mission of St Joseph in company with my friend and guide, Mr Melton. I could not help smiling again to myself at the ungainly, long-legged manner in which he sat his horse and thinking what a laughable figure he would make at an English hunting meet, although to his credit I must say that he always kept his horse in good control.'"

Mr Melton had blushed severely at first, but now he rose in indignation : " He doesn't tell, I suppose, about how he had to change horses twice before he got one he could manage! "

Judith went on : " ' We passed through a barren country of brown hills supporting a few skeleton-like cattle which gnawed at the roots of the scanty grass. My morning's ride confirmed my belief that the richness of California is a mere legend.' "

Even Juan was indignant : " But it was the drought year! Doesn't he say that? "

" Not that I remember. And he says we have to import wheat, without saying that that was the only year since anyone could remember that the crop failed.

" ' On our arrival at Rancho Amarilyo I was pleasantly surprised. The cookery indeed did not equal for excellence and delicacy that of Old England, but was at least superior to that which I had enjoyed, or better, suffered from, elsewhere in California. The chief dish, as at other ranches, consisted of tough beef stewed with plentiful hot peppers. The fare, however, was varied by the inclusion of a coarse wheaten bread, a few vegetables such as onions and carrots, and preserved fruit. To my amazement I was offered—a degree of luxury which had not appeared at any other ranch—my choice of coffee, tea, or chocolate. Yet in spite of being better than elsewhere, the fare was, for an Englishman, extraordinarily coarse and poor.' "

Judith stopped, and she could feel herself panting a little with indignation :

" And he never once mentions that we gave him the best we had, even though it was the drought year."

" Serves you right for entertaining the damn' Englishman," said Williamson jovially. " Go on."

" ' The ranch-house at Amarilyo is not without a certain charm. The newly built addition is two-storied in front, and surrounds a small patio possessing a suggestion of old Spanish delight. Rose-bushes and fruit-trees have been planted in front of the house with an attempt at æsthetic embellishment, although the effect is crude.

" ' Rancho Amarilyo is also notable or unique in California for its possession of facilities usually lacking in that country, much to the embarrassment of the modest traveller. It has, in short, two well-constructed latrines, one for the family and one for the servants. The mistress of the house planned these improvements, but she is, I am informed, much chagrined that the Indian servants still frequently prefer the out-of-doors, and even when they condescend to employ the modern " convenience " they disregard its duofold nature and mingle the sexes indiscriminately, subordinating modesty to sociability.' "

This was already a joke up and down California, but everybody laughed to find that Judith's discomfiture had got as far as being published in London. Williamson mixed her another glass of brandy and water. " I can see you're going to need it," he said.

" I'm going to need it worse than you think," she said, and plunged into her own description.

" ' The mistress of Rancho Amarilyo is, strange to say, of American birth. She is further notable for the possession of such very blonde hair that the Indians call her " Señora Blanca," a term for which an English equivalent might be " Snow Lady." This remarkable person keeps herself well supplied with books and magazines from Boston, and it was with amazement that I found myself discussing with her such matters as the Corn Laws, the menace of Chartism, and the works of Boz.' "

" A lot he knew about Boz," commented Mr Melton. " I think he might have looked at some of the illustrations to *Pickwick*."

But Judith was continuing: " ' In fact, in this most unlikely of all places, I was forced to conclude that my hostess was a veritable Blue Stocking.' "

" Show 'em! Show 'em! " shouted Williamson, in delight, and Judith, with a grimace at him, pulled up her skirts far enough to show that they were really black.

Then came the part which Judith had flinched from reading—but perhaps it would be a good thing for Juan to hear it, after all.

" ' The master of Amarilyo is as dark as its mistress is fair, and in other ways also their contrast is so great that their marriage must be explained only upon the magnetic principle of attraction of opposites. The only civilized trait which he possesses is a good ear for music, which is coupled, as often happens, with the ability to speak foreign languages. During my visit to Oregon I had become familiar with the common American frontier types. The master of Amarilyo resembled these, but still retained a little of the nonchalance and grace of some far-removed Spanish gentleman in his ancestry. Perhaps the closest analogy which I can bring to bear would be to compare him to some petty Irish landlord in the wildest and farthest-removed parts of that unfortunate island. There he lives surrounded by his own half-savage bog-trotters, nursing his ignorance against the world. So he of Amarilyo might be considered an epitome of provincials. As such he might be defined by his dislikes. As I gathered in my brief visit his dislikes included almost every class of person—Indians, priests, townspeople, all ranchers who kept sheep, all the Southerners of his own country, and, for personal reasons, a large proportion of the Northerners. As his marriage would indicate, he seems to approve of Americans, and I am forced to state that his reception of me indicated a decent respect for the subjects of Her Britannic Majesty.' "

Judith finished. She saw Juan's scowl so dark that she was afraid it never would lighten. By the look on Mr Melton's face and on Uncle Enrique's she could tell that they felt the Englishman had not done such a bad job at striking off Juan's character. It took Williamson's biggest laugh to bring good feeling back :

" Let's all have another drink, and drink it to the damnation of all Englishmen who write books! "

Perhaps that one more drink was the one which sent things over the line from the jovial into whatever the next stage was for each individual. Julio went to sleep. Juan sank into a black taciturnity. Williamson picked up Juan's guitar and started to sing, although nobody would join in or even listen. Uncle Enrique and Mr Melton drew their chairs together and with super-sober faces and much nodding of heads began what was obviously a very deep philosophical discussion. Judith felt her own head spinning, but she drew up a chair beside Mr Melton and Uncle Enrique.

"What is life? " Uncle Enrique was saying in a voice almost sepulchral.

"Yes, yes," said Mr Melton. " What? "

This reply seemed profound to Judith, and apparently to Uncle Enrique too, for he nodded several times before going on :

"If you will permit me I shall express for you something which I have often thought of, but never put into words—lacking until this moment the golden opportunity. The life of man, I feel, is like a stream of water. The banks of the stream hold in and restrain the water, just as the world and our surroundings and the pressure of other people hold us in and restrain us in life."

He paused. Mr Melton was nodding assent; Judith nodded too, but she wished that her head would not whirl so fast. She decided not to drink the rest of her brandy and water, and she began to roll a cigarette, hoping that it would clear her head. She thought that she had read somewhere in a book things like those that Uncle Enrique was saying, but they seemed none the less profound for that. "Go on," she said.

Uncle Enrique nodded, and continued gravely, taking his time: "There is much more to the comparison. Sometimes the stream flows gently and beautifully through open meadows, quietly and well within its banks, scarcely seeming to feel their restraint. So some people, and perhaps all people for certain times, live quietly and happily and at home in their world. There is little or nothing to tell of the lives of such."

"Happy the people whose annals are short," Mr Melton murmured.

Judith's head was spinning still, but she felt that Uncle Enrique had said something of importance. Her own life of the last few years on the ranch illustrated what he meant. It had been a life of quiet and happiness, of deep love, of children growing first within her and then outside her, of planting trees and building a house, of watching the hills turn from green to brown and back again.

"But," Uncle Enrique continued, gesturing with his hands, "the stream leaves the meadow and enters the hills. It runs more rapidly, then breaks into rapids and cataracts. The banks press in, and the stream fights back trying to force its will upon them in a fury of foam. Is the comparison with life still clear?"

"Yes," said Mr Melton, and Judith felt that he had commented very philosophically. Again she thought of her own life; when she had run off with Juan and when she had first come to the ranch—then had been the time when her stream of life had fought its banks.

L

" But is that all of the comparison? " she asked.

" No, there is one point more. In the end all rivers flow into the ocean."

In California, thought Judith, they may disappear into sand, but she did not say so, for she realized he had spoken poetically. She knew what he meant, and she thought of Juan's comment that the grass was ripe, not dead. Perhaps it was death only if the river ended prematurely and ignobly in the sand; if it flowed home to the sea then perhaps it really came to fruition, like the grass. Mr Melton was quoting again, from the Bible this time:

" ' All the rivers run into the sea; yet the sea is not full.' "

In the hush Judith became conscious of Williamson thrumming unskilfully on the guitar; Julio was snoring. Judith felt that she must ask a question, even though it might be a foolish one:

" But does the stream, as it flows through the meadow, ever know that it is about to enter the hills? "

" Why not? Your life has been quiet for the last few years, but I can tell you this evening that it will not always be so, and probably not much longer. And I do not mean that I am a prophet, even "—he sipped his glass meaningly—" under the stimulus of Rancho Amarillo brandy. But the year is the year of our Lord, 1844; the place is California. I am an old man; you, Judith, are a young woman. In the course of nature I may perhaps die before the break comes; you will not."

Williamson's big matter-of-fact voice broke into the pause; he had come across to listen: " You mean what you Californians call the closing circle—Indians on one side, foreigners on the other."

Bother, thought Judith, it really seemed as if we were getting at something deep, and now it's only politics!

" If you ask me," Williamson went on, " the talk about one half of that circle is all bunkum. These Californian Indians don't amount to anything."

" Did you ever fight them? " It was Juan's clear baritone.

Judith felt a sense of gratification at the sudden way in which every one deferred to Juan; when it came to Indians he knew.

" These Indians," he went on, " aren't bad fighters. I should know. There are only a few reasons why we hold them off—they haven't any leader to unite the tribes yet; they haven't learned the use of horses yet; they haven't fire-arms—yet. What if this fellow Sutter or the New Mexico traders start selling them guns? They almost have a leader now—Felipe, that renegade from Santa Clara. What if they start stealing horses to ride, not just to eat? "

Judith felt herself shudder at the coincidence of the name: Felipe—that is, Philip. There had been a Philip who had led the Indians in New England too.

" But," Williamson protested, " most Californians say the Indians aren't much."

" That's because they live back from the frontier. But look how things are even now. North of the Bay the Vallejos are driving the Indians back some. Here we hold our own; so they do about Los Angeles too. But look at San Diego. Half the ranches are abandoned; the Indians have raided clear up to the town! "

Mr Melton and even Williamson had long faces. They nodded gravely, for as traders they knew how hide exports had fallen off from that district.

" Well," said Williamson, " probably we'd better ask the Americans to come in and help us against the Indians."

Juan nodded noncommittally, but Judith knew that, like many of the ranchers, he was nearly ready to accept American annexation as the best way out. Only Uncle Enrique piped up lugubriously:

" But even if the Americans come in that means change; and change means trouble—at least, until things get adjusted."

" All right, all right," said Williamson—" but why talk only about the outside of the closing circle? How do you know there won't be trouble on the inside too? "

Judith saw that it was as if some one had suddenly drawn masks over the faces of Juan and Uncle Enrique. Mr Melton they might trust, but they did not know Williamson so well; and for all his snoring Julio might have an ear open. Trouble on the inside of the circle; that meant trouble between the native Californians and Micheltorena, the Governor whom Mexico had foisted upon them with a battalion of convicts at his command to see that he stayed in power. The former Governor, ambitious Don Juan Bautista, was beginning to stir restlessly. Judith knew that factions were forming; she had heard talk of ' blues ' and ' greens.' Yes, Williamson might ask the mistress of the house to show her stockings, but even with the license which the brandy granted him he had now overstepped the line. Uncle Enrique's politeness was almost pointed :

" You must all pardon me; I am an old man, and I have drunk more brandy than I am accustomed to. You must pardon me for going to bed. Do not allow me to break up the party."

Next morning at breakfast-time Uncle Enrique was still in bed; so was Julio. Judith was shaky herself, and so obviously was Mr Melton. Juan was morose. Williamson was the only jovial one. He kept saying, " What a night! What a head! What a morning! " Then he would remark something about the hair of the dog that bit him, and take a swig out of still another bottle of his French brandy. He did not seem nearly so funny as he had seemed the night before, but at least he was good-humoured, and that was more than the rest of them were.

He and Mr Melton were leaving, but the latter found an opportunity to draw Judith aside.

" How's your stream of life find itself this morning," he said, only half joking.

" I feel," said Judith, " as if I were in that little quiet pool just before the stream goes over a waterfall."

" You've got yourself a fine place here at Amarillo now," he said. With a sweeping glance he took in the new house, the fruit-trees and the vegetable garden, the rose-bushes, the vineyard on the hillside beyond the house. " Well, sometimes it's easier to get than to hold. If your stream needs any help—fighting against its banks, that sort of thing, you know—well, let me know." He paused. " But the old man was good last night, wasn't he? He talked like a poet, or a prophet, even if it was the brandy. He's getting to look pretty decrepit though, isn't he? "

She thanked Mr Melton, and could feel herself growing very sentimental, almost having tears in her eyes, as he rode away. He was an old, old friend now, and one you could always count on. But when she thought more soberly of his offer of help if troubles came she was a little amused. She remembered Cape Horn and Mr

Melton sick and huddling in corners; if troubles came he would be running to her for help, not she to him.

Mr Melton and Williamson had dipped out of sight at the ford, but now they came into view again. Williamson turned about, rose in his stirrups, waved his big hat, and let out a resounding "Hyip- pee!" Mr Melton, tall and ungainly in his saddle, took off his hat to her, but if he called anything she could not hear it.

She watched the two horsemen gallop across the valley. They were well behind their vaqueros and the herd of spare horses. From under the horses' hoofs faint puffs of dust rose off the brown grass and drifted away in the breeze. To get, he had said, was sometimes easier than to hold. But she could not feel much for her to fear in the prospect; for old men like Uncle Enrique it might be different. But she was an American and had been born to civilization. She had left it, but when it caught up with her again she would wel- come it. Civilization was good.

Then she found herself thinking of Mr Melton's last words. What a lovable old faker Uncle Enrique really was! Every one seemed to think that he was about a hundred, whereas she had the family records to show that he was only fifty-three, and so probably not more than ten years older than Mr Melton himself.

THAT MORNING THE SOUND OF HOOFS brought Judith awake with a start. Going to sleep every night with the realization that Juan was away had made her a little jumpy. It was not really light yet, but through the gridiron of the wooden window-bars and the tracery of the leafless young peach-trees she could just make out the horses passing, beyond the fence. It would be fine to think, she reflected, that you had such a godly household that a good part of it would get up before daylight to go to church, but of course it was really not the Mass itself so much as the sports and merriment which followed it. Right now, too, everything would be especially spirited, for some of the men from the Division of the North, as the revolutionists liked to call themselves, would probably be at the Mission too, even Juan himself might be there. If it had not been that some of the servants seemed to deserve their turn Judith would have liked to ride down to see Juan, even all the way to San José. It was a delightful feeling which made you seem almost like a mistress—to come riding brazen-faced to visit your husband in broad daylight. Well, she couldn't to-day, and she might as well get another nap.

More hoof-beats came by as some one who had made a late start galloped off to overtake the others. Uncle Enrique had been right; life had changed. Everything now seemed to go swiftly, to the pounding of hoofs. This whole present matter had started just that way. She could remember the young fellow spurring his horse up from the ford, flinging him back on his haunches, and jumping off. She had seen that he was a gentleman, even if a callow one, and had gone out to meet him herself. She knew that she ought to recognize him, and she felt sure that he was a Castro—but there were dozens of Castros. So she tried to make the warmth of her greeting compensate for its vagueness. The boy—he was hardly more than that—did not seem to notice at all, and said that he had a personal message for Juan, who of course was off riding over the ranch some-where. He seemed insistent and worried. As it happened, most of the vaqueros were out behind the quarters breaking horses; Judith sent four or five of them off in different directions to hunt Juan.

The boy wandered about nervously, twisting his hands. And that mannerism made Judith see that he was wearing on one finger a little ring which he had braided out of green grass. It was a childish thing to have done, she thought. She gradually became aware that the boy looked curiously overdressed; it must be because of his jacket and neckcloth—and they were both largely *green*. At that some-thing clicked in her mind. Afterwards she laughed to herself that the first thing she did was to look to see whether the children were all at hand and safe. Of course, the boy was a 'green'—so was Juan. The boy being just the age to enjoy mystery was showing off his party in this ridiculous way.

An hour later Juan had come in. She had been surprised at how cold he had been about the whole matter. She would have imagined his liking a revolution of any kind, particularly one against the Governor sent up from Mexico. But, although Juan believed in California for the Californians, among his numerous dislikes were the Castros as a family.

"How about Don Juan Bautista?" he said. "Is he in with you on this?"

The boy stammered doubtfully.

"Well, tell them I may be along later."

The boy, crestfallen in his fine clothes, had ridden off a little pitifully.

"It looks like a bar-room plot," said Juan later. "Some hotheads started it down by Monterey, and the first thing they did was to run off the Governor's horses. That warned him, and didn't hurt him. Now they want us from the outer ranches to come in and do the work for them. Let them fight their own Governor."

That night a messenger came from the Fuentes saying that they too had refused to join the rebels. Their feelings, Judith could imagine, had been just about the same as Juan's.

But next day ("Hoof-beats all the time," thought Judith) a mes-senger had come from Don Juan Bautista. That was different.

Juan had been through one revolution already to make his cousin Governor; he had just come back from that affair when Judith had first met him. She knew that he was Don Juan Bautista's man just as Sir Gawain was King Arthur's.

That same day Juan was off, Miguel and Ramón as usual behind him. He would pick up Pablo García as he went along. " Riding with three men under his banner to join his liege lord," thought Judith There was no banner, but she still liked to interpret things in California in terms of Sir Walter Scott.

Juan had no belief that there would be much fighting—" just the way it was eight years ago " was his prediction. Still Judith did not just like the idea that there would be any fighting at all, for she was sure Juan would be in all there was.

She was not much concerned about herself or the ranch. There were the Indians, of course, but they would never attack a place where there were so many people. If they took some horses, what was the difference? The ranch had too many horses, anyway. They ate up grass which was more valuable for cattle, and she never could get Juan to get rid of them.

Nevertheless, she had been glad when Don Alonzo Fuente rode up to the house with two of his men. He said that while Juan was away he and his brother would keep a look-out over Rancho Amarillo too. Judith had never liked the Fuentes much, although she knew that Juan trusted them and counted upon them. They were little men who seemed to come not much over Judith's shoulder. They had narrow faces with teeth badly out of line, and their eyes seemed too close together. But during these weeks Judith changed her opinion entirely. It was good to know that every Tuesday and Friday afternoon—the little men were methodical— either Don Alonzo or his older brother, Don Diego, would be along. Whichever one it was always came in for a drink of brandy, and indeed, since it was the middle of the rainy season, they were often wet and cold. In manners they were Spanish gentlemen, but in ideas they were frontiersmen. Neither of them had ever read a book, and they had little to talk about—grass and weather, cattle and horses, Indians and grizzly bears, and occasional gossip about what was happening in the revolution.

On that last subject Judith gave them most of their information, for she had been in touch with Juan, and twice had even ridden down to see him. There had been no fighting at all. The two armies, each about two hundred strong, had come together at Alvires' ranch, and with both parties very well dampened by a heavy rain they had signed a treaty; the Governor and his troops were to leave California. But all through December the revolutionists had kept a body of men at San José, fearing that the Governor might change his mind. Juan had stayed with this troop, but Judith supposed that he would soon be coming home.

Don Diego or Don Alonzo heard these different items of news with much interest, and always very politely sent a thousand best wishes to Juan. The last time one of them had been at the ranch had been two days ago, and he had begun to leave with the usual formula that it was a long way back to his own ranch and he supposed he had better be going. He—this time it was Don Diego— had lingered as usual long enough to have another glass of brandy; it was the same brandy that Williamson had made such a fuss about. Don Diego, tough little range-rider. took it neat and without a chaser. Then he had ridden off. Was his roan really extraordinarily tall, or did it look so because Don Diego was so short-legged?

That had been Friday afternoon, and now, the day after to-morrow, Don Alonzo would be coming in to have his brandy and wish Juan a thousand good wishes, and assure Judith that Indians were nowhere to be seen. She felt herself looking forward to seeing him—but perhaps Juan would be back before that and Don Alonzo would not even come.

Now that the last of the servants who were going to church this morning had ridden off everything was very quiet. Judith might have gone to sleep, but she did not. Either it was too light, or else the very quiet itself bothered her. Silence could be more disturbing than sound if a person's nerves were set the wrong way for it. Far off somewhere she heard a cow lowing, most lugubriously. Gradually the sounds of the ranch began ; roosters crowed and the jackass brayed stridently. The two younger children began to make noises in the outer room, and she heard Antonia talking to them. She felt easier, and got up.

The children kept things noisy enough at breakfast, but after they went out to play the silence settled down again. Judith went out to the kitchen; only old Lupe and one of Catalina's squat half-grown daughters were there.

"Has everybody gone down to Mass?" Judith demanded.

"Almost," said the girl, sullen that she had not been able to get away.

Suddenly Judith felt that she did not like it. "How about Juanito?" she asked.

"He went," said the girl taciturnly.

Judith liked it less than ever. She did not blame Juanito much; he was only sixteen, and could not be held very responsible. Still, with Juan and Miguel and Ramón gone, he was the only man around the place who was trained to use fire-arms. The trouble was, she reflected, that she had let Julio himself go, and, not liking to ride too hard, he had gone the evening before. Once the major-domo was out of the way the others had drifted off whether they had permission or not. Well, it didn't matter, they would be back before dark.

Going around to the front, she saw that the horse-corral was empty. *That* was inexcusable and made her angry. Being without horses made one almost as helpless as being without feet. She sent word out to the quarters for one of the vaqueros to bring in a horse-herd, and soon she saw old Tomás trying to round up the blacks. Tomás had smashed his knee five years before, and had not been much in the saddle since. Was *he* the best the ranch could offer to-day? The blacks seemed to sense that Tomás could not ride very fast, for they kept scampering away, seeming to enjoy it.

Then little Luis came running up to Judith:

"Mamma," he cried, excited at the opportunity, "let me go out and help get the blacks." Judith had the shock that her seven-year-old son had suddenly come of age. But it was a good idea; the pony would be doing the work, and Luis could stick to the pony any-where.

With Luis delightedly shouting and old Tomás directing, they got the pinto bell-mare headed into the corral, and the blacks followed. When three of them had been saddled and tied up to the rail Judith felt better. But the silence was still oppressive. It was a lightly overcast day with scarcely a breeze.

Luis, feeling that it was a time for manly achievement, was demanding to be allowed to shoot his pistol. This sport was reserved for times when his father was there, but to-day Judith felt that it might be a good idea. Luis's pistol was the little old one that Judith had first found in the old chest. Juan had taught him its management, and given him good instructions about how not to shoot himself or anyone else.

Luis shot at a stick of firewood set up in the orchard. He could hit it too, for he had a knack at shooting. The pistol made a very satisfactory noise. Judith superintended, wondering all the time at her guile. She knew that she had allowed Luis to shoot his pistol so that anyone hearing it would think that there was an able-bodied man at the ranch, and she had him shoot it in the orchard so that no one could see that he was only a child.

Just the same, she was not surprised when the dogs barked. From where he was playing in front of the house she heard little Guito cry out, " Some one's coming." With Luis she ran for the house.

It was only a rider! He had popped up over the hill, and was down on the valley floor already. " It's Juanito," said Luis, who had a quick eye.

A minute later, on a badly blown horse, Juanito spurred up from the creek.

" Indians? " yelled Judith, as if she knew already.

" Yes! " cried Juanito, and then, " No! "

Then things were happening confusedly, instead of in orderly fashion one after the other. The dogs barking; children crying; Lupe and old Tomás and all the others running together. Indians, Americans, Sutter. . . . What about Sutter? Somebody was coming—but was it Sutter or Indians? Juanito losing his head and breaking into Indian gibberish instead of Spanish. . . . " At Gómez." Luis holding her hand, looking pinched and frightened. . . . Was that some one coming over the hill right now? Little Guito starting to blubber. . . Run to bed and pull the covers over you; you're little Judith Hingham of Appleby, Massachusetts. Why is everybody looking at you for orders?

Then across the valley, over the tops of her rose-bushes, she saw the great green hills lined with dark tree-filled ravines. There everything was still standing firm. Her brain cleared. She tossed her head quickly—once. She did not know what was happening, and probably no one else did, even Juanito. But something must be done. Things must be made to happen, not all at once, but one after the other.

She started to give orders.

"Tomás, go down the road to the top of the little hill. Stay there, and warn us if anyone comes. . . . Felipe and Ignacio, get horses ready for all of us. . . . Lupe, pack up all the food you can. . . . Antonia, get warm clothes and blankets for the children. . . . Juanito, stay with me. . . . The rest of you help where you can, and get ready to go, if we have to ride for it."

In a moment she was alone with Juanito and little Luis, who was looking scared, but still was dry-eyed. It took her three minutes' careful questioning of the excited Juanito to get at what was happening. They were Indians, yes. But they were not wild Indians from the great valley. Why be afraid then? Oh, but they had guns; Sutter gave them guns; they were Sutter's Indians, hundreds of them. And there were Americans too.

"Did you see all this, or did some one tell you?"

"I hid in the chaparral and saw them, señora."

"Where are our other people?"

"They were ahead. They must be taken prisoner, maybe killed. I was the last to get started this morning."

"Were the Americans dressed in red?" She tried to trap him by a leading question.

"Oh, no, señora—leather mostly, with fringes. They were like trappers."

"How did you know it was Sutter?"

"I saw Gómez; he was driving his horses into the hills; the Americans were coming to take them; he said Sutter had joined the Governor and is going to kill all the Division of the North and let his Indians plunder the ranches."

More questions showed that Juanito knew nothing else of importance. She dismissed him, and looked around her. A mile away across the valley she could see old Tomás already sitting on the grass just where he could overlook the crest of the hill; below him, out of sight from the other side, was his picketed horse. In the corral the two other old men were roping and saddling horses. Inside the house the baby was still howling miserably, but Guito and Leticia were quiet; Judith could hear sounds of activity from Antonia and Lupe. Beside her stood Luis, worried, but still clutching his pistol.

Judith tried to piece together Juanito's story. It held water. Of course the ranch people were not killed, and Juanito's ' hundreds ' of Indians meant nothing. Still she knew that the revolutionists distrusted the Governor and were afraid of Sutter. If Sutter decided to strike he would come down from the north on a long loop to the east of the swamp country, and into Mission San José by the road where Juanito had seen the army. Thus he would take the revolutionists in the rear, cutting them off from their homes and recruiting grounds. On their front would be the Governor's troops. They would be caught front and rear and outnumbered. But of course they would not be caught; they would merely scatter into the hills. So far Juanito's story held together. But surely with such a campaign in view Sutter would not allow his men to stop to plunder ranches—no, he might need horses, or his men might be deserting to plunder on their own account.

Still old Tomás sat quietly looking over the hill; she was keeping an eye on him in case he should start signalling.

Now her immediate thought was to mount and ride. She could not defend the ranch, certainly. So why risk herself or the children? But the memory of Juan held her. She thought how he always strode along the line for just a minute before he gave the order to mount and ride. She must think too.

Then she remembered that Sutter had armed his Indians, and for a moment she was so hot with indignation that she could not think. The Californians would pick out trusted half-breeds like Miguel and Ramón and teach them to shoot. But their Indian vaqueros they let get along with a lasso and a knife, and perhaps a bow inherited from the old tribal life. Now this German upstart, who had come begging into California and been so hospitably used, was trying to overthrow and plunder the Californians by arming Indians against them.

The more she thought the more she felt sure that she would not abandon the ranch until something more definite threatened. But she would make everything ready. Going into the outer room she saw by the clock that it was eleven. She took up a little hand-bag. It was not the same one which she had taken that night when she had eloped, but nevertheless the analogy struck her. She was going out into the world again as she had eight years before, but having accumulated the not inconsiderable baggage represented by four children. She went to the old chest and took out the money-bag. It was much heavier now than it had been when she first looked into it. From the chest she took also the old parchment which was the Governor's grant of the ranch to Juan's father. She could think of nothing else which was of outstanding importance; there was so much that she would like to take and so little which she really had to have. As a whim, she took the Chinese bowl from the mantelpiece. She decided to have one book, with the vague idea that if the Governor threw them all into prison it would be pleasant to have something to read. She chose *Gulliver's Travels*; it was small enough to go into the hand-bag easily, and she treasured its reference to California. She put in a few clothes.

"I won't forget my nightgown this time," she thought, smiling.

Luis still trailed her. In spite of his protests she took his pistol, loaded it, and put it at the top of the bag, already heavy with the coin and the bronze bowl. She laid the bag in a handy place, and beside it put a serviceable bonnet and cloak. Still there had been no sign from Tomás.

She called to Lupe to serve every one a heavy meal as soon as possible. She began to feel more cheerful. At a sudden thought, wondering she had not done it before, she sent Juanito off north to carry the word to the Fuentes. She began to think rather well of herself as a general-in-command. Juan would be proud of her. If only she had an army that did not consist altogether, now that Juanito was gone, of children, women, and crippled old men.

Tomás had come in for his dinner, and one of the other old

men had taken his post. Every one had orders now. If the alarm came all were to mount and, scattering, ride away singly so as to leave no easily followed trail. They would take shelter in the hill-ravines, and their point of rendezvous would be the little valley at the northern edge of the ranch—the one called Ojuelo, or Little Eye. Every one must leave. Building on a current story, Judith told them that Sutter's Indians were cannibals and would eat them; her real reason was that she wanted no one left behind to steal or to give information about where the family had gone. The weak point in the plan was that with the short warning they would have some old woman would be sure to be too slow, and the raiders would catch her.

The thing to do was to send some one to a point in the hills where there was a view of the road several miles beyond. But who? The old men could not ride fast enough, even after they had seen the enemy. She did not dare to risk the disorganization which would follow if she went herself. Then with a pang she thought of the way the horses had been brought in that morning. Luis's pony was fast and sturdy. Old Tomás could watch, send word, and then slip off into the hills while Luis raced for home. She gave Luis back his pistol, exacting a promise in his father's name that he would use it only as a soldier should. The boy was in the highest heaven of enjoyment, but Judith felt nearer to tears than she had been yet that day as she watched the old man and the child ride across the valley and disappear over the lift of the little hill. It was early afternoon.

At dusk the two of them rode in again together. They had been able to watch the road almost as far down as the García place, and no one had come up it. There was little danger of anything happening by night, and the dogs were vigilant. Nevertheless the three old men divided watches, and no one undressed. Judith lay down only to doze, and made the rounds every hour.

Just at daybreak came a rushing of horses from the north. It was the Fuentes with fifteen men; Juanito was with them, drooping in his saddle from weariness. The two little men were white with rage against Sutter. Here they had been fighting Indians at heavy odds for years, holding their own only because the Indians had no fire-arms—then this pig of a German! . . . The Fuentes had never bothered about the revolution; now they were ready to fight Sutter till they rode their horses thin.

They went on to the south, scouting. Late in the day they came back, bringing with them the Rancho Amarillo people who had ridden off to attend Mass. These last had to stay all night at the Mission, and Sutter's men had taken a few of their best horses. But there was no more danger of a raid. Sutter had gone on south, and the Division of the North had dodged the Governor and was going south too, keeping a safe hundred miles ahead of Sutter's American riflemen.

And so, thought Judith, the excitement had all ended in anti-climax after all, and she was glad that she had not turned tail and bolted for Ojuelo. But she felt better when Don Diego and Don Alonzo came in together, very formally, to congratulate her on her courage and thank her for the example she had set. Don Diego put it very grandiloquently in Spanish, the kind of language which sounded silly when you translated it into English. But she knew that he meant it, and she was glad to know that in time of danger she had behaved in a way that made these seasoned Indian fighters approve of her.

Also, they rated the servants for deserting the ranch, and they left two of their own men there as a guard.

Two months afterwards, one day in early March, Juan and his men came riding back. Judith had not worried much about him, for all the news which had come up from the South had been reassuring, and she had had enough worries of her own about the ranch. But it was good to feel Juan's hard body against hers, and to sense the responsibility taken from her. Juan was disgusted with the whole campaign, just as he usually was when he came back from chasing Indians. If the Governor could have caught up with them at first he might have beaten them, but by the time he got to Los Angeles his Americans were sick of the business and the revolutionists were ready for him again, and after firing a few cannon to save his face he had surrendered, and Sutter along with him. Juan thought they should have shot Sutter for arming the Indians, but instead they had merely let him go and not even confiscated his lands. Well, the Californians would have to put on a big campaign against the valley and foothill tribes now, burn some villages just to show them who was master still.

"And why didn't the Governor chase you harder?" Judith asked.

Juan began to laugh: "Why, the poor man had piles and couldn't sit on a horse; he had to go in some kind of a carriage pulled by vaqueros with their lassos."

Judith laughed too, and cradled Juan's head on her breast. They were both sleepy. History, she thought, what a funny affair it was! You read the big books and they had the big theories, but perhaps all the explanation of something or other was that Napoleon or Julius Cæsar or Alexander had eaten a bad egg, or slept in a bed full of fleas the night before, or been troubled as the Governor had been.

Then again Judith had the consciousness that she was part of history. This revolution—it would be in the books, and she had stood on the edge watching it go by. When she was an old lady some historian might come to ask her questions about it. If she lived to be a hundred—why not imagine it?—the year would be 1916. She and the historian would sit on the veranda looking out to the south. Her peach-tree would have died and been replanted before that; even her apple- and pear-trees would be old and gnarled. But the line of the hills would look just the same, and the trees would still grow along the ravines. Then she would smile to herself and begin, "In those days . . ." Perhaps she would keep the Governor's secret, or perhaps being a very bold and licensed old lady she would tell the historian bluntly He would, of course, not dare put it in his book; historians never did.

Juan was asleep. She was sleepy too. She supposed she would have another baby now; it was time. History or no history, babies kept coming. If they didn't, she reflected with the gravity of one more than half asleep, soon there wouldn't be any history at all. Anyway, she had lived through a revolution. Perhaps Uncle Enrique had been right, and she had finished the placid stretch of her life. Perhaps history would strike again. In her half-sleep she felt herself thinking of history as a snake. At a picnic she had wandered off, and suddenly the rattlesnake had buzzed; as she sprang back it had struck and missed. History was like that. You seemed to wander along calmly controlling your own steps, and then something you could not control—a war, a revolution, a failure of banks—buzzed and struck, and did not always miss. But she thought of the wide stretches of the valley outside, and the calm profile of the hills to the south, and the knee-tall, gently waving grass. It seemed too quiet and far-removed a spot ever to be much troubled. " Well," she thought, " Juan is back, and I got through *that* revolution all right, anyway."

CHAPTER III . . . . . MAY 1845

-ʖ-———-ʖ-

LUIS WOKE UP with a more-than-usually light feeling of being happy, although it took him a moment to remember just what he was being happy about that particular morning. It was not his seventh birthday, for that had already happened back in March. Then he remembered that Rancho Amarillo was the meeting-place of all the different men who were going out on the biggest raid against the Indians there had been for a long time. Luis himself couldn't remember anything like it.

He understood things very well. It was simple. The trouble was that his father had had to go away to put the old Governor out and see that another was put in. While his father was doing this he could not pay any attention to Indians, and so they had raided a lot of ranches and carried off a lot of horses down around San José. And now the Californians were getting together from every-where this side of the Bay and as far south as San José, and they were going to show the Indians what about it. The San José men had come in last night, and were camped over across the creek.

Luis pulled on his clothes all by himself, refusing any help from Juanito. Guito, although he was only going on six, tried to do the same, but had to have some help with his bootlaces. Luis felt some satisfaction at this, for it was pretty hard work keeping ahead of Guito, even though you were a year and a half older. But any-way it was a lot better now that they didn't have Antonia as a nurse any more, and didn't have to sleep in the old outer room along with Antonio and Leticia and the baby. Now they slept upstairs over in the new part of the house, and had only Juanito to sleep there too, just to see that they did not fight too much after they were sent to bed.

Most mornings Luis could put up a pretty good argument at breakfast. Guito would always back it up too, and that was a very decent thing for him to do. Leticia of course wouldn't, but then she was a girl and too young, anyway; she didn't really like her porridge any better than the boys did, but her way of being superior was to eat it and pretend she liked it. Luis and Guito stood for their right to have beans and tortillas, the way their father did and the way the García and Gómez boys did. But their argument never got them anywhere, for they had to have porridge, and eggs, and wheat bread with butter and jam, and just one tortilla.

This morning Luis did not take any time to argue; he was too anxious to get across and see the encampment. He left the table on the run with Guito behind him. They headed for their ponies, but just as they got to the horse-rail both of them knew they couldn't go just yet. So they went round by the out-house first, and when they got back Juanito also was there by the horse-rail. Luis didn't like being trailed around by Juanito, but of course Guito being so young needed some one, and, after all, Juanito was a good sort and much better than a baby-nurse like Antonia.

The three of them rode their horses through the ford, and came first to where the San José Indians were camped. Luis knew all about them, for his father had explained very carefully. Luis had been pretty well puzzled about these Indians, for it seemed mixing matters to have some Indians to fight other Indians. It looked as if you or they might get turned around and forget just who it was you were supposed to kill. But his father had told him that these San José Indians went to Mass, and wore clothes, and raised things in gardens; so they weren't like the wild Indians; the Mission Indians liked to fight the wild ones because they belonged to different tribes and were enemies.

Luis took a good look at them this morning. Going to Mass and raising things in gardens might be true enough, he decided, but he couldn't see that his father had much of a point when he said they wore clothes. Some of them had cast-off pantaloons, and some had cast-off shirts and hats, but you would have to take the best clothes off any four of them to get a suit good enough even for a García. A lot of them had nothing but blankets and rags around their middles

Luis didn't think much of their weapons either. Some had knives and some had lances. Mostly they had just bows and arrows, the same as those the wild tribes had. Their bows were weak-looking and their arrows rather short—not cloth-yard shafts as they were in the stories his mother told him about Robin Hood. The Indians' horses were poor too, and had ribs sticking out.

The Indians were still eating their breakfast from a steer they had just killed. They had made an awkward job of the butchering and had left the guts strewn around. Their camping-ground was messy and smelly.

Beyond the Indians were camped the soldiers. Luis counted them carefully, and found there was just enough to match for his fingers and thumbs. They had uniforms of blue and red, but, as Luis had discovered the evening before, the uniforms looked better from a distance. When you got close up you saw how ragged they all were, and how greasy and wrinkled. They looked as if they had been worn a long time, and had been out in the rain a lot, and been slept in. Besides, only about half the soldiers had all of a uniform. The others had maybe the pants or maybe the coat. Some of them had leather jackets, and Luis knew that that was a very sensible thing to have for protection against arrows, and he wondered why they all didn't have them. But then he knew that soldiers didn't know much about fighting Indians, and really belonged down in the forts where they could fire the cannon; his father had told him so. The soldiers had good guns—short ones they could shoot from horseback.

Next they came to the camp of the San José men. "They're a mixed lot," he remembered hearing his father say. A mixed lot usually meant a herd of cattle of all ages and kinds, but this morning he could see how it applied to the San José men. They were all ages and kinds too. Some of them had clothes just like those his father wore when he went Indian hunting, and others had just common ranch clothes, and still others were togged up in a lot of finery as if they were on a picnic. Some had guns or pistols, and some had lances, and they all had lassos and knives.

Three Americans were with them. Two of them Luis knew lived in San José and had Californian wives and could talk Spanish; so they really counted as Californians just as his own mother did. But the third man was dressed all in leather with fringes on it, and had a great rough beard. Luis had seen trappers before. The three Americans were camped by themselves at their own fire. The two from San José were smoking cigarettes, and the trapper was chewing tobacco and spitting into the fire. All three had knives and pistols, but what fascinated Luis were the three big rifles which the men held balanced over their knees as they sat by the fire. Something about those rifles made Luis's heart go faster. He didn't see why his father who could buy anything he wanted didn't have one of those rifles and learn how to shoot it the way the Americans did.

As the boys sat on their ponies and looked the trapper glanced up at Luis; he raised his hand in salute.

"Hi-ah, Major."

Luis knew he was being made fun of, and he wanted to say the right thing in reply, but before he could think Guito spoke up:

"Major yourself!" he said very firmly.

The men roared, but Luis was embarrassed. Guito was pretty dumb; he thought Major was some kind of a bad name the trapper had called him, so he just called it back. The men were really laughing at Guito, and at him too.

After that the trapper showed Guito the rifle. Guito wanted to snap the trigger, but the trapper said no, that was bad for the flint. Anybody, thought Luis, ought to know that much, even Guito.

The trapper seemed to like Guito.

"Crimeny," he said, "I wouldn't be surprised if I hain't got a little papoose back among the Crows, just about your size. That is, if the goddam Blackfeet hain't caught and skelpt him yet."

One of the other Americans asked Luis if he wanted to see a rifle, but Luis felt superior to Guito, and said naw, he'd seen plenty of rifles.

When they were leaving the trapper fished two little red stones out of his pocket for them.

" Them's genu-wine roo-bies," he said. " Come all the way from the Navajo country."

Luis saw him flutter an eye at one of the Americans, so he knew they weren't rubies, but they were very fine stones to have, anyway. He thanked the trapper, and tried to kick Guito to make him remember to say thank you too. But Guito was such a dumb one he just sat in his saddle, looking at the red stone with a kind of silly grin on his face, and forgot all about saying thank you as their mother told them to. That was all wrong too, for Guito's stone was lots bigger and better than Luis's.

The next exciting thing was seeing the Fuentes come galloping in. They had their own men and some who came from the ranches in the north—the Contra Costa and the country over towards the Bay. They unsaddled and camped beyond the San José men, and the boys went to look at them. Luis felt better when Don Diego came over and clapped him on the thigh and said:

" Well, Luis, have you and old Tomás been out fighting any more Indians? "

Luis could only grin and say no. This made little Guito look very downcast, for that riding out with old Tomás was the big thing Luis had done that Guito hadn't. Luis was glad for a moment to see Guito look that way, but in a minute he was sorry, for Guito was such a little fellow, anyway, and only five. So Luis liked it when Don Diego slapped Guito over the thigh too, and said:

" Here's little Guito too; first thing you know he'll be going out to kill himself an Indian."

They both liked Don Diego, and they had seen a lot of him at the ranch when he used to ride down to see about the Indians. They showed him their red stones.

But the men who came with Don Diego—Luis decided that they were a mixed lot too. Don Diego's own men were good fighters, but the men from the Bay ranches were pretty much like the men from San José; they didn't have any Americans with them either.

Luis could hear Don Diego telling the men that they must picket their horses and be ready to march with the rest of the army that afternoon. Then Don Diego rode over towards the house; Luis, feeling that things were going to happen in that direction next, rode after him. And behind Luis trailed Guito, with Juanito behind him still keeping an eye on the two of them.

Guito would have ridden right up to the house, but Luis made him stop, and they left their horses at the rail with Juanito. They walked towards the men standing in front of the veranda, Luis holding Guito's hand. He was always ready to take very good care of Guito, even though Guito didn't have much brains Trying to ride right up to the house, for instance—that wasn't a good idea, Luis knew; for if they had come clattering up on horseback along with Juanito they would have been sent away, but if they just wandered up as two little boys nobody would pay them any attention. And Luis was pretty sure that something important was going on.

Captain Jaramillo was there. He still had on the fine deerskin riding-boots and the pantaloons which went with his handsome uniform, but he was wearing a leather jacket now and looked ready for fighting. With him were Luis's father, Don Diego Fuente, and Don Jaime Lozano, who commanded the San José men. There was also old Gallo from San José, who walked with a limp. Luis knew he limped because somewhere in his knee was an arrow-head he had got in a fight years and years ago; all the boys knew about old Gallo.

'This group in front of the veranda was a mustering of heroes, but the heroes themselves were all scowling, and looked like a lot of strange dogs circling around and getting ready to mix up, all except Don Jaime from San José, who was smiling a little as if to say that this wasn't his fight.

"I repeat, gentlemen," the captain was saying, and, with his arms folded across his chest, he looked magnificent, "the order of march is this. First division, Ensign Fidalgo in command, and under him each rancher to command his own men; in this division all the contingents from the outer ranches and the Contra Costa. Second division, the Indians, Ensign Garza in command. Third division, the San José men, Don Jaime in command. Headquarters, the military under my direct orders."

Before there was enough interval for anyone politely to reply the captain called to a very young-looking officer standing at a little distance:

"Ensign Fidalgo, we must inspect." They rode off together.

Luis saw his father very deliberately spit, and he knew that his father seldom spat because he wanted to clear his mouth; he spat to express himself, just as some men swore.

"I am sure," said Don Jaime, "that you gentlemen should not be irked; Ensign Fidalgo is a very gallant officer."

Luis's father spat again. "Gallant," said Don Diego—"but what does he know about fighting Indians?" Old Gallo said a lot of words which Luis's mother had told him not to say; Luis hoped Guito wouldn't remember them. He didn't think Guito ought to know such words, but for himself of course he knew them already and rather liked them. They were good words to say to yourself or to your pony when he shied, provided your mother didn't hear them.

There was so much to see in the next hour that Luis and Guito fairly ran and rode around in circles. You could hear the most talk over among San José and Contra Costa men; they were all telling about how many scalps and Indians' ears and captive squaws they were going to bring back. The San José Indians had started some games of hand, and were yelling and laughing and having a high time. The men from the outer ranches were not talking much, for going out after Indians was nothing new to them. They were lying around smoking, or whetting knives, or playing games with some packs of old dirty cards.

About noon Luis saw that something was happening down by the creek, and he made for the place. It was another gathering of heroes. His father was there, and Miguel and Ramón, both the Fuentes, the two Americans from San José, the trapper, old Gallo, and his two half-breed sons. Luis came up and stood behind the trapper, who turned and winked at him.

His father was speaking: "I appreciate your wanting to join me, but even if you came into our division you would be fighting under the command of Ensign Fidalgo."

The trapper turned to Luis, and spoke aside:

" What's he sayin', Major; I don't know much Mex."

Luis explained, and of course missed the rest of the talk while he was doing so. But it appeared that his father and Don Diego were telling old Gallo and the Americans that they had better stay with their own division. If the men were as poor as Gallo said they must be in bad need of all the stiffening they could get from their few veterans.

" Why they worryin' so much about that little pimp Fido? " said the trapper in English to one of the other Americans. " Tell 'em I'll go over and pick a fight with him and scare the pants off him so bad he'll run home to mamma."

" There's enough trouble in this camp without starting any more," said the American shortly.

'' Well, tell 'em anyway not to worry; it's the same all over the world. I've been out with the Americans too, and the milit'ry allus hogs the show—until the fust Injun whoops. It'll be the same here. These here fellers with the pretty-coloured pants will be plenty glad to take advice mighty soon."

The gathering broke up. The trapper walked off holding Luis's hand, and Guito tagged along holding Luis's other hand. The trapper was discussing Californian Indians with the other American and saying that some one called Old Greenwood said they weren't much account as fighters. The American said that they weren't so bad either.

" Well," said the trapper, " the only Californy Injuns I ever fout was Moharvies and they run like hell. But then anyone, even Americans, will run like hell if you catch 'em wrong. I've fout Blackfeet and Sinaboines and Rickarees mainly, but I've mixed up with most other tribes one time or another, even with some Crows when some young bucks jumped our camp one night just for a lark. There was an Englishman out hunting on the Missouri once, and he said I was a ' connysoor ' of Injun fighting. So I'll be mighty glad to see how these Tokolummies of yours go 'bout it."

At his camp he held his rifle so that Luis could sight along the barrel and pull the trigger; of course the trapper really held the rifle and took the recoil on his own shoulder. But it was very much as if Luis were shooting. Then he reloaded and let Guito do it too. He told them about the time he fought a two-headed Ute over by the big salt lake, and how he shot a carcajou, but to do it had to make a silver bullet by melting up half a Mexican dollar he got in Taos. He was going to show them the other half of the dollar to prove it to them, but when he looked in his pockets he couldn't find it, and said he guessed he must have lost it that time he jumped off a precipice to get away from the Shoshones. Guito's eyes got bigger. Luis didn't believe those stories much, and he had heard that old yarn about the carcajou before. But still he enjoyed them, and pretended to believe them so as to be polite.

When they left Luis was polite again, for he had got to like the trapper; so he said as he had heard his mother say:

"If you are ever passing this way please drop in again to see us."

The trapper laughed at this and so did the other Americans.

"I guess you heard that from your mammy, Major. Your mammy's that white-headed gal I've been seein' and she's a Yankee. I guess she wouldn't be too pleased to see a Missouri Rixson a-comin' in to call, and settin' down on her best parlour cheer. Your pappy and me, we might talk turkey on Injuns an' sech, but I won't come botherin' your mammy none. She don't want no truck with a Rixson, an' a hairy one at that."

Luis noticed then, although he hadn't thought of it before, that besides the long hair and beard the trapper had heavy black hair on the backs of his hands, and at the opening of his shirt you could see long curly hair coming out. As he went back to the house with Guito Luis could remember the trapper as he laughed, his long yellow teeth, and two or three of them broken off.

Just after lunch the men mustered in very irregular lines according to their divisions, and Captain Jaramillo inspected them. Luis could see that his father seemed to look on the captain more kindly at this. Some of the Indians' horses were in bad condition; so they were allowed to take Rancho Amarillo horses. Seven men were told off to guard the camp at the ranch; they seemed too old to make the campaign. The rest of the men were counted off—

one hundred and thirty-six in all. It was the most men that Luis had ever seen, and he was sure they could lick all the Indians in California.

In the early afternoon as the men rode away Luis stood holding his mother's hand. He knew that she worried when his father went off this way, and he wanted her to feel that he himself was with her. He had his little pistol in his belt; it was not loaded, but still it seemed reassuring. He had his red stone clutched in his other hand; even though it might not be 'roo-bie,' he liked it.

The men rode off by divisions. First of all went Don Alonzo and four men as scouts. Then Ensign Fidalgo, whom the trapper had called Fido, rode in his uniform at the head of the men from the outer ranches and the Contra Costa; among these were Don Diego and his men, and Luis's father and the men of Rancho Amarillo. Next went the Indians; then Captain Jaramillo and the soldiers; last of all Don Jaime and the San José men.

It was a long time before they were all out of sight, for at the head of the valley they took a trail on which they could ride only single file. In spite of this, Luis and his mother stood looking until they had all disappeared. He knew that she was wanting to cry, but didn't. He asked her how long it would be from the head of the line to the tail; she was quiet for a minute working the sum out in her head, and then she said that it would be maybe half a mile. Half a mile of men! That made them seem more than ever to Luis. He wished he were old enough to be riding with them, and said so.

"I hope by that time," said his mother, "there won't be any more Indians."

That was a funny thing to say, thought Luis. He was very fond of his mother, especially when his father went away and left her in his own charge; but her saying something like that showed how funny women were, even his mother. He felt sure his father would have a dull time at the ranch if there weren't any more Indians for him to chase.

THEY CAMPED THE FIRST NIGHT at a place called the Ranch of the Little Wolves. The people there were very glad to see so many men going to the Indian country, for they had been badly harried, and had lost so many horses that they had scarcely been able to round up their cattle. A few more men joined the expedition here.

Next day they crossed the plain, and camped in a grove of trees along the nearest branch of the San Joaquin River, having seen no Indians.

On the third day they crossed the different channels of the river. It was high, for snow was melting in the mountains. They had to swim their horses, and to wallow through several swamps full of tall reeds. After getting through the marshy country they swung off northward, and in mid-afternoon scouts came in with news of a small village in which the Indians seemed unsuspicious of any Californians being near by.

The San José Indians and some of the San José white men went out, surprised the village, and came back saying they had killed all the Indians. Juan and the other men from the outer ranches sniffed at this. You might boast or you might honestly think that you killed all the Indians, but most of them always got away and hid in the reeds. Anyway, they had burned the village and killed a few Indians, as shown by the scalps and ears that they brought back. There had been several horse skulls around the village.

The San José men brought in five young squaws, two of them with babies, all tied together on a rope like a gang of convicts. This capturing of squaws for household slaves was a bad business, Juan thought; but the Californians had always done it. Juan did not care much about its being against the law or about the right or wrong of the matter or about the squaws' feelings either. But capturing women always demoralized an expedition. That very night the men untied the squaws (because you can't get much fun out of a squaw when she is tied up with a lot of others). Two of them managed to escape, and one bit a man who was trying to hold her. Next morning the bitten man and three others set off to take the squaws back to San José. It was ridiculous for four men to escort three women, but that was the way things went when you started squaw-chasing.

On this day the expedition set out to make a long march, for they had had three easy days. Old Rixson's saying came true too, for before breaking camp Captain Jaramillo called a council. He was facing the great plain which ran from the river to the foothills of the big mountains; he couldn't see any Indians, and he didn't just know how to go about finding them, or catching them after he had found them. He had brains enough not to be too puffed up about the first little success down by the river, although some of the San José men seemed to think that that showed they were real Indian fighters.

At the council Juan gave his plan. It was to divide into three sections, each with some white men and some Indians, and advance towards the mountains several miles apart, but keeping in touch through scouts. Then if any division found a village it could halt and the others could swing round on a pivot and catch the Indians in the rear and thus trap them. Old Gallo supported Juan, but the others were doubtful about splitting their forces. Juan said it was not really splitting, for in this open country you would almost be able to see from one division to the other, and being on horseback you would outmanœuvre any Indians. Rixson seemed to favour Juan, but he would not speak out; he said he didn't know anything about Californian Indians.

They finally marched in one body with scouts flung out widely, but they found no Indians that day. They kept their left flank along a small river which was one of the feeders of the San Joaquin. The day was very hot; one man came down with heat-sickness, and had to be left among some trees by the river with two men to guard him. The main body camped in the first rise of the foothills among some fine oaks and some scrubby pine-trees.

Next morning they advanced higher into the foothills. Don

Diego Fuente, Gallo, and Juan himself had been in the country before and knew its lay-out, but they could not tell where the Indians were at this time of year. What they really wanted to find was Felipe and his band of Tokolumnes who had been doing the most and boldest raiding of late. They saw many hoof-prints in the trails; so they knew that the Indians must have driven stolen horses that way. They advanced slowly, keeping scouts out in all directions. Towards evening Don Diego came in with the news that a large village, which he thought was Felipe's, was not more than five miles away; it seemed peaceful and undisturbed, and there were many horses grazing; he had been close enough to make out the brands on some of them.

The captain ordered camp made at once, and called another council. Juan was disgusted that the captain was now all for separating his men and attacking from two or three directions at once. In the last two days the captain had been impressed by how little damage they would be able to do if they merely charged upon a village and let the people scatter into the hills. They might burn the village, but that amounted to nothing. Juan was all against dividing now; it was proper to divide mounted men out on an open plain, but here in the thick-wooded hills separated bands were as good as lost, and it was all luck if they ever turned up where the fighting was. He spoke his mind. There was a lot of argument then. Juan kept quiet through most of it, for he did not like wordy arguments.

In the end the captain decided to keep the bulk of his men together and attack from front and one flank. But he would send a small detachment around to attack from the rear of the village and block the escape. In that way he hoped, if not to surround the Indians, at least to pinch them badly. The captain asked who would lead this small party, and Juan spoke up at once. He volunteered because he had opposed the idea, and opposing a dangerous idea always leaves you open to the charge of being afraid of it personally. So if you oppose something and it is carried against you you must always volunteer for it; that was part of the code which Juan's father had taught him. Old Gallo still protested that the whole idea was a bad one.

Juan was allowed to pick fifteen men. He took his own, of course,

and some of the best of Don Diego's. He would have liked to have
Gallo, but under the circumstances he couldn't very well. He was
pleased when Rixson came over and said he guessed he'd come
along.

"Looks to me," he said, "like you fellows might have the most
fightin'."

Rixson was a free-lance, and so could go where he wanted. Juan
knew he must be a good fighter, and, besides, he would be good at
finding his way about in the woods, and that might be more important even than fighting.

An hour before daylight the whole army started. First went two
half-breeds on foot along the Indian trail. Then came the men on
horseback, at a walk, merely letting the horses find their own way.
They came to a glade about two miles from the Indian village. The
scouts had located this the day before as a good place to leave the
horses. By this time you could just see your way around. The men
picketed their horses, and a small guard was told off to stay with
them.

Juan ordered his men to leave their lances and lassos with the
horses, and to draw up in a line. He inspected them as much by
feel as by sight. They were all from the outer ranches, and were
better armed than most of the Californians. Every man had either
a carbine or a pistol, and all had knives. Juan gave his own carbine
to Pablo, and kept his two pistols and knife.

Juan and his men left at once, for they had to circle and come
down on the rear of the village. The captain said he would give
Juan half an hour's start, and then begin his own march.

One of the scouts who had located the village was with Juan,
and Juan told him to lead straight for it. From the hill Juan looked
out through the half-light. He saw horses grazing, and Indian huts
scattered about among oak-trees. The village was still not half-
awake; it was a big one. From the hill it seemed to lie in a level
valley, but Juan knew that once you were down off the hill there
would be so many hummocks and trees and man-tall granite boulders
that you would not think of the ground being level at all. The main
body of Californians would attack from the point at which Juan now
was; the San José Indians would come down on the village from the

ridge to his left. His own problem was to take his men around beyond the village somehow. He would have to keep out of sight, and so might easily lose himself in the ravines or get held up in a thicket. And he might as well not arrive at all as arrive late. "Attack from the rear of the village"—that might sound easy enough to the captain. But where was the rear of the village? An Indian village in thick woods wasn't definite and compact like a group of ranch buildings in open country. Instead, there were a few huts in one spot; then in the narrow valley would be a rough place with boulders and brush and trees, then some more huts, and so on. From where he looked Juan could see several such little clusters of huts, and he supposed there would be more of them farther up where he could not see. Rixson, spitting tobacco juice, agreed that it looked like a pretty hard job.

They more or less kept in touch with the village through a couple of scouts who worked along the ridge. Juan led the rest of his men, scrambling through a ravine full of blackberries and poison-oak. He hated being on foot, and he hated being in the woods; the trees and brush kept him from getting a good look around and made him feel uncomfortable and smothered. But he was a soldier, and a soldier went ahead. They seemed to be going a long way, but distances on foot through the woods always seemed very long to him.

Finally the scouts signalled them in. Juan stuck his head through some deer-brush at the crest of the ridge. He could see a few huts. The sun had not quite risen yet, but its light was at his back, and that indicated that he had swung around in a half-circle and was in a position to attack. So quietly that Juan did not hear him at all Rixson slid up at his left hand; he was still chewing and spitting, but he was not making any noise about it.

Juan went back to where his men were waiting in a little hollow behind the ridge. Like well-seasoned fighters they were taking their ease, resting before the attack. Juan gave his orders:

"Spread out until you have a horse's length between men. Don't bunch so they have a clump to shoot at. When you go over the ridge take a look at the place farther down where the valley draws together. That's our direction. If you lose touch keep headed that way. Each man watch the next man towards the centre, and go

N

ahead when he does. Don't whoop. Maybe we can hit them before they see us."

He assigned Ramón to lead the right flank, and Nicanor, one of Don Diego's men, the left. The men disappeared quietly. Juan took his place again at the ridge. To green men, he reflected, he would have had to give more instructions. To these veterans he hardly needed to say even what he had.

On his right he could see Pablo García; to his left, Rixson. Both kept their eyes on him, watching for him to start. Pablo was loosening his knife in its sheath and seeing to the priming of his carbine. Juan waited; he would have to give the men several minutes to deploy.

The arrangement had been that he was to attack first; then at the sound of firing Captain Jaramillo would charge.

Below on the slope, nearer him than to the huts, a squaw was wandering; she was hunting grubs or beetles probably—an Indian ate anything. If they charged now she would shriek an alarm immediately. Juan waited. The deer-brush which sheltered him was a mass of feathery white blossoms; their sweetish fragrance filled the air. He felt as he always felt before a fight. His pulse-beat was strong and steady. He was half sick with suspense, and yet he felt a certain wild joy. The moment the action began he would shoot more accurately than at other times, move more quickly, and think more surely. Only he must watch that the ecstasy of fighting did not carry him away. That was right for a boy, but he was a captain and must shepherd his men. He commended himself to St Barbara, as his father had taught him to do before a battle.

The squaw moved out of sight into a clump of bushes. Juan rose quietly, pistol in hand, and started to walk down the hill, taking what cover he could behind tree-trunks and bushes. Left and right he could catch glimpses of his men likewise dodging from cover to cover. The woods were very quiet

A shriek from the squaw was the first sound. She broke from cover like a deer, and in great leaps bounded through the bushes towards the huts, screaming. Spontaneously a yell broke out along the scattered line of Juan's men, and they charged.

Scrambling through bushes and jumping fallen trees, Juan raced

for the huts. Indians were swarming out of them and all around.
A big buck running naked and unarmed . . . a little girl scuttling
. . . an old man hauling a child by the arm. Juan heard shots
right and left, a scattered fusillade. Rixson's rifle roared close in his
ear. A grey horse bolted out from nowhere and ran right through
the clump of huts. Then Juan was among the huts himself. He
ran through to the other side. There were only a dozen houses; the
Indians had run. A squaw lay dead. Already some of the men
were taking sticks from the Indians' own fires and lighting the
flimsy shelters of sticks and grass. Thick smoke went up. That
would let the captain know, even if he had not heard the firing.
Juan kept his ears cocked for the roll of musketry from down the
valley. He ran hastily along the line right and left. The men were
reloading; several of them claimed to have shot Indians. They had
met no resistance; the surprise was complete.

Then a flight of arrows came rattling in among the bushes. It
was time to be moving; this this was only a small part of the whole
village. Never stand on defence was the first rule of Indian fighting. Juan glanced around to get his bearings; then he shouted,
and charged the thicket ahead from which the arrows were
coming.

At the second jump his foot caught in a trailer and he fell flat.
He came up spitting blood from a cut lip. The men were ahead of
him. He heard pistols crack and the rifle roar again. He burst from
the thicket into another glade with a few huts in it. A dead Indian
lay sprawling, his head torn open by the slugs from a carbine. His
men were among the huts, setting fire to them and crouching to
reload; they were dodging about for safe places, for arrows were
falling among them. Juan heard the shouts of Indians to the front
and on the right. Rixson was sheltered behind a tall boulder reloading.

"These here Tokolummies ain't so goddam bad," he said,
grinning.

"They'll run when the captain attacks,' said Juan.

An arrow pinged against Juan's helmet; it hit so squarely that it
did not glance; the stone arrowhead split, and the shaft fell to the
ground. The arrow had come from the right; they were outflanked

—time to be moving. He called to the men to fan out; they had bunched badly in the last charge. Then they rushed again.

An Indian was running in plain view. Juan fired his first shot. The Indian yelped and dropped his bow, but kept on running. He's out of the fight, anyway, thought Juan. More shots and more arrows. Juan heard one of his own men cry out. He fired his other pistol at another running Indian, and missed. They came out among more huts. A wounded Indian was trying to crawl away, but one of the men put a knife into him. They did not set fire to these huts; instead, they sheltered behind them, reloading. Miguel was cursing; the side of his face was running blood from where an arrow had ploughed along the cheek-bone. Nicanor was white-faced; one arrow had pinned his left arm to his side, and another was through his calf. Squatting beside him Juan broke off one arrow-shaft and freed the arm. The arrow must have been power-fully shot and at close range, for it had pierced the arm and leather jacket and entered the man's side. The head would have to stay there for the present. Juan broke off the feathered end of the arrow which had pierced the leg, and pulled the shaft through. Nicanor said he could still walk.

The huts had given good shelter for a minute, and the men had been firing as they saw Indians moving and shooting from among the bushes. As he straightened up from removing the arrow Juan for the first time heard firing from farther down the valley; it was a dropping fire, not the sudden roar which he had listened for. But the Indians around him did not vanish at the sound, as he had ex-pected. Instead, the arrows seemed to be coming faster, and from more directions. It was time to move again. Indians could never stand up against a charge; they had no weapons for hand-to-hand fighting.

They charged so quickly this time that they trapped two Indians in a gully; knives flashed and the charge went on. But the men were too closely bunched, and arrows came fast from the flanks against the good mark they offered. Juan heard an arrow go home somewhere with a *plunk*; a man cursed, but no one cried out for help. An arrow struck Juan's side. The leather stopped its force, but he could feel the prick. He dropped on one knee behind a rock, broke off the shaft, and went on. They came to the narrows of the valley; the place for which they had been heading ever since their first charge.

Needing no orders, the men halted to reload. It was a strong position. Tall weathered granite boulders gave good cover Arrows were coming in from all sides. Juan saw his men beginning to squirm deeper down, and to raise up stones and dirt in front of them. They realized as well as he that they were on the defensive now. They would fight where they were until the Indians got sick of it and left, or until the other Californians fought through to relieve them—or until they were wiped out.

Rixson was dodging back and forth looking out from behind a rock, his rifle at the ready. Juan felt like apologizing:

" Something must have happened to the main attack."

They could still hear firing, but it seemed to make no difference to the Indians around them.

" Sure," said Rixson, spitting, " it's what comes of tryin' to attack from sixteen directions at once. I could'a told Pretty Pants just like you done, but it weren't my party. Maybe it weren't Pretty Pants' fault, anyway. Them Injuns o' his maybe cut stick on him, an' his white men——"

Rixson brought up his rifle and fired in one motion. He looked along the barrel an instant, spat noncommittally, and began reloading. Juan started to crawl away

" Say, Mex," Rixson called after him, " lemme tell you somethin' I was goin' to tell after we got back, but maybe I better tell you now. Y're a good Injun fighter; y'handled this attack just fine. And don't mind about me; I been havin' a good time with your Toko-lummies."

Juan grinned, and crawled off. You couldn't say thanks or hand a compliment back when a man said things like that at such a time.

The men had distributed themselves well. Two of them, badly wounded and out of the fight, lay in a protected hollow. Four held the front, and four the rear. Two, well placed on a little knoll, covered the right flank. Rixson and two others were on the left; that was the danger spot, for high ground there gave the Indians command of much of the position. Rixson's rifle held them in check, but even so most of the men had to depend on concealment rather than protection to save themselves from that angle. When arrows began to fall close the only thing to do was to wriggle away.

Several men had been wounded slightly, but their leather jackets protected their bodies. Nicanor was out of the fight, and Miguel was bleeding badly. Juan could feel the arrowhead in his own side galling him

The first attack came from the rear. It was foolish, unless its idea was merely to try out whether the white men still had ammunition. Indians came leaping up among the boulders, dodging about, and shooting arrows fast. Guns roared; an Indian dropped; and the attackers vanished. But one man had an arrow in the flesh of the buttocks. Ramón crawled to him; forced the arrow through the flesh until the barbed head came out the other side; then he broke off the head and pulled the shaft out. The man, his Indian blood standing him in good stead, did not murmur. He joked coarsely about the place in which he had been hit, and kept his place in the line—but he was biting his lips.

How time passed Juan had no idea. Attacks came from the front or flanks, but they were never pushed home. In the lulls they could hear renegade Indians shouting taunts in Spanish. In one attack Juan glimpsed a tall, middle-aged Indian with a scarred face; this he knew was the famous Felipe.

The dropping fire from the left was the worst. Juan, crawling from point to point to direct and encourage the defence, was the most exposed. He wondered that he had escaped so long. Then as he crouched by a rock an arrow struck at the base of his neck. The edge of his leather jacket saved him partly, but the arrow drilled deeply in among his neck-tendons. He felt his right shoulder and arm paralysed, but he rolled down into a gully for shelter, groaning in spite of himself. With his left hand he found his brandy flask and gulped hard. Ramón broke off the shaft, and the pain grew duller. He felt some life in the arm again, and could move it from the elbow down. Holding the pistols between his knees, he reloaded them with his left hand. A burst of firing from the rear brought him back to his duty. Scrambling to his feet he discovered that his legs still worked.

Behind the big rock he found Rixson lying dead. An arrow had struck him in the back as he turned to load. It must barely have reached the heart, for the shaft stood far out. A leather jacket would have saved him.

Suddenly Juan realized that the sound of guns down the valley was louder and was coming closer. It was now or not at all. He called to his men to be ready. He went to where the three most badly wounded men were lying. One of them had died. To the others he gave brandy, and they said they could walk. He assigned a slightly wounded man to help them. He gulped some more brandy himself, wondering whether he could make it.

Shooting as best they could, they went forward. It was good to get out from that dropping fire on the left. But this was no charge. It was the desperate advance—or retreat—of wounded men, weary of battle. They all loaded and fired rapidly, scarcely stopping to aim; the noise itself kept the Indians off. Ramón and three others who were still untouched led the way. Juan, shooting left-handed, took the post of honour at the rear. He was biting his lips to keep going, and sometimes he saw black spots. Miguel and Pablo kept close to him, but Miguel himself was weak with loss of blood from his face-wound.

They could hear the shooting ahead more loudly. Then suddenly the Indians vanished from in front, and there was shouting, and white men in leather jackets came leaping through the bushes—the Fuentes, the two Americans from San José, Ensign Fidalgo and a few soldiers, old Gallo, and some score of men from the outer ranches.

The joining of the two parties made the Indians draw off, but the time was still critical. One of Juan's wounded men fainted, and a big vaquero of Don Diego's flung him across his shoulders. No one suggested going to get the bodies of Rixson and the other man ; the squaws would have mutilated them already. Don Diego sent skirmishers out to drive away the Indians who still hung on the flanks and kept up a long-range arrow-fire. Half-way down the valley they picked up the body of a rancher with an arrow through the throat.

They found the main part of the village on fire, and Captain

Jaramillo's men plundering it. They had pulled a blind old Indian from a hut and knocked him on the head. Somewhere in the woods they had caught two screaming squaws. They had rounded up some thirty stolen horses, most of them bearing the brand of Los Lobitos. Scouts brought in word that the Indians seemed to be retreating deeper into the mountains. There would be no use in pursuing, even if they had not been hampered by so many wounded. They camped beside the burned village, sending word back for the horses to be brought up.

Rafael, one of Don Diego's men, was a surgeon by instinct, and into his hands was given the work of cutting out arrowheads and cleaning and bandaging the wounds. The arrow which had pierced Juan's leather jacket and gone into his side had turned on a rib and could be felt just under the skin. Rafael cut cleanly from where the arrowhead had entered to where it now was, and lifted it out along with the remnant of the shaft, all in one piece. He washed out the wound with hot water, bound it up, and said it was nothing. He shook his head over the end of the broken shaft which protruded just where the neck and shoulder joined. First he cut deeply into the flesh around the shaft so that the wound bled freely. He pulled the shaft; the arrowhead was barbed and would not let go its hold; Juan's head swam with the pain. Rafael said that he could do nothing; it was for the Virgin. The arrowhead could not be pushed through or pulled out; it was in too deeply to be cut free. By the Virgin's help in two or three months the sinews which bound the arrowhead to the shaft might loosen and the shaft be removed. Again by the Virgin's help, after other months the arrowhead itself might work out, or failing that the wound might heal over the arrowhead.

"Shall I have the use of my arm?" asked Juan.

"You are asking *much* of the Virgin."

Juan could see that Rafael did not expect him to live. Juan had seen many men die, but the idea of his own death had not seemed real to him, and did not seem so now.

From Don Diego he had learned what had happened. Captain Jaramillo had not surprised the Indians; it had been the other way around. He had fought them off, but his men had funked an advance. Then the Fuentes, raving with anger, had called for any men who would follow them to come, and had charged in the direction of Juan's firing. Charging, firing, and stopping to load, they had fought their way up the valley.

All that afternoon Juan lay on the cedar twigs beneath the shelter of boughs which had been erected for the wounded. Ramón hung over him, bringing him water and watching him. From the talk he knew that one of his men seemed to be dying. Near by lay Miguel; Rafael had tied up his face, but he was so weak from loss of blood that he could not walk.

Juan hoped to live to get back to the ranch. He wanted to see Judith again. He would like to die in sight of his own hills—if he was going to die. He wanted to talk with Don Diego again, to tell him some things to tell Judith. Those were men you could count on, the Fuentes; if they had not led that charge he and his men would never have got away from that place with the big rocks where they had made their stand. But he could not see Don Diego now, for the Fuentes were off scouting to guard against a surprise. Felipe might attack; everybody had much more respect for Felipe and his Tokolumnes than they had had twenty-four hours ago.

Lying in his pain, he heard the buzzing talk of men at work near by—unwounded men, who had skulked when they should have charged. They were building horse-litters to carry the worst of the wounded. These men agreed that the expedition had won a great victory. They had lost only three killed, and they had now recovered all the bodies, although two of them were badly hacked up. Two or three more of the wounded might die, of course; the men talking admitted this with regret, but with great resignation. Besides, about twenty-five were wounded: but not dangerously; unless, of course, some of the arrows were poisoned

But this, said the men building the horse-litters, was a small price for a great victory. They had found the whole tribe of the Toko-lumnes camped at one place and had burned the whole village. They had taken thirty horses and two squaws. They had killed a great many Indians; fifty, said one; oh, a hundred at least, said another. Here a wounded man began to curse them for a lot of bragging fools. One of the talkers apparently held up a pair of ears to show that he had done some fighting. The wounded man uttered the foulest word that the Spanish language afforded and said:

"Anybody can cut ears off a dead man."

Juan sent Ramón to tell the men to stop talking. He noticed that Ramón dropped his hand to his knife as he left; the talking stopped.

Juan fell to wondering whether it was a victory or not. The burning of the village might be some hardship, but at this time of year it was not very serious: and it might even lead the Tokolumnes to more horse-stealing. As for Indians killed, he himself could remember about six, and one of those was a squaw. Of course that did not mean much, for when you fired into the moving bushes you didn't know whether you killed an Indian or not—only usually you didn't. Very likely they hadn't killed more than fifteen, for all their shooting. Fifty or a hundred was fool's talk, and Juan started to shrug his shoulders—but that was the part of him that he couldn't move.

"G O INTO THE KITCHEN and get some breakfast," said Judith. The man must have been travelling since dawn, and he looked tired and hungry.

She read the letter, standing in the patio, where she had been when the rider handed it to her

YERBA BUENA
July 29, 1845

MY DEAR JUDITH,
   The French frigate *Diane* anchored here this morning. I managed to see the chief surgeon. He seems to be a competent man and was extremely polite. He says, however, that it will be impossible for him to leave the ship or even to send his assistant. The frigate will be here for a few days, and in that time I shall do what more I can. Will you be so good as to let me have news by the bearer.

Most sincerely yours,

. . •

That letter, she thought, was thoroughly Mr Melton—kindly, considerate, prompt, ineffective; it did not even ask, "How is Juan?"; tactfully refraining for fear that Juan might already be dead. Yes, it was Mr Melton in every line, and suddenly she crumpled the letter in her hand and threw it from her. "Impossible" —it was just like Mr Melton to be stopped by a word like that. What did the word mean—merely perhaps that the surgeon was lazy, or that he preferred to go shooting quail rather than to ride into the country to treat an arrow-wound? She had heard that word "Impossible!" often and often in the days when she was building up Rancho Amarillo to suit her dream; she had learned to look upon it as only a challenge to a stronger will.

Tossing her head, she strode into the kitchen. Her vehemence startled them all. Mr Melton's messenger sprang up awkwardly from where he was eating his breakfast. He upset his cup of chocolate, and the thick brown liquid dripped to the floor as she spoke:

" How did you come? "

" I—I—on horseback," he stammered, open-mouthed.

" Yes, you fool! By what road? By Santa Clara? "

" Oh, no, señora. Señor Melton had me brought across the Bay in the boat from a hide ship. They are loading hides at San Aristeo. I got a horse at the ranch."

" Will the boat be there all day? "

" Yes, señora. The men were getting ready to camp to-night near the landing."

Judith swung around to Lupe:

" Get me Miguel and Ramón—at once! "

Juan was sleeping. He was feverish, but still he should not be waked. It was just as well not to have him know that she was going. A quick panic like a nightmare came over her at the thought of leaving; he had grown worse so fast in the last few days. If she were a Californian, thought Judith, she would merely sit by his bed praying to the Virgin, and Juan would be dead in a week, and it would be the will of God, to which wives must be resigned. Possibly that was a better way of life—but it was not her way. Now her desperation and her very panic drove her on to do something.

She gave sharp orders to Antonia. " I'll be back to-morrow evening. Don't touch the bandages. And no poultices of fat mutton or chickens quartered alive. Pray to all the saints, and make all the Indian charms you want "—Antonia crossed herself—" but *don't touch the bandages*! "

She threw a few things into a saddle-bag. She stopped to give orders to Miguel and Ramón. (Miguel still had a raw-looking scar running from the point of his cheek-bone back to his ear.) From the chest she hurriedly took out the smaller bag containing the gold. She had added to it of late; there must be more than five hundred dollars; now might be the time to use it. She kissed the children quickly. They were such healthy little brats, she thought thankfully, that she had no need to worry about them. Guito and Leticia, busy playing, paid her no attention. Luis, sensing something unusual, followed her to the horses. His worried little face touched her, and she spoke to him from the saddle:

" Don't worry, Luisito, I'm going to get a doctor for papa."

She looked at the two vaqueros. They had their lassos and knives.

"Go get your carbines," she said. They looked surprised as they obeyed. Judith thought furiously for a moment whether she had remembered everything. Then they were off.

They took the hill-trail. Ramón and Miguel had very little conception of time. When Judith asked whether it would take three or four or six hours to San Aristeo they agreed to each figure. When she asked whether they would get there before sunset they cocked their eyes at the high sun and said, "Oh, yes." It was slow work by the hill-trail, and they could have made just as good time by way of the Mission. But Judith realized that she must take the way of fewer miles. She was four months pregnant; that was the reason she was glad to leave when Juan was asleep and could not forbid her. Even though she rode a little every day, she knew that she was taking a chance. It was great luck that they could get a boat at San Aristeo; to have gone by Santa Clara and up the peninsula would have meant two or three times as much riding; she might not have been able to do it.

The hills were brown with summer. It was hot as they wound along through the narrow valleys, but on the ridges the air was fresh with the breeze from the Bay. Judith halted conscientiously once an hour, dismounted, and lay down for a few minutes. She was feeling well, but it was the long pull that counted.

As she rode her mind seemed to rest; but when she lay down she kept planning her attack. She felt confident. "Impossible!"—she would show Mr Melton something about that. She kept making up speeches to the surgeon or to the captain of the frigate:

"Señor"—no, she should say "Monsieur," perhaps. Anyway, Mr Melton would have to translate. "My husband was wounded twice in an Indian battle two months ago. The wound in his side healed quickly. We could not remove the arrowhead from the wound at the base of his neck. He suffered greatly, and the wound discharged continually. My friend Mr Melton when he came to see my husband agreed with me that our only chance of getting a good doctor would be to obtain one from one of the warships which occasionally visit the coast." (This would flatter the surgeon, and

Mr Melton must be told that when translating he should pause here for the surgeon to bow and acknowledge the compliment.) "About two weeks ago the sinews loosened, and we were able to remove the arrow-shaft. The wound closed, and we were in good hope, but apparently it closed too quickly. My husband's fever has risen, and the wound is swollen and painful."

It was time to mount and ride on. At the next halt she took up her thoughts. She would say that she had hoped the vessel arriving would have been one of her own country's ships. Then she could say something about the chivalry of France, and French friendship with America, perhaps a reference to Lafayette. Should she stand up tall, looking queenly, her hair for a diadem? Or should she be the helpless and appealing female? But Juan needed a surgeon, and by one way or another he was going to have one. "Impossible"—that was a word for Mr Melton to accept, not for her! In one way or another, yes; she smiled. If you lived on the frontier you might at least claim the advantages of the frontier. She looked up at the two vaqueros:

"Ramón and Miguel, could you kidnap a Frenchman for me?"

They were startled for a moment, but reacted with an unswerving loyalty which touched her and a professional enthusiasm which amused her in spite of everything. Really, they were born bandits. It would be easy, Ramón was sure. One of them would drop a lasso and pinion his arms. They would have to take the Santa Clara road. They might have to hide in the hills if pursuit was hard; but they had friends at some of the ranches who would help them. They would have him at Rancho Amarillo in two days.

"Three," said Miguel.

The two discussed the problem professionally, considering such matters as the length of time it would take to throw pursuers off the trail and to pass certain places by *détours*. Three days, they concluded.

"If he comes of his own accord we can have him there in one day," said Judith. "Besides, a kidnapped man might not be in the mood to be a very good surgeon. We won't try it unless we have to."

The vaqueros looked disappointed. It was too bad, thought Judith; even though she was the mother of four children, she still felt young enough to enjoy the excitement. Besides she might stir up an international situation and make history. Well, as her father used to say, it was still a shot in the locker.

In the late afternoon they topped the last ridge and looked westward. The beauty of it made Judith swallow hard. Below them was the broad shore-plain of brown grass set with dark green oaktrees. There were the ranch buildings of San Aristeo; the long tidal creek running from them down to San Francisco Bay was gold in the afternoon light. Over the Bay itself hung a partial mist dimming the sun, masking the outlines of the western hills, laying a pathway of brighter silver than any moonlight across the water towards the sun. Somewhere across the Bay, in the little village of Yerba Buena, the sunlight caught two glass windows and made them flame out. The strait leading to the ocean was hidden in the haze, but she could see where the hills fell off towards it. The masts of two ships rose from the mist; their hulls were hidden. Those must be the frigate and the hide ship.

They found the boat-crew loafing about at the landing, waiting for the next load of hides to come down. In her hurry Judith had not even asked the messenger what nationality the hide ship was. Fortunately the men at the landing were talking English with a Yankee accent; they were under the command of a wiry little third mate—a Marblehead man. Judith offered him five dollars and a dollar to each of the crew to take her and the vaqueros to Yerba Buena. The mate asked fifteen for himself and three each for the crew, saying the captain would skin him. He would probably have bargained down to ten, but Judith agreed to his price; it was no time to argue. She might as well have bargained, for they had to wait an hour before the tide was high enough to float the boat through the creek. It was twilight when they came into Yerba Buena Cove and up to the landing.

Thirty or more people, being a rather large fraction of the whole population, were standing along the top of the ten-foot bank, at the base of which the boat grounded. Mr Melton was among them.

"Where's the surgeon?" said Judith. It appeared that he and the other officers and seamen had all gone off to the frigate some half an hour ago.

"There's nothing you can do till morning," said Mr Melton.

"*Isn't* there?" said Judith, and she struck a bargain with one of the villagers to take her out to the frigate immediately. Mr Melton and the others too were appalled. No one, they said, especially not a woman, could demand admission to a ship-of-war at this time of night. Judith stuck to her resolution, but she let them persuade her to go and get something to eat. That was good advice, she thought. She was hungry and tired and going on her nerve. She would put up a better fight after supper.

It was almost dark now, and they blundered along through what was supposed to be a street, but was only a sandy path winding among bushes.

The talk, Judith realized suddenly, was in English. Yerba Buena was more a foreign than a Californian settlement. She looked around curiously; she had never been here before. It was a poor little place, with twenty or thirty houses, and many of these little shacks or shanties. Most of the better houses looked queer to Judith, for they were built of sawed lumber in the American fashion. Mr Melton seemed enthusiastic about the place; he said he owned several lots, and expected to make money on them. He pointed out the chief buildings—the old Hudson's Bay Company store, Spear's store and mill, and, well up on the hill, the adobe which people called ' casa grande,' or the big house. They came out on a little plaza on the side of the hill, and Mr Melton gestured proudly to the new and as yet unfinished custom-house on the upper side of it. Judith had to grant that it was a very imposing building for California, being an adobe about sixty feet long.

They came to the house of Señora Luna, where Mr Melton boarded when he was in town. Señora Luna was a dumpy little woman, very kindly and very much worried when she found that Judith had ridden so far in her condition. During supper they still tried to dissuade Judith, but after supper Señora Luna said that she would go along. Is she just being friendly, thought Judith, or has Mr Melton told her that I need a chaperon? The boat was so small that they had to leave Ramón and Miguel at the landing.

"It's a wild-goose chase, I'm afraid," said Mr Melton; but he went loyally.

The wind had turned bitterly chill, and was blowing wisps of fog before it. In spite of the serape which Señora Luna had lent her Judith shivered. The frigate's watch must have been slack, for Mr Melton called out something in French before they were seen and challenged. Mr Melton asked to talk with an officer. The officer had trouble understanding Mr Melton, but finally Judith saw him catch the idea and throw up both hands as in utter futility.

"Tell him," said Judith, "that we'll stay here until we can come on board or talk with the surgeon."

At this the officer shrugged his shoulders so vigorously that they could see it from the boat; then he walked away. Judith promised the boatman another dollar and told him to keep the boat where it was. Mr Melton looked at his watch.

The wind got colder. When Mr Melton looked at his watch again fifteen minutes had passed.

"I'm afraid we're not getting anywhere," he said.

Judith grimaced impatiently. What was fifteen minutes, even in a cold wind? Juan must have that surgeon. Besides, they were getting somewhere; they were attracting attention; she could hear little murmurs of conversation and see heads lean out towards them. She took off her bonnet and sat up with her best carriage so that they could see her hair and tell that she was a lady. Give time for the famous French gallantry to work. The buzz of talk was growing a little louder.

Next another officer, an older one, came and talked with Mr Melton. The conclusion seemed to be the same as before, but Señora Luna spoke up. She had lived so long in a seaport that she knew enough of any language to get along. Judith gathered she must be telling the officer that the lady was pregnant. The officer said something back rather sharply, and Judith could feel even in the dark that Mr Melton was blushing.

They must have waited fifteen minutes again. Then still another officer hailed them, and at the same time some sailors let down a kind of stairway. All three scrambled up. The surgeon, Mr Melton said, had agreed to talk with Judith.

Judith felt a great sense of elation as she stood on deck. Under the light of a lantern several officers stood about looking at them, and farther back she could see sailors moving about as if at work, but really trying to get a glimpse of what was happening.

The surgeon was coming, and Judith held her breath. Here was the real test. He stood looking at her, and she realized that he was seeing whether she was pregnant or whether that had been a lie to help gain access to the frigate. She hoped he could tell; at four months she did not show her babies much; a doctor had other ways of telling probably; but a naval surgeon wouldn't know much about pregnancy. Funny that so much might depend upon that. But the pause let her look at the surgeon too, and decide what approach to take. He was not a handsome man; he was bald and round-headed, not long-headed like Americans or Spaniards. A deep scar ran across his bald skull. He had fine, steady, dark eyes, and she liked his face. He must be between fifty and sixty. When he spoke it was in Spanish—not fluent, but at least intelligible. Judith's pulse pounded with delight; this was luck; now she would not have to depend on Mr Melton.

The surgeon was all politeness. He apologized for his Spanish, which was rusty. He had learned it as a young man, long ago, when he had campaigned in Spain two years under Marshal Soult.

Judith thought of the scene in her Froissart where the pregnant Queen Philippa, entreating for the lives of the men of Calais, went down on her knees before King Edward. But no, the surgeon did not look as if he would appreciate melodrama. So she put her case directly, in few words—and in almost the same words which she had planned that afternoon.

The surgeon was polite. He lamented her situation, and would be happy to serve her. Unfortunately his duty tied him to the frigate. He would, however, go so far, in the name of humanity, as to ask the captain for leave to go with her and treat her husband. He saluted her, and left.

Whether he really meant it or not, that was the first question, thought Judith. He might merely be shifting responsibility; he might not even ask the captain, or he might ask him in such a way that the captain would be sure to refuse. Yet the surgeon did not look like that. Well, let it happen that way—and she remembered Ramón and Miguel.

In the meantime she must make a good impression and an appeal to the officers who were standing around her She wondered where she had learned her guile, but she knew that any kind of bond which she could establish might help towards her great end.

She was a sea-captain's daughter; she knew something of ships—that would surprise them, and might be a bond. She glanced desperately around for something about the ship to comment intelligently upon. She could see the officers following her eyes, wondering what she was looking for. It was eight years since she had left the *Spanish Belle*, and she had forgotten much. But as she looked upward she caught her cue.

" Tell them," she said to Mr Melton, " I like their ship, but why are their topmasts stayed so far forward."

When the Frenchmen grasped this idea they all talked at once, and Judith could see that they were expressing both astonishment and pleasure. When Mr Melton had a chance to translate it appeared that Judith had made a great stroke in her comment, for there was a certain trick to the frigate's topmasts, and the officers were immensely pleased with Judith for having noticed them.

In a minute Judith found herself seated, wrapped in another blanket, and sipping a glass of cognac. She hoped that some officer had gone to urge her case with the surgeon or the captain. She thought hard for another opening, and found it.

" Ask them," she said, " if any of them were on the *Victoire* when she came to Monterey in '37."

This caused more excitement, for there were two such officers, and they had made themselves somewhat unpleasant by airing their previous experience in California. A sailor was sent below to the wardroom to find them.

One of these officers had had the bad luck to be on duty during the night of the ball in '37, but he was gallant enough to say that he had heard at that time of the señora with the remarkable hair. The other officer Judith recognized at once as having been the beanpole midshipman with whom she had danced. Since he could talk a little English, they exchanged reminiscences like a pair of old friends.

By now she was on such good terms with the group of officers that one of them went to speak to a special friend of his who in turn had some particularly close relation to the captain and might say something for Judith's case.

It must have been half an hour altogether before Judith saw the surgeon coming back. He was not wearing a greatcoat or carrying an instrument case. Judith felt suddenly cold even inside the blanket; she thought of Ramón and his lasso. Then the surgeon said, so simply that she could hardly realize it:

"Señora, I have obtained leave from the ship to go with you to treat your husband."

The little group of officers broke into a murmur of approbation. Judith felt that now was perhaps the time to go down on her knees, but instead she held out her hand to the surgeon. He bent deeply and a little awkwardly, and kissed her fingers. Plump little Señora Luna was weeping.

"I shall be ready," said the surgeon, straightening up, "to go with you at whatever hour you set in the morning."

"We must go at once," said Judith firmly.

The surgeon looked startled; he glanced at her doubtfully.

"But you yourself, can you stand the journey?"

Judith felt herself tired, but she had confidence in her own strength of body; it had seldom failed her. Señora Luna was urging her to spend the night at her house.

"We must go at once," said Judith again. "I can stand it."

"You are right," said the surgeon. "In such a case, to arrive late is as bad as not to have gone at all."

The boatman took Señora Luna back to the shore, and returned with Ramón and Miguel. Mr Melton had merely said quietly that he would go with Judith to the ranch; she had known all the time that he would. They left with the surgeon in one of the frigate's boats, under the command of a boyish midshipman.

Judith huddled beneath a blanket, keeping under the shelter of the gunwale. Mr Melton sat with the surgeon and the midshipman at the stern, talking. He's taking the opportunity, thought Judith, to improve his French.

The cold, damp breeze from the ocean was a fair wind for them; the sails stood out steady. It was a night of shifting mist, with the fog threatening to settle down, but never quite doing so. To cross San Francisco Bay on such a night was no mean feat of seamanship, and the midshipman was happily excited. He kept shouting to the lookout standing in the prow, and asking questions of Mr Melton about the local geography.

They steered out until they saw the bulk of the island ahead of them. They coasted around it so closely that even in the darkness they could see the white line of the little waves breaking. The midshipman shouted boyishly at a vague shape on the beach, and it dissolved into a dozen goats stampeding up the hill. Mr Melton said that the water was deep close inshore; so they rounded the south point within what Judith remembered her father used to call " a biscuit toss." Beyond the point they stood out for the Contra Costa, feeling for the creek-mouth, and finally having to strike sail and work along with the oars.

" I'm a very bad horseman," said the surgeon suddenly in Spanish.

" Let's put Ramón and Miguel ashore here," said Mr Melton, " and have them bring the horses down to the Mission building. We can go there in the boat; it will save twenty miles of riding." From the quickness with which he spoke up Judith knew that he and the surgeon must have planned this while they talked French, and that they were trying to save her the ride rather than the surgeon. But it might be a good idea, for she had slumped down now and was hopelessly tired and having pains. Besides, she thought, sailing down to the Mission landing would get them to the ranch almost as soon as riding from San Aristeo.

Instead of working up the creek they landed Ramón and Miguel on the first solid ground and let them walk to San Aristeo. In getting out to the open bay again the boat grounded on mudbanks twice. Judith was sinking into sleep in spite of her pains, but she heard Mr Melton telling the midshipman to lay the course east-south-east; his French sounded enough like Spanish for her to understand. The steady cold breeze, still with tongues of mist in it, was taking them on the beam now. The boat was heeling over, and she could feel and hear the prow hitting the waves with a *slap-slap*. She didn't think that Mr Melton could find the Mission landing in the dark; probably no one could. That would not make much difference; it must be past midnight by now and it would be daylight by the time they were trying to land.   . She was cold, but she was falling asleep. . . She felt proud of what she had done during this day and night. " Impossible," Mr Melton had written—*impossible*. . .   A sudden pain took her in the middle of the thought. . This surgeon was a fine man Would he let her give him a hundred dollars of the gold for his fee, or two hundred? Rancho Amarillo could afford it. What was his name?—funny, she had never found it out. How little names mattered when people were doing something important. His bald head and the ugly scar across it had almost prejudiced her against him to begin with. Where had he got the scar—the Spanish campaign perhaps, or a naval engagement? It looked like a bullet wound.   . . She came up suddenly from a doze with a cold fear of what might have happened to Juan while she was away. In the excitement of the evening she had half forgotten. But she was too sleepy now to think, even though she was cold and her face felt clammy with fog. . . . The waves were going *slap-slap*. . .

" At dawn what guided us into the landing was catching sight of the two men with the horses who had ridden down during the night to meet us. The littoral is so level there that, even when they were miles away, they stood out black against the sunrise. The strange loose-jointed American who talked such atrocious French and was so proud of it showed us the creek-mouth (he was a very efficient fellow really; I came to like him), and we had no trouble bringing the boat in. I can remember it vividly—the dark outlines of the horsemen against the yellow light; it seems strange that it was a year ago."

Jean Louis-Robert Lamarque, chief surgeon of the frigate *Diane*, paused in his story, and looked across the marble-topped *café* table at his brother. Thirty feet away at the edge of the quay he could hear a tiny *slap-slap* of waves; they sounded intimate and familiar—French waves. He was French enough to be glad to be home after a round-the-world voyage. He took a sip of his wine; it was from the Côtes-du-Rhône, and thoroughly French too. With a glance which was almost worshipful he let his eyes wander out across the harbour. There was his own frigate at anchor; beyond was La Seyne, and the wooded point of Tamaris, where the young Napoleon had planted his batteries, and the spit of sand which was Les Sablettes.

"It is all France," said his brother, oracularly interpreting the glance. "There is no land its equal."

Jean Lamarque nodded, and yet he had reservations. He knew wider horizons; one could not, he reflected, be for thirty years a physician in Aix-en-Provence, as his brother had been, without becoming actually as well as literally provincial. That ranch in the Californian hills—and he swung back to his story:

"When we reached the ranch I found the husband in bad condition. I opened the wound, and by good luck got the arrowhead. He would surely have died if I had not arrived; perhaps he died, anyway.

"But it was a remarkable place, that ranch. Even though the grass was dead, there was a sombre beauty in the sweep of the valley and the sculpturing of the hills. The house was the best that I saw in California. There was a paved court with a fountain in the Spanish style.

"They seemed well-to-do, and the American fellow told me that the ranch was one of the best-managed and best-paying in California. But when she offered me five hundred dollars in gold as my fee I am glad to say that I refused it. Yet I saw that she would like to give me something; so I asked her for a curious little Chinese bowl. Then I was afraid that it might be an heirloom; but she said she had found it in an old chest, knew nothing about it, and would be glad to be rid of it. I know that she lied in the last part, but I took it. I have felt sheepish since; I should better have taken the money. Our *savant* on the frigate said that the bowl was old and very valuable. In honour I could not sell it, so I gave it to him; it will go to some museum. He was very curious about how it could have got to California. The Spaniards in old times, he says, sent a yearly galleon from Manila to Acapulco; it probably brought the bowl, and then some one took it north to California. There is also a legend, he says, that the galleon was once wrecked on the coast near San Francisco Bay.

"And the children at the ranch were charming too. They rode like Cossacks. The oldest boy, a serious-faced little fellow, realized why I had come. The next one, called Guito, was precocious and talkative; he was my favourite.

"Then I remember the two vaqueros who waited for us to come in to the landing—centaurs, if there ever were any; dark, villainous-looking fellows with coiled ropes and long knives. One of them was badly scarred. You would have thought they were bandits, and, if I remember my mythology, the centaurs were sometimes bandits. When they closed in behind us I imagined a grim look in their faces, and I felt I would have to go on then, *nolens volens*."

The brother was smiling:

"I can understand your going, but I cannot understand your captain's granting you leave."

Jean Lamarque's eyes glittered as with French zeal he shaped his repartee:

"Ah—there, brother, I differ. I do not wholly understand my going, but I know why the captain granted me leave. After I had decided that I should go I pondered in my cabin fifteen minutes. I was afraid to approach Captain Dondeau, knowing that he was conscientious and a strict disciplinarian. But a man has always the weakness of his virtues, and I finally made my petition on purely professional grounds. I declared—what is probably a fact—that no French naval surgeon had any experience with the treatment of arrow-wounds. So much for the captain.

"But as for myself. You will say that I was romantically touched by the woman herself. Yet she was taller than I; her pregnancy showed in her face; she was roughly clad; she was dishevelled and ungroomed for her long ride—and I am fifty-six years old. It was rather a certain power, a determination to force her will, which emanated from her, I think, as it must emanate from all great persons. Our Emperor had that power, though he was short and grew pot-bellied. Your own Marshal must have had it. For remember, my brother, you were not always the leading doctor of a provincial capital; you too followed the eagles in your youth."

Jean Lamarque smiled as he saw his brother's face light up with the loyalty of an old Third Corps man.

" If Davout had not had that power how could we, unaided, have beaten the Prussians at Auerstadt? "

" And yet there was more than that to explain why I went with her. You and I know as doctors that measles and the plague are catching; as old soldiers we should realize the same of courage. She was four months with child; yet she rode all day on the slim chance that some Frenchman might be fool enough to come to the aid of her husband She must have known what she was doing—and that afternoon she miscarried. I, surgeon of a frigate, attended her."

The older Lamarque nodded; there was a light in his eyes again as he smiled across the table :

" Yes, it was gallant; it was French—the last charge of the Guard."

Instinctively Jean Lamarque raised his hand to the scar across his bald head. Surgeon that he was, he had gone forward in that last charge.

" Yes," he answered. " She was gallant But was it worth it? She lost her baby; she perhaps shattered her own health. The husband had a fine body; he bore the pain of the knife like a stoic; in spite of the pain he thanked me like a gentleman when I was done. And yet he is not a great man, I am sure; and I might be inclined to call her a great woman. . . . But I wonder—and you will pardon my professional curiosity—how he got on."

"WHAT ARE YOU wearing that helmet and jacket for?" said Judith. "They won't be any use against bullets." Juan could see that she was pale; she didn't like the idea of his going out to fight Americans. But she was right in what she said. He had just put them on from habit. The old helmet and the hard-tanned bull-hide jacket were good against arrows, not against rifle-bullets. The helmet was heavy and warm, and the jacket was likely to chafe under the armpits in hot weather. And it was the end of June now, and likely to be hot.

He took them off; Judith brought him a hat. But it was his old hat. "I want my new one," he said. Judith looked displeased, but got it. It was a fine big sombrero, brand-new, with a wide turned-up brim all round, black with a green braid worked upon it in an elaborate design.

"That's too fine a hat," said Judith, "to be wearing on a campaign; every time you camp you'll be letting it lie around in the dirt."

"Oh," said Juan, "I'll bring it back all right." He put it on, and slipped the chin-strap into place. All these years, he thought, and still Judith could never understand that a man liked to dress up when he went off to fight; it was fun to wear good clothes, and you might as well wear them when you went away to fight just in case you never came back to have another chance to wear them.

He had his usual weapons—carbine, two pistols, and knife. He hesitated between his sword and a lance. The lance would probably be better, but the sword was more a gentleman's weapon. Ramón and Miguel had lances. So he took the sword; it was his father's sabre—long, slightly curving, but not very heavy.

Judith went white as he kissed her good-bye. She had got for a while so she didn't mind when he went after Indians, but then he had got that arrow in the shoulder, and it had shaken her nerve more than it had his. Besides, she knew as well as he did that going to fight Americans was different. But she didn't cry.

"You had enough bad luck last time," she said. "Maybe that will carry you through now."

It was good to be riding again. It was good to look ahead at Miguel and Ramón, wearing their leather jackets, their carbines slung over their backs, whooping and singing. Juan lifted his right arm experimentally, and swung it as if he were throwing a rope. A twinge of pain made him wince. That was the one thing he could not do yet. It was a month over a year since he had been wounded; he could do almost everything as well as ever, but there was something about that motion of throwing a rope that caught him every time. Well, he had been proud of being able to rope as well as any vaquero, but there was no great reason why he should have to.

It was queer, thought Juan, to be riding to fight Americans He had an idea it would be nasty work. He didn't know quite how you should go about it. They wouldn't run like Indians when you charged them. He was sure of that. More likely they would only squint more carefully along their long rifles, and, as the Americans themselves said, there would be the devil to pay. Once you got in among them with lances you could kill them fast, for the Americans would either be on foot, or else, if they were mounted, they couldn't ride very well or fight well from horseback. The trouble would be getting to close quarters, for the riflemen would get two volleys in probably, and by that time your best men, who would be leading the charge, would be out of their saddles, and the men who were coming behind would lose heart and turn about, just when, if they charged home, they could do something.

Well, the whole thing would probably have blown over by the time he got there; he had heard a lot of rumours, but he hadn't much faith in them. Maybe he could find out something definite at the ranches on the Contra Costa.

But when they dropped down from the hills and came to San Aristeo they got only what sounded like more and worse rumours. The younger men were all gone. Some of them were with the army, and the others, Juan guessed, had sneaked off to the hills so that they couldn't be conscripted. The women and the older men left at the house had their stuff packed and horses ready in the corral so that they could jump and ride for the hills if the Americans came. Juan felt glad that Rancho Amarillo was so far off all the main routes of travel; there was nothing for Judith to worry about. She had had her scare last time with that Sutter business, and even so nothing had really happened. He had given Julio and the others a good wigging for going off that way and leaving the ranch stripped of able-bodied men. That wouldn't happen again.

Riding away from San Aristeo northward, Juan tried to reckon out what it all boiled down to. The Americans north of the Bay, or some of them, had revolted. They called themselves the Bears, and had raised a flag with a bear on it, and had made a proclamation that California was an independent republic. They held the town of Sonoma. The rumour was that Frémont and his trappers had joined the Bears. That was likely enough, for Frémont had just been driven out of the country south of the Bay for being impudent to the Government; he was probably glad of a chance for revenge. And of course Sutter would help the rebels; the Californians should have shot Sutter after that last affair, if they had had any sense.

At Rancho San Emilio things were much the same as they had been at San Aristeo, but there was a whole new crop of rumours. An American warship was giving ammunition to the Bears. The Americans at San José and Yerba Buena had risen to take the Californian army in the rear. The Bears had killed some Californians, and other Californians had retaliated by executing some prisoners they held.

If the whole thing meant that the American Government wanted to annex California, why didn't they send some marines ashore and do it? Juan felt that he would be glad to see it happen; it was going to happen sooner or later, anyway. But to have a riff-raff of emigrants start stirring up trouble—that meant danger of burning and plundering and shooting. Besides, it was insulting to Californian gentlemen like himself to have such a thing happen. Juan was ready to admit that he liked Americans as a general rule. But a new kind of American was coming to California. They used to be hide-traders like Mr Melton or trappers like old Rixson. The hide-traders often married Californian women, and the trappers, without bothering to marry, took up with squaws or half-breed girls, and they all mingled with the population. But lately along with a lot of farmers with their families had come adventurers who had very little money, but who talked as if they had a tubful. Some of these had come to the ranch; Juan had disliked them, and Judith had disliked them even more. They were always talking confidentially to Judith, and assuming that because they were Americans they were close friends. They would shake half a dozen silver dollars in their pants' pockets and talk in terms of a million of laying out a town-site and selling lots. One of them had wanted, with a salary for himself of course, to start driving stakes in their own valley. He had even made Godoy City sound reasonable for a minute; it was Judith who had laughed at him. Such fellows would never work, and could get ahead only in times of change. Somebody like that may have started the affair of the Bears; Judith thought so too. " They want to upset the apple-cart, so they can pick up a few apples for themselves "—that was the way she put it.

Night fell as they still rode north. Ramón pointed out a little cluster of lights across the Bay. There must be as many as twenty or thirty of them, although they blurred into one another at this distance; Yerba Buena was beginning to put on quite a show at night.

At Rancho San Pablo they found the advance division of the Californians under Captain Torre. Juan reported. Miguel and Ramón started a fire, and began to broil a hunk of liver and some ribs which they cut from a newly slaughtered steer.

It was a pleasant night. The Californians, about fifty men, were bivouacked in the open. Their horses were grazing. The fires were burning up brightly, and Juan walked about from one to the other; he knew men at every fire, and most of them knew him. They asked politely about his shoulder, and said that they hoped he was quite well again. He had hoped to find the Fuentes, but they were not there. That was too bad. As a fighting force the ' army ' did not impress Juan. There was a handful of regular soldiers, but most of them were youngsters picked up from the ranches around San José and along the Contra Costa. They were poorly armed, and most of them had never campaigned even against Indians. Several of them told Juan that General Castro with the main army would move up in a few days to support them; their telling him that was a bad symptom. Even from fighting Indians Juan knew that men who lack confidence in themselves start talking about reinforcements.

They lay at the ranch all next day. A few recruits came in from the outer ranches. Towards dusk they marched down to the Bay, and began ferrying across in a clumsy launch which belonged to the ranch and was used for transporting hides. Even at the narrow point the Bay was three or four miles wide, and getting the men and horses across to Point Quentin on the north side was slow work. Not being in the regular army Juan was only a gentleman volunteer, and in spite of all his experience at fighting Indians no one consulted him. He gathered that they were crossing after dark so that no one on the other side could observe them and oppose the landing. But why was the advance division crossing alone? Juan remembered some rules of fighting which his father had taught him; his father had said they applied just as well whether you were leading ten men or ten thousand. One of the first of them was never to let your force be caught astraddle a stream or some other obstruction so that part of it could be wiped out before the other part could come to its aid. And yet here was Captain Torre putting three or four miles of water between himself and General Castro.

They marched on during the night through Mission San Rafael and joined forces with some twenty Californians who had been skirmishing around during the last few days. They had captured two Americans, and then killed them in cold blood. One of these Californians was called " Three-fingered Jack " from having lost a finger, the way vaqueros did, by having it caught between his saddle-bow and the coil of his lasso. He was a ruffian, and boasted of having mutilated the two Americans.

Juan was not disturbed at the thought of mutilation—he had been through too much Indian fighting. But from the point of view of the campaign he saw that the whole affair was bad. These Californians knew now that if they were captured the Americans would do the same by them, and so they were jittery and jumped every time a horse shied.

By dawn everybody was tired and hungry; they still kept riding north. Juan wondered what the emergency was, and why they had to make this night march. It would mean that they would not be good for much fighting that day. But he was a soldier, and did not question orders. He looked over the country with interest, for he had never been north of the Bay before. He did not think it was such good cattle country as his own ranch; there were more woods and thickets, and the more of them the less grass. For the same reason it was not good country for cavalry; every thicket would give cover for the Americans and make half a dozen riflemen a match for any number of lancers. That might be the reason for Captain Torre's hurry; he wanted to get into open country where his horsemen could act.

They halted finally for breakfast at a ranch-house. It was a poor little place. They did not unsaddle. But they put their extra horses in the corral a little distance behind the house. The old man and his daughters who lived there received them hospitably, but could give no news of the Americans. The men killed 'a beef,' scattered about in front of the house, and got their breakfast. The old man had heard of Juan and his wound, and, having been an Indian-fighter himself, he asked Juan into the house to eat at the table.

Juan was just finishing off his beef-bone when one of his senses sent him from somewhere a quick message of warning. He stopped chewing and sat a moment open-mouthed, the saliva flowing about a bit of beef. He thought he could hear hoof-beats; he wondered. Had Torre been such a fool as not to throw out vedettes? Then came a sudden confused shouting.

Juan had to upset a bench and unscramble himself from the table and jump around it before he could make the doorway. He grabbed his hat as he went, and had his pistol out. Men were running every way, each for his own horse. Some were jumping into the saddles; horses were plunging and squealing with fright. From somewhere a few shots crackled out—" Rifles! " thought Juan. He started running, and then Miguel and Ramón came galloping down, his own horse in tow Juan vaulted up without touching the stirrups; Miguel tossed him the reins.

He glanced both ways—men riding in every direction, a man on foot chasing his frightened horse, two horses colliding and one going down. Whatever it was must be behind the house. A man shouting some orders, another screaming in panic, more shots—pistols and muskets mingled with rifles

Right or left, no matter! Juan swung his horse to the right, and struck spurs. Around the corner of the house he saw the corral and the horses in it screaming, kicking and piling one on the other. A Californian in a soldier's uniform lay in a crumpled heap. At the corner of the corral a tall man in buckskin had just fired; the smoke was still around his rifle-muzzle. He vaulted the fence, and started running like mad for the trees beyond the corral.

Juan pulled aside to dodge a riderless horse galloping wildly with stirrups swinging. Then he went straight after the running American; he stuck his pistol back and pulled out his sword. Shouts and shots from the trees, the buzz of bullets, the running man glancing back. Juan swung the sabre upward—three more jumps. Then all in one motion the man dodged, swung round, and fired a pistol point-blank. Juan felt his sabre swing through the air without biting; the horse had shied off to the left at the pistol-shot. The man was running for the trees on a new angle.

Juan knew that he could not pull his horse round and catch the man again. He wondered why Ramón or Miguel had not swung out on the flank and lanced the man when his own sabre-stroke missed. Then with a shock he realized that neither Ramón nor Miguel was with him. He sheathed his sword and pulled out his pistol, but his frightened horse had already taken him out of range. The only Californians he could see were galloping in different directions, but all were headed away from the grove of trees. Everything was suddenly quiet; even the horses in the corral had stopped squealing. In a moment Juan came to a little hollow; some Californians had dismounted and were reloading. Miguel and Ramón joined him there.

"Where have *you* been," Juan said viciously.

They looked at him silently, their great black eyes pitiful, like children asking not to be struck. He struck bitterly with words: "You half-breeds—you can kill Indians, but when you get up against white men you run."

The Californians lying along the bank began firing. It was only a gesture, for the Americans had good shelter and were at the extreme long-range for the muskets. On the other hand, it was only medium range for the Americans' long rifles. The Californians probably hit no one, but in a minute a rifle ball clipped one of them on the shoulder.

Juan, the two vaqueros following him now, rode off to see what had happened and what Captain Torre would do next. Juan had lost his hat somewhere. Miguel dutifully offered his own hat, but Juan cursed him. They found the captain cursing too. Half his men, he said, had jumped on their horses and ridden off at the first alarm. It seemed to have been as much a surprise on one side as the other. The Americans had seen the extra horses in the corral, thought they were merely the ranch horses, and had come riding in to take them.

Juan could feel himself working up into a rage. Why should he be angry at Ramón and Miguel? He had run away just as they had, and not very long afterwards. Most of the Californians had been cowards, and he had not been much better. If this sort of thing was allowed to happen the Americans would despise all Californians rightly. And he had lost his hat; it was his new hat, and he wanted it back; he didn't want Judith to say " I told you so."

Then his rage left him, and he felt a kind of coldness all over. His mind started to work faster than normal and more cunningly, as it always did when he was going into a fight.

He dismounted and began plaiting a loop on his horse's mane. It was a trick the New Mexicans had learned from the Comanches— New Mexican traders had brought it into California; most boys on the ranches knew it. Ramón and Miguel looked puzzled, but they started doing the same.

" Stop it," said Juan. " You're staying here; I'm going to get back my hat."

He rode up to the little ridge and cantered his horse along in sight of the Americans among the trees. He could see the hat, a black spot lying close to the corral, and in easy range of the riflemen. There was still a dropping of shots from both sides. Juan let his horse canter along in full view; he wanted to be seen. The

P

range was too long for anybody to shoot at a moving horseman. He laid his plan carefully. The Comanche trick was to put your left arm through the loop in the horse's mane, and, dropping behind the horse, shield your body from the fire while you were at close quarters. To make things come out right he would have to swing around in an S-curve, with the house inside the first loop and the corral inside the second.

By the time he came out from behind the house he knew that every one on both sides would be watching him. He swung round on the first loop and started back between the house and the corral, his right-hand towards the grove now, still at a canter. It was long-range, but three shots came from the trees; one ricocheted close by. Good, thought Juan; they'll hardly have time to load again. He quickened to a hand-gallop, and went behind the shelter of the corral; he could see the line of Californian heads watching him. As he came into view of the Americans again he let out his horse to a gallop and swung round on the last loop of the S. His left hand was towards the trees. Three more Americans fired, although every second they waited he would be in better range.

The hat lay in full view ahead, one edge of the brim sticking up, inviting his hand. That would be easy. He shouted to the horse for a last burst of speed, and as another shot came he put his left hand through the loop and fell out of sight behind the horse's body. The hat seemed rushing towards him. There were no more bullets; he smiled. The best shots, the unhurrying ones who had been drawing their beads so carefully, had lost sight of him. They thought perhaps that last shot had knocked him from the saddle; when they saw him again they would have to shoot quickly.

His right hand trailed the ground. His fingers closed on the brim. He swung into the saddle again, and waved his trophy defiantly at the Americans. The smoke of rifles burst from the trees in a volley, but they were snap-shots, making no allowance for his own motion. He pulled his horse to the right, and in a few seconds was beyond effective range.

He rode back again in front of the house; the old man waved delightedly at him. He kept in view of the Americans, riding a-canter, but they did not want to waste powder at that distance.

He brushed the dust from his hat. There was no bullet-hole in it; it must just have blown off; in his excitement he had forgotten the chin-strap. He felt a very deep, grim satisfaction about the hat. The Americans held the battlefield and would capture the horses in the corral, but they could not say that all Californians were cowards.

Later in the day Torre retreated. If his men could not fight the small body of Americans who had come raiding the ranch they could certainly not meet the main force, now that Frémont had joined with the Bears. Torre and his men spent a few nervous days before they could get back across the Bay.

Finally they recrossed, and found General Castro with the main army of a hundred men or so at San Pablo. They all marched south to Santa Clara, hoping without much confidence for reinforcements from the down-country people sufficient to enable them to face the Bears. Then came news that Mexico and the United States were at last at war. From the Californian point of view it looked as if they had been at war for several weeks. But now it was above-board, and not a treacherous rising in the night. Responsible officers were in command—gentlemen whose word you could trust. Commodore Sloat had occupied Monterey without resistance; he sent to the camp at Santa Clara some copies in Spanish and English of his proclamation.

Juan managed to get one of the English copies, and then with his vaqueros rode for home. Most of the other ranchers were doing the same. Castro was trying to keep the army together, but that was only, Juan knew, to save his face with a show of resistance. They had not been able to beat the Bears; they could certainly do nothing against the warships and against the troops that would be sure to come soon. Mexican rule in California was over; the ranchers, as they rode off from the camp at Santa Clara, agreed on that. Most of them said they were glad of it. Mexican rule had given them nothing but bad government and heavy tariffs which put the price of Boston goods too high. And the way Castro and Pico had been squabbling about the Governorship was a scandal.

At the ranch he told the news, but Judith had been expecting it, and was not surprised. On her part she surprised him by the care with which she went over the copy of the Commodore's proclamation. Juan had learned to pay very little attention to proclamations. During every trouble in California the rival generals and politicians burst into proclamations the way a sick man breaks into a sweat, and to as little purpose. Juan had been fooled with proclamations when young; since then he never bothered about them.

Judith said American proclamations were different; they really meant something—like the Constitution and the Declaration of Independence, which had lasted fifty or sixty years, and were still, if you believed the Americans, as good as ever. Judith seemed much pleased as she read him parts of the proclamation: "'California will be a portion of the United States, and its peaceful inhabitants will enjoy the same rights and privileges as the citizens of any other portion of that territory' That means we can't be imprisoned without a fair jury trial. . . . 'All persons holding titles to real estate shall have those titles and rights guaranteed to them.' So Rancho Amarillo is ours still. And listen to this: 'All provisions and supplies of every kind furnished by the inhabitants for the use of the United States ships and soldiers will be paid for at fair rates; and no private property will be taken for public use without just compensation at the moment.' I think we ought to go down to Monterey just as soon as we can and see if we can't get a contract to supply beef; I've always heard there was a fortune in Government contracts. I think it would be good not to kill as many as we usually do just for the hides, but to save some to drive down and sell on the hoof.'"

Juan grunted uncertainly. He had always made plenty of money by selling just the hides and tallow. He did not like changing the ways of the ranch, especially on the strength of a proclamation.

"We ought to make an American flag," said Judith, thinking of some red cloth she had had for a year without using. "It might be a good thing to show that we accept the new Government."

Juan grunted again. He was thinking that it was high time to get back to work and finish killing.

Judith had taken up his hat, and was brushing dust off it.

"You ought to take better care of a good hat, and not let it lie around in the dirt." Probably she had expected him just to grunt again, and that was the reason she looked up in such a surprised way

"*Jesús María!*" he was saying; he was grinning from ear to ear.

THAT MORNING THE CHILDREN had all come down with some
kind of stomach-upset, and were vomiting, so that Judith and
Antonia were running from one to the other with pots and hoping
that not more than two of them would have to at once. Judith had
moved the two little ones into the inner room to get them out of the
way, and she was with them there when she knew from the noises
that some one must be coming, but she was too busy to pay any
attention. She realized she did not think as much about who might
be coming, now that they had been under American rule for four
months and things had settled down.

Then she had to get some hot water from the kitchen, and she
started to make a dash for some, holding a badly smelling pot in
one hand to give to one of the servants to empty. Whoever had
come to the ranch would have gone into the office probably, and
she hoped she would not see them, for she was in no condition
to see anyone. She had thrown on herself an old shapeless house-
dress, and to keep her hair from dangling she had wrapped a pillow-
case around it like a turban; she was wearing bedroom slippers
without any stockings; she had the pot in her hand, and was pretty
sure her face was smeary.

Then the moment she stepped through the door she knew she
was facing another emergency, just at a time when, with the children
sick and all, you really would have thought emergencies might have
waited.

Juan was standing there, looking as he did when he was just
about to start a fight. Facing him were four men dressed like
Americans of the frontier. They all swung round as she came in
through the door, and she noticed the sudden start of their hands
towards their pistol-butts, stopping half-way when they saw she was
a woman. The one who stood in front broke into a wide-mouthed
insolent grin.

"Hi-ah, old woman!" he said. They all kept their hats on. Judith tingled with the insult. Perhaps he did not think she could talk English, and perhaps the untidy wisps of hair from under the pillow-case did look white like an old woman's. She wanted to draw up to her full height and let her eyes flash out and toss her hair and tell that greasy backwoodsman to take his dirty feet out of her house. Then she knew she would only seem ridiculous if she tried, looking as she did, and with the pot in her right hand. She wanted to put the pot down, but she held it, thinking it and its contents might make a most disconcerting missile.

The man stood grinning a minute. One of his dog-teeth was missing, so that he looked distorted and uglier than ever Judith suddenly hated Americans because she despised this one so. She hated the very look of him, short and bull-necked with shoulders broad enough to block a doorway He swung away from her, and spat tobacco juice in the middle of the floor. He had calculated so carefully that the brown drops spattered on Juan's boots.

Then Judith saw Miguel over beyond Juan, with Ramón behind him. Had they been there all the time, or had they slipped in noiselessly, as they could?

Abruptly the man spoke to Juan: "How many horses you got on this ranch, you goddam Greaser?"

"Go and find out'

"You better be civil, I'm tellin' yuh. You want to be tied up there to your horse-rail? An' find out what a rope's end feels like? Come on now—what horses you got, and where are they?"

She saw Juan standing with his left leg bent, the toe on the floor, and the heel moving back and forth She knew it must be a signal; men who fought Indians together could signal without speaking. She saw Miguel's knife-hilt, and remembered how he threw a knife with a quick underhand snap, quicker than anyone could draw and cock a pistol. If any man touched Juan it would mean blood; there were four Americans in the room, and more outside; it must not start She summoned her dignity, and moved forward to stand between the American and Juan.

"What is it you want?" she said, trying to be coldly polite and put the man into his place. But he grinned again; she could see the wad of tobacco in his mouth; then he spat, so closely that she knew her dress must have taken some of it.

"For Christ's sake, old woman, take that puke out and empty it! We want horses, and we're goin' to get 'em. And you Greasers being so goddam uppity, we might even look around and see whether there's any little trinkets we might fancy."

"But the Commodore's proclamation promised us safety and pay for anything taken."

The man made a loud obscene noise with his lips, very realistically:

"That for the Commodore. I'm takin' my orders from Colonel Frémont. If you tricky Greasers want to revolt and kill Americans you'll have to take what's comin' to you, includin' a few kicks in the pants, until you learn what your place is, now this is a free American country. Waugh!"

It must have been a signal, for the pistols all came out together. She was glad Juan made no attempt to fight. Unarmed, he let himself be backed up against the wall. One American jerked the knives away from the two vaqueros, and they were shoved over to stand by Juan. Two Americans stood guard.

The big-shouldered American with the missing dog-tooth went through the house rapidly, spitting as he searched. He tore the papers out of the desk in the office, scattering everything around the floor. He found the purse there with about a hundred dollars in gold which they kept for running expenses. That and his being in a hurry saved the larger sum in the chest, for when Judith unlocked it for him he merely pawed around in the clothes which lay on top; he probably did not suppose that they would have more money than he had found. Judith followed him from place to place; she suffered acutely every time he touched something. Yet she would rather know what he was doing than imagine worse things. She even got a little inverted pleasure out of watching him, for it let her imagine all the satisfactory ways in which she might kill him.

The inner room was the worst. The two younger children were in bed there. Leticia had been sick and vomited all over her blankets; she seemed to realize that something was wrong; she lay still and eyed the intruder with a cold stare of hatred. Little Enrique, sitting up in his bed, merely howled.

" Shut up, you little bastard," said the man, and gave the four-year-old a slap across the face. The howling stopped for an instant, and then shifted to a frightened whimpering. Judith had a flaming vision of the man tied to a stake with a slow fire about him. There was nothing to say, she knew. She held herself in, thinking of Juan unarmed and backed against the wall. She took Enrique up for a moment, cuddling and patting him, and telling him to be quiet.

The man was tearing her dresses out of the clothes-press. He seemed to be enjoying the wantonness, for he would surely not care to steal dresses and it was not a likely hiding-place for valuables. In her bureau-drawers he pawed over her underwear, and held up one piece with a salacious grin. Going out, he spat full upon one of her dresses, and she watched the brown stain spread upon the lavender silk as it lay crumpled on the floor.

In the outer room again Juan, Miguel, and Ramón still stood against the wall. The American took Juan's arms down from where they hung on the wall, and looked at them. He laughed at the leather-jacket and the helmet, and threw them down. He hit the two carbines against the hearth so as to smash the locks. Judith noticed that one of the other Americans had already stuck the two pistols into his belt. Another took the sword which had been Juan's father's; he had always wanted to have one, he said.

Outside, the other Americans had taken the horses from the corral and rounded up the herd of bays which was grazing in the valley. There were plenty of other horses near by in the hills, but the Americans did not look for them. They had about forty as it was, and perhaps that was all they wanted, or all they could drive. They rode off, shouting and whooping, without even bothering to keep a look-out behind.

Everything in the house seemed to be lying in confusion on the floors, and tobacco juice was everywhere. For the first time in years Judith had to break down and cry before she could pull herself together.

What made her stop was her realization of Juan's calmness. It was sinister. He had not cursed once, or spoken a threat. He did not notice her, or the confusion around the room. He was looking carefully at the two smashed carbines; one of them, he said to Miguel, might possibly be made to work. Ramón had vanished. That Spanish temperament, thought Judith, she never could reckon it out; little things excited it, and big things it took calmly. Juan was speaking:

"We have knives and lances; you two have your carbines in the quarters; I'll take the little pistol we gave to Luis."

He paused, thinking, and Judith wondered what was happening.

"We won't need much food," he went on, talking chiefly to himself. "We can kill a steer, or sneak into a ranch when we need something else. Be ready to leave when Ramón gets back with some horses. We'll pick up Pablo at García."

Then Judith knew, and came suddenly to the alert.

"But you can't fight all the Americans yourself," she cried. He shrugged his shoulders—meaning, thought Judith, that when your honour is touched you don't count noses. Then he said:

"Don't worry about my being alone. This will be happening everywhere. Half the ranchers between here and Monterey will be in the hills right now."

The hills, thought Judith, "from whence cometh my help." And this Spanish blood—why, the very word for 'guerrilla' was Spanish! They had taken to the hills in Spain, and the great Napoleon with his Marshals and his army corps had never got them out again. And in all the coast country of California for every level mile there must be ten miles of hills. Juan was speaking:

"I'm leaving Juanito with you, and you'll have Julio—for what he's worth!—and the vaqueros. We can defend the ranch better by keeping the Americans busy somewhere else than by staying here."

Judith saw that it was his way of apologizing for leaving her.

"Don't mind me," she said shortly, "I'll be all right." After all, she was a sea-captain's daughter, and had been Juan's wife for nine years. And she was really much more worried about Juan than about herself. She knew what guerrilla warfare meant—descents by night, reprisals, prisoners shot or strung up to trees. Yet as she looked at the havoc about her she set her jaw, and knew that she would say no word to turn Juan from his purpose. And these had been

Americans—in spite of the Commodore's promises! For the first time in her life she felt wholly a Californian and ashamed of being American. She could not reckon it all out, but Frémont's men must need horses to fight the Californians who had revolted in the South. Then little Enrique cried from the inner room

"Mamma, I feel sick"

Sick herself, she thought of how he had cowered whimpering. "Yes, dear, I'm coming," she called, and ran for the pot.

DURING THE FIRST FEW WEEKS after Juan went away it rained most of the time, and was no kind of weather for any raiders, even Indians, to be out in. As the big storms sent the water out from Ojuelo and all the valleys behind Brushy Peak the creek came pouring down bank-full, and once spread out into a lake over all the lower end of the valley. The grass grew tall and rank. The adobe bricks of the house were never dry, and the rooms felt dank; moss showed green in the corners of the patio. No one at the ranch could remember such rains.

There was little for Judith to do. She saw to it that horses were always saddled. She kept the children's clothes ready packed. Every day she sent the vaqueros out to scout the hills. She stationed one man at the Garcías all the time, for that was the direction from which trouble was likeliest to come. One night, with only Luis to help and to remember the place, she took up a floor-plank, and buried most of the gold from the chest; what she did not bury she put into a money-belt, which she wore

For a week at a stretch she would see no one from the outside, and then it would probably be only one of the García boys riding up to see if she herself had any news Not once did the Fuentes come riding from the north; probably, she thought, their ranch had been raided, and they too had taken to the hills.

Twice Pablo came back to get new supplies of ammunition and clothing. Each time he hid in the hill-ravines during the late afternoon, watching the house to see whether any Americans were around. Then after dusk he rode in, dried himself out before the fire, and was gone again before daylight. She tried to press little luxuries upon him, to be carried back to Juan—sugar and tea and chocolate, and clean cloth for bandages in case it should be needed. She had little enough at the ranch itself these days; they were out of coffee and getting short of salt and corn-meal. But Pablo would never take much; he had to ride light.

She could gather little from him about what was happening. Sometimes, he said, they were with larger bodies of Californians; sometimes the four men from Rancho Amarillo rode by themselves. Occasionally they had to sleep in the wet underbrush shelters, but usually they were at some outlying ranch. There seemed to have been little fighting, but a great deal of riding about, and stampeding of Americans' horses, and galloping off with rifle-bullets whistling by.

Each time after Pablo left Judith went into a fit of despair. This kind of guerrilla fighting might go on for months or years, and as the Americans got more troops into the country there would be counter-raids, and plundering, and ranch-houses burned in reprisal. And all the while supplies would be running out, until they would be living on nothing but beef, and the children would go wild, and fear would lurk in every hill-ravine, and the little attempt at civilization which she had built up would go slipping back into barbarism.

It was stupid, the way the Americans had done. A year ago half the ranchers would have welcomed American intervention, and probably none of them would have thought the matter worth fighting about. But the way it had happened was wrong. First had come Frémont with his bullying ways, then the " Bear Flag " revolt, and then the breaking of promises in the Commodore's proclamation. If the American Government had spent a few hundred dollars in buying horses and had exercised a little common courtesy not a rancher in all the up-country would be in arms. And even in her despair Judith felt the quick glow of anger at what seemed the stupidity of it all.

After the middle of December came a break in the rains, but the days were so short and gloomy that things hardly dried out. On the twenty-first Judith kept thinking that this was the shortest day of the year and the longest night; that was something which even war-time could not change.

About mid-afternoon Judith, as she often did these days, went to a window, just to see how things looked. The sun was still well above the hills, but it was a dull winter sun giving no warmth, and even, it seemed, little light. Twilight coming already, she thought. Then her heart bumped as she saw a man break from the cover along the creek and at a quick walk make for the house.

Juan—on foot. Something was wrong. She was sick with fright as she ran to unbar the door. His cloak dark with wetness, beads of water on his hat, a strangely gay smile, his lips first cold and then suddenly warm against hers. He had flung open the wet cloak, and taken her to himself within it; as he held her she could feel his muscles firm and hard as they always were. A cold wind about her ankles let her know that they were standing in the open doorway. She felt suddenly conspicuous, as if standing against a skyline; it was easy rifle-range from the bushes along the creek. She drew him in and closed the door.

" What's wrong? " she asked.

" What's wrong! " he echoed. There was a contagious gaiety about his tone and his little laugh, something that mocked at prudence. " Here I've been away six weeks, sleeping in the cold and wet, and I come home and my wife asks me what's wrong! And it's the longest night in the year too."

She should have blushed perhaps; then all she remembered was that it was war-time and her husband had come home, and nothing was sure beyond the present. He was holding her again; she flung her head back and looked up at him, smiling what she hoped was his own gay smile :

" Well, if that's the way you feel it's three hours till dark, and that's a lot of time to waste."

There was Antonia standing, smiling in her knowing way. Juan flung her his wet hat and cloak.

" Don't take them into the kitchen," he said. " Build up the fire here and dry them. Did anybody else see me come in? "

" I don't think so, señor."

" Good. You watch here. Don't tell anybody that I'm here. It will be safer."

Safer from what? thought Judith. Then she did not care. They had the present. There would be a time for questions; she would take the present while she could. . . .

The sun must almost have set now, she thought. With all the shutters closed the inner room was nearly dark. Juan lay quiet; he must be dozing; his body was warm beside hers. But Judith felt herself in some state of preternatural alertness. All the little noises of the house and ranch came in to her, and she registered each and clicked it off, as if she were some kind of machine. She felt sure that something was going to happen, that she was going to deal with it.

Then all at once she knew by the noises that some one was coming, and she heard Antonia pounding on the door. She was out of bed in one movement, and pulling on her dressing-gown. She was not in the least frightened, for she had been expecting it. Juan, awake all at once as usual, was out of bed on the other side, and fastening on his clothes.

"They're coming," Antonia was calling.

"Who?" said Judith, without realizing that she was asking Juan rather than Antonia.

"The Americans that chased me, I suppose," he said. Then he added apologetically, ashamed of being caught, "I thought I'd thrown them off the track; I didn't think they'd come up to the ranch." He pulled on his first boot.

"What if they catch you?"

"Hang me, or take me down to San José for trial and then hang me." He grabbed the other boot.

Judith's mind seemed to grasp the possibilities all at once. No time for Juan to get a horse from in front of the house; no time for him to get away on foot.

"You stay right here," she said, realizing it was the first time she had ever given him a command. "I'll take care of this."

She did not have the slightest idea what she was going to do, but she felt capable of anything.

She looked through the peep-hole in the shutter at the front window. Just beyond the creek eight horsemen were halting; her mind worked so fast that she knew there were eight of them without really counting. She saw the long rifles lying across the saddle-pommels. The men were prudently looking the place over. The thicket along the creek, she knew, suggested an ambush, and the house stood up behind in fortress-like solidity.

As she looked they suddenly swung their horses round and galloped off in panic, shouting and hanging low over their horses' heads. She felt a sudden relief, and then knew that it was all a trick. By pretending flight they were trying to draw the fire of any ambuscade. A little way off they began to pull in Several had difficulty with their horses.

"Call me as soon as they cross the creek," she shouted through the door to Antonia. Then, with sudden thankfulness that the Americans' prudence and bad horsemanship had given her a minute or two, she sprang into action. Clothes first of all—she remembered how her house-dress had ruined everything when the other Americans came. She let her dressing-gown fall from her and, standing naked, threw open her clothes-press. She spent two precious seconds considering, for the decision was momentous. Not the black, not the blue—yes, the new bottle-green one. It was the right touch, and bottle-green had good associations. She slid into it with one snake-like movement. No time for petticoats. She called for Antonia to come and fasten her, and for Juan to get his hat and cloak from the outer room and then to watch at the window. Antonia worked at the back of the dress; Judith pulled on stockings. Thank God, she thought, as she slipped her feet into black pumps which had no call for lacing! But her hair was loose. No time to do much with it. She leaned forward, dipped her head, and let the mass of white fall freely. She shook the worst snarls from it, and with a motion of her hand she coiled it into a great ball at the base of her head. Antonia spiked it there with a huge Spanish comb

"They're coming," said Juan.

Judith took another second to look in the mirror. She patted the hair above her forehead to give it a little fluffiness. Another look to be sure that the dress was not falling off anywhere. She ran to the window.

The Americans had crossed the creek, but instead of advancing they had swung off to the right in single file Judith decided that the horses which she kept saddled in front of the house made it look as if there might be several men inside; the Americans were taking no chances, and were going to circle the ranch buildings for a look round. They would see little, Judith thought; the sight of American rifles would be making everybody keep very close by this time. On the other hand. this encircling would give her just the chance she wanted to see what kind of men she had to deal with.

Two in buckskin—one old and bearded, one young and with

yellow hair almost like her own—trappers, both of them. Two in nondescript clothing, with sallow dull faces—clodhoppers from some Mississippi Valley farm, ox-team immigrants of the last summer. Two others who rolled about curiously and uncomfortably in their saddles—sailors from some hide ship or whaler. (Judith smiled; she should be able to handle sailors.) But the two in better-looking clothes—one of them obviously in command. Even as they swung round the ranch buildings at a canter Judith could notice a certain restlessness of mind showing itself in quick glances this way and that. She knew the type; they were the adventurers, the filibusters, the incipient Napoleons, who came talking millions and wanting to lay out ranches into town-sites. And they were the most dangerous of all. Clodhoppers could be browbeaten or tricked; sailors would be your friend for a bottle of brandy; trappers were clodhoppers at heart, or you could appeal to a vein of chivalry in them. But the adventurers—she would have to wait for inspiration there

They dismounted and tied their horses to the rail. The older trapper pointed to the horses already tied there, and Judith imagined that he was saying that they had not been ridden that day. Then the Americans moved in towards the front door. In the lead was the adventurer who was in command; he held a pepper-box pistol in his right hand. At either shoulder walked one of the trappers, his rifle at the ready.

Judith went to stand by the front door. Nervously she gave her hair a pat. She hoped the silk of her dress was stiff enough not to show, too obviously, that she had nothing on beneath. She looked to see that the door into the inner room was closed, and Juan behaving himself.

She heard the *tunk-tunk* of the pistol-butt on the door. Although she could not see, she felt sure that the leader had rapped and then stepped aside out of any possible line of fire When she opened the door she would stand facing the muzzles of the trappers' rifles. Well, she had the advantage; they would be surprised and she would not; they would not expect a lady, or her hair, or a greeting in English. She waited another second for suspense. She drew herself up and shook her hair. She flung the door wide open, stepped forward, and waited another moment :

"Gentlemen," she said, smiling graciously and pitching her voice low, "what can I do for you?"

The effect was all that anyone could have asked. The rifle-muzzles wavered and went down. There was a blank, foolish look on all the faces. The jaw of the young yellow-haired trapper dropped until his mouth stood half open. There was silence, and Judith felt a triumphant joy; she was mistress of the situation; the others were on the defensive this time; she could feel their embarrassment.

"We was just a-chas——' the older trapper started to say and then stopped between syllables as if some one had kicked him.

"Oh, but pardon me," said Judith, "for keeping you standing here; won't you please step in?" The words sounded foolishly trite and formal, but she felt that she had had her inspiration. As long as she could maintain this shell of politeness things were safe; guests could not very well demand to look into their hostess' bedroom.

They shuffled nervously, still embarrassed, at her invitation. Then the leader lowered the hammer on the pepper-box pistol and thrust it into its holster, Judith stood back, and he passed into the house, glancing around a little nervously. The other whom she had put down as an adventurer came next; he was a big man with a little swagger of pomposity in his walk; he took off his hat ostentatiously The trappers followed a little awkwardly but still maintaining a certain confidence in their own self-sufficiency. Then came the clodhoppers, shambling, and forgetting to take off their hats. The sailors, on the other hand, had their hats off and were fingering them nervously; they looked as if they had been summoned aft for a wigging from the captain. Judith sat down: "Won't you be seated, gentlemen; I do hope there are enough chairs." She was overplaying her politeness enough to keep them ill at ease.

Their getting seated caused as much milling around and commotion as cutting a steer out of a herd. Two of the rifle-barrels collided with a loud clang. One of the clodhoppers dived into the arm-chair just as the leader was about to sit in it. The latter looked momentarily as if he were going to throw the intruder out, and then sat on the bench and relieved himself by scowling at the old trapper, who had unceremoniously squatted cross-legged on the floor. The two sailors remained standing.

Q

The room's getting dark, thought Judith. Every minute I can keep them in play the better. When it's dark we can cut a bar from the window, and Juan can get away.

"Oh, but I'm sorry," she spoke up. "I should have asked you to hang up your hats and put down those horrid, awkward rifles." She came as close to a simper as her face made practical. There was a sudden silence, and she felt the moment was critical.

The young trapper rose, put his hat over the muzzle of his rifle and stood it against the wall by the door. The others began to do the same.

"Stand them against the wall, boys," said the leader, appearing to give an order, although that was what was already happening. He added, "We still have our pistols."

Judith wished that he had not said that last, but it was a warning for her to be on her mettle. Only the old trapper kept his rifle lying across his knees.

"I should like very much to have some of the news from below," Judith led off, when they were seated again. "What with this unfortunate trouble and all, you know—and being so cut off here at the ranch, I really haven't heard much. Almost our last news was the Commodore's proclamation—the one, you remember, when he promised the Californians all the rights of American citizens" (and forbade plundering, she wanted to say, but that was too obvious for the part she was playing). "Won't you tell me something, Mr——" And then she paused and threw her hands out in a little gesture of embarrassment, as if by mere mischance she had missed getting his name.

"Baxter, ma'am—Major Cornelius Baxter, ma'am, at your service." The leader rose as he spoke, and bowed ceremoniously. Kentucky or Tennessee by his accent, thought Judith. She held out her hand graciously, and Major Baxter stepped forward, took it, and bowed again.

"Of the Tennessee Baxters?" she asked, for it seemed a harmless chance.

"North Carolina, ma'am. But the Tennessee Baxters are, I believe, a branch of the family." He seemed pleased.

By this time the other adventurer was on his feet, and Major

Baxter introduced him as Judge Wingram of Kentucky. Then the others came in turn. The room was getting darker, for the ceremony took time. Judith smiled inwardly, for she knew that among themselves the men must pass as Joe, and Mac, and Butch, and Shorty. But when it came to being introduced to a lady even the sailors became *Mr* Black, and *Mr* Richmond.

These last two she looked at quizzically.

"And you—jolly tars, if I mistake not." It was pure melodrama, but they would like it.

They did, and stood grinning. In a minute she had learned that one was from Nantucket and the other from New Bedford; she told them of her father and the *Spanish Belle*, and they grinned more widely.

Then it was time to light candles. Major Baxter, interrupted now and then by Judge Wingram, told the news. Judith kept making polite exclamations, but she was really putting all her thought to summing up the situation. The clodhoppers were ciphers; she had won the sailors; she thought that she had flattered Major Baxter sufficiently; the young trapper seemed fascinated by her hair. But Judge Wingram was obviously struggling with the Major for the leadership, and could be counted on to jump in the opposite direction, and the old taciturn trapper had, like an Indian, merely grunted from where he sat without getting up to take her offered hand. She could see him moving his head back and forth, taking in every noise. The worst of it was that they would have to stay all night, and would probably throw out sentries. Yet she felt a certain confidence; it would be hard to hang a man when you had just accepted his wife's hospitality and taken her hand. But there was always the chance of accident.

She could not let the Major run on too long. He enjoyed talking, but it gave the others a chance to think, and to wonder what was on the other side of doors. As he paused once she begged his pardon, and clapped her hands vigorously. Ordinarily she would have gone to the door and shouted to the kitchen, but the hand-clapping seemed somehow more elegant. She felt sure that Antonia was just outside and would be smart enough to catch the signal. And, in fact, Antonia entered immediately. Judith gave her the orders in Spanish,

and then spoke to the men again in English, keeping up her best
hostess manner :

" I shall be most happy to have you accept our poor hospitality of
the ranch. Our chief meal is in the middle of the day, but those of
you who are hungry will, I am sure, find a simple but plentiful fare
in the kitchen, and if any of you wish to drink tea with me in front
of the fire I shall be charmed."

It worked. The two clodhoppers almost bolted for the kitchen,
and the sailors followed. They were hungry, and the drawing-room
atmosphere was much too rarefied for them. The old trapper rose
slowly, spat into the fireplace, and moved silently towards the
kitchen, carrying his rifle with him.

This left the Major and the Judge eyeing the young trapper
askance. They evidently considered him scarcely gentleman enough
to drink tea with a lady. But he ignored their glances and even a
deliberate " Hu-hem! " from the Major.

The tea-party, thought Judith, was a success—but then it had to
be. The young trapper, whose name was Graham, turned out to
have as good table-manners as either of the others. That was not saying so much, for the Judge left his spoon in his cup, and the Major
guzzled his tea quite audibly. Judith steered off politics, and tried
to play the perfect lady by keeping the conversation on a very high
plane. Talk about books fell flat. The Major gave a little oration
on the beauties of our English poetry, and stopped short. The Judge
had apparently read some of Scott's novels, and pretty well forgotten
them since. Young Graham probably could not read at all. Drama
proved to be a better subject, for the Major and the Judge had seen
plenty of Hamlets and Richards in the theatres of backwoods
towns. On American scenery they grew very oratorical, but Judith
noticed that Graham was the only one who showed real feeling.
He spoke of the great canyons of the Sierra and a blue lake among
the mountains; Judith could feel a certain reverence in his
voice.

It was a master-touch for Antonia to dress up the four children
and bring them in to see the visitors. The Major said, " Well, well,
young man," to the nine-year-old Luis, and showed him his watch.
Luis looked embarrassed. The Judge gave each of the children an

American penny, and pinched Leticia's cheeks, who stuck out her
tongue at him. The children took much better to Graham.

" Can you throw a lasso? " said Guito to him.

" Not much."

" I bet you can shoot, anyway "

" Well, yes, I can shoot."

The only thing Judith did not like was when the Judge in his
big, booming voice suddenly asked of Luis, " Well, son, where's
your pappy? "

Luis froze into instinctive silence, but Guito piped up quickly,
" He's out shooting damned Yankees.'

Judith could see young Graham scowling at the Judge, but the
Major and the Judge laughed loudly and the Major said, yes, he
had always believed he would like to shoot some damn'—begging
your pardon, ma'am—Yankees too, especially if they were abolitionists.

But Judith knew what the Judge had tried to do, and although
she could not imagine anyone hanging Juan after they had drunk
tea with her and played with the children, still she did not know
just how obnoxious Juan had made himself or how many Americans
he had killed. It was dark now, and the Major ordered Graham
and one of the sailors to go on guard outside. So she knew that
Juan would have a hard time getting away, and it might be better
to keep him till the Americans had left in the morning. In that case
she would have to be sure that they did not have too much time to
think things over and talk among themselves during the night.
Drink was the obvious way to keep them amused, and she ordered
in a bottle of port just to see how the Major and the Judge took to it.
They took to it very well. But the trouble wih drink was that you
never could trust it; instead of lulling a suspicion it might make
that suspicion work all the harder in a man's mind.

If not drink—what then? And she had what seemed an idea.
By now it was late enough to be thinking of going to bed. The
men, she said, could find room in the quarters or in the storehouse;
she showed the Major the bed in the guest-room upstairs and the
Judge the cot in the office; then she returned them to the table in
front of the fire and a second bottle of port. In the doorway to the

kitchen she whispered hurriedly to Antonia, and saw her shrewd eyes light up. Then she excused herself to the Major and the Judge, went into the inner room, and bolted the door. Juan, fully dressed, was stretched on the bed, asleep; good thing, she thought, he doesn't snore. She knelt by the door with her ear at a crack.

The two men apparently had nothing to say to each other, but she heard the bottle clink against the glasses. Then she barely heard some one come into the room and the click of dishes being removed.

" Not bad, *not* bad." It was the Major's voice.

" I saw it first, Major."

" Try your fascination then, my boy; but you might ask if there's two of it."

The Judge said a few words in Spanish; they were very simple, direct words of a kind that a man travelling in a foreign country is likely to pick up. The Judge had to repeat them, for his pronunciation was very bad. Then Judith heard a *tap-tap* of something small and hard against the table, then a loud laugh from the Major:

" I win; your Spanish don't talk like my half-dollar."

Then came a sudden flow of Spanish in a woman's voice; Paquita was explaining that she had a friend. Judith suddenly shook with silent laughter. In some illogical way she thought that she was evening a very old score against Paquita.

Half an hour later Judith slipped quietly from the inner room, and closed the door behind. The outer room was dark except for the little flickering light which the dying fire cast about. No one was there. Everything was quiet. She disliked leaving unguarded even for a minute the door of the room where Juan lay sleeping, but she felt that she must see how things stood. Quickly and stealthily she went across the room and out into the patio. No rain yet—it was snappy cold, not far above frost. Negrito, the hound which had the run of the patio at night, came up fawning. She crossed the patio diagonally, and listened at the door which led into the office. No sound. The Major was in there, and Paquita.

Upstairs, listening, Judith heard a girl's laughter. She wondered what other slut Paquita had picked up out in the quarters. She shrugged her shoulders, and silently wished her luck. Two bottles of port plus two wenches—no, the Major and the Judge wouldn't lie awake speculating on the whereabouts of that Californian they had been chasing, or wondering what lay behind that closed door of the inner room.

In the other upstairs room Luis and Guito were sleeping as usual. In the outer room downstairs were Leticia and Enrique, but Antonia was not in her bed. Judith thought of the older trapper, and remembered the way Antonia's eyes always rested upon such thick-necked men. Why, to-night her respectable Rancho Amarillo was nothing better than a brothel! The thought came how shocked she would have been at all this a few years before. But now she was even seeing that it got started, merely to serve her own ends; you couldn't live ten years in a Latin country without developing an easy-going attitude towards the ways of men.

Then, going back towards her own room, she wondered whether there was so much difference after all between herself and those girls in there. In a moment she would pass through the door and shoot the bolt behind her and wake Juan, telling him things seemed safe for a few hours. And then—so why should she feel superior to those others? Yes, she and Juan had stood before the priest, but that seemed a long time ago, and it had been such a scurvy-looking priest at best, with his bare hairy legs sticking out below his robe. She felt her excitement rising. What could sober wives back in the States know like this—those who nightly went to bed in mono-tonous safety? But this was life and love at their heights—as she crept by stealth to her husband, with the house full of enemies, and sentries with their rifles pacing outside. This would be a night to remember.

And yet, two hours later, still lying wakeful, she knew that it had not been a time of perfection, of a great height of love. She could feel Juan beside her, but she was not even sure that he was sleeping; surely he was not in that deathlike sleep of perfect attain-ment. It was not that he feared the armed men all about them; such a thought, she knew, would never bother Juan. But that night he had had too many other thoughts upon his mind, and some of them had come between her and him. She had tried to keep him from talking of such things, but still he must. Perhaps, she thought, it was the difference between men and women. Men seemed the slaves of their bodies, and yet even in the great moments they seemed not able wholly to forget the outside world and to give themselves up to love.

First he had had to tell her about the day. About noon, as he was heading for the ranch, they had ambushed him. He had ridden through them, and got a good start before they could mount; but they had wounded his horse, and knew it. They followed hard. When his horse failed Juan had taken to the thickets in the creek-bed, got across the flooded creek on a low sycamore limb and worked up to the ranch, keeping under cover. What worried him, Judith knew, was not the danger, but the being chased, particularly on foot.

Then he had told her of what he had done since leaving the ranch.

" It's not much," he said bitterly.

The old story of guerrilla fighting, thought Judith, as he talked. American garrisons held the towns; the Californians kept to the hills and swept down on horseback to fire a few shots and cause what trouble they could. Each town was as good as isolated, for no courier dared to try getting through.

" They'll beat us in the end," he said, " of course."

His voice did not sound hopeless or bitter, merely matter of fact. But Judith knew there would be no use in urging him to quit fighting; he was in the field to avenge the personal insult of the plundering of his ranch when he himself had been threatened and backed against the wall. He was fighting also to vindicate his own and his people's courage. But could it be done? That, Judith realized at last, was what worried him most.

After a pause he spoke ·

" Yes, the Americans hold the towns, and they hold something more too." There was bitterness in his voice now

" What else? " said Judith.

" Wherever there are Americans they hold all the ground within range of their rifles. Our men won't face them." He paused, and then went on, talking as if he were tired " I can't figure it out. Ramón and Miguel will rope a grizzly bear just for fun; they will play with a wild bull and dodge him on foot, and ride the wildest horse. They take the longest chances fighting Indians. But they run away from rifles."

After all, thought Judith, can you blame them? They haven't any weapons to fight rifles with.

" I'm still trying to figure it out," he went on. " I have an idea. If I get everything right maybe I can do it. . . ."

Next morning Judith in her most correct morning gown ate breakfast with the Major and the Judge. Neither seemed very alert. There was only one bad moment before the Americans left. That was when the Judge, seeming to come to himself for a moment, asked if she would not show them over the house. But since she was still keeping up her part as hostess he had to put it as a request, and Judith passed it off lightly with an excuse.

The Major also bristled up against his rival, and unconsciously came to her aid:

" Tut, tut, sir," he said, " don't you know no lady likes a lot of men tracking all over her house. And I'm sure, ma'am, that I speak for all these gentlemen when I say that your hospitality would do honour, ma'am, even to the South, and that we appreciate it to the full—yes, ma'am, to the full."

From the porch Judith watched them leave. As they rode up the slope from the creek-crossing most of them turned, looked back, and took leave of her with various gestures. The Judge raised his hand stiffly in a military salute. The Major took off his hat, and swept it downward in a generous curve. The young trapper called Graham, the one with the yellow hair, was riding last. With a motion graceful as a wild bird's he rose in his stirrups, and swung his long rifle up above his head. And—it was too far off to be sure —Judith had a definite impression that, slowly and meaningfully, he winked.

FROM THE COVERT OF THE OAK-TREE Juan looked out at the Americans. At a good rifle-shot from where he was lying was the little clump of oaks along the stream; for the last hour he had been sure that the Americans would camp there. He felt just a little new satisfaction, therefore, on seeing the guide halt, glance at the low sun, motion in two or three directions, and convince the officer that this was the right place.

As they made camp Juan watched carefully. There were five of them, with a dozen horses. The leader wore the uniform of a lieutenant of marines—a mere youngster; but, from the way he kept his men in hand, a good officer. Still he was very young, and Juan calculated coldly that you could count on a youngster to be rash and to be looking for ways to distinguish himself. With the officer were two marines; their uniforms still showed a touch of nattiness in spite of rain and mud. The guide and the other man were nondescripts, hard to classify. But they were not mountain-men or trappers—Juan was sure of that; if they had been he would never have dared be within so short a distance of their camp. They seemed to know something about the country; so they might be Americans who had been in California for a while, ranchers from the north Bay country.

These two and the officer had rifles; judging by the shorter barrels, the two marines had muskets. Juan could see that most or all of them carried pistols. The officer and his two men had swords.

He guessed that they were a scouting party sent from Monterey to swing around southward through the hills to see if any armed Californians were in the region. They were heading towards Mission San Juan now, and would get there by the next afternoon. Juan had sighted them about noon, and since then he and Miguel had dogged them, keeping them in view from a distance, while Ramón and Pablo stayed farther back and drove up the spare horses.

The Americans rode with one man out ahead as a point, but otherwise they were not very wary. They paid little attention to watching their back trail. They could have seen no traces of an enemy, Juan was sure; for there were none in the region except his own band. The others were off around San Juan, or had gone north to join Francisco Sanchez in the hills behind Santa Clara. Sanchez had raised something of an army, but Juan had no interest in joining it. He didn't like Sanchez, and he hadn't thought the army would accomplish anything. He had been right too, for now word had come that Sanchez, after a futile brush with the enemy, was negotiating for terms. The time for fighting, Juan realized, was about over. Whatever he was to do he must do quickly; in a few days he would have no more standing than a bandit. He was glad that he had sighted these Americans just when he had, and he felt a great satisfaction to be lying where he was, watching them and knowing that his own men were safely hidden in the hills a mile or so away.

As he looked Juan found himself thinking of the Americans all as dead men. Ramón, Miguel, Pablo, and himself—they were four and the others were five. Nevertheless, in spite of their rifles, the Americans were as good as dead men. He had worked this out right this time. The Californians had beaten the Americans at San Pasqual and at Natividad in just a blundering accidental kind of way. But to-morrow morning there would be nothing blundering or accidental. In the last two weeks since he had come down from the ranch and rejoined his men he had worked out the plan, and even rehearsed his men at it. That was why he would rather have only a few men; a few dependable ones were better than Sanchez' army at this sort of game. Besides it would be better to remember that the Americans outnumbered him and still he beat them; that was what he was fighting for, anyway—honour; he had no hope of driving the Americans out of California. " Remember," he had drilled into his men, " Americans don't ride well; they can't reload or shoot straight when they're galloping." He had talked that way for a week now, until he knew that he had built up a spirit of victory; as he had spoken, he had seen the blood-lust of their Spanish and Indian race beginning to glow in their eyes; they would not run away from a few rifles now that they felt sure of whetting their lances.

And yet could he be certain? Even Miguel and Ramón had gone into panic in the fight against the Bears. He shrugged his shoulders; he had made up his mind. He would charge, anyway; if his men didn't follow him he would kill an American or two before they finished him. He was tired of running away and keeping hidden.

The Americans' horses had been hobbled and were beginning to graze over towards the place where Juan was lying. It was a hard year on horses; there had been so much rain that the old grass had rotted and the new grass was still thin and watery Juan saw that these horses were in worse shape than his own. That was good, for it would make the Americans quick to snap at the bait he was going to offer them.

He took a last look, and then wriggled away. He led his men around through the hills. While they made camp he took advantage of the last of the daylight to see just how the land lay. A mile from his own camp he came over a low rise, and through the dusk could see the Americans' fire about two miles away, farther up the valley. It would work out well enough. In the morning the Americans would come riding down the valley, and at the proper moment he and his men, driving the extra horses in front as a bait, would ride over this little rise. The two parties would come into each other's view about a quarter of a mile distant; it would have been better at half that distance, but you could not expect everything to be ideal.

At the camp the men were eating jerked beef around a fire. Gnawing a piece of beef, Juan went to make sure about the horses. Those which they were to ride were picketed and grazing. The others, as Juan had ordered, were tied to trees; it was better to have them hungry than to run the risk of losing time in rounding them up in the morning. Back at the fire Pablo was cleaning and reloading one of the two carbines which they had among the four of them.

"Don't bother with that," said Juan, and he found himself a likely looking stone and began whetting the edges of his lance-point.

"White arms"—that was what would count in the morning. Juan could remember his father telling him that in armies in the old country they called the bayonet and the sabre and the lance "white arms." "The white arms must settle this affair," they would say. The words reminded him of Judith. They sounded more like love than war. And yet love and war had something in common—the wild excitement, the thrust sent home, the fulfilment.

The others now had followed his example. He heard the faint *wh-ee-ee*, *wh-ee-ee*, as the stones rubbed the lance-points. They were only the products of local blacksmiths—not steel at all, just wrought iron. They would not take any real edge, Juan knew that, but the sense of preparation encouraged the men, and at least they could see to it that the points were as sharp as could be managed.

No two lances were alike. They ranged from seven feet to nine in length; the leather wrist-loops were set at different points; the weight varied according to each man's fancy and the kind of wood used. Miguel stood up and began practising strokes—underhand, overhand, to right, to left. The balance of the lance did not quite please him; he whittled a little weight off its butt.

Juan heard some horses snort, and went off to see what the trouble was. Nothing much, he concluded; the scent of a bear probably. Around the fire he heard the men singing—a mournful ballad of a cruel one and of the lover who rode off and whose horse came back riderless. Juan thought of his father again; his father had known the ways of fighting men. "Men," he had said, "sing sad songs when they are in good spirits." By the time Juan had come back to the fire the song was over and the three men lay rolled in their blankets. It would be a cold night, they were agreeing, for they were high in the hills and far inland. . . .

It was still pitch dark when they got up. They had kept the fire going all night for warmth, and so lost no time by having to start it again. They chewed their jerked beef quickly, standing with first one side and then the other towards the fire to thaw themselves out. Through the darkness there was a faint gleam of frost from the grassy spot where the horses were picketed.

It was faintly light when they rode down towards the main valley, driving the dozen loose horses ahead of them. Juan galloped on in advance, making for the little rise where he had been the night before. There was small chance that the Americans would be off so early, but he wanted to be sure. He dismounted below the skyline, hastily stuck some bunches of grass into his hat-band, and crawled to the top. In the half-light he could see the Americans' fire blazing brightly;

they were standing around eating breakfast, warming first one side and then the other, just as he and his own men had been doing half an hour earlier. Juan signalled back to Ramón to halt the horses in the swale.

The frosty morning was clear, and it grew lighter rapidly. Across the valley beyond the eastern ridges the sky changed from inky blue to bright blue. Lying in the frosty grass was cold work, and every few minutes Juan had to crawl back down the slope and then run around beating his arms to keep his hands from being numb. The eastern sky began to show just a rim of faint pale yellow; it was full light now. The Americans rode out from the grove, and started down the valley. First came the one who was acting as guide and scout. Then came the half-dozen extra horses. Next was the other rancher, or whatever he was, driving the horses; Juan could see his arm waving at them, and just catch the sound of his shouting. At the rear rode the officer with his two men just behind him.

Juan felt sick with excitement; this was different from fighting Indians. The worst of it was that for five minutes he would be able to do absolutely nothing except wonder, as the Americans approached, whether they would take the bait and behave as he thought they would.

The little figures grew bigger rapidly. Now Juan could see the guide's rifle held in readiness across the saddle-pommel. It was time.

He wriggled back, then scuttled for his horse, signalling to Ramón. As he mounted he saw his men riding about the loose horses, whirling their lances. The horses sensed the excitement, and swept up the easy slope at a gallop. Juan swung around and rode at one side of them, lance in hand. Everything seemed strangely peaceful; the enemy was out of sight; there was no sound but the gentle swishing and thudding as the horses swept through the tall grass.

They burst over the rise and into view. For a full second or more they galloped on before the Americans saw them. Then the guide whooped and threw up his rifle; *fwee-ee* came the bullet close overhead, the sound of the shot just behind it.

Juan shouted as if in sudden alarm, and pulled his horse around, making the loose horses rear up, and start milling confusedly. They were squealing as Pablo pricked them from behind with his lance-point. Good, thought Juan, we must look exactly like some scared Californians, surprised and trying to save our horses, but having trouble with them. He looked around just in time to see the young officer of marines shout and strike in his spurs. Good. Juan called to his men.

Driving the horses ahead of them, they galloped back along their trail. Another shot came from behind. At the top of the rise Juan looked back. The Americans were in wild pursuit—first the guide; some yards behind him the other rancher; a hundred yards farther back the officer and one marine; still farther the other marine, having trouble with his horse. Then out of sight again.

It was only for seconds. The leading American broke into view again over the rise behind them. This was the moment, thought Juan. Would his men turn? He shouted. He had a glimpse of Miguel's face, excited but not afraid. Then all four of them had swung around and were riding at the first American. His horse's gallop was carrying him on, and he had no time to turn. His companions were too far behind to be of help. His rifle was empty. He was pulling at his pistol, but his horse reared as the Californians charged. Juan saw Miguel and Pablo thrust with their lances. He did not bother to look, but rode after the second American who had had time to turn. But Ramón was close behind him and on a better horse.

The officer and one marine were at the top of the rise. They pulled in their horses instinctively at the sudden change in affairs. They grabbed out their pistols and fired, foolishly, at Ramón who had just lanced the American in the back. Miguel, coming up from behind, his lance-point bloody, rode at the marine; Juan charged the officer.

The youngster had his sword out and parried the lance-thrust skilfully. Juan flung his horse around on its haunches and thrust again—too quickly—he missed. The other tried to ride in and sabre Juan, but he was not a good horseman. Juan pulled to one side and dodged the stroke. The blow swung the American off balance, and before he could recover Juan thrust home.

Juan jerked his lance loose before the youngster had time to fall from the saddle. But as he glanced around he saw that everything was about over. Up the valley the last living American was riding desperately for the shelter of the trees. But he was the one who had had trouble with his horse at first, and he was the poorest rider of them all. Ramón and Pablo, lances ready, were coming up on him to left and right, as they might close in on a steer at round-up.

Then the marine pulled in his horse, jumped off, and swung around at bay with his musket levelled. Juan saw the burst of smoke, and saw Ramón go headlong from his saddle. Pablo rode the marine down.

Juan galloped across towards where he had seen Ramón fall. Pablo, wild with blood-lust, was spurring back and forth driving his lance into the marine's body Ramón was dead, his chest shattered by the musket-ball at close range. Miguel rode up; he was unhurt.

Juan felt suddenly very tired. He would like to lie down and sleep. " White arms "—yes, it was much the same : the excitement, the release, and the death which seemed to follow

But Ramón was really dead. They must take him in, bury him at some ranch; perhaps they could find a priest. Things would be different now; Ramón had been riding behind him ever since they were children.

Miguel and Pablo were starting to roll Ramón in a blanket. Miguel was Ramón's brother, but he was not weeping or showing any sorrow; he had enough Indian blood not to. As far as that went, thought Juan, he was pretty sure that Miguel and Ramón were his own half-brothers. It wasn't a thing to talk about or admit; it wasn't right to look back upon what your father might have done. Yet he was pretty sure of it; that was why he had always counted upon Miguel and Ramón.

And yet Juan could not be sorr, Ramón had died as a fighting man—as a Godoy—should die. And deep within Juan felt a new, boundless satisfaction. Come what might in the later years, he would always remember that place and the fight in which he had met the Americans and beaten them. Now he could go home.

A glitter fell over the frosty valley. Juan started. The sun had just broken the line of the eastern hills. It had all happened as quickly as that.

"IT'S BEEN A LONG TIME since you were here," said Judith; she smiled and held out her hand, for she had always enjoyed Williamson and the jollity he brought with him.

"Plenty long—but say where's Don Juan?"

"Out riding over the ranch; he'll be back in an hour for dinner. You can see him then, *Captain* Williamson—as I ought to say."

"Captain—oh, hell, yes! But look here, couldn't you send some one out after him? Got to see him in a hurry."

Only then did he get round to introducing his two companions. Judith did not catch the names, and did not think that it mattered particularly. They must be new immigrants from the States, come in now that everything had been peaceful for a year. In the old days every American's coming was an event, and you remembered it; now they were arriving by hundreds.

Judith, recollecting Williamson's old weakness, went for the brandy bottle. When she came back the three men were still standing on the porch; she started to pour out a glass. "Oh, no, thanks; no, thanks, not for me," he said. The others refused too. Surprised, Judith looked curiously at the three of them. For a moment she thought that they might be drunk already, but it was not like drunken men to refuse more drinking. They seemed rather to be floating along on some kind of hidden excitement which made brandy unnecessary. One of them was working his fingers nervously. Williamson had not tried to crack a joke since he had arrived; he kept glancing about to see whether Juan was coming. Then the two strangers whispered together, impolitely, it seemed to Judith.

"We're going to take a walk down along the creek, and look it over," said one of them.

"The latrine's out there; one of the boys will show you." Judith spoke sharply; they irritated her, and, besides, she did not like people wandering about everywhere; it wasn't tidy.

Williamson broke into a long, cackling laugh, but it was more as if he were relieving nervous pressure than being really amused.

"Good, good," he said—"but they really want to look at the creek-bottom."

Well, let them, thought Judith. The creek-bottom was very unattractive; they would get their boots muddy, and might stir up a rattlesnake. But if they wanted to, all right. It was obvious that there was some matter of business with Juan, but she didn't like people being secretive.

After they had gone she began again to try to talk with Williamson—captain as he was now, since serving with the California Battalion. She asked about Mr Melton.

"Dan's gettin' on fine," he said. "Saw him three days ago. Said he thought he might give up hides. Spends his time buyin' and sellin' lots up in Yerba Buena—San Francisco I should say. It's gettin' to be quite a town now. Ought to come and see it some time. Dan Melton'll be a millionaire some day if he keeps on—if he doesn't go broke."

Captain Williamson was polite enough to ask about Indians; that seemed more like old times. No, said Judith, the Indians didn't amount to much any more. Juan still rode around patrolling, but there wasn't much point in it, and he got disgusted sometimes. Amarillo wasn't an outer ranch any more; there was a whole line of ranches beyond it, some even out in the big valley.

"Yep," he agreed, "things has changed. You know, I've thought a lot about that talk we had up here—musta been in '44, just before all the boys got busy and revoluted against old Micheltorena. You know, that night I sure thought little old Don Enrique was crazy with my cognac when he started that talk about things goin' to start happenin' like hell. But he sure was right—revolutin' and raisin' flags, and marchin' and fightin' all over the place."

"I guess it's over now; everything's been quiet for a year now."

"Ye-ah, ye-ah, prob'ly. But I ain't setting up to be no prophet like old Don Enrique. Maybe they ain't goin' to be so quiet neither."

Judith noticed he seemed suddenly nervous again. He had his right hand in his side-pocket and was jerking it up and down idly. She could hear a little *ker-chuck*, *ker-chuck*, like quinine pills shaken gently in a bottle, but fainter and duller. She went in to see that three extra places were ready for dinner.

When she came out again a quarter of an hour later Juan was there, and the two other men, their boots very muddy as a result of their strange desire to go wallowing along the creek. Judith could see that there was some argument.

" . . . sound right to me," she caught a tail-end of Juan's sentence. "I've been in those mountains lots of times; I never saw any."

"Course you been in those mountains lots," Williamson answered. "That's just the point. Soon as I heard of it I says, 'I'm goin', but I don't like the idea of gettin' lost in them goddam canyons or runnin' into a tribe o' Injuns and gettin' scalped.' 'Where the hell you think you goin' to get a guide? They ain't no guides,' says my friend here. 'Hell, they ain't,' says I. 'We'll swing round and pick up Don Juan Godoy. He's chased more Injun bastards through them goddam mountains than any man alive. He knows all about 'em, and he's a straight-shooter besides.' That's what I said."

"Thanks," said Juan. Judith did not know just how ironic he meant the word to be. She stood by the door, and in their vehemence the men had not noticed her. It was eavesdropping, but she was frankly curious, and she always enjoyed hearing a man like Williamson swear when he did not know a lady was present.

"Why, man," he went on, "we've been waitin' here for a whole hour and a half, and we wouldn't ha' waited that long for Jesus Christ. I tell you, I got this thing straight. What if you didn't see nothin'? You was lookin' for Injuns. It won't jump up and bite at you, like a goddam rattlesnake! It don't shine out like a candle in the dark. I tell you I got this thing straight. I had to pour whisky down that damn' Irishman of Sutter's for an hour, but I got the straight of it at the end."

Juan was still cold: "I don't think you'd get the straight out of an Irishman with that much whisky in him."

"*You* say so!" Williamson snapped back, with a sudden truculent confidence in his voice "Maybe this ain't the straight of it then? What if I did give him twice what it's worth?"

The four men gathered quickly around one of the plain wooden chairs that stood on the porch. Judith pressed in among them to see. Williamson had pulled a little bottle from his side-pocket—a quinine bottle, sure enough, thought Judith. From it he poured about a teaspoonful of something or other upon the seat of the chair With his finger he stirred it around a moment, as a person plays with spilled sugar at the table.

To Judith it looked like a little sand or fine gravel; there were two or three tiny irregular pebbles no larger than small peas. What about it? thought Judith It was dull and quite uninteresting-looking, yellowish with a silver glint here and there But Williamson was bursting out into what was almost a wild chant:

"There it is; there it is. Get the heft of it. Dip it in acid, Hammer it out flat. That's no iron pie-rights. Gold! Gold! It's gold from the American Fork. There's lots of it there, and we're going to get it. You can pick it out of the cracks with jack-knives. In ten days there won't be a man left in San Francisco, but we lead the crowd, and we get the pickin'"

Williamson and the other two must have seen the gold many times before, but they went on their knees, peered at it, and stirred it, as eagerly as Judith and Juan did. None of them doubted any more its being gold, even though it looked so little like gold. Dinner waited while they gazed. Then they began to test it, less from doubt than from mere fascination with the stuff. Some muriatic acid from Judith's medicine-chest made not the slightest bubble. Williamson chewed one of the pebbles, and showed them his tooth-marks deep in the soft metal. Laying the same pebble upon the flat of an axe, Juan pounded it out thin with a hammer. It did not break or splinter Williamson had a bit of pyrite in his pocket, brought along for comparison. It looked much more as gold ought to look, but at a blow from the hammer it shattered.

Judith knew that Juan was going, even before he began excitedly to shake Williamson by the hand. She could feel the intoxication; she wanted to go herself; brandy was nothing to this. They all lost their heads. The first thing Judith found herself running to get was an elk-skin bag big as a wheat sack; it would be good for carrying the gold in. Juan started shouting for the men to saddle horses. It was suddenly like a panic.

The only thing that pulled them out of it was Lupe coming and shouting that dinner had been waiting an hour. A good heavy meal of beef and beans sobered them, just as it would have sobered them if they had drunk too much. The men rather meanly began to laugh at Judith's gold-bag. The idea of their being able to fill it seemed not particularly ridiculous, but by that time they said it would weigh a ton or so, and no pack-horse could carry it.

After dinner it seemed late to Judith for anyone to be starting out, but none of the men seemed to think of that. Besides Miguel, who went as a matter of course, Juan took three other vaqueros. They were his men, he said, and they might as well come along and dig for him. He wasn't going to do any digging himself. They collected all the picks and shovels around the ranch. They took guns and pistols, and jerked beef, corn-meal, and wheat flour. What they needed other than picks and shovels for getting the gold none of them seemed to be sure. Williamson stuck to his idea of picking it out of crevices in the rocks with knives; and they all had knives. One of the other men had an idea that spoons might be useful; so they packed up half a dozen iron tablespoons from the kitchen. It was then that Judith began to think, and she remembered what she had heard about the gold-workings which some one had discovered a few years before in the San Fernando Valley near Los Angeles. She went and got three wash-basins.

"For God's sake," said Williamson, "I can wash my face in the river!"

Judith said that you could use them for washing the mud away from the gold; you slushed the water around, and the gold being heavier went to the bottom some way; she talked boldly, but she was not very sure herself about the process. Nobody knowing anything to the contrary, it was half decided to take the wash-basins along for luck. Then one of the men who was from Alabama recollected having heard that in the Georgia gold-mines they used something of the sort. At that one of the vaqueros spoke up diffidently, saying that his grandfather had come from Sonora, and all Sonorans were miners, and he remembered his grandfather saying you could use a pan that way, but he himself could not remember just how. So they decided to take the pans. Williamson said that Judith had a great head, and gave her a resounding kiss.

Then everybody was mounting, and Juan rode over, and leaned down from the saddle and kissed her. She had a sudden feeling of desertion and loneliness, in spite of all the excitement. The younger children were running about yelling good-bye, but Luis stood beside his mother. He seemed to understand in such times. He was ten now, and she did not have to lean down to put an arm around his shoulders.

"It isn't like going to fight," said Luis. "They haven't any lances."

Judith was thinking how much things had changed in the ten years since she had first stood watching Juan ride away to chase Indians; that day Luis had been jumping around inside of her and the pains had frightened her. And look at him now! And now the Indians were as good as gone, and California was American. And if there really was all this gold they might get on a ship and go to Boston for a trip, and even go to Europe and see those things she had read about during all these years on the ranch in the books which Cousin Carrie had sent out.

Gold—she thought of it as a bucketful, brighter than the dull stuff she had seen to-day; the glitter dazzled her in imagination.

WHEN HE WOKE UP the sun was already glowing hot in the east. He had slept a little, and feverishly, with many dreams. He moved his muscles cautiously, and shook his head experimentally to see just how bad he was. The right arm was wholly useless now; as he moved it began to throb clear down to the finger-tips. Otherwise he was not as badly off as he had feared he might be; he was in his right mind, and felt strong enough to sit up, and perhaps to ride.

He sat up. The movement cost him some effort, and his arm throbbed worse than ever. He looked around the little glade where he had camped. His horse was grazing at the end of the picket-rope, still saddled. It was a terrible thing, he thought, not to unsaddle, but if he had taken the saddle off he knew that, one-armed, he could never have got it on again. Well, this would be the last day's ride; even on a tired horse he ought to be able to cross the hills and get to the Mission before night.

Some cattle came wandering up, and stood at a little distance bawling thirstily. The stream at this time of the year was a mere succession of dirty pools, and he had shut them off from one of these. Well, let them wait a little; he was leaving as soon as he could.

He did not stop to make a fire, but chewed grimly on his jerked venison. It sickened him, but he knew he must eat something. He wished that he had coffee or whisky, but they had been finished weeks ago; everybody at the mines had been running out of supplies, and living mostly on deer and quail. Laboriously getting to his feet, he walked shakily to the water-hole. He did not wash, but he filled his canteen, drank in gulps, and refilled it.

He sank down again on his blanket beside his saddle-bag, his pistol, and his money-belt. One book lay there too; he had stuck to it so far through all his troubles, but he knew that to-day he would leave it behind.

At the thought the whole weight of his depression suddenly came in upon him. Close to fifty he was now, and had worked hard all his life and tried to do things decently. Yet here he was alone, and ruined, and in pain, and probably dying, beside a smelly water-hole in the Californian hills. And if he died no one would care. Perhaps Judith Godoy would wonder what had become of him, and old Don Enrique down in Monterey would miss him for chess and for conversations about Thomas Paine and Deism. Nothing more—and the pistol was handy. . . . He would have strength enough to walk over and unsaddle the horse, and take the picket-rope off. That would be his last duty in the world, and he had always done his duty.

But as he still was thinking it over his eyes fell on the book, and the idea faded. It was his volume of Shakespeare's tragedies; he had had the three-volume set of the plays for thirty years, and how many times he had read them he could not have told. He had even taken all three volumes to the mines. The comedies had fallen into the river and been lost, and he had left the histories behind when he lightened the pack. But he had stuck to the tragedies.

It was strange, he thought, that the recollection of the tragedies should take his mind off suicide, for Shakespeare seemed to approve of it, and people in the tragedies killed themselves—Brutus and Cassius, for instance, and Othello. Lines began to click themselves off in his brain:

> Othello's occupation's gone . . .
>
> I'm more an antique Roman than a Dane . . .
>
> No more a soldier: bruised pieces, go;
> You have been nobly borne.

He wasn't sure of that last; it was probably all mixed up; but it was Antony speaking just before the end. Yes, suicide was for strong men like those—men who could die with poetry on their lips. He, Daniel Melton, was not a strong man; he would have to crawl through to the end.

By now the sun was beating in upon him. He seemed to feel his fever mounting. There was something vindictive in the sun, something personally hostile, that it should be so hot so early in the morning. He must move now, if at all.

shovel or a pick—not by a long shot, for shovels and picks had got to be worth quite a bit. San Francisco would never come back; it was no place for a city There would be a city over on the Contra Costa, or up along the straits—that new place called Benicia probably. If he had even left for the mines earlier it would have been better Then he could have got some decent partners, not two like Whitey and Mack who as good as left him in the lurch when he hurt himself. And if Whitey hadn't had the crazy idea of digging into the hill the rock would never have fallen and hurt him.

Full of bitterness and pain, he came to the hills. Some bushes gave a little shade and shelter from the wind. He sucked some water to give him strength, lifted himself from the saddle, and collapsed as he struck the ground. Keeping his grip on the bridle-reins, he crawled the few feet to the shade. He took off the money-belt, and eased himself. He tried to suck a little of the jerked meat, but his stomach revolted. Then he tied the bridle-reins about his left wrist. It was a long chance to take with a Californian horse, but he knew that he was going to lose consciousness for a while, and he could not risk the horse's straying away even a few yards. In the heat insects buzzed here and there; they made a sound like rattlesnakes, but he was too old a hand to be fooled. The horse staled close by, and the acrid stench was in his nostrils, but he was too tired even to turn his face away.

He slept feverishly. When he awoke the sun was well over to the west. He quenched a raging thirst with most of the water left in the canteen. He felt a little stronger than when he had lain down, and thought that he might mount again. The horse had grazed around in a half-circle at the end of the bridle-reins.

He sat up painfully. Just where was he? He could see the road; it was not much more than a trail, but there were the wheelmarks where wagons had gone through. Up a little side-ravine he could see a trail turning off. His thoughts swam a little, but he pulled himself together to piece out his geography. He was at the beginning of the last stretch of hill-country; at the other side of it was the Mission. There were two ranches on the road, but ranches didn't mean much for a sick stranger these days. That side-trail . . he figured painfully. Then he had it. That must be the back-trail to

Rancho Amarillo, the one that came out under Brushy Peak. It couldn't be so very far to Rancho Amarillo that way, and Judith would take care of him, surely. And yet he did not like the idea of riding to her the way he was. What if she did not recognize him and came out with a shotgun the way the other woman had? Or what if she came out with the same pitying smile which he remembered—that would be worse yet.

He decided to take the side-trail. He could certainly not get to the Mission. Probably he could not get to Rancho Amarillo. So what was the difference?

He drank the rest of his water, and lay a few more minutes bracing himself. First he got up on one knee, and then struggled to his feet, with every movement an effort of the will. He got his foot into the stirrup; there he stuck. Left-handed, he could not lift himself into the saddle. He put his foot to the ground again, unfastened and let fall the empty canteen, took off his coat and let it drop. Last he unbuckled the money-belt. It fell with a heavy *chunk* about his feet. He felt suddenly lighter. He put his foot up again, and, with a convulsive letting out of breath which was half a groan and half a scream, he got himself into the saddle. The pistol was still in his belt.

Decisively he pulled the jaded horse into the side-trail. . . .

The sun was low down now. The wind did not seem so hot, but perhaps he was just past being bothered by anything outside of himself. The grass looked more than ever like some brown dusty fur. Dispirited, the horse plugged along, head down, at a walk. How long—no telling. . . . Something in the trail, staring . . . horse stopping. . . A bear—no, a bull. Hard to say. There, it's running. . . . Downhill—must be a bull then. Bear runs uphill—or does it? Somebody ought to make a rhyme so you could remember . . . if it runs downhill must be a bill. Bill who? Ha . . . didn't rhyme, anyway. . . .

The captain . . . big fellow . . . shouldn't have walked out . . . asked what he means. . . .

Sun behind the hill . . . bettter on the eyes. . . . What you know!— a lake! Silly, no lakes here . . . must be a valley . . . can't be fooled like that. Fire behind the hills—no, sunset. . . . Know a fire from a sunset. . . . Hawk from a handsaw. . . . Must be Amarillo. Judith Hingham—mean Godoy. . . . Fine girl . . . wanted to marry her once. Maybe should have. She lives here in a 'dobe house—" worm-eaten hold of rotten stone . . ." Old 'dobes always like that. . . . ' Ragged ' stone maybe—no difference. . . .

With a horseman's instinct he pulled up the horse's head, and made a suggestion of striking spurs when the tired animal stopped to drink at the scarcely flowing creek. Funny, he thought, coming up to the house—no horses at the rail, no servants about, just dogs. Where is every one? . . . He pulled out the pistol; he remembered once before some time he had fired a pistol when it had something to do with Judith Hingham. Monterey one time, he thought.

He pulled the trigger. The horse, too tired even to shy at the report, stood head down in front of the house.

Then he saw her coming; the white hair floated like a cloud. She was coming herself . . . no servant. An honour to him, surely. . . . There was that look on her face—pity, yes. . . . He didn't seem to mind. . . . Had thought he would. . . . Must do something . . . show honour appreciated. . . .

With a momentary strength of delirium he waved the pistol over his head. " And this worm-eaten hold," he began. . . .

He reeled, and slid quietly out of the saddle.

H E CAME SO SUDDENLY into Judith's arms as a dead weight that she almost dropped him. She managed to ease him down without too much of a bump; he groaned painfully, and she knew that he must be hurt somewhere. His left foot had caught in the stirrup; she loosened it, and pulled him away a little from the horse's hoofs. She stood, half bowed over, feeling helpless, holding him under the armpits. He groaned again. Her back gave a warning twinge; he was heavier than she would have thought. She could not lift him, and to drag a hurt man might open his wounds. She shouted for help.

Silence came back at her with almost the reality of an answering shout. She had feared so. The vaqueros were gone to a man, slipped off to the gold-mines; most of them had taken their women with them. Only children and decrepit old people were around the quarters. Gold had demoralized the whole countryside. The house-hold servants had slumped; Julio the major-domo was drunk; her own children were off 'digging gold' in the creek-bottom. But Antonia and Lupe and Catalina must be somewhere about. She shouted again.

Under the shelter of the house even the wind made little noise. The sunset still lighted the valley rosily. The air was crisp with dry heat. Mr Melton's horse stood dejectedly. Two dogs romped about, acting as if they were being helpful. From inside the house came a faint sound of singing; it was the drunken Julio. The voice was a thin half-falsetto; Judith scowled as she thought of him— pudgy, pasty-faced worm! She would discharge him surely this time. Then Antonia stood in the doorway.

"Hurry," called Judith. "Where have you been all the time?"

"At the latrine," said Antonia insolently, as if adding mentally, "Believe me or not, I don't care." Count on Antonia to turn insolent when things went badly. But she came running; you could also count on Antonia to enjoy an emergency.

With Judith at the shoulders and Antonia at the knees they got Mr Melton to the bed in the outer room. He half came to himself, but they did not question him. They found the shoulder bandaged with soiled remnants of a shirt. The look of the wound made Judith half sick. Something sharp and jagged had torn deeply for four inches into the muscle below the shoulder-point; the wound was partly healed over, but there was a show of pus beneath. The skin all around was bright red, and the flesh was puffy.

Suddenly the children burst in, hungry for supper, muddy, happily noisy. " We got some gold," yelled Guito, holding up some pebbles with streaks of glitter in them. " Whose horse is it? " said Luis. Little Enrique was shouting aimlessly and holding up more pebbles. As Judith turned to hush them it was Leticia who first glimpsed the man on the bed. The look on their mother's face and the quick realization of something wrong quieted them. Judith sent Leticia and Enrique to get their supper, and Luis and Guito to unsaddle the horse. In some way or other, Judith thought, children would have to be sent to their suppers, even though men died and the heavens fell.

She and Antonia began to wash Mr Melton. Washing seemed to be hardly what he needed as much as some attention to the wound, but it seemed the natural thing to do first, and it gave her a moment to collect her thoughts. This was her affair, she realized, and felt herself getting cold. There was that man of Don Diego's who had a knack of treating wounds, and a doctor—at least, a man calling himself one—lived now at San José. But there was no use sending, even if there had been anyone to send; everybody had gone after gold. She must do this job herself.

The boys came in, large-eyed with excitement. " We had a terrible time," said Guito, talking rapidly. " The saddle-cloth stuck, and a lot of skin came off; somebody must have treated him something terrible. The flies will get into him and he'll die. We better shoot him. Can't we? " Guito looked excited and hopeful; Luis was sober and worried.

s

" No," said Judith shortly. " Go get your supper."

They made Mr Melton as comfortable as they could, putting him into a nightgown, but leaving the right arm out; they wrapped the wound lightly with a clean bandage. Leaving Antonia to watch, Judith went into the inner room. There were her medicines in a wall cabinet safely high against the prowlings of small children; on top of the cabinet were a few books. It was getting dark, but she knew the titles by heart. *The Farmer's and Drover's Own Veterinary Book*—even in the emergency Judith smiled—a veterinary book had been Cousin Carrie's own quite natural idea of what people at Rancho Amarillo would want. She could not have known that no one ever treated sick cattle. All a sick horse ever got was gunpowder, and on most ranches not even that; he was merely let go to get well or be finished off by the coyotes and mountain lions. In all these years, thought Judith, as the gilt letters of the title glared at her, gentle Cousin Carrie had never been able to realize what life in California was like.

The other three volumes had proved more useful; they dealt with human ills. *Household Guide to Medicine*, a ponderous volume in dark green and gilt, loured down at her in the twilight. It was the fullest and seemed the best of these books; it covered everything, even to such matters of beauty as removing freckles and building up the busts of embarrassingly flat-breasted women. She put her hand up, and then drew it back. Her desire to read about wounds in the book was, she realized, only inspired by a wish to put off time and action. No, she must deal honestly. She knew well enough what the *Guide* said on the treatment of wounds. What she must do was to act, not read. She must accept the responsibility, even though Mr Melton's life lay in her hands.

She opened the cabinet below, and found the little knife. Cousin Carrie had sent that out too. Judith did not know what it was called. It had a handle six inches long and a blade like a narrow segment cut from a circle, the cutting edge on the outer, curved side. It was of fine razor steel. She found Juan's hone, and whetted the blade a few times. The faint *whee-whee* made her feel cold all over.

She looked again into the cabinet wondering whether anything there would be of use. There was not much. Quinine, calomel, Brandstreth's Pills, Hoffman's Liver Pills; a cathartic made from a recipe in the *Guide*; a home-made cough-syrup of honey, cherry-juice, and some herbs; bear's grease. mutton tallow; mustard for plasters. There was also a jar labelled " Mother Beaty's Salve," made from a recipe in the *Guide*; it was largely beeswax, and looked like beeswax. Judith could not remember what else was in it, but she remembered its fine power of drawing pus from oozing cuts. In the old days Aunt Leticia had learned the recipe and been very fond of using the salve. Judith took the jar down.

She gazed also at a little bottle containing a small chunk of a dark smoky-grey waxy substance. There was no label except an eloquent death's head. Judith eyed the opium dubiously; as always, it fascinated her, and frightened her. She had never used it. It might be just the right thing now to keep Mr Melton quiet while she opened his arm; but she was still afraid. A ship's captain who had traded on the China coast had given it to her once, but neither he nor anyone else seemed sure of its strength or of the dose. No, it would be better to depend on brandy and on Mr Melton's own delirium.

Judith gave the little knife to Antonia. " Wash it," she said, " with soap and hot water, and rinse it with as hot water as you can get." The *Guide* said nothing about this, but it seemed common sense to Judith to have the knife clean.

On the opposite side of the bed from where Mr Melton was lying she put a table, and on it six candles; behind them she stood some tin trays from the kitchen as reflectors. She wished it could be daylight—but she dared not wait, and this gave a fairly good illumination

After his bath Mr Melton seemed to be a little better. She gave him a stiff drink of brandy, and told him she was about to open the arm. He looked at her a little pitifully, like a very sick child, but merely nodded.

Antonia held a clean towel and a basin of warm water. " Indian blood," thought Judith. " I can trust her; it won't bother her more than killing a chicken. I wish I felt as sure of myself." Then as the moment for action came she felt herself getting steady. She held the knife poised for a last moment. "The big arteries are on the inside, I'm sure; Lord knows what I may hit, though; but it has to be done!"

With as clean a stroke as she could manage she drew the knife from the point of the shoulder along the length of the wound. The flesh curled back on both sides. Near the end of the stroke it seemed as if the blade-point suddenly went into a hole. A gush of yellowish pus flowed out, sickeningly. With a sudden hope that she had struck the seat of the trouble, she let the knife cut its way out with an upward lick.

She gave the knife to Antonia and took the towel. For the first time she was conscious that Mr Melton looked very white and was groaning. "Get the hot compresses," she said, without looking around. She looked at the wound a moment. No spurt from an artery—good! Blood was flowing everywhere, but in places it was mixed with pus. She clapped the towel over the horror of the wound. Then Antonia came again, and they changed the towel for a thick-folded cloth soaked in hot water. Outside in the patio she heard with sudden loathing the high-pitched voice of Julio trolling away at some song.

At nine o'clock Judith left Antonia watching the compresses, and went out to eat. Lupe had a hot beef stew with peppers all steaming, but Judith saw the oozing wound and the blood everywhere. She got down only a few mouthfuls. Then she went into the patio, and peremptorily ordered Julio back to his room. At least, she tried to be peremptory. But Julio replied with what she supposed he intended for a leer, although it was hard for him to leer with that pudgy face. He began to argue; he was major-domo, and could sit in the patio if he pleased. All right, thought Judith, but you won't be major-domo or anything else after to-night. She felt he was not in condition to have that made plain to him at the moment; so she went on through the office, and out in front of the house.

Overhead she could feel the wind passing with the steady force of a flowing stream, but here she was sheltered. The day had been hideous with the glare of the sun and the beating heat. But what had made the day hideous had made the night beautiful. It was balmily warm. The strong, dry wind from the north swept the air clean, so that the stars glittered as if close enough to be touched from the ridge-pole. She felt calm again for a moment, and looked out towards the firm, unchanging profile of her southern hills—the hills that she had loved so long. Then she glanced back, and saw on the porch the saddle and the saddle-blanket lying where the boys had piled them. The blanket must have bits of the poor horse's hide still sticking to it. . . .

The ugliness of the thought blotted the stars and the hills out of her brain. She must go in and face the blood and the pus again, to help Mr Melton fight for his life. There was a certain nobility in that. But why, she thought, couldn't things happen one at a time in life—or at least things of the same kind happen together? The next thing probably one of the children would begin vomiting or a coyote would start all the dogs howling. Of all nights, why should Julio choose to-night to get drunk? She could hear him still caterwauling.

She sent Antonia to sleep in the inner room on call. Before long she stopped using hot compresses, for the blood seemed to be flowing freely, and she did not know how much she dared let him lose. Mr Melton was pale, but otherwise a little better; he was beginning to doze off.

She looked at him curiously as he lay there. He had always been clean-shaven and had looked thin-faced. Now the unkempt beard made him look rougher and more masculine, and covered up the thinness of his cheeks. It made him look strangely older too. He must still be under fifty, Judith considered, and his hair was not much greyed. But the beard was heavily grizzled, and made him seem almost patriarchal. He had wanted to marry her once—many years ago that was, on the old *Spanish Belle*. The brig was a sunken hulk now, but she and Mr Melton were again in the same room. She began to feel close to him—closer even than she had felt in those days on the *Spanish Belle*.

She wondered why he had never married, and whether he had ever had a little half-breed girl to wait for him in some house in Monterey or Yerba Buena. He had always seemed a lonely man; she hoped he had not been too lonely.

It must have been nearly eleven o'clock when Judith decided that she would stand Julio no longer Tragedy might call for a comic offset, but this was farce. But when she told Julio that he must go to his room he rose and put an arm around her. She could not have been more surprised if a chicken had attacked her. She tried to slap him, but he was too close. He was suddenly stronger than she would have imagined, but she pushed a determined hand into his face under his big sombrero and broke away. As he stumbled drunkenly around the table she slipped into the outer room again and bolted the door.

She was not alarmed—Julio amorous and attacking was almost funny. But she was suddenly angry It must be my insulted dignity, she thought; I don't often get really mad. She felt sick with anger, and there were twitchings in her stomach. Julio was pounding on the door; although the poundings were not very hard or very determined, still they did not make her feel any the less angry.

First she looked to see that Mr Melton was as well off as could be expected. Then she walked determinedly to the fireplace and took down the loaded pistol which these days she always kept above it. She went around through the office, and came out at the opposite corner of the patio from where Julio was.

" Julio! " she called. He came across towards her. She swung the pistol up and fired. She saw the big sombrero suddenly seem to jump half off his head and slew around. A ragged sliver hung down from the brim. She had not really meant to come that close, but perhaps it was just as well. It was too dark to see how pale Julio must be. Then he leaned forward, and vomited. She walked back to the outer room, not even troubling to bolt the door.

The pistol-shot had brought Antonia out questioning. " It went off by accident," said Judith; she enjoyed using the same believe-it-or-not tone of voice that Antonia herself had used that same afternoon.

A moment later Luis came in, big-eyed and serious, in his nightclothes. She sent him off with the same excuse. In a few minutes she heard the sound of horse's hoofs. Julio must be leaving. He would be cold-sober now, and afraid—the pudgy little coward!—to face the morning. She wondered what he had stolen as he left.

She did not care; she had put up with Julio a long time, for major-domos were hard to find.

Mr Melton did not seem even to have heard the shot. The wound had stopped bleeding now. Judith put a liberal amount of Mother Beaty's salve between two layers of cloth and laid it on the wound, so that it could act through the cloth, but not actually get into the wound.

She sat by the bed all night with a single candle burning on the table, shaded from the wounded man's eyes. She felt certain that he would die; yet he seemed to be sleeping a little and to be less feverish and delirious. It was strange, she thought, how quickly and fiercely the gold had worked through California, like some fever in the blood. Everything topsy-turvy: Mr Melton and how many others dying, the ranch half-deserted, and the old settled feudal life suddenly smashed to pieces in a few months—and all because Sutter had been building a sawmill and they had found gold. She had disliked that Sutter ever since he had conspired with Michel-torena and armed the Indians. Now she found herself blaming him for the gold in a personal way. She had not quite realized before how she had come to love the old life. In those days she had wanted civilization—books, the theatre, the contacts of a city, security from the ever-present Indian threat. Then had come the gold—"like a thief in the night"; she felt the words come to her. The old life might survive revolutions and wars and conquests, the ranch-owner might change, but the ranch went on. But could the old life survive this gold and the wild frenzy which it brought to men, so that even vaqueros born on the ranch—and perhaps their fathers before them—deserted their salt and ran away in the night. Now that it might be gone for ever she knew that she loved the life of the ranch—the valley, the grass, the cattle, the unaltering skyline to the south, the steady rhythm of the change from green to brown and back to green unendingly. In that life a man or woman could feel in touch with things deep, constant, and certain.

But this gold! . . She remembered what Williamson had said: "It won't jump up and bite at you, like a goddam rattlesnake." Perhaps not in the mines. Yet that was just what it had done for her She had been walking steadily ahead, her eyes upon the hills.

wondering whether she might not again soon feel a child within her. Then beside her path, sudden and unexpected as always, the snake had buzzed and struck. It had not missed either. Where was Juan? Where were the vaqueros and the old life? And Mr Melton —awkward, dependable, kindly Mr Melton—here he lay

In the first grey of dawn he was sleeping more quietly. Judith went outside for air. There was not much wind, but there would be more later. The stars had paled. There was no touch of the usual bay-fog and early morning chill. In an hour or so the sun would rise, scorching, brilliant, and horrible, and the hot wind would pour down from the north. But for the moment the dawn had a blessing in it—warm, still, and tender. A man would not die just now Later, perhaps. . .

The chickens were coming down from their roosts. Judith caught one. It squawked discordantly. In sudden contradiction to the peace of the dawn she wrung the hen's neck; she plucked it, cut it up in the kitchen, built up the fire, and put it on to stew for broth. Eat or be eaten, she thought harshly—that was life for human being or for chicken. She had always been among the strong. The strong lived on, even when the ways of life changed; the weak went under. She felt a sudden pity, and walked softly into the outer room to look at Mr Melton.

He lay awake, too weak to move or to speak, watching her with a strange mournful and questioning look in his grey-blue eyes. But his fever seemed to have fallen, and there was no touch of delirium in his face. Cautiously she lifted the pad with the salve. On the lower side it was thick with blood and pus it had drawn out. Around the wound the edges of flesh were pale, almost white, where the salve had sucked the blood from them. The whole wound looked cleaner and less fiery. For the first time she began to hope. . . .

It was nearly the end of the month before she ventured to let Mr Melton take his first longish ride. The arm was still in a sling, but after all it had been merely a flesh-wound; once the pus was out it had begun to heal rapidly. A younger man would have been up and off about his business already.

They rode north over the brown hills towards Ojuelo. It made

Judith think of that ride she had taken with him to Mission San Carlos on her first day in California. Then they had just shared that long voyage around the Horn; now they had voyaged together in even more dangerous seas.

They went only as far as the crest of the ridge above Ojuelo. Next to the valley where the ranch-house stood, this was the spot on the ranch which Judith loved most. It was only a few acres in extent, with the hills rising sharply around on all sides, quiet and secluded. "The Little Eye" some one had named it, not inappropriately. It was well watered; even in autumn there was a touch of greenness in it, and along the stream-bed in the centre was a thick copse of bushes and small oaks.

But even the beauty of Ojuelo could not lift Mr Melton's gloom as they rode back. The hide business was probably ruined, he said; and even if not he was too old now to ride about from ranch to ranch competing with younger men. What money he had made and saved was gone with those cursed lots. He might get to be a clerk with one of the new firms that would be sure to come in now; that was about the best he could hope for. He was getting old, but he knew Spanish and French, and he knew the country—that might help.

He was clean-shaven again, but he looked older than ever to-day, thought Judith, even though the grizzled beard was gone. Yet a man under fifty was not very old.

"Come live with us," she said. "Julio's gone; you would make a good major-domo." He would too, she thought; but at the same time she knew that he would never come.

She herself was feeling more cheerful about the ranch. "They'll need food," Mr Melton had said, "all these people who are coming to dig gold. Don't kill your cattle for hides, even when Juan and the men get back. Save them to drive in and sell for beef. Prices will go up with all this gold—bound to." It was shrewd advice, Judith could see. Mr Melton had some points as a man of business, although he had not made money for himself. (Judith herself with Luis and Guito had ridden back to find the money-belt; but people had passed that way already, and the belt was gone.)

When they came over the hills above the ranch-house they saw horses standing. Judith felt an old familiar lightness about herself again; Juan was home. They had had word, and had been expecting him for several days.

She kept looking to see Juan any minute, out striding around somewhere in his usual energetic way. She had to ride slowly on account of Mr Melton, but even so she did not see Juan as they approached the house.

Mr Melton faded tactfully away; entering, she found Juan sitting at the table in the outer room. She gave a gasp of relief to see that he was well and unhurt. Yet there was something wrong too. There was a gone look about his face; his jowls seemed fallen. He was sitting back heavily in his chair, and did not seem to notice her. She crossed to him quickly. He put up his face, and kissed her. He needed a shave badly—that was to be expected; but there was a dull look to his eyes. The brandy was heavy on his breath. That could not be the trouble, although it was strange too that Juan should be drinking by himself; he seldom drank at all.

" Did you get any gold? " she asked.

" Look." He pointed to the two squat bags of fresh deerskin on the table. " That's ours; the men have had their shares." He reached out, and at arm's length lifted one of the bags with difficulty. He let it down with a dull thudding *sqush*. Judith loosened one of the thongs and felt the coarse grains inside; she pulled out a rough irregular lump as big as the end of her finger. She felt suddenly dazzled; she had never imagined so much gold. They were rich! Why was Juan sitting so dull and heavy when they should be prancing around rejoicing that they were both still young enough to enjoy their wealth?

Then she noticed the rifle; it was leaning against the fireplace; it had the long, sinister barrel which she had come to associate with the Americans. Juan followed her look.

" I got it from a man in the mines," he said. " It's a good one, and I can shoot it pretty well now I'm going to get one for Miguel. Look at this too."

He laid on the table, not his old Spanish pistol, but one of the new-style revolvers—six-shooting, long-barrelled, big-bored, cleanly built—an epitome of sudden death. Judith thought of all the times in the old days when she had urged him to buy new and better weapons, and he had gone on content with old things which might have served with Alva in the Netherlands.

"Things have changed," he said before she asked the question. "A lot of rough ones are coming in already, now that there's gold. We'll have to watch out for ourselves."

Change—even Juan feels it coming, thought Judith.

Mr Melton entered. There was a restraint in the air; even old friends seemed to feel the difference which the gold upon the table could make. Mr Melton congratulated Juan.

"It was everywhere," said Juan. "You weren't there long enough to see. When the streams shrank in the fall I saw bars where the gold lay and glittered like fish-scales. And we—the ones who went this summer—were the first to get at it. They're coming from everywhere now; I saw men from Oregon and men all the way up from Sonora across the desert. And who else do you think I saw?"

Suddenly Judith knew that here was something which was lying very deep in Juan's heart.

"Who?" she asked.

"Old Felipe himself—and pretty nearly all his Tokolumnes, warriors, squaws, babies and all."

"Did you fight?"

"Fight? He had a bottle of whisky in one hand and was half drunk, but he knew me, and came over holding out his hand and grinning and saying 'Hello,' the way they learn from the Americans. The men were digging out gold and buying whisky with it, and the squaws were hiring themselves out to the Americans at an ounce a throw. It's the end of the Tokolumnes. One buck stabbed his squaw that night when he was drunk, and two nights later a buck fell in the river and drowned."

With a quick feeling of horror Judith glanced at the brandy-bottle on the table. She had never thought of it as a threat before; the Californians did not drink much; their Latin blood found its release in other ways. Now she knew why Juan was drinking. He too felt the old life with its deep satisfactions crumbling away beneath his feet. No longer would the ever-present thought of Felipe's Tokolumnes give him the touch of excitement that he needed. The ranch might go on after a fashion, but it would not be as before. It was the end of an era; perhaps the only graceful thing they could do would be to die. They had money now, but what could they buy with it to equal for Juan the established ways of living to which he had been born?

Juan poured one of the bags out on the table, and played with the gold, heaping it here and scooping it out there—as a child might in sand, thought Judith, making hills and valleys. And that brought to her mind what Uncle Enrique had said so long ago about the stream of life. They had left the old quiet valley behind, and were still swirling violently down through the hills; somewhere ahead, but still out of sight, might lie another valley. Who could survive and reach quiet waters again?

She looked at Mr Melton. He had sat down. His arm must be hurting again. He looked pale and old.

She looked at Juan. There was strength in his dark face, but she saw again that gone look, and the brandy-bottle seemed the symbol of a man at war with himself.

What of herself? She still felt strong, and with her old fighting gesture she threw her head back and gave the little toss to her white hair. But her spirit did not rise as it might have, and for a moment she felt a little coldness of fear mingled with uncertainty and a touch of weariness.

THIRTY-FIVE THOUSAND—dollars, gold, and spot cash," said
the man—Bamman, Bramman, or whatever his name was. He
was a flamboyant fellow; had made money with a store up in
Sacramento City, and had come down-river to play a bigger game
now. He wore blue coat and trousers, a crimson gold-embroidered
waistcoat, and an ornate sombrero; beside him Mr Melton felt very
sombre in black broadcloth and conventional ' tile ' hat; his only
ornaments were a massive gold watch-chain and some modest em-
broidery on the waistcoat. Yet Mr Melton did not feel wholly put
into the shade. He knew that there was richness and quality in all
that he was wearing. He remembered that Englishman saying just
the other day, " By God, Melton, if it weren't for your Yankee
loose-jointedness and that yellow-tan face I'd take you for a duke
who's on his way to a governors' meeting of the Bank of England! "

" Thirty-five thousand . . ." Mr Melton repeated meditatively;
he was uncertain. He drew out a big handkerchief, and, playing
for time, leaned over to brush the ever-present San Francisco dust
from his varnished Wellingtons.

" Hell, thirty-seven-fifty," said the other, with the air of one who
would rather spend a few thousand extra than waste any more
time talking about it on a street corner. He'll go forty, thought
Mr Melton, still busy with his boots, but I don't want to sell it.
He straightened up and stood looking meditatively north across
the plaza. He could see the fifty-foot lot in question. Covered
with a straggly-looking two-story corrugated-iron building bearing
the name " Hudson and Curme, Bankers," it certainly did not
look worth forty thousand dollars. The other, seeing Mr Melton
was considering the matter, took out a big cigar and set to work
getting it lighted—no small task in the breezy spot where they
stood.

It was Sunday afternoon. Around and across the littered sandy plaza were walking scores of men of all races and nations, in all costumes, talking and shouting various languages, and—generally speaking—in all stages of drunkenness. Half a dozen horsemen dashed whooping down Kearny Street scattering the crowd; they swung round the corner and went out of sight down Washington Street. Mr Melton started; he had heard that Juan Godoy was in town, and he was pretty sure that the leading horseman had been Juan. He wanted to get rid of the present business and go and find him.

"No, I don't want to sell—sorry," he said.

"Forty thousand," came the reply.

Out of mere politeness Mr Melton had to consider again. It was a good price and actually more than the lot was worth—that is to say, the money could be better invested elsewhere in San Francisco. There was a lot right now going at a bargain price on Sansome Street, and on the outskirts over along Market and Spring Valley you could pick up lots at five hundred which were sure to rise. Still, his rule was not to sell, and it had worked well enough to make him a millionaire, or close to it. Strange, when he had left Rancho Amarillo a year ago he had thought himself a pauper, but as he had been lying sick Benicia and the other rival towns had been fading out of sight, and his lots in San Francisco had been doubling in value every week. If he had been here he might have sold out on the first rise. Being ill had made him a rich man in spite of himself. Bad luck was good luck; that was the way it went. That lot across the plaza there—he had paid eighty-five dollars for it a few years ago—when was it?—just before Judith Godoy came up to Yerba Buena after the French doctor. It was a high price then; now it brought more than that amount a day in rentals. He had bought that lot when they were building the new custom-house, which people called the Old Adobe now. He looked at it where it still stood on the upper side of the plaza; the five-year-old building actually had a touch of antiquity and long-permanence as compared with the surrounding shacks and flimsy overnight construction of raw wood, corrugated iron, and canvas.

Mr Melton decided that he would manage to buy that Sansome

Street lot some other way. He felt sentimental about the plaza lot; it was one of his first holdings. He felt suddenly what was almost a love for the whole city He let his eyes sweep over what he could see of it: the tall wooden structure of the City Hall looming up on Kearny Street; beyond it the sharp, bare hill rising up to form the northern skyline, the new semaphore on top; the smokes from hundreds of stove-pipe chimneys, streaming off eastward in the breeze, the cove of the Bay, with scores, maybe hundreds, of tall-masted ships laid up at anchor because their crews had run off to the mines.

"No, thank you; I'm going to hold that lot." He hoped this was the end; he wanted to find Juan.

"Just as you say, Mr Melton; business is business; no hard feelings, I'm sure."

Mr Melton noticed the placating note in the man's voice; it flattered him. Even a big boisterous fellow like this, his revolver in plain view, did not want to be on bad terms with Mr Melton, one of the richest men in San Francisco—perhaps the richest. "Financial wizard," he had heard some one say the other day as he walked past.

Mr Melton strode off to where his horse was tied. "Big Mike" Shane, his bodyguard, followed close, his long-barrelled revolver and a knife to every one's sight in his belt. "Big Mike" always made Mr Melton feel very conspicuous, but a man as rich as himself, and not a fighting man to boot, couldn't run around loose—not in San Francisco in November 1849. Mike was a good protector; the only trouble was that Mr Melton was rather afraid of Mike himself. Mike claimed to be a law-abiding citizen from County Wexford, but he had a face which was tough-looking enough to convict him before any jury. Mr Melton was afraid he might be one of the escaped or paroled convicts from Australia who were flooding California; people called them " Sydney Ducks." Sometimes Mr Melton was afraid that Mike might prefer tapping him on the head some night and making off with a year's pay all at once instead of waiting for weekly instalments.

He let Mike ride ahead, for people always opened right and left when they saw Mike coming, either on horseback or afoot. With

Mike bellowing for gangway, they forced ahead through the crowds on Clay Street at a canter. The street was merely a sandy, dusty thoroughfare, cut with wheel-ruts and littered with horse-droppings and refuse. We ought to get some planking down before the rains, thought Mr Melton, feeling a stir of civic consciousness. They turned south into Montgomery Street, which was just as bad. Here and there horses were tied up outside hotels or bars or gambling-houses. Mr Melton kept looking for the long-legged black stallion which he had seen going around the corner of the plaza; it looked like one of the breed which Juan cultivated at Rancho Amarillo.

After searching back and forth they tried the " Flor de California "; it was run by a man from Ecuador and patronized chiefly by Latin-Americans. Mr Melton had never been inside, but the doorman bowed deferentially; either he recognized Mr Melton or he was afraid of Mike. There was the usual bar along one side; on the other side were the games—roulette, faro, monte. A few girls—rather more decent ones than Mr Melton had expected—circulated here and there. There was Juan too. He had apparently just won at roulette, and had stepped over to the bar with some friends to celebrate with a round of drinks.

Mr Melton had not seen Juan for a year, and was shocked at the way he looked. He was not really drunk, but he was carrying plenty; he had put on weight, which did not become him; his cheeks sagged, and his eyes looked tired.

He greeted Mr Melton warmly, and there were introductions all round. Mr Melton always felt embarrassed introducing Big Mike as Mr Shane—but it was democracy these days, and that was how things went in California. He noted that Miguel hung back; Miguel was of the days when a vaquero kept his place. First Juan introduced Judge Wingram and Mr Reynolds; they shook Mr Melton's hand very warmly and said in such tones as to leave no doubt about it that they were very happy, sir, to meet him. They spoke the truth there, thought Mr Melton; they'll talk of their friend Mr Melton from now on. He hated to see Juan with such fellows—adventurers, political hangers-on, gamblers. The other man with Juan was hand-some and young; Mr Melton liked him as naturally as he disliked the other two. Perhaps it was the hair, for he had hair almost like

Judith's, except for its being a little yellower His name was Jerry
Graham, and there was a familiar ring to his speech.

" What state are you from? " said Mr Melton.

" Pennsylvania; born out in the Two Lick Hills " He pronounced
it ' Toolik.'

" I thought you sounded like it; I'm from the Juniata Valley
myself."

" Never been that far east," said Jerry Graham. " Ran away from
home and came west when I was sixteen."

Mr Melton had little chance to talk with Juan, for Judge Wingram
and Mr Reynolds conducted most of the conversation. They kept it
on a very high plane to show what men of the world they were.
They talked politics, becoming indignant about the way Congress
was treating California in not making her a state right away; from
the way they spoke you would have thought that they considered
themselves personally aggrieved at not being consulted by the
President in the matter, but they let you feel in some subtle way that
they would have their revenge when one of them was Governor and
the other United States Senator. Then for Juan's benefit they talked
about land titles, and how unjust it was for the Californians not to
have their ranches confirmed to them as the treaty had promised,
and to have to fight the squatters off. Then for Mr Melton they
shifted to real estate; they as much as offered to give him a few
tips as to where some bargains could be picked up; you gathered that
between them they owned about half the frontage on Montgomery
Street. But they weren't selling—no, sir, they were sitting tight and
waiting for things really to go up; this was going to be the biggest
city between New York and Canton—yes, by God, sir, maybe
between London and Canton! Then they called for a toast, and the
Judge made a speech, ending, " Gentlemen, I give you San Francisco, in a hundred years the greatest city of our globe! " Everybody
around the bar drank to it, and over some protests from the Judge
and Mr Reynolds the bar-keeper scored it up against Juan.

After that Judge Wingram looked at his watch and said, " By
God, Reynolds, our appointment with General Twinning almost
slipped me! Quite a compliment to present company, ha-ha! But
we must close that deal before two-thirty. The General will be

T

at the Esmeralda; we'll find him, settle things, and be back in ten minutes."

"We'll wait," said Juan—"and then we'll all go to the bull-and-bear fight."

The two hurried off. The only important business they have, thought Mr Melton, will be transacted facing a wall. Now was the time for him to get Juan out of the hands of those two; but he could not think of just what to say, and, as often, he cursed himself for not being a glib talker. Besides, Juan had said that he would wait, and it was always a hard job to change an old-time Californian when he had given his word even in the slightest matter.

As a beginner, Mr Melton said that he did not want to drink any more and was ready to leave. Juan called for the bar-keeper, and pulled out a leather bag of gold-dust which seemed to hit the bar with the weight of two or three bricks. The bar-keeper began taking out his pinches to pay for the drinks. Mr Melton was astonished that Juan should have so much gold; it was lucky he had both Miguel and Jerry Graham to guard him if he was going about San Francisco with all that in his pants, and maybe as much more in his belt.

"Is that what you got in the mines?" he asked.

"Hell, no!" said Juan. "That's gone long ago; this is from selling cattle. You couldn't guess what cattle are selling for."

Mr Melton did not need to guess; he knew what the butchers were paying in San Francisco, and it was plenty. Still, there were a lot of cattle in that bag of gold-dust; he had a fear that Juan might be cutting in on the breeding-herd.

"Where's all that fortune you got in the mines?" he asked carelessly.

"Oh, everywhere. Lawyer's fees—we're getting ready to defend the title to the ranch. And I had a run of bad luck at poker in San José. But a lot of it I've got invested in lots up at Benicia."

Swindlers have got hold of him, thought Mr Melton. He's gambling, and when a Spaniard starts that! . . . And lots in Benicia. . . . The babe in the wood! What swindler sold him those?—Woods or Lemaitlan, probably.

Judge Wingram and Mr Reynolds came back, and everybody

went out to mount. Mr Melton had no desire to see the two animals
tear each other to pieces, and in fact rather dreaded it. He had seen
such fights often enough in the hide-and-tallow days, but getting
older he was getting more soft-hearted. Nevertheless he went along,
thinking vaguely he ought to stick by Juan. He, Daniel Melton, did
not fit in very well with this crowd, he thought; and in a way he
disliked even being seen with them. But as they were mounting he
realized that they all looked so different that no one of them could
seem conspicuous. Himself in his tall hat and black broadcloth.
The Judge and Mr Reynolds in tall hats too, but one in blue and
the other in brown, and both with high boots. Juan with his big
sombrero and black cloak and scarlet jacket. Miguel with his lasso,
and his head stuck through a serape. Jerry Graham in fringed
buckskin. And Big Mike in corduroys and a soft felt hat and a
miner's red shirt.

They started north along Montgomery Street, the horses' hoofs
sinking deep and raising up clouds of dust. With Big Mike in the
lead they might have gone faster, but people did not get out of the
way so quickly for Judge Wingram. It was no crowd to fool with
either—all men, most of them on their Sunday afternoon 'drunk,'
and all with revolvers. It was a fine place for a man whose hobby
was languages; as he often did these days, Mr Melton rode with an
attentive ear. In this part of the city it was mostly English of all
dialects, with a good deal of Spanish. But before they got to Washington Street he had identified French and German, picked up a few
words of Kanaka, and heard what he thought was Dutch. He had
recognized Chinese without understanding it, and had heard two
languages which baffled him entirely.

Judge Wingram led the way; then Juan and Mr Reynolds; then
Miguel; then Mr Melton and Jerry Graham; Big Mike, like Miguel,
kept his place as bodyguard.

Jerry Graham had never been to San Francisco before, and Mr
Melton was quick to take the opportunity of pointing things out.
Here on Montgomery Street was the big business district—auction
houses with goods piled high in front of them, commission houses,
buildings containing offices of bankers, lawyers, and land-agents.
Mr Melton indicated with pride the beginnings of an occasional

brick structure. On their right, between the gaps in a single row of buildings, he pointed out the mud-flats, the wharves extending out towards deep water, the barges busily unloading, even though it was Sunday, and farther out the ships at anchor.

" A lot of people are for filling in the mud-flats," said Mr Melton. " I don't know about it; might be better to make a system of canals or tidal basins."

At Jackson Street they crossed the old lagoon on a solid ridge of earth. " I can remember when there wasn't even a bridge," said Mr Melton. Here on their right was a wharf and on their left what remained of the lagoon, now not much more than a big smelly mud-puddle. Ahead they could see the cliffs bringing the street to an end, and on the hill the shanties known as Sydney Town.

Mr Melton was glad that the Judge turned left at Pacific just as Montgomery began to peter out. This brought them past the new City Hall, four stories, with galleries all round; rather imposing, thought Mr Melton, and let it work on Jerry without saying anything more.

At the livery stable diagonally opposite the Judge and Mr Reynolds' horses wanted to turn in, but the Judge went to the right along Kearny and towards the hill again. This was a low district, no denying it; mostly Mexican, and of the worst class. On both sides were shacks and hovels. Here for the first time they saw women. Frowzy, half-naked, tipsy prostitutes screamed provocatively, sensing good game among the well-dressed horsemen. Judge Wingram waved grandiloquently at them, not understanding the Spanish. Juan shouted back in kind, saying he would see them later. Mr Melton felt disgusted. A gentleman like Juan should not be talking even jocosely to such filth, scourings of Mazatlán and Acapulco.

At the end of the block they were close under the hill, and turned into Broadway. Here Spanish yielded partly to a vile whining Cockney, the lingo of the Australian convicts. " Just here," thought Mr Melton, shaping the phrases to himself, " the worst of the Anglo-Saxons impinge on the worst of the Latins." A free-for-all fight was in progress; Irish against English apparently. The air was thick with cursing. From the hovels on the hill a few English whores hurled down epithets.

Half-way down the block Spanish was the language again; here the hill above was covered with the conglomeration of shacks known as Little Chile. Mr Melton was chagrined; if they had to ride into the outskirts they might at least have gone into some of the more decent districts, south and west.

He saw the little new Catholic church ahead, and beside it the small, roughly built, wooden bull-ring. Nationalities became more varied again, for the bull-ring was a magnet drawing individuals from all the colonies of the city. Mr Melton picked up the sound of Swedish, and looked around to see two blond giants walking with the roll of sea-legs.

Various men offered to watch the horses at a dollar apiece, but they all looked so much like congenital horse-thieves that it was deemed safer to leave the job to Miguel and Big Mike. Some small stands had been built; the rest of the crowd inside the enclosure had to stand on the natural hillside. At five dollars apiece the party bought the right to sit in the stand; when they got inside it looked as if they had made a purely theoretical purchase, for the stand was full, and other people like themselves were waiting for seats. Fortunately some men got up to leave, and the Judge led a dash for their seats. Some miners were closer, and would have got the seats if two men sitting just in front of the vacated places had not refused to let the miners through from that direction. One of the miners wanted to fight, but the crowd wanted the next event, not personal squabbles, and its sentiment backed him down.

They were just in time; the announcer was standing in the rough, trampled space which served as the arena.

" Ladies—and—gentlemen! " (The " ladies," thought Mr Melton, must be out of deference to three Mexican prostitutes who, with American escorts, sat in the top row.)

"Ladies—and—gentlemen! The—next—ee-vent will be the grand com-bat to the death between a wild fighting bull and a great Cali-four-ni-ya grey-or-griz-lee-bear, the ty-rant of the western wilds." A low anticipative roar went up from the crowd, but the announcer was a born speechmaker, and went on : " The bear is the monarch of his race, and the bull is a rip-snorter, a ree-al he-bull, gentlemen; you will be able to see for yourselves." A clod of earth whizzed by the announcer, but his love of oratory overcame his prudence. " It's the old case, gentlemen, of the irresistible force and——" Here a well-aimed whisky-bottle took him in the Adam's apple, and he doubled up coughing. The crowd laughed.

" Reminds me," said Mr Reynolds; he pulled out a bottle of whisky and passed it along. Mr Melton only pretended to drink, but he felt the rot-gut burn as if it were eating through his lips.

There was some betting, at even odds. Juan was backing the bear. The men in front, the ones who had helped them against the miners to get the seat, seemed to have money; each of them took a hundred dollars of Juan's offer, and they passed their brandy-bottle back. There was a little delay

Mr Melton was sitting between Jerry Graham and Mr Reynolds; beyond Mr Reynolds was Juan and then the Judge. Juan was just behind the two men who had taken his bets. Mr Melton began to feel that he had been shoved out of the party. There was something suspicious in the look of things. He turned to Jerry.

" Why do you suppose," he asked casually, " those two men in front helped hold these seats for us? "

" You've got round to that, have you? " said Jerry, below the clamour of the crowd, grinning in friendly fashion. " Well, I'll ask you another. How come the ones sitting here got up and left just as we came in, and just before the big ee-vent? Funny, eh? Couldn't be a put-up job, could it? "

Mr Melton must have looked his consternation.

" What the hell? " said Jerry. " No, we can't do anything about it either. He's off for hell, faster than powder burns."

Mr Melton had a vision of Judith, and felt suddenly miserable. But he liked Jerry.

" Where'd you come from, anyway? " he said.

" Me? Oh, I blew into Rancho Amarillo one day during the time of the war. Me and a few others from Cap'n Weber's company—the Judge there was with us—we chased Don Juan himself up through the hills one day. Damn' near caught him too. If we had, guess we'd have shot him. Might have been a good thing too—damn' sight faster than the way it is now. But the missus stood us off—guess you know about that."

Mr Melton nodded.

"We knew he was in there all the time—me and old Abe Hand-side did. But we liked the missus, and didn't tell the old Major When Abe went to the kitchen for his beans he slipped me the wink to stay and watch things. Hope to die if I ever thought I'd be drinkin' tea with a lady that way. Old Abe sure slipped me a dirty one that time."

"But how did you know Juan was in there?"

"Hell, there was a chunk of fresh mud from the creek-bottom lyin' on the floor, big as your finger-nail. A blind man shoulda saw it."

"How do you happen to be at the ranch now?"

"Oh, after I tried the mines and didn't like it I remembered how I liked the missus down there and the place and all, and I went and struck her for a job. She's white!"

"You stick by her. She's an old friend of mine. You watch out for her, and I'll make it worth your while."

"Sure, I'll stick. I like *her*. Last, I'll stick long as I can stand that guy over there. How come she'd marry that beaver-gut, any-way?"

Mr Melton's old loyalty stirred:

"Oh, Juan's a pretty good sort."

"Used to be maybe."

The crowd was getting so noisy that it was hard to talk. Then a gate opened, and the bull came in. He was not much of a bull—a three-year-old probably. He had good enough horns, but was not very spirited. He trotted around the ring uncertainly; a whisky-bottle taking him with a *clunk* in the ribs went unnoticed.

A cart with a wooden cage was backed up to the ring. The bear at first refused to come out. That was nothing unusual, Mr Melton remembered from the old days. They lassoed a bear in the hills, and it might be a good bear then, but by the time they had kept it in a cage for a week, thirsty and half starved and bedevilled with poking sticks, all the fight went out of it.

When the bear had finally been prodded out he looked better.

As he reared up on his hind legs he would have dwarfed even Big Mike. He growled. The bull looked uncertain. The bear made no advance. The crowd hooted, and threw bottles, but the confusion only seemed to disturb the two animals.

"Tie 'em together with a chain!" Juan was shouting. "That's the way to make 'em fight!" The crowd liked the looks of the bear, and the odds jumped to two to one. Juan was placing more money with the men in front, although the Judge seemed to be restraining him.

The owner of the ring lighted three or four little Chinese fire crackers and threw them into the ring under the bull's nose. The animal suddenly came to life, lowered his head, and charged. The bear lurched forward to meet the rush. In the quick hush the sound of the impact came with a heavy thud.

The right horn drove into the bear's side. The bull's backers set up a yell. It's all over, thought Mr Melton, looking to see the bear rolled clear over and gored to death before he could get to his feet. But the bull was small, and the bear's forward rush and his own weight had saved him. Maintaining his balance, he seized the bull by the neck; growling, he bit into the big neck muscles towards the bone. For a moment or two they wrestled, blood spurting from the bull.

The odds shifted to the bear again. Shouting wildly, Juan was giving three to one. The men in front put up two hundred more apiece. Funny they don't hedge, thought Mr Melton.

Something seemed to be happening to the bear. His claws kept slipping from the bull's neck. The bull broke from the grapple, whirled round, and stood threatening a second, bleeding horribly from along the neck. He lowered his head and charged again. The bear tried to dodge, but was caught broadside and rolled clear over. The bull was upon him, goring again and again. In a few moments the bear was a shapeless mass of bloody fur and flesh, pierced and trampled.

The crowd had risen to a wild pitch of excitement. Now it began to quieten down. Bets were settled. Juan had lost something over two thousand dollars; he arranged coolly with the men to weigh out the gold-dust at a certain bar-room which had the proper scales. The crowd began to disperse. In the ring Mr Melton saw two men rope the bull, and then cut his throat. So much for the victor.

As they came to the horses Mr Melton had a new idea. " Come with me," he said to Mike. At the entrance to the ring a man tried to bar their way, but he fell back as Mike shouldered him. Already men were at work skinning the bull. Mr Melton went to the bear; it was a horrible mass of carrion, the flies already buzzing about a long tear that had laid open the intestines. Mr Melton felt his gorge rising, but he knelt and looked carefully at the bear's fore-paws. No wonder those men in there did not hedge their bets. The ends of the bear's claws had been neatly clipped off. Not more than a quarter of an inch probably—no one could have seen it from any distance. But with those points intact the bear could have ripped the bull's hide to shreds or held him fast until he chewed through and snapped the neck-bone. Nice business! How many had been in the know, and how many thousands had gone into their pockets? Two more men came in and began skinning the bear; it would be in some butcher's shop before dark.

Mr Melton found the others waiting for him. He said nothing; there was no use. If you ran around with gamblers this was the kind of thing you had to expect. He suggested supper at Delmonico's at his own expense. Again he sensed that the Judge and Mr Reynolds were against him; they probably realized that he was trying to get Juan away. They expressed their sorrow, but they had already arranged for a poker game in a private room at " The Golden Girl "; they could have plenty to eat during the game. They invited him to join them. Mr Melton felt that the invitation was somewhat perfunctory, but he accepted—half out of bravado, and half out of a fast-waning hope that he could do something for Juan, or for Judith. Once he had accepted Mr Melton could see that the two gamblers were highly pleased; it isn't every day, he thought, they have a chance to fleece the richest man in San Francisco. Well, let them try; he wasn't their dupe.

The only other man they picked up for the game was a miner in a blue shirt whom they all called Rufe. He was just down from somewhere on the Yuba River Middle Fork with a big bag of dust. Mr Melton staked Jerry Graham with a couple of hundred to get into the game. Big Mike and Miguel sat back on chairs tipped against the wall. Mr Reynolds, a little too ostentatiously perhaps, opened a new deck of cards.

The hours moved on, slowly for Mr Melton. The stakes were high. Once when Mr Reynolds was dealing Rufe cried out something at a peculiar flick of a card. There was an ugly moment of suspense. Big Mike and Miguel had tipped their chairs down from the wall and were standing each behind his master. Mr Reynolds had stopped dealing, and his right hand rested on the edge of the table in a handy position to be snapped back towards his pistol-holder. Rufe had already drunk so much that he was not frightened, but the same drinks had made him good-humoured. Seeing how seriously Mr Reynolds took the matter, Rufe laughed and said he had been mistaken, and apologized for holding up the game. Mr Reynolds went on with the deal, and Mike and Miguel went back to their chairs. Judge Wingram seemed to have something the matter with the right sleeve of his coat; probably he carried a derringer there, and had been getting it into position for a quick draw; now he was making it comfortable again.

Mr Melton held three tens natural on that deal. Only when he had raked in the pot did he realize that he was breathing quickly and in the last few minutes had somewhere lost a string of heart-beats. He too had been watching the dealer, and he didn't think there was anything wrong—especially not when he himself had held the best hand. He thought the game was straight. Why shouldn't it be? Rufe was rapidly getting drunk, and Juan at poker, drunk or sober, was easy picking for these professionals. But that little interlude showed how easily things happened. " Prominent Citizen Shot "—that would be the newspaper heading, and about one inch of space below it would be the epitaph. Getting shot over a card-table counted as a natural death these days; it scarcely rated as news for the papers. And the coroner's reports were a joke; the saying was that he put those deaths down as " heart-failure," " cerebral-lesion," or " acute indigestion "—according to where the bullets hit.

By ten-thirty Jerry Graham was cleaned out; Mr Melton offered him another stake, but he shrugged his shoulders and retired to a chair beside Big Mike. The room grew heavier and heavier with cigar-smoke, and Mr Melton began to have a headache. He had never considered himself a poker player and did not enjoy it much, although in the old days he had often sat in with the other traders. He played conservatively. For a couple of hours he held level or was a little ahead; even by eleven o'clock he was not more than a hundred behind, not counting his stake to Jerry; that wasn't enough to be bothered about. But the gamblers were not out after *his* scalp. Juan was losing steadily, and if Rufe kept on losing and then taking a drink for better luck he would not last long.

About midnight they called a halt for a few minutes and ordered some fried eggs to be sent up. As the door stood open a pair of girls came down the hall.

" Hi-ya, Gret? Come in," called the Judge.

Gret was a big-framed girl with fading blonde hair, and the other was a little ordinary-looking half-breed. They must be pretty high-class, though, to be taking time off on a Sunday night. Mr Reynolds pulled the little Mexican down into his lap and kissed her with a resounding smack; she pretended to struggle, and succeeded in show-ing most of what she had. But Mr Melton with a hopeless feeling saw that Gret had gone over to stand by Juan in an ' old friends ' sort of way, and with what seemed an accustomed gesture he had thrown his arm around her waist. Only, since he was sitting down and she was rather tall, his arm was hardly around what would be called her waist except out of politeness.

The fried eggs came in; the girls refused to eat any, but said they were busy and went on down the hall. Mr Melton gulped down two eggs, but he did not feel hungry, and his head ached more than ever. He felt hopeless. When he excused himself nobody seemed to care.

The fog had come down thick. The streets were dark. Few people passed, and those in groups of three or four. It was a bad business being out so late on a foggy night, even with Big Mike and on horse-back.

He was too dispirited to worry. He kept thinking about Juan as he had been in the old days—so quick at picking up languages, so good at the violin and guitar, such a figure on horseback. And that Gret! . . . Those girls came out on ships, half a dozen of them perhaps and a couple of hundred men. They were full of rottenness, flowing over with it. All right for some one like the Judge to take his chances with, but not for any man with a healthy wife at home. Yet what seemed to make Mr Melton sickest was not any practical matter, but merely that dingy blonde hair. It seemed a kind of blasphemous parody. You would have thought Juan would have had enough sense of decency left to pick himself one with black hair, or a red-head.

THE CHOCOLATE WAS VILE that morning, although perhaps not worse than it had been for a week or more. It was bitter and thin, and the foam which Lupe had beaten up on top of it had a dirty look and soon sank down into a scum-like covering. Ordinarily Judith would have been the first one to notice it and send it back to the kitchen with a sharp reprimand to old Lupe. But now with a kind of slinking feeling she drank her own as if it were excellent. She was glad that Juan was not up yet, and she hoped that none of the children would say anything. But of course Leticia did :

" I won't drink this chocolate; it's bad."

" Oh, no, dear, it's the same as we always have. Look, I've drunk mine." Judith tried to speak calmly, but she could sense the snarl in her own voice. Then Antonia, standing with a tray in her hand, spoke up :

" That last lot of chocolate you got, señora, is no good; Lupe can't do anything with it."

" It's the best there is in the stores at San José," Judith snapped back, the snarl in her voice quite open now. " Since the gold-rush everything's adulterated."

" It's all right," said Luis.

" It's the best chocolate I ever drank," said Guito.

Judith saw Leticia make a face at the boys; one of them had probably kicked her under the table. Judith felt a little better for the boys' support, even though she realized that it was mostly a brother-sister fight with the boys backing her up against Leticia. They had lied gallantly; she could see by their faces as they drank that they hated the stuff. Who wouldn't? Yet maybe it had been loyalty to her that made Luis speak up; she could count on him more than any other.

She felt thoroughly sick as she finished breakfast and left the table. She hated lying—not so much for moral reasons perhaps as because it seemed a small, sneaking, and cowardly way of doing. To have to lie to a servant was worst of all. And yet she knew that every word she had spoken to Antonia was a lie. There was good chocolate to be had. She had bought a cheap quality, in panic, thinking of how little money she had and of how badly things were going. Cheap chocolate was not the only thing. Even the vaqueros' beans were second-rate; she had imagined seeing a sneering smile on the store-keeper's face as she bought them.

Well, the vaqueros deserved second-rate beans. They had come sneaking back from the gold-mines to sit around the quarters, expecting to be fed again, just as if nothing had changed, just as if the price of food hadn't gone up three or four or maybe ten times over. There wasn't even much for them to do, for the herd had suddenly got so much smaller that so many men weren't needed. But you couldn't go out and discharge your vaqueros; they wouldn't quite know what you meant. They were retainers; she had realized that a long time ago. They weren't New England hired-men. In the old days she had liked the idea of their being retainers; she did not like it so well now.

Juan was sleeping in the big bed in the inner room. Judith had been sleeping on the cot lately. It was just the opposite of the way it used to be when they slept apart. Juan seemed to like the soft bed now. Even when he went down to San José or San Francisco for a few days, as he often did, she kept on sleeping on the cot. She was still his wife, but things had changed somehow. Juan had changed. Perhaps she herself had changed—but not so much as Juan had. She was sure of that.

He lay now on his stomach with his head twisted at right angles. She could just hear the sound of heavy breathing. He had a two-day black beard, but in spite of that she could see that his cheeks looked a little fat and puffy, not firm and hard as they used to.

It was time to wake him. She jiggled the edge of the bed. He came to, opening one eye reluctantly. He cleared his throat, stretched himself under the covers, and yawned. It took him a minute before he was able to gather resolution to throw back the covers and sit up on the edge of the bed, still yawning.

Afraid that she would start to cry, Judith turned and went out.

Trying to forget about it, she put on her gloves, took her clippers, and went out into the rose-garden. Strange that ten years ago there had not been a rose-bush on the ranch, and now some of them were old and gnarled; they changed faster than human beings. But did they? How long had it taken to change Juan?—less than two years of money and a soft life. Some people couldn't stand it. What was the use of trying to forget things? Even the rose-bushes reminded her.

Soon the popping of the pistols began, and that was an additional reminder. They were out behind the storehouse, she knew. Juan, Jerry, Miguel, Pablo, Juanito, Luis and Guito—quite a little army. Later on they would shift to rifles. It was appalling the amount of money they must be using up for powder and lead. And what use? It might have meant something in the days of Indian fighting, but now all it meant was that Juan was enamoured of American ways of doing things. He was always getting himself drawn into a shooting contest with side bets down at San José, and losing; by American standards he was still not much of a shot, probably never would be. Jerry Graham was the only one out there who was a decent rifle-shot; he was first-class, but he was an American to begin with. Luis (he was thirteen now) had a knack with the pistol; at wheel-and-fire he could even beat Jerry. Judith was glad Luis could beat Guito at something. Guito, though he was younger, was better than Luis at everything else—riding, roping, even rifle-shooting. But Luis had that touch of cold steadiness which counted with the pistol.

The pistol-shooting did not last long that morning. There was a pause, and then she heard Juan calling her from the house. His voice had a certain note in it which brought her up sharply; it was a new tone of vigour and decision—that is, the same tone his voice had carried in the old days. She hurried in.

He even looked different, standing there in the outer room. He had shaved. There was a vigour about him, and a light in the eyes, and his jowls were not so fallen. He was holding a piece of fresh cow-hide about a foot square.

"Look," he said.

It was the piece of hide bearing the brand. She saw the tied-X of Rancho Amarillo, the scar old and long healed; below, changing the tied-X to an hourglass was another line, a raw, unhealed burn.

"Those squatters at Ojuelo," said Juan. "Some of the men drove the cow in. We just slaughtered her."

It was the sheer bravado of it that appalled Judith and angered her. Brand-changing was something new in California; she had hardly heard of it before the Americans came. But that anyone could start changing brands on Rancho Amarillo within three miles of the ranch-house and not expect one of the vaqueros to spot the fresh scar before it healed! The whole action seemed a deliberate dare. "We're stealing your cattle—and what are you going to do about it?" These men had seen Juan only in the last few months—a middle-aged Californian, drinking and gambling, getting paunchy. How could they guess the fighter that lay beneath?

"We're going up now to run them off."

There was a sudden lightness in her heart at the almost gay tone.

"What if they won't run?" she asked provocatively.

His answer was a quick little laugh. He stepped forward and caught her in his arms. She clung to him with an almost forgotten happiness. She had hardly thought that she could ever feel it again. Then he spoke:

"You see, I've got to run them off; I won't be able to sell Ojuelo if there are squatters on it."

Judith was suddenly cold and sick. The reaction shocked her like a slap in the face. She squirmed loose. Even Juan might have noticed the sudden look of dismay and hatred on her face, but he spun about on his heel and strode out eagerly.

Sell Ojuelo! Like selling a child! It had stood, in the wordy official Spanish of the original grant—"to the topmost point of the hill beyond the valley known as Ojuelo." But, apart from sentiment, there was the real foolishness of it—to start selling land when obviously the only thing to do was to cut down expenses, and build up the herd. To get out of a tight place by selling land only meant that you would be the sooner in a tight place again and would have to sell more land, and then again.

But what was the use? In the old days Juan had never wanted money. She had kept the books and bought the supplies, and what he had spent was hardly noticeable Now it was different. He wanted money faster than the ranch could supply it, and he had used up the reserves. Legally or practically, there was nothing that a wife could do.

She felt a wild desire for freedom, and out of the blackness of her heart welled up a consciousness of the only way in which freedom could come. She did not force the thought down. Honestly, she looked upon Juan through a black veil of hatred. She hoped he would never come back. Those four Texans, the squatters, with their long rifles and lank yellow cheeks did not have a sinister look to her mind. She wished them luck.

A moment later she was half appalled at what she had been thinking, although she could not honestly take it back entirely. She heard the men mustering outside, and, still hesitating, she went to the window to look

How often in those thirteen years at the ranch had she seen the men mustering? Ramón was dead, and in the course of years the older men had dropped out Miguel was still there, dark-faced and taciturn, to ride behind his master Jerry Graham was there now, with hair so strangely like her own. Pablo and Juanito were there; they had been just boys when she first came to the ranch. That was all Juan was taking—himself and the four others. They would out-number the Texans only by one, but they were all good men. She saw Juan on the long-legged black stallion, casting his eye along the line for the last time, making his inspection.

Then, without knowing when or how it had happened, she knew that she had changed. This was her husband, and these were his men. Her heart would fight with them. She wanted to run out with a wild cry, to hold him again, to tell him to be careful. But he struck his spurs in, and the black jumped. They were gone.

It might have been that very first time he rode off—she was as much frightened. Yet that was so long ago. Even the black stallion was the grandson of Black Boy, whom Juan had ridden then. They had been his favourite horses, and had had English names. First Black Boy, the Black Hawk, then this one called Tall Boy, besides various cousins and uncles, like Blackfoot, who was killed that day the Americans had chased Juan.

U

Luis and Guito burst in, yelling that they were going to follow the men. Well, here was something different, anyway; she hadn't had two big boys around that first time. They both had pistols.

"You're *not* going; don't be crazy! You know your father wouldn't let you." Then, even before they had time to look crest-fallen or start to argue, she had a new idea: "Yes, you are going, and I'm going too. Get the horses."

She ran for bandages; that was an excuse at least. The real reason she was going was, she knew, that she could not stand the sus-pense.

They were not more than ten minutes behind the men, but Judith put her own horse into the lead, and held him in; it would never do to catch up. The boys were jumping with excitement; in the trail they watched the hoof-marks of the horses which had just passed. Mostly they saw the marks of a big-hoofed horse with a trick of throwing his right hind foot out a bit; that must be Miguel's horse, they decided. He would be riding last. Judith kept listening for the sound of shots.

Half-way to Ojuelo she pulled her horse out of the trail, and went off uphill to the right. The hills were easy, rolling ones here; you could ride across them anywhere. The boys looked puzzled, and wanted to ride ahead.

"No," she said, "they don't want a woman and a couple of boys tagging along."

They looked rebellious.

"And look here," she went on, "you're going to have to stay here to look after me." She had them there, she knew. They looked glum, but followed her.

She kept her horse at a walk; there was no pressing need for get-ting anywhere. Now for the first time she began to notice how hot it was. The perspiration was running from her; the horses were lathering. It was well on towards noon, and not a breath of breeze —oppressive. Insects buzzed in the grass. The grass—it brought her back. It was too long, too little grazed. That showed there were not enough cattle left on the ranch. She felt black thoughts at work again.

But what good outcome could there be? If Juan should be killed, could she ever face herself happily again? And if not, she felt herself caught as in a nightmare with a slowly tightening net—the ranch shrinking, debts, a mortgage, poverty, and the children to think of.

She sat slumped in the saddle. She felt the boys looking at her. She knew that her face must be woebegone, but she had no desire to cry. Too much hatred was mingling with her sorrow. The boys could not tell what she was thinking, and whatever happened they must never know.

She dared ride no farther now; only a ravine and another hill separated them from Ojuelo.

A shot! More! Half a dozen rattling off almost together. A pause while she and the boys breathed half a dozen times, open-mouthed and alert. Another, and two more. Then silence profound and un-broken, not even a breeze rustling in the grass.

She saw Luis looking big-eyed and worried, perhaps at the look in her own face. Guito's face was intensely alive.

" Rifles and pistols both," he said professionally.

All the shots must have come within twenty seconds. They waited two minutes perhaps, and then heard two more shots spaced a breath apart—*pung, pung.*

" Rifles those," said Guito.

They waited. " Which way? " Judith was thinking. " My God, which way? " It seemed no more than a minute, but it must have been longer.

" Look," said Guito, pointing over the ridge towards Ojuelo.

" Smoke," said Luis.

It was a few moments before Judith could make out anything, although the boys kept pointing. Then she saw the whitish-grey pillar—wispy, spreading out just a little as it rose, leaning a trifle towards the east as an imperceptible air-current carried it. It was silent, softly beautiful against the shiny blue of the sky; yet it was sinister. For a moment Judith thought only of the fire. She remem-bered the great fire that September when Guito was a baby, the one that had swept down with a north wind behind it; the men had managed to stop it only at the ridge behind the house. Her first impulse was to ride hard for the smoke; the boys were quite old enough to help fire-fighting.

Then she remembered the shots. She hesitated. If there was a fire wouldn't everybody stop shooting and help put it out? Or would they? Suddenly she was conscious of the boys in a quick, eager discussion.

" It won't be bad," said Guito. " The grass is hardly dry."

" There's no wind either," said Luis.

She saw a sudden light break upon Guito's face.

" That's not grass smoke," he cried. " It's not yellow enough."

They all three looked at one another puzzled. Judith was thinking, as she knew the boys were, of the tangled copse of Ojuelo. It must be years since it had been burned through; it was thick with old dead blackberry vines and dried twigs and branches; brown leaves of last year lay caught in the tangle. Once afire, it would blaze like a furnace. But it would be hard to get started; that was the funny thing.

" Look," said Guito, " there's another! "

Clear and distinct, another column of smoke was beginning to rise. The first one was big and thick now; it was starting to billow about as the heat waves rose in it. With a hollow feeling of something ugly and not understandable Judith led the way irresolutely downhill and back to the trail. She paused, not knowing which way to turn.

" Some one's coming," said Guito.

Judith had heard nothing, but she knew that Guito had caught the click of horseshoes as a rider went over a stony place; he had his father's eyes and ears for things in the open.

A rider broke into view. The boys' hands went to their pistols, and then relaxed. It was Jerry Graham

At a hand-gallop he came along, caught sight of them, and raised a hand in greeting. He held his long rifle across his saddle-horn; from beneath his hat Judith could see the long yellow hair curling out; he rode well, but not with the natural seat of a Californian. He's in no hurry, she thought; he rides like a man coming home after the work is finished. In a moment now she would know; whichever way it would be wrong.

He must have seen the strained look in her face.

" Your husband's all right, ma'am," he said.

Judith felt the blood go to her face. Yes, she was glad. Quickly, before she had time to think, she had felt herself suddenly glad. Whatever happened it would always be good to know that in the test she had been loyal.

"How about the others?" she asked mechanically. (What difference did it make?)

"Miguel's dead."

She heard a sudden cry of anger from Guito. She herself was looking at Jerry. Something was wrong with him; he had an ugly look of sullen defiance. And why, with a fire to fight, was he riding off?

"Where are *you* going?"

"Sorry, ma'am, but I'm quittin'. I'm goin' to pick up my traps at the ranch. I'm mighty sorry to be leavin'—to be leavin' *you*."

"But what happened? Why don't you fight the fire?"

He stood looking blank for a moment, and then Judith felt herself, as in the old confident days, flaring with quick anger.

"Speak up, man!" she snapped, as if talking to a servant. "What's wrong?"

"Well, you don't need to worry about them squatters any more. I shot one, and Pablo lanced another, and the other two got off into the brush, both wounded. Then we found they'd got Miguel, and I guess your husband went kind of crazy. He began yellin' his own brother's dead, and he started settin' the woods on fire. I come away. I don't mind killin' when you have to. But I don't like the idea o' burnin' wounded men alive, or settin' down with your rifle to wait for 'em to break cover."

He paused. There was nothing more to say or do. The silence lengthened out.

"Good-bye, ma'am," said Jerry, taking off his hat.

She felt that he was expecting her to hold out her hand, but she could not. She felt suddenly humiliated before him.

"Good-bye, Jerry," she said. As he rode off he did not replace his hat, and she could see his long yellow hair bright in the sunlight. Some deep feeling within herself went out towards him; they were the same kind, more than just by virtue of yellow hair. She knew how he felt. There was something hawk-like, of the honest open country, about Jerry—the strong flight, the quick swoop, and the clean kill.

The trail went over a rise. He did not look back. For a moment after he was gone, by a trick of eyesight, she still seemed to see the glint of his yellow hair against the sky. The boys sat their horses irresolutely beside her. As Jerry, the grown man, had ridden up and told his story their little self-confidence had collapsed. Now she saw that they were only little boys, looking towards their mother for guidance. She found herself wishing, almost for the first time in her life, that some one else—even the boys—would make a decision for her.

Finally she pulled her horse around and rode back towards the house. The boys followed without a word. She kept her horse at a walk; she wanted to let Jerry have time to get away from the ranch.

Again she had only black thoughts of the future—the ever-narrowing circle. If there were no Juan—that was as far as she would go—she might fight her way out. Jerry was a good man, and he could leave. She was a wife, and couldn't. And more than that, the old loyalty held her. Stronger than reason, she felt it, like something alien to herself within herself, and stronger—a last remnant of that same wild passion which years before had made her leave all her old life behind and scramble down from the *Spanish Belle* to be rowed through the darkness to where a black-haired horseman waited on the beach.

Just the faintest yellow shadow fell upon them, and they all glanced up. A wisp from the column of smoke had passed across the sun. Looking back, she saw that it was all one column of smoke now; the whole copse must be blazing.

Judith shuddered. Somewhere, as an old heritage of Juan's blood, she knew, there lurked a cold-blooded cruelty. Those campaigns against the Indians—there were questions she never dared ask or think about. And those men over in the burning copse at Ojuelo who had killed Miguel and were paying the price were Americans, not very good ones—but still, her own people. All she felt herself hoping was that, since Juan must kill in cold blood, he would at least kill quickly. She hoped the boys did not understand. She would never know for sure; she realized that. Pablo and Juanito, close-lipped with their Indian blood, loyal to their master—neither prayers nor torture would drag a secret from them.

Even at the ranch-house she could still see the column of smoke. The vaqueros had seen it, and were mounting to ride out and fight the fire. She ordered them in again. They looked at her wondering, but she did not even make up any excuse.

The fire burned for more than a hour, but did not spread. There was no wind, and so Pablo and Juanito must have had no difficulty in keeping it under control.

In mid-afternoon Juan and the two others rode in. Miguel's body lay across a horse; they brought no other bodies.

What story Pablo and Juanito told in the quarters Judith did not know. She herself asked no questions, and Juan said nothing. His face was black with soot from the fire, and the expression made it seem even blacker. Yet for a moment Judith pitied him, and wanted to run to him as of old. For she could see the sorrow in his face too—something deep which time would not heal, the passing of youth. Miguel had stood for something old in Juan's life, older and deeper even than herself—for the life of the cattle and horses and Indians and open grasslands, before there was gold, or Americans came. Miguel had stood for that which even Judith found herself speaking of regretfully as " the old days."

Without washing, he sat at the table, a brandy-bottle and glass before him. Lupe served him up beef with chile, beans, and tortillas. He ate mechanically, but heavily—with the blood, thought Judith, still on his hands.

He sat drinking through the afternoon, seeming to get no pleasure from it, but growing more and more sodden.

Judith saw to laying out the body, and sent down to the Mission for a priest to come up for the burial. Pablo had a wound in the upper arm; a revolver bullet had ploughed up the flesh, and was still embedded. With a quick, determined knife-stroke Judith cut the bullet out. She was not queasy at the rush of blood, nor did she feel any sympathy at Pablo's spasmodic wince of pain. All such matters seemed childish and far off.

The evening, after the children were in bed, was the worst of all. Miguel had not been married, but in the quarters a woman was wailing. Juan still sat at the table. A bottle and glass were before him, but he was no longer drinking much. He had slumped down in the chair. Smears of soot were still on his face, and the blackness of his beard was again beginning to show. His cheeks looked baggy and fallen.

Judith made ready for bed. It seemed the worst day she had ever known, and nothing but blackness ahead. Worse than all the thoughts of debt and poverty and humiliation was her horrible feeling about Juan. How, she wondered, would she ever be able to lie beside him again? She lay awake through the darkness, and saw the dawn come.

WHEN JUDITH WENT TO HER ROOM she threw herself on the bed and lay there a few minutes. More than at any time since the news had come, the press of her emotions weighed her down—despair, loneliness, and grief. She waited for the sounds which would show that Mr Melton had got up from the big chair in the outer room where he was sitting so glumly and gone off to the room where he was to sleep. She did not want to go to bed, but she wanted to be alone with her own troubles. Everything seemed to have ended so quickly. She had to think; she could not stand being there any longer with Mr Melton. He was kind and sympathetic, and suffering just as she was. He kept trying hard to do something helpful, when there was nothing helpful to be done. Even his attempts at conversation to take her mind away from things always ended gloomily; they were such obvious attempts that they never lured either of them into forgetfulness.

It was eleven o'clock when Judith came out. She went through the empty outer room and out of the front door. The moon was rising—an almost full moon, showing just a little wearing down along one edge. In the moonlight she could see the long-loved profile of her hills to the south, and below it the dark lines of the trees along the ravines. Close at hand she saw her fruit-trees still in leaf, and her rose-bushes.

One of the dogs came up and nuzzled her. She patted him mechanically; he was Chu-chu, Guito's pet, a lanky hound.

A breeze was setting in from the west; there was a chill of bay-fog in it; by midnight the moon would be behind mist.

That touch of chill and fog in the wind snapped her thoughts back. She remembered that other time when a boat, close-hauled to catch the western breeze, was steering south for the Mission landing. From five years back she felt the chill of that fog, and heard the *slap-slap* of waves under the prow. Then she was lying down, sinking off to sleep, happy in her own power which had brought her success. In the stern she saw the dark, cloaked forms—Mr Melton and the French doctor, and the boyish midshipman, so excited to be for the first time in command of his own craft. On that voyage they had come bearing life.

And now another boat steered south, and the waves must be *slap-slapping* under the prow just the same. But the three bodies that lay in the boat's bottom did not hear—Pablo and Juanito wrapped in their blankets, Juan in his coffin.

She would not even see his face. She understood. He had been shot twice at close range. She was just as glad that she need not see him again. He had changed in the last few months. She would rather remember his face as it had been in the years before—wearing that sudden look of rapture, as when he had turned and seen her first on the deck of the *Spanish Belle*; quickly alert as when he rode the trails looking for signs; eager yet restrained, like a tightly reined horse, as when he was mustering his men.

Since that night of madness when they had galloped off together through the streets of Monterey it was thirteen years and a few months She would remember the years, not the last few months.

It was like Mr Melton to arrange everything, and to come himself. She had tried to thank him, but he had looked at her a little strangely.

" Juan was my friend," he said.

He was thinking a long way back, Judith knew—back to days when San Francisco was a few houses among the windswept sandhills and the world seemed to stand still rather than to move. He was thinking all the way back to the days when Juan was little more than a lad, and the two of them had traded languages to each other—Juan fluent and quick, Mr Melton haltingly grammatical.

There seemed to be nothing practical that she could do about it. There was little justice to be had in the San Francisco courts as yet, said Mr Melton; and anyone brought to trial would plead self-defence and have his own witnesses. Probably Juan had been right, and there had been cheating—but it would be impossible to prove it.

" It would have happened——" Mr Melton had started to say and then stopped. She knew what he had meant: it would have happened sooner or later, anyway, the life Juan was leading.

Without being told, Judith could see it all. The room with the cigar-smoke drifting heavily about, the whisky-glasses on the table, stakes high and the hour late and the nerves worn thin with tension. Juan's quick accusation at the suspicious turn of a card, men reaching for their guns, the sudden roar of the shots, Pablo and Juanito closing in, but the bullets too quick for the knives. Just another brawl in a gambling den, men would say. But this time it was Juan Godoy and his two men who were carried out. Before they got him, Mr Melton said, Pablo had slashed one gambler from the shoulder-point to the middle of the back; that would be all the revenge Juan would ever have.

From the quarters she heard the wail of women. Catalina was mourning her eldest son, that little Juanito who had been only ten years old when Judith had ridden up from Monterey as a bride. She remembered him, happy-faced with excitement, at the time of the first Indian raid, when Juan had sent him riding south with the warning. And Pablo too. When she had first come to the ranch with Juan they had stopped at the Garcías, and she remembered Pablo, a lithe youngster of fifteen. Even that day Juan had talked with Pablo; Juan always had an eye for lads who might make good fighting men. Now they were all gone—the dark-faced men with their knives in their boots, who had ridden behind their master— Ramón and Miguel, Pablo and Juanito. And their master was gone too. . . .

She could see the mist coming in high over the western hills now; it had not yet reached the moon. She walked back and forth close in towards the house to keep out of the wind. In a way she felt calmer to-night than she had for weeks. She had been waiting for the worst to happen; now things were down to rock-bottom. To be killed in a gambling brawl was not the most honourable of deaths, but there might have been worse. She had had her moments of fear that Juan might take his revenge upon the Americans and the new ways of life as many an old-time vaquero and rancher had done—by turning to cattle-stealing, holding up pack-trains in the

mines, or waylaying solitary miners. That at least had not happened.

Now she could start things again, by herself. It would be hard
to get going. Ojuelo was sold and the money spent; the herd was
depleted; the lawyer was demanding payment; they owed money
to storekeepers in San José. But it could be done. Her face grew
hard. She would get rid of some of the useless vaqueros. For a
year they would live on their own cattle and what they could raise.
She would plant a field of wheat again. Luis was old enough to
help. They could raise vegetables, and they had fruit. That was
more than they had in the old days. In a year or two the herd
would build itself up. There was money in cattle in California; the
miners had to eat, and would pay in gold. The only thing was
not to bleed the ranch too fast as they had been doing. She could
manage things, now that she had the chance.

She looked up, and saw Mr Melton standing by the doorway.
His very attitude looked an apology for his intrusion. She felt a
tug of affection for his dogged old friendship.

"I'm glad you came out," she said. It seemed the only polite
thing she could say, and she more than half meant it; she had had
her chance to think the matter over.

"I don't want to intrude," he said, "but I couldn't sleep, and
I heard you out here, and I thought maybe I could help some. I've
thought of one thing. I owe a lot to you and Juan, you know.
Well, things may not have been going very well lately—with the
ranch; if you need anything, money, you know, let me help; I've
got lots now."

It had come pat upon her thoughts, but in a way Judith felt
sorry. She had been making up her mind for something heroic;
with a loan from Mr Melton it would be easy.

They talked plans. Mr Melton said she should round out the
ranch again by buying back Ojuelo. In that case, said Judith, she
would keep all the vaqueros. The thought made her happy, for
she still liked to think that they were retainers, not hired-men.
She was lucky, said Mr Melton, in having an iron-clad title to the
ranch. Judith thought of the yellowed parchment which had
knocked about so long in the chest. Since the Americans came it

had become important. Lawyers looked and grew suddenly respectful, for it bore the seal and signature and rubric of a Spanish Governor. It was none of your flimsy grants that Don Pío had showered on his friends during the last doubtful days of the Mexican rule.

They walked back and forth a long time. They did not talk much, but they kept walking on account of the chill in the air. The mist had covered the moon, and the valley began to look dimly silvered.

She remembered that once long ago they had walked together along the deck of the *Spanish Belle* on a chilly moonlit night, and stood looking out at some island in the Antarctic—what was its name?—with the mountains and the snow running down in the ravines. That was just the opposite to what it was here, with the ravines standing out dark instead of white. That was long ago. A lot had happened since.

" Do you remember," she said, " the night old Uncle Enrique talked about life being like a stream dashing down through the hills for a while and then wandering along, slow, in a valley? "

" Yes," he said. They walked the length of the house again.

" We've had plenty of dashing down through the hills lately, haven't we? Wars, and raids, and the gold-rush, and squatters, and Indians and revolutions before that. Maybe we're going to have a rest now."

" You can't tell. California is nothing but a powder-barrel still; anything may blow it up. If Congress doesn't admit us, people are talking about a Pacific Republic. Yet, you can't tell. Perhaps we'll have a quiet time; perhaps, even, we'll live quietly all the rest of our lives."

Suddenly Judith realized that she would probably not want to live a quiet life always. For a while, yes. Mr Melton might like it for always; he was not very strong, or much of a fighter Again, as on the *Spanish Belle* long ago, she felt the difference between them. There was Juan too. He had needed the hard life of a fighter. As soon as life had got easy he had gone to pieces. " It's ripe, not dead," he had said once of the grass; she had always remembered the phrase. She wished that she could think of him as having ripened, but she could not. He had been part of the old ways of life, and when the new ways came he could live only by feeding upon some kind of false excitement.

"It's strange," she said at last. "During all those quiet years on the ranch I looked forward to when civilization would come; and when it came it brought only trouble and disaster—like this."

"Yes," said Mr Melton thoughtfully—"but this isn't civilization We're still in the turmoil of one way of life changing into another Give us a few more years—better steamers, a railway across the Isthmus of Panama, maybe one across the continent, people pouring in from everywhere, Asia and Europe mingling with America. You'll see. We need time to settle down and mature. Give us a few years, and we'll be civilized as well as any part of the world. We'll have a civilization you can be proud of."

IN 1851 JUDITH GODOY AND DANIEL MELTON WERE MARRIED. It was nothing to occasion comment; with ten men to one woman in California the early remarriage of widows was taken for granted. They had been close friends for years, and now both were lonely. She was thirty-five years old; he was fifty. It was a very satisfactory marriage.

They built a great mansion on the Stockton Street hill, and Judith brought the family up from the ranch to live in it—not only the children, but the house-servants too. The children liked the new arrangement, and throve. But it did not work as far as the servants were concerned. The children were getting too old to need Antonia as a nurse; Catalina could never come to conceive the duties of a chambermaid on Stockton Street hill; cookery in San Francisco called for something more than Lupe's beef, beans, and tortillas. Then old Lupe herself settled the matter by snuffing out with lung-fever in January of '52. After that Judith pensioned off the two others, and they went to live at Mission San José where they would be close to two of Catalina's numerous children. Antonia was a little dried-up old woman now, still shrewd-faced; Catalina was nearly as old, and was very fat. They both wept when they left, and Catalina, who never had had very good control in times of stress, forgot her Spanish and started babbling some Indian gibberish. In spite of herself Judith wept too; it was the breaking of another link

Judith soon dried her tears, and engaged a butler and a chef. Before long she had a French maid, and a housekeeper, and a governess for Leticia and Enrique, besides a coloured coachman and Big Mike as bodyguard, and whatever minor servants were needful. There was much social life and much keeping up with one's neighbours in those years when San Francisco was getting to be one of the chief cities of the country.

Mr Melton grew richer. He kept to the simple formula: " Lease; don't sell." As fires and business panics swept across the newly built city his holdings might fluctuate in value, but in the end they were always worth more than they had been before.

The children almost came to forget that they had Spanish blood and had once lived on a ranch. Luis and Enrique took to spelling their names ' Lewis ' and ' Henry.' Mr Melton and Judith wanted Lewis to go East to college, but he preferred business to a profession. When he was eighteen (men started life young in California) he became junior partner in " Thompson & Godoy." Mr Melton's money backed the new firm, which specialized in marine insurance.

" Marine insurance! " thought Judith sometimes—Juan would not have known what it meant, and anyone would have had difficulty even in making him understand the suppositions upon which it was based. The development of such a business showed the way in which life was growing more complex. Between 1850 and 1856 California was settling down. Gentlemen were talking of ' business,' and ladies of ' culture.' Gold production was still the basic industry, but it too was becoming a business. The adventurous single miner with pan and cradle was yielding to the capitalized company which built quartz-mills, or ' flumed ' whole rivers, or washed away hills with hydraulic monitors.

The career of Judge Wingram epitomized the history of that time. In '46 he came to California with the " great immigration." He was thirty-six years of age, and his resources were seven hundred dollars in gold, a membership in the Kentucky bar with a complimentary title of " Judge," and a personality excellently adapted to his environment. To cross the plains in '46 was much like attending the right college; it gave you a chance to make the proper contacts. The Judge arrived in California as the good friend of Hastings, Grayson, Reed, Bryant, Lippincott, and others who were to be worth knowing in the next few years; in '47 he met Frémont, Brannan, and Sutter. Disappointed in his hopes of becoming an officer in the Californian Battalion, the Judge served as volunteer in the irregular force mustered at San José by Captain Weber, and in this capacity he pursued Juan Godoy and came to spend the night at Rancho Amarillo. In '48 he went to the mines, but he soon decided that more money with less work could be made in San Francisco In '49 he was little better than a professional gambler; helped by Mr Reynolds and many others, he assisted in the fleecing of Juan Godoy. At that time he and Mr Melton first became acquainted. The Judge was neither brilliant nor profound, and he made a poor impression upon Mr Melton; but he had a vein of shrewdness, plenty of energy and determination, and a complete lack of anything so hampering as a conscience. While his cronies like Mr Reynolds sank into obscurity the Judge progressed. In '50 he left gambling with cards for the scarcely more respectable but much more profitable business of city politics. In '51 he was a " Law and Order " man, and the Committee of Vigilance had him in its books; but he weathered that blustery, brief gale. By '52 he was getting out of direct participation in politics, and was becoming an " investor." He obtained from the legislature the franchise for a toll-road, and manipulated it very profitably; he organized companies for a brewery and a foundry. At this time he left off wearing a revolver at the hip and substituted a pocket-derringer. In '53 and '54 he built the Glorietta House, bought the San Francisco *Gazette* and three up-country weeklies, and acquired title to much real estate, including a good half of the sporting district of Stockton. In these years also he gradually left off driving his two fast trotters through the best San Francisco streets while he sat in an open carriage beside his French mistress. With the Judge, wealth and respectability advanced in equal strides. He began subscribing to charities and Church funds; he continued to swear like a gentleman, but he dropped from his ordinary vocabulary certain obscene terms. In '55 he married pretty little Alicia Delong of Alabama. Alicia's southern accent was so soft that it seemed squashy, but, concealed behind her simper, she had brains; she definitely swung the Judge over the line into the safe grounds of respectability. They bought a house on Stockton Street hill only a block from the Meltons.

The summer of '56 was momentous in San Francisco. Casey shot James King of William, and the Committee of Vigilance reorganized. From Fort Gunnybags its cannon kept the city quiet while the work of civic reform went forward. Lewis Godoy served

x

with the artillery that summer, and Guito with the cavalry. Mr
Melton, although well past military age, was a member of the
Committee and helped largely with contributions. And, as a final
evidence of respectability, Judge Wingram was a member also, and
even sat in some of the inner circles.

This fellowship may have made Mr Melton feel less cool towards
the Judge; besides, little Alicia had twice picked Mr Melton up
in her carriage and driven him up the hill, although he protested
he was walking for exercise. (Alicia had not gone very far in
social circles as yet, but she had plenty of time and was playing
her cards.)

Some weeks later the Meltons were planning a dinner, and
Judith was surprised when Daniel suggested asking the Wingrams.
"You can't hold a man's past too much against him," he said.
"Not in California, anyway. The Judge seems pretty respectable
now, and he's got a nice wife."

Judith, with the Rancho Amarilla affair always in her memory,
had never liked the Judge, and she had an instinctive mistrust of
Alicia's soft accent and simper and sloping shoulders. But still
she was glad to ask the Wingrams if Daniel wanted to. There
was certainly no important reason for snubbing them; many of
the more careful hostesses in San Francisco had already received
them.

But the on-coming of that dinner gave Judith much worry. To
cap everything, at the last moment Mrs Grainger sent regrets on
account of a sick headache. Judith hurried off Big Mike with a
note to Guito, but Guito answered that he couldn't come to dinner,
having an engagement with some friends at a shooting gallery.
Well, she knew she couldn't count on Guito to go out of his way
to help in a pinch, but she could count on Lewis. She would go
and find him; besides, there was some trouble about the wine,
and she had better see Daniel about that. Then there was the
queer business of the note from Mrs Donovan, whoever that was.
She could just as well have put this last matter off till the morning, but since she was going down-town anyway she could attend
to it now. She told Mike to have Sam get the victoria ready.

PART THREE
1856–1861

CHAPTER I . . . . . OCTOBER 1856

IT TOOK JUDITH several minutes to get herself properly settled in the seat of the victoria. Dresses were dresses that season, with all their flounces and ruffles and underskirts. By the time she had got herself comfortably and becomingly arranged and had tilted her parasol properly, more for show than for protection, Sam had already swung the greys off Stockton Street and the victoria was tipping forward with the slope of the Sutter Street hill.

Judith looked approvingly at the backs of the two men on the driver's seat. Sam, the coachman, was in his new plum-coloured uniform, and even the back of his shiny black neck seemed to glow with an added sheen of approbation and pleasure at the appearance which he felt himself making. On his left, Big Mike was a massive figure in black; it was only semi-livery, but they had been afraid that he would object even to that. Mike was something of an anachronism, anyway, Judith reflected; bodyguards had been out of fashion for several years now in San Francisco.

"Turn up Montgomery Street," she said, "and keep a look-out for Mr Melton, or Mr Luis—Mr Lewis, I mean."

"Yessum," said Sam.

Judith was a little irked at having used the old name; the very fact of her doing so showed, she supposed, that she disapproved of the change. It did seem quite a needless smashing up of one more old cherished association. Not that she had raised any objections when he had consulted her. It was his own affair, and she could easily see the inconveniences of the Spanish form and the business advantages which would result from the change. Still . . .

As they turned north into Montgomery she began looking about for either her husband or her son. She could stop of course and

323

send Mike in to the offices, but either of them was just as likely to be on the street. Lewis was always running here and there about his insurance business, and Mr Melton was often going from one to another of the buildings he owned. Sure enough, at Pine Street she saw Mike wave, and Sam pulled over to the kerb.

Lewis came up, handsome and smiling. Dark like his father, thought Judith, for perhaps the millionth time, but otherwise not much like him—an inch taller, anyway. She gave him her hand. a little formally.

"How are you, mother?" he said. "I haven't seen you since Sunday."

Judith smiled inwardly at the touch of Spanish intonation in his voice; Lewis had always had it. He might Americanize his name, but not his tongue.

"I wanted to see you," she began.

"Just a moment, just a moment. I'm going to compliment you first. The dress is splendid That shade of green was always your colour. And the hair and the rest of your appearance—perfect!"

Judith did not even try to disguise her pleasure—after all, a compliment from one's son when he was eighteen and you forty! . . . She was about to return a compliment upon his own appearance—for Lewis always dressed with care; but then she noticed that the ends of his trouser-legs were wet and draggled.

"What's the matter?" she said, pointing.

"Oh, there's a little excitement in the marine insurance line; the *Orizaba* sank at her dock, and when a ship as big as that does something we all jump. I've been poking around her. Somebody must have left some valves open—on purpose maybe; I don't see how the bottom could just fall out of her. But she ought to be easy to raise—not much loss."

"Did you hold any insurance on her?"

"Yes, she's too big for any company to handle alone. Not much, though; nothing to worry about as things stand."

"Since it's no worry, what I wanted to see you about was dinner to-night."

Lewis did not look particularly pleased.

"Oh, but you have to come, I'm afraid," she went on, giving

him her best smile; she knew anyway that he would never turn her down. "Mrs Grainger just sent regrets. I tried to get Guito to fill in, but he couldn't—or wouldn't. It leaves me with nine instead of ten, and that's impossible. So you must come; it's important."

"Very important! Anyone can see that. Of course, I'll have to come."

"Fine. It's going to be a good dinner, in the best Melton style."

' Sounds like a threat. But tell me who'll be there, so I can get ready for the worst."

"Judge and Mrs Wingram and the Buxtons——"

"That's a pretty stodgy beginning, except Mrs Wingram."

"Well, then, Lieutenant Grainger; he's not stodgy."

"Not that clown, no. He's capable of anything. His idea of a really bright joke is to paint some buckshot green and mix them with peas."

"And there's Sir Robert Tyneman——"

"Lion-hunting, eh? The visiting English sportsman I've been reading about in the papers."

"The last man is a Mr Burke. I don't know him; Mr Melton wanted him asked."

"Not *Tony* Burke? He'd be ' the last man ' as far as I was concerned."

"Anthony—yes, that's it."

"That wild Irishman! I know him, but I didn't think Mr Melton had taken him up. Well, he's not really so bad, after all, and he can be amusing. At seven-thirty, as usual."

As he moved off Judith found herself about to shout, " Be sure to change your shoes." But she thought better of it. After all, Lewis was nearly nineteen, living in bachelor quarters, getting a business started. He could look after his own wet feet; besides, he never took colds, anyway. She liked the idea of his being connected with marine insurance—at least the ' marine ' part. It was not like actually being a shipmaster, of course, but still it seemed to give him just a little touch with his grandfather and all the Hinghams before him who had followed the sea. She came of a seafaring family, Judith reflected; in spite of all her years among the hills, she had never quite forgotten the salt water It was good to be in San Francisco, and to look out from her window and see the clippers. Some time. she felt, she would like to return even more intimately to the sea.

She had to send Mike in after Mr Melton.

"Well, my dear," he said, " you look wonderful."

" There must be something about me to-day," said Judith. " Lewis just complimented me too. But I mustn't keep you. I wanted to tell you there are only two bottles of your Saint-Émilion left, and that's not enough to be safe for to-night."

" Good. I'll see Fourchard about it. As it happens, though, it was your business I was just busy with. Foster sent in another long letter from the ranch. That man should be an author. Put six or eight of his letters end to end. and they would be as long as a novel by Charles Dickens. Just as fictitious too, but not as funny. This time he even has the inventive power to tell me that Joaquin Murrieta is still alive and is devoting his special talents to stealing our cattle."

" Murrieta means Foster, that's obvious. I suppose we'll have to try some one else. It's discouraging. Will we lose money this year? "

" We'll probably not actually lose, but it will be a little profit where it should be a big one. That doesn't matter, of course."

He paused, and she could see a little worried look in his kindly grey-blue eyes; the hair was still plentiful above his forehead, but it was mostly grey.

"You know," he went on, " the money isn't it, but I'm sentimental, I suppose. I hate to see the old ranch abused and a man like Foster running it. Even if he were honest—still he has no feeling for the place. He'd be just as likely to overgraze, and start gullies on all the hillsides. I'd like to do something that would be right for the place, even if it cost us money. Lord knows, we're making plenty here! "

She saw him cast his eyes right and left at the buildings fronting on the other side of the street. In this single block she knew that he owned three buildings on one side and one on the other— and it was the best business district in San Francisco.

" Speaking of the ranch," she said, " I'm on an errand right now which has some connexion with it. Did you ever know Jerry Graham —that young fellow with the bright yellow hair? I had a note from him to-day "

" Oh—yes. I remember the hair. I saw him once with Juan in San Francisco here; we went out to a bull-and-bear fight. I liked him. So you had a note from him? "

" Well, not exactly, either. It's from his landlady. He's in trouble, and of course he'd be the last sort of person to write for help when he was in trouble. I imagine she heard him mention me, and so she wrote."

" Wants her board money? "

" It's worse than that, I'm afraid. Jerry's sick."

" I see, Mrs Ivanhoe-Marmion, and you're going down to look after the man who once ate your salt at Castle Amarillo."

Judith tried to pout at his making fun of her, although she knew he approved But her face was as badly adapted for a pout as for a simper; so she had to smile instead.

" Where's the address? " he asked.

" Torrey Street. Mike says he knows."

" Hm-m. Pretty bad district. Six months ago I wouldn't have let you go there even with Mike and Sam. The Vigilance Committee has things so well cleaned up now that I'll let you chance it. Got plenty of cash? He may need it "

" Yes, plenty, thanks."

Sam clucked, and the grey moved along. Torrey Street, according to Mike, was a little alley-way over somewhere towards Pacific and Battery, on the new land where the cove had been filled in.

The cobblestones were rough, and the streets were thick with drays. It was slow going, and Judith settled back comfortably on her cushions.

She was feeling very well satisfied with herself and her surroundings. Two compliments in a morning was not bad after you had passed your fortieth birthday. And indeed the image in her own mirror just before starting out had been reassuring. Bottlegreen had always been her colour. And now she really felt that she had come into a kind of late summer or early autumn beauty. She had always had her hair, but her face had been too strong-featured, and her figure with the square-set shoulders also was strong rather than beautiful. The shoulders still stuck out, but maturity and a little increased weight had mellowed the rest of her figure. Her features were large, but no one expected a woman of forty to have a girlish beauty, and now she made up in dignity what she lacked in prettiness.

And there was no denying that the backing of Daniel's money would help any woman's poise. She could not pass a block here on Montgomery Street without seeing a building or two which were Daniel's, or else built on land leased from him. San Francisco was no longer a city of shacks either. Right and left, Montgomery Street was a solid wall of buildings, many of them substantial brick or stone and three or four stories high. There were not many streets in Boston or New York, she imagined, that made a better appearance. Some time soon she and Daniel planned to go back and see for themselves.

She hoped it would be soon. And then, as if that had been a signal, Judith became aware of a feeling of which she had been more and more conscious lately: she was bored. She had had safety, and luxury, and riches, and prominence for five years—and she was bored. Already in the mansion on Sutter Street the French cook was at work upon the dinner for to-night; the Sauterne was cooling, and Fourchard had probably by now sent up the special Saint-Émilion which Daniel favoured. Suddenly Judith wanted Lupe's beans; she wanted the rough texture of tortillas between her teeth, and the sting of the raw red wine which came from the vineyard on the hill behind the ranch-house.

She had no complaint against Daniel. He was fifteen years older than she, and getting very grey. With him she could never recapture the splendour and the glory of her love for Juan during those years on the ranch. But then she herself was forty; perhaps no woman at forty could feel as she had felt in her twenties. And she was very fond of Daniel.

Sometimes she thought she would like another baby. But that failure she could not honestly blame on him. During the last five years when she had lived with Juan she had had no children either

She had strained herself, she realized, that time when she had ridden for the French doctor and miscarried afterwards. She had never been quite so well since; that would probably account for there being no more babies. Anyway, she was not sure that a baby would make any real difference. She had four children now, and they were all growing up and doing well—except Leticia perhaps; she never seemed to be able to get along with Leticia.

By the time the greys turned into Pacific Street she had got as far as thinking that perhaps she needed to fall in love again. It was being done, she knew. Many a simpering little thing whom you saw sewing garments at the meeting of the Ladies' Assistance Society was really tl inking about what she would do when her husband was gone to Sacramento. In San Francisco you could find ten eligible young men for every lady, with plenty of money too—and not all of them were content with Pacific Street.

Yet the whole matter rather disgusted Judith—a hole-and-corner business. It was not her style. Of course it meant nothing to think about it in the abstract; you had to meet the particular man. She had received plenty of oglings, pressings of the hand, assiduous adjustings of the cloak, quite respectful advances of foot and knee under the table. But those particular men had left her where she was.

All this life—what was there in it? Receptions, balls, charitable fairs, excursions on the Bay, the Ladies' Assistance Society, ten-minute calls, the theatre, *musicales* with Mrs Some One singing *Juanita*, a fashionable watering-place with its dust and mild flirtation in the summers. There were times when one liked it, as when Mrs Hayne played *Camille*, lovely in her golden-brown hair with that little fluff always about it. But take even her own dinner to-night. It would be a ceremony, a lusty rite; you would eat and drink your way through it as you might sit down to besiege and capture a fortress. All the way you would go from oysters to dessert, or by the liquid route—champagne, sherry, claret, Sauterne, liqueurs, coffee, and then port in the drawing-room afterwards. And when it was over you were done, and only felt fuller than you wanted to be.

And this was what California had changed into—that land east of the giants, where anything might happen! And now it was nothing more than marine insurance, and Judge Wingram's soap company, and the chitter-chatter of the Ladies' Assistance Society.

She barely noticed that as they went along Pacific Street the appearance of things got worse. A drunken man shouted some remark at the clean-limbed greys and the black-lacquered victoria. Mike scowled. They probably put me down as some politician's mistress, to be driving alone here, she thought. No, I forgot, the Vigilance Committee has stopped that sort of thing—so openly, anyway.

Vigilance Committee—that was the strange thing. Her own life had been quiet since she came to San Francisco, and yet it was not because life in San Francisco was quiet. Yes, when you thought of it that way California was still not so far perhaps from the land of the giants. She had lived through two Vigilance Committees and several big fires; ships had sunk and steamers blown up, cholera had raged, speculations had puffed up and collapsed and the ruined men had shot themselves; men had hurried off by thousands on this or that rumour of new gold-fields; 'down-and-outers' had starved to death in the streets. Yet through it all she had passed as through a meadow. It did not make sense. She was too far from where things started. She ate her roast beef without seeing the steer it came from, without seeing the blood flow, often without even seeing the red meat before it was cooked.

Sam had pulled the greys to a halt, and Mike was inquiring the location of Torrey Street from a shabby-looking local inhabitant. Mike was an anachronism—well, so was she. She had left civilization to go to the wilderness, and now that civilization had overtaken her she found that she did not much admire or like it. Most of the old-time Californians who had been her kinsfolk and companions for so long were frankly anachronisms now, unless—as was so often true—they were dead. Here and there one of them like Don Mariano Guadalupe had come out on top. But mostly they were in a bad way, like the debonair Don Juan Bautista, Juan's cousin, who had led the revolution of '36 but was now sitting quietly and drinking. Castros, Fuentes, Jaramillos, Osanas, Cavarros —they were a broken people now; pillaged and shot by squatters,

hounded into banditry, fleeced by land-agents, bled white by litiga-
tion costs. And most of it, Daniel said, was all because the United
States had not lived up to the spirit of the treaty rights.

Paugh! In her disgust something primitive as of the old days
came to the surface, and Judith spat. It was most unladylike to
spit, especially from a victoria. She hoped that Mike and Sam had
not seen. But she was glad she had done it. When she used to go
riding on the ranch she had spat when she felt like it, and Juan
always laughed at her.

They must be very close to Torrey Street now. Yes, she was an
anachronism, worse than Mike. She ought to have died—well, say
about the time Juan did, or a little before. That was the way to finish.
That would have been the time to finish off cleanly. Yet after all
there wasn't anything unusual in being an anachronism. She had
read plenty of history People—individuals—couldn't all die neatly
at the end of what historians called " periods." And that kept most
lives from being shaped like stories. Even the great men lived too
long, or else they died too soon. The ones who died too soon made
the *ifs* of history—" If Brian Boru hadn't been killed at Clontarf "
. . . " If young Prince Henry had lived " . . that sort of thing.
Napoleon lived too long and spoiled the ending. Only occasionally
a man like Lord Nelson had sense enough—artistic sense, that is—
to go into battle with all his medals on, so as to be a shining mark
to the sharpshooters and die at the proper moment. There weren't
many Nelsons. She herself was more ordinary stuff; she let herself
live on.

T HE ROOM WAS SMALL and gloomy and damp, with an earthen floor. It was really a sort of cellar. At times of very high tides the water backed up and stood in a smelly puddle in the lowest corner of the room. Then the walls got a little damp too, and sweated a lot and smelled. But that did not happen very often—not more than two or three times a month probably. To-day there was only a little show of water in the corner.

Jerry Graham lay rolled in his two blankets on a pile of dirty straw in the corner of the room farthest from where the dampness was. But the room was so small that his feet were not more than a yard or so from the damp spot.

Jerry was lying quite still, except that now and then he coughed. Once he sniffed. As usual, he reflected, there was some kind of new smell in the room. That was the trouble. You could get used to any particular smell, but when the smell changed you minded it. He had got pretty well used to the damp and the chill, for they didn't change much. His feet had been half numb for so long that it seemed natural.

He tried to lie still again, but soon he itched and had to squirm. With one hand he scratched weakly in his untrimmed yellow beard and his long, stringy yellow hair. One advantage of the cold and damp was that the fleas and flies and mosquitoes left him alone, but the grey-backs were working on him pretty hard. Besides, he hadn't had a bath for a long time, or even a chance to wash very well. That made a man itchy, and sore on the skin of the joints where he had to lie.

No, it wasn't the cold or the damp he minded so much. Many times, a week on end maybe, he had slept in the rain or the frost or the melting snow out on the mountains when he was trapping. But on the mountains you always had good air, and lots of it. Here the air was always the same, and you breathed it over and

332

over until it seemed foul. Then at night you got suddenly too stuffy and warm and broke out into horrible sweats and dreamed, and then woke up suffocating. And the air would still be close and foul even after you woke up; and you couldn't do anything about getting better air. And really you would not be too warm, even though you had sweated, but so cold that you shivered. That bad air was the worst thing; it made him feel trapped and shut in, and he was a man who had always lived in the open.

Well, pretty soon he would be getting well, and could go out again. He had never been sick really in his life before, except for that fever in the gold-mines; and when a strong young fellow like himself got sick he just laid up for a while and then got well and went about his business. Maybe it was having that accident first, getting his ribs smashed, that made it so hard for him to get over this sickness.

In the spring he had taken the room upstairs because it was cheap and had a little sun and a scrap of a view out over blue water in the Bay. And Mrs Donovan had seemed a pleasant sort of person then. He had thought his ribs would be well in a month and he would be over his cough too, and that would have been long before he used up all the money they had given him after the benefit. But the weeks had gone on, and he wasn't strong enough to go out, and after his money was gone Mrs Donovan got nasty and moved him down here and started pawning his things, or probably selling them. Pretty nearly everything was gone now, even his rifle. That was a good rifle, and ought to have brought money enough to last quite a while.

Sometimes he got afraid, especially when he coughed a lot and there was blood. And he hated the smells and the crawling feeling on him. But mostly he was too weak to care much. Sometimes he was so shaky he couldn't go upstairs and out to the privy; so he just crawled over into the damp corner. He hated that horribly, especially because he was afraid it might be worse for his sickness.

It was strange for him, such an active fellow, to have to lie up all summer when so much was happening in the city. The only way he knew the Vigilance Committee had taken over the city was when search-parties had come through the house twice looking for some one. The tall skinny man who led the last one had warned Mrs Donovan to clean up this room. But she hadn't, and nothing had happened. The Vigilance Committee was probably busy enough with other things.

So mostly he was too weak even to care about anything, and to get away from things he had learned to let himself slide into a kind of dream, thinking about what used to be, far off. He must have thought over most of his life, he guessed, about sixteen times. He tried not to think about the worst things, like the time when pap got drunk and larruped him with the horsewhip, and the time when they found Whitey and old John after the Apaches had had them. But he liked to think of the Two Lick Hills with the wild turkeys calling, and his first deer, and one or two girls. Those old things were harder to bring back to mind; so mostly he thought of what was closer at hand and he could remember better, like the time he had been at Rancho Amarillo. He liked the señora there and the boys, but Don Juan sure was a ' beaver-gut.'

Most of all he thought about the time when he had been with the troupe, for that was what had happened last of all. He hated some things about the troupe—the way he had to show off and all. But he liked old Sol who owned the outfit, and José and Mario who did the riding and roping stunts were all right. Even Walter Sterling, the lead man, wasn't so bad; he was stuck up, but white just the same; and he sure could say his lines so that he didn't sound like any ordinary talking. It was great.

Sol called the outfit " Jaggard's Old English Equestrian Troupe." Jerry couldn't ever make out why, for Sol's last name was Friedman and he was Jewish. And nobody in the troupe even claimed to be English, except the soubrette, who was most likely lying. They put on their shows in a big tent like a circus—usually shows that called for a lot of riding about and shooting, like *Nick of the Woods*, and *Putnam, the Iron Son of '76*. In between the acts they would put on kind of circus stunts. José and Mario would ride bucking horses and throw steers and flip knives and pick up things off the ground at full gallop, and do things with ropes that made you think they were magic. Sol always introduced José and Mario as the " champeen buckaroos of all Mexico and Central

America." Really they had grown up on a ranch down by Los Angeles, and weren't much better than some other vaqueros Jerry had seen.

Between a couple of the other acts Jerry came on for his own stuff, and Sol would introduce him as "Jerry Graham, the master scout and trapper, companion of the great Kit Carson, and sharer with him in the glories of the great Pathfinder, Colonel Frémont." Jerry didn't like that because he had only seen Kit Carson once, and Frémont not very often—and from what he'd heard from the other boys he figured he didn't admire Frémont. And he was always afraid one of the real old-timers from the mountains would be in the audience and would get up with a big ha-ha and say, "Jerry Graham, who's he?—nothing but a little bastard of a youngster who ain't dry behind the ears and never saw the mountains till after '40!

But that never happened, and Jerry always got through his act pretty well. Old Sol would say. "Jerry Graham shooting from a range of fifty yards will now put three bullets into a piece of paper so that the bullet holes make only one hole." The range was never much more than about a hundred feet really, and with good rifles well loaded there was nothing to it. Besides he always had big-bore rifles and the softest kind of lead bullets, so they would splatter plenty and make a big hole Sol made him spend a lot of time loading and aiming, so that it would look harder. And while he was doing this the men they had planted in the audience would make bets.

After Jerry had done it to three pieces of paper he would make his mark on each of them, and they would sell them to the people in the audience for souvenirs. Jerry could have written his name all right, but Sol said it was better for him to seem not able to write. Sol was particular about everybody keeping up a reputation. He wouldn't let Jerry pick up money when people threw it down to him. Instead, one of the boys picked it up, and Jerry got his share all right later.

It was the same way when anyone started getting vulgar. One of Jerry's stunts was to shoot the pips out of cards. The ushers would pass a deck of cards around, and a man would take maybe the eight of clubs and say, "I want the left-hand upper pip shot out." Then if Jerry could do it, and he usually could, the man would buy the card back as a souvenir. And almost always some one who was drunk or thought he was funny would pick out a queen and yell out, "Queen of Diamonds—shoot the left tit off her!" The audience would laugh, but Jerry would fold his arms and look hurt, and Sol would be indignant and hold up his hand for silence and make a speech about the true-hearted scout and his regard for the nobility of women. Then the audience would turn right around and hiss the man and want to throw him out, and sometimes there would be a fight and the man really would be put out. Sol always gave the man back his money, so that he wouldn't be too mad. But Sol liked things to happen that way; he said it made the audience and the actors feel more at home together. Sol was really mighty clever.

There were other stunts too that he would work with Jerry when he saw some sport in the audience with a lot of loose money. He would announce: "Jerry Graham will now, ladies and gentlemen, perform a feat of shooting known only to himself. He will with one rifle ball put two holes through the same sheet of paper." Then there would be a kind of gasp from the audience, and some would yell out it was crazy and couldn't be done. Then Sol would get indignant, and he would pick out the right man as if that man were doubting his word personally. There would be some argument, and Sol would say, "Well, sir, if you're so sure of it maybe you'd like to put up some money." They would make the bet, and there would be much fussing around with paper and Jerry aiming. After he fired everybody would whoop and laugh because they could see there was only one hole in the paper, and Sol would scratch his head. Then Sol would take the paper down and spread it out to show that it had been folded, and there of course were two holes where the bullet had gone through both folds. Nobody had thought of that and they would all shout and laugh. And usually the man who had bet would see that the joke was on him, and would let his money go. If he got nasty and said it was a trick Sol always gave him back his money. So either way the audience liked it.

Jerry never did any real acting with speeches, but he went in for the riding scenes. Often the last scene was a big chase, with the heavy carrying off the *ingénue* on horseback. José and Mario always helped the villain, and Jerry chased after them along with Sterling, the lead man. It was fine, with lots of shooting and men falling off horses, and the heroine rescued in the end.

The biggest time they ever had was when they put on *Macbeth*. Jerry liked to think of that. It was all on account of Walter Sterling, who wanted to play Shakespeare. So he kept telling Sol to put on *Hamlet*. Sol trampled on that idea. "Us Jews has had a lot put on us," he said. "They've been tellin' us for a couple of thousand years about how we killed Jesus Christ, and I guess maybe we did. But I'll be damned if I give anyone the chance to say it was a Jew that first played *Hamlet* with actors ridin' around on a lot of cayuses!" But Sterling kept on arguing, and since he was so important, Sol was good-natured and sort of went half-and-half with him to try *Macbeth*. Once he got started Sol got interested, and he was mighty clever the way he fixed up the scenes so they could be on horseback.

Sterling thought the witches ought to come on riding black horses with skeletons painted on them in white, and they rehearsed it that way once. But everybody laughed. So Sol said, hell, they didn't have to have all the scenes on horseback—the witches could just as well come in on foot!

The performance, Jerry thought, was great. The audience seemed to like it too, except for a bunch of gentlemen down in front who kept laughing their heads off even at the most serious scenes.

After the witches, for the scene with the wounded captain, everybody was on horseback; that was great, and was just the way it ought to be for a battlefield scene. At the end the wounded captain fainted and took a grand fall right off his horse, so that even some of the gentlemen down in front forgot to laugh, and applauded.

In the third scene Macbeth and Banquo came riding in to talk with the witches, and that was right too, for they surely wouldn't have been walking home after a battle.

The murder of Banquo was the best of all. José was a murderer who didn't have to say any lines. Instead of surprising Banquo

Y

they had to chase him and his son all the way round the ring whooping and yelling and riding like mad. Then José whipped out his knife and threw it twenty feet into Banquo's back. He made the butt-end strike of course, but you had to be good to do that; the audience couldn't tell the difference. Banquo took a fall with José jumping his horse right over him to chase after the son. The audience went wild. But of course the play didn't let José catch the son, and he got away through the exit. Even Sol got excited about that scene, and he said he bet that Shakespeare would have liked it too. He gave José a dollar, and said it was the first time a murderer stole the show.

The trouble came with a sarcastic article in the *Daily Gazette* next day. It made fun by pretending to be very favourable. The writer said he was only disappointed that they hadn't brought Banquo's ghost back on horseback like the spectre-bridegroom, and hadn't done a sleep-riding instead of a sleep-walking scene. Sol said it was good publicity, and was for going ahead, but Sterling got huffy and sulked; so they gave up *Macbeth*.

In the plays they put on the chief actors and the trick riders like José and Mario did all the fancy horse-work. Jerry did the shooting, and all they asked of him was just straight riding. But there was always some danger in it; they couldn't fake anything, and they had to ride hard, for that was what the audience liked. And taking quick turns around the little ring inside the tent could mean trouble. That was how it happened.

Jerry's horse slipped and fell at a turn. Jerry rolled free, but the horse behind him clipped him in the ribs going by. Some way or other Jerry didn't remember his being hurt as anything very unpleasant. Everybody was so decent to him. Even Walter Sterling quit being conceited for a few minutes, and Mario cried as he helped carry Jerry out. They gave a benefit for him two days later, and passed on to him quite a chunk of money. Sol paid him up to the end of the month, and said he wished he could carry him on the pay-roll. But Jerry said of course he knew that couldn't be done. Then in a couple of weeks the troupe went off on tour up to Nevada City and the other mining towns. Jerry had heard rumours that it had met hard luck and busted up.

As far as he was concerned it didn't matter. He'd probably never be able to do any more hard riding, or even be much good at shooting for a long time.

He had been almost in a dream, but these were unpleasant thoughts, and they began to bring him back. Again he noticed that the air was bad, and he began to cough. The cold was now half-way up to his knees. He tried to breathe more quietly to still the cough, and he stirred about to get his circulation started. Some time passed—hard to guess how much. Probably it was getting on in the afternoon, but he could hardly tell when all the light came in from a little window high up and shaded by buildings outside. After a while he began to hear voices.

He couldn't make out the words. But one voice was Mrs Donovan's, shrill and high as it was when she was angry or arguing. The other voice was a woman's, and it sounded familiar too, although it was not any of the women's voices that he had heard here before. He could sense a feeling of power in it; it was low-pitched, but he felt some way that there was anger behind it.

The voices sounded nearer; suddenly he realized that the people must be coming down to his room. He became fearful with shame and embarrassment. Quickly he tried to arrange his blankets more decently on the straw. But it was too much, and he collapsed, coughing weakly, with his blankets every way and his arms and shoulders in the dirty, ragged shirt sticking out in plain view.

Then he saw the white hair and recognized her. He did not want to believe it. He couldn't stand being caught this way—he, Jerry Graham, trapper and mountain-man—lying here with blood flecked on his blankets, and dirt and vermin all about him, and his own filth in the corner, where the rats had scattered it!

He saw her nose tighten at the smell. She looked around blankly a moment, for the room was dark to a person coming in from the light. Then she saw him, and he watched a look of horror come over her face. He felt only shame—shame at being thus come upon. He drew the blankets up around his shoulders and lay looking at her, wondering why she had come to spy on him in his squalor.

Then he saw that she was crying. She came to his side with

two quick steps, and went down on one knee upon his straw. He cringed back, afraid of sullying her cleanness. Her white hair seemed to light the room like a lamp; his own was dingy now and streaked as if yellow with egg-stains. He felt her hand on his forehead.

"Don't," he said, thinking of the vermin in his hair, and tried weakly to draw away.

He felt a sudden soft wetness of a tear on his face, and then before he knew it she had kissed him on the forehead.

Jerry felt himself weak and confused, and then all at once she was on her feet and everything was different. Her voice was no longer low-pitched and restrained; she could not be weeping now. Her deep, wild fury seemed to shake the room. She was threatening Mrs Donovan with the police, hell-fire, and the Vigilance Committee. Tyrannical Mrs Donovan was wringing her hands and wailing.

There were men in the room—a big fellow with a murderer's face, and a black man with a kind of purple suit on. How could a nigger afford clothes like that? The big man at his shoulder and the nigger at his hips—they were lifting him up. The light dazzled him as they carried him out into the street.

"We can't lay him in the victoria, and it'll be bad to sit him up," the big fellow at his shoulders was saying to Señora Godoy. Then she did a thing which worried Jerry and he couldn't straighten it out. For a bus was passing—a regular public bus with some passengers in it. And the lady went out and wanted to hire it. You couldn't hire a public bus—anybody knew that. And the driver told her so, and laughed; the men in the bus laughed too.

Then the two men who were holding Jerry laid him down in the street so quickly that they bumped him, and the nigger stayed by him and the big fellow jumped over and stood beside the lady.

But she was merely saying to the driver:

"It is an emergency. I want you to drive this sick man to Mrs Green's Nursing Home. Everything will be taken care of. I am Mrs Daniel Melton."

When she said that last the driver took off his hat, and one man in the bus called, "Everybody out!" The passengers came out with their hats off. She was trying to give them a dollar apiece (it didn't make sense, thought Jerry), but they wouldn't take it. Instead they helped lift Jerry into the bus.

Then in a minute he was lying flat in the bottom of the bus, bumping over the cobblestones, with the big man sitting on the seat looking down at him. Now and then he could catch a glimpse of the grey horses' heads or the nigger's hat, and he knew that the victoria must be following along behind.

B Y THE TIME JUDITH was nearing home it was five o'clock. She was still shaken with the shock of seeing Jerry Graham trapped in that horrible cellar, with the mark of death on his face. It was years—not since she had been on the ranch—since she had had to meet such an emergency or to face life in such ugliness.

Seeing the house soothed her down a little. Sometimes it seemed rather dull and gloomy, but now she felt its comfort and safety and stability. It was solidly built of dark red brick. She let her eye sweep upward from the heavy foundations over the tall windows of the first and second stories. the mansard roof on the third floor, where the servants lived, and the cupola on top.

A high fence of iron bars with spikes on top cut off the small front garden from the street, and she noticed that there seemed to be some unusual activity going on in the garden. She heard Daniel's voice, and he was swearing. That was something of a shock in itself, for he hardly ever got excited enough to swear.

He and half a dozen workmen were standing about an opened crate. Then she saw that the iron bull had arrived from Boston. It had been ordered for over a year, and its pedestal had been waiting while the ship bringing the statue came round Cape Horn. Both Daniel and she had liked the idea of the bull. It would be different from the iron dog and deer which stood about everywhere, and at the same time it would be reminiscent of the old hide-and-tallow days of which they both were a little sentimental.

There was the bull on the pedestal, and the men were laughing. Daniel saw her.

" Look at the damn' thing! " he called.

She looked, and at first it seemed a fine bull. It had its head lowered threateningly, with nostrils wide and long horns, and along the neck the big swell of muscle that bulls had. Then when you looked farther back you became conscious that, whether from

342

ignorance or accident or prudery, the bull was lacking those parts which you might say were really most essential for a bull.

But the whole thing struck her as funny, and she began to laugh. Then Daniel laughed too.

" Well," he said, " it's funny too all right, but just the same I won't accept the statue. I'll take it to court first. That would be fun; I could get all the cattlemen in California as expert witnesses to swear that that isn't a bull, as I ordered. I'd heard Boston was getting pretty prudish, but I didn't know it had come to this."

Going inside, Judith made a quick trip to the kitchen and found everything moving on well for the dinner. She saw that Fourchard had sent up the right Saint Émilion. Two hours before she had felt that she could not even eat a dinner. Now habit and the stability of the house and the household seemed to move in upon her with waves of normality, steadying and strengthening her.

Just the same she was still shaky. " I'll have to talk with Daniel about it," she said to herself. " Otherwise I'll be jittery and won't be able to keep my mind on what people are saying." That was something about Daniel as a husband, she realized; she could talk to him about a problem and find advice and comfort. She would never have thought about talking to Juan on such a matter.

She went up to her dressing-room. Félice, her maid, was flutter-ing about saying that the bath was ready and it was time to start dressing. *Jesús María*, thought Judith vulgarly to herself, and it's two hours till dinner-time! The light was fading, but from her windows she could still see the line of the hills on the Contra Costa. She liked the room particularly for that view; somewhere far to the south-east among those hills was Rancho Amarillo. Dis-regarding Félice, she went through the bedroom and into Daniel's dressing-room. He was not there; so she crossed the hall and knocked at the door of his study. He was sitting with his secretary, young Hoffman, about to dictate a letter most likely something to do with the " Society for the Propagation of the Opinions of Thomas Paine." Catching her look, he dismissed Hoffman.

" What's wrong? " he asked. " That business down on Torrey Street? How was it? "

" Pretty bad," said Judith, and told him about it. " I've got

him comfortably fixed up at Mrs Green's now," she ended. " Dr
Cunningham's coming to examine him, and is going to send me
a report to-night."

" It's horrible that such things can happen."

" That Mrs Donovan was terrible."

• Yes, but she's only a poor human being like the rest of us."

Yes, Daniel was right; she realized that he was usually right.
She sat silent a minute. Yes, Mrs Donovan couldn't be too charitable to a sick man, for she had to pay her rent to some man who,
in turn, had to pay his taxes. So it went—civilization.

" Civilization," she said bitterly. " I waited for it all those years
on the ranch and when it comes it's this—crueller and worse than
what we had then." She remembered saying that once to him before, and he had said to wait—that it wasn't civilization yet.
Could he say that again? He went in the other direction :

" But the old days were cruel too. I've seen heifers that men
had roped and cut a steak out of, living, and then let go. I've
heard stallions scream when some mule-breeder was cutting them
open the way they thought they had to. And then the way they
treated the Indians. The world has always been cruel; maybe it
always has to be." . . .

Félice was knocking at the door—" Madam's bath." There was
nothing more to say, anyway. Daniel had sympathy, but no comfort. There was only fatalistic acceptance in his final words. She
felt tricked and trapped in civilization. It had taken Jerry
Graham, that free creature of the wilds, and thrust him to die in
a foul hole with the rats and his own filth. She might rescue
him. But how many others were there?

Back in her room under the careful ministrations of Félice she
felt habit steadying her again. It was good to think that she could
depend upon Georges in the kitchen. The champagne would come
in iced, and the Sauterne at twenty degrees below room temperature, and claret at room temperature, and the coffee hot.

She was wearing a blue silk for the dinner—dark enough to give
contrast to her hair, but not dark enough to take the richness from
the colour. Dubonnet had only been fairly successful with the
design, she thought, but the bustle thing that they had to wear

this season was enough to spoil the line of anyone's figure. He had done well with the shoulders, and had cleverly managed to mask somewhat their harsh grenadier squareness.

Félice did her last bits of work, and backed off for inspection. She seemed to approve. That is, thought Judith, as much as she can ever approve of my appearance. Félice, like every one else, admired little wax-figure, baby-doll prettiness.

There was still time for Judith to go in to say good-night to the children and be looked at. Leticia was going on sixteen now; her Spanish blood had brought her out early; she had a fine, fully developed figure, and was very conscious of figures in herself and others.

'That blue dress covers up pretty well the way your shoulders stick out, doesn't it, mother?" she remarked. Judith almost lost her temper; Leticia always seemed to rub her the wrong way. But the two of them managed to exchange a perfunctory kiss, and Judith went into Henry's room.

She could see by Henry's eyes that he approved of her appearance, but he was not the kind that would say anything. His face, she noticed, seemed worried about something; he always looked serious, but this seemed more definite.

" Is something the matter, dear? "

" No; I'm all right."

She remembered a sudden movement of his left arm as she had come in.

" Is something wrong with your hand? "

" No; nothing much."

" Let's see it."

There was an ugly deep scratch on the thumb, and she could see that he had been working unsuccessfully to get a splinter out; there was probably pus.

" I'll get Mrs Martin to come and take care of it for you," said Judith, thinking how lucky she was to have a housekeeper who was so good with the children now that they were too old for nurses.

She went to ring for Mrs Martin. How like Henry that was—to try to take care of his own cuts and not to say anything! Funny, she thought, that each one of her children in order was harder for her to understand. Lewis she had always seen eye to eye with; she could count on him. Guito she felt she knew too, but he was like his father, and had a primitive unreasonable vein which baffled her. Leticia she always quarrelled with, but even so, quarrels gave people a certain common meeting-ground. But Henry she felt that she hardly knew at all; he was one who drew in to himself.

She hurried into the dining-room to have a look at the table. Everything seemed perfect. The silver glowed richly in the light of many candles burning in the candelabra. She gave a last-minute reconsideration to her seating arrangements; a good deal depended on that. Seven gentlemen and only three ladies—but that was not a bad proportion, as things went in San Francisco. Now that the excitement over the Vigilance Committee had gone stale the presidential campaign was the troublesome problem for hostesses. But this party didn't seem very likely to get to arguing politics. Mr Buxton and the Judge were old Democratic stalwarts and would be voting for " Buck and Breck " as a matter of course. Daniel, being something of a radical, was probably going to vote for the new Republican Party. He approved of their platform; but, like most old Californians, he didn't have much admiration for their candidate Frémont. The lieutenant, being in the army, was supposed to have no politics; Lewis was not of voting age, and was not interested much as yet. Sir Robert was English; Mr Burke, the unknown, was Irish; probably neither of them would have any interest in the American campaign. It seemed safe.

Mr Buxton would be on her right; he would appreciate having the conventional place of honour. He was fifty, and a bore, but his wife entertained lavishly. For compensation Judith had the lively lieutenant on her left; it was also good to have him under his hostess' eye so that he would restrain his tendency to practical jokes. Pretty little Mrs Wingram was beyond the lieutenant, and then Lewis. Since Lewis had been so decent about coming at the last moment he deserved the pleasure of having a pretty face to look at; he was young enough to appreciate it. Sir Robert was between Lewis and Daniel. Mr Burke, being Daniel's friend, she had put at his left. Then came Mrs Buxton and Judge Wingram completing the circuit.

The door-bell jangled. . . .

Oysters on the half-shell, *potage Julienne,* sand dabs *à la Limousienne,* entrée, salad Impératrice, squab for the game course, roast lamb (and it was lucky she had not trusted to getting through on only two bottles of Saint-Émilion), Roman punch.

Everything was going well. Mr Burke had turned out to be handsome and intelligent and apparently civilized, although he wore his evening-clothes rather carelessly. Politics had raised its head only once, and the lieutenant had sent it scurrying with a laugh by his declaration that as for politics he had none—" No, sir, not a single politic."

Sir Robert had proved to be quite an affable lion. He told them about his ' shooting ' trip, as he termed it, into Oregon Territory; he had been very successful with elk, although he called them ' stags '; he had had no luck with grizzlies. He must return to England now, but in a few years he hoped to come to California again and make a regular expedition to the interior; he would go as far as the Crow country and have a try at stalking mountain-sheep and at running buffalo.

He was tall and ruddy and hawk-nosed with greying temples. He had been an army officer; two fingers were missing from his left hand. Judith kept wondering why such a man, no longer young, should be so restless. What force drove him to penetrate the wilderness for the mere boyish satisfaction of bringing back some pelts and heads of animals?

In a minute now the fruit and cheese would be coming on, then the liqueurs; then the ladies would leave the gentlemen for a while.

Mr Buxton at her right had just finished a pompous platitude; her end of the table rested a moment in silence. Then, as if the stage had been set, they all heard Mr Burke's voice from the other end, clear-toned, a little loud in its vigour, resonant, with a touch of fervour:

" History, sir—you call upon the record of history? *What* is history? *Thirty centuries of poverty and carnage!* "

Every one drew breath and waited. It did not seem a dinner-table remark. He had addressed his words to Judge Wingram, and the two men were leaning forward talking across Mrs Buxton, who was leaning back with a well-well-how-extraordinary expression on her face.

"But, sir," the Judge rallied, "you cannot pass by the difficulty with an epigram. How, I ask you, in the record of history or by the experience of our own day, in the clear light of the failures of New Harmony, of the failure of Brook Farm, of the failures of a dozen, nay, of scores of other ventures, how—I say . . ." The Judge lost the thread and floundered a moment. "How can you theorists declare that an association of some scores or hundreds of families will work smoothly, when ordinary experience should teach us that an association of even two or three families comes quickly to grief, especially on account of the jealousies and heart-burnings created by the females?"

Before the Judge's mouth could close Mr Burke was upon him. He waved his hand, and spoke as if addressing a parliamentary body:

"The gentleman argues—shall I say?—by a kind of combination of analogy and *a fortiori*. Does his argument hold? No. Is it not common knowledge that people living in small villages create back-biting, jealousy, and constant bad feeling, whereas people in great urban centres exemplify and have actually led to the creation of the word *urbane*? Three or four men enforced to camp together are notoriously liable to quarrel, but in a military company or battalion men pass from contact to contact and so live happily. No, the failures—and I should rather say 'partial failures,' for such they really were—of New Harmony and of the phalanxes illustrate only the fallibility of particular instances, not the fallacy of the general principles."

As he paused Judith felt her duty as hostess requiring her to change to a less quarrel-breeding subject; she might ask the lieutenant about plans for the coming military ball at the Presidio. But the ring in Mr Burke's voice had stirred something in her blood. His battle-cry—"thirty centuries of poverty and carnage" —had brought the sudden memory of Jerry Graham to her again.

Deliberately, with a feeling of abandoning herself to malice, she stirred the flame:

"Mr Burke, please go on. Are you a Foo-er-ist?"

She was not even sure of the word, but it was close enough.

"No," cried Mr Burke, "I am not a Fourierist, or an Owenite or an Icarian, or a Rappist, or a Transcendentalist, or a Zoarite, or a Perfectionist—I am myself. But I share beliefs and feel sympathy with all these and all others who believe that the world is to be made over root and branch, who believe that men may live in the world as men co-operating, and not as beasts fighting tooth and nail among themselves for scraps of meat."

As he spoke he gestured with his right hand; his thick hair, wavy and reddish-brown, seemed to vibrate above his forehead with the very vigour of his enunciation; his bright blue eyes had a level, far-off look. He spoke as if in prophetic trance, contagiously. Judith sensed in herself a strange feeling of ecstasy; it was as if he were saying things she had known deep down for a long time, but never recognized consciously. The cheese had come in, but on most plates it lay untouched; Mrs Buxton was eating with determined good manners, looking at Judith askance as if she had committed treason. But the men seemed to be enjoying themselves. Mr Buxton cleared his throat and began to come into action, slowly, as if he felt himself a siege-gun.

"Mr Burke," he said, suave and ponderous at once, "could you be so good as to answer me, how does all this contemporary enthusiasm for communities differ from the exploded theories of that Frenchman Rousseau—the natural goodness of man? Your communities fail—and why? Because they trust to natural goodness, and fail to apply the necessary social restraints."

"As for Rousseau," cried Mr Burke, "I am under no more constraint to defend him than to defend Owen or Cabet. But as for restraint, sir, I throw the word back at you. Why does society need restraint? I sum it up in a few words. It needs restraint to prevent the poor man's taking back what the rich man has hoarded from the common store of mankind. But look more widely. Here is the earthly globe"—Mr Burke held his right hand cupped, as if it actually presented to them the world—"and here is the race of

mankind "—he held his left palm flat, as if men in their millions
were walking there. "What is the destiny of man? To support
himself and make himself happy by cultivating and beautifying
this world, by making to bloom its deserts, by draining its noisome
morasses, by sowing forests upon its mountains, by regulating and
keeping pure its crystal streams. But instead, our present society
leads him to fight other men for his existence. To bring men back
to their true destiny—towards this, all these new communities
strive."

He paused breathless, and Judge Wingram took up the cudgels:
"Look at the Mormons, Mr Burke; they are a community. And
what is the corner-stone of their social life—the unutterable and
foul degradation of polygamy!"

"Brigham seems to have been successful, anyway, in getting a
lot of women in the same household to co-operate." This was the
lieutenant breaking in.

Everybody laughed, but it was hardly a joke worthy of the lieutenant's reputation. People, thought Judith, had to laugh at a joke
like that, the ladies especially; there was nothing for them to do
except either to laugh or to gather up their skirts and leave the
room. Again she felt she might shift the conversation, but she
paused, and Mr Burke swept on again.

"Yes, look at the Mormons. They are not a real community,
but I welcome them, anyway, and do not let the one fact of polygamy blind me to all else about them. I have been in their city of
Deseret—it is clean and beautiful. Streams of pure water flow
through it. Their children are happy. I have seen your Gentile
towns on the frontier with their piles of garbage and tin cans half
as tall as the houses and smelling with their brothels and their
whisky-mills. Some day, in a hundred years perhaps, America will
know that the Mormons were its best colonizers and Brigham
Young one of its greatest men."

Judith caught the ladies with her eyes, and they withdrew.
But when the men came in the argument was going on as strongly
as before. Mr Burke, looking younger and more vigorous than
ever, was florid with excitement; the Judge and Mr Buxton and
even Lewis appeared a little hot under the collar; the lieutenant

looked disgruntled at not having an opportunity for jokes; Sir Robert looked bored; only Daniel seemed really to be enjoying it.

Mr Burke was on the offensive now. Not all the communities had been failures. In Oregon Territory even now, just to the north, the Aurora Community was flourishing. Amana was thriving, and was just removing to new and better lands in Iowa. There was the North American Phalanx, and Hopedale, to represent the strict Fourierists. The Oneida Community was highly successful, and the Icarians, who had taken over the old Mormon city of Nauvoo, were prosperous. There were probably a dozen others of which he was ignorant.

An hour before Judith had hardly heard of Fourier or Owen, and had never heard of Cabet at all. Now Mr Burke's eloquence had made her think of them as the greatest leaders of modern times. An hour before she had thought of communities, on the basis of a few magazine articles, as associations of religious fanatics and other queer people, harmless and rather funny. Now she saw them as scattered seedlings, destined to burgeon inevitably and grow and scatter more seeds, until they embraced in their growth all society. She had never dreamed that there were so many of them, and that in spite of some failures so many were prospering. She had never dreamed, either, of their diversity of opinion and practice; yet, as Mr Burke emphasized, behind all their diversity lay their unity—the idea of co-operation, not competition. She was proud also that her own country was leading the way and making possible this revolution in the history of man. Here in America, as Mr Burke pointed out, cheap and unexhausted lands gave the community idea its chance to make beginnings.

A determined onslaught by Mrs Buxton got the conversation away from communities and upon the safe subject of a society excursion being organized for a trip around the Bay by steamer—a ' water frolic,' Mrs Buxton liked to call it, although the idea of her engaging in any kind of a frolic was a little hard to imagine.

It was past midnight when the guests took their leave. A lovely dinner, my dear," said Mrs Buxton. " I'll see you to-morrow afternoon at the meeting of the Ladies' Assistance Society." Then, with a shake of the finger, " Be sure you have your treasurer's report in order." This reference, Judith knew, was for Mrs Win-gram's benefit, for the Society was snobbish as well as charitable, and Alicia had not yet been taken in.

They were gone, each bowing himself or herself out in his or her own manner. She had rather expected Mr Burke to apologize for having so nearly monopolized the table conversation until he, not Sir Robert, seemed the lion. He had not apologized. Yet he was a gentleman certainly, in spite of all his unconventional ideas; her head was still spinning with them as if she were intoxi-cated. She had said to him that she hoped he would call soon.

By the time that she had collected herself Daniel had already gone upstairs; a dinner-party always made him very tired. The servants were straightening up the rooms a little, and beginning to blow out the candles. She said good-night to them.

In her dressing-room she started to undress alone, having told Félice not to wait up for her. Then she noticed an envelope on her dressing-table—from Dr Cunningham, of course, about Jerry Graham. In the excitement of the evening's conversation she had almost forgotten, she had to admit, all that bad business.

MY DEAR MRS MELTON,
   Unfortunately I cannot give you a very hopeful report upon the condition of the patient, Jeremiah Graham. The injury to his chest and the shockingly bad living conditions to which he has been sub-jected have either aggravated or initiated a phthisical condition of a galloping degree of intensity. It is unlikely that improved conditions and treatment will much help at this stage.

                                        Very truly yours,

                                              . . .

She looked at the doctor's scrawled illegible signature. Then she winced as the import of the note came in upon her. She had been too late. Not again would Jerry ride out, that free creature of the open, his yellow hair bright in the sunlight. She thought again of the dank chilly room, the filth and the smell, and the rats squeaking in the walls. This was the best that their civiliza-tion, that great new city of San Francisco, could do for Jerry.

Daniel was already in bed. His hair was neatly brushed, as if he were at the dinner-table. The hair was silvered, but life showed in that boyish wave above the left temple. He looked at her and smiled, but she did not say anything about Jerry. He had not known Jerry much, but still it was the kind of thing that might make him worry and not go to sleep. She crawled in at the other side of the big four-poster bed.

The moment her head touched the pillow she knew that she was going to have a hard time going to sleep. It had been too much of a day. Her thoughts swirled round in all directions, and she could not let herself relax: Jerry Graham and the visit to Torrey Street, the general discontent with her life which she had been feeling, the dishonesty of Mr Foster down at the ranch and Daniel's worry that he might be over-grazing, and then the dinner, and, most of all, the amazing Mr Burke's amazing conversation—the communities and the world being remade while you saw it. What was history?—"thirty centuries of poverty and carnage!" Like Jerry Graham's case. . . . But it could change—not competition, but co-operation. . . . The thoughts went whirling round in a circle.

She could never go to sleep this way, and to calm herself she thought of Mrs Buxton's remark about the Ladies' Assistance Society and the report which she as treasurer was to deliver to the meeting. She had been over the figures so much that she had them in her head. The total sum was $2455.87; of this $125.67 remained in the bank and $2330.20 had been distributed in direct gifts to the needy and in purchases. Purchases for distribution included 269 garments, 154 yards of material, and 111 packages of groceries.

Judith had a sudden sense of disgust and futility. It was patch-work. It was mere doling charity, getting nowhere, nor to the roots of anything. It did not touch the causes of this poverty and suffering which they went around superficially—and often superciliously—relieving. Paugh!

She took refuge again in the figures. They were—in themselves, anyway—exact and complicated and honest. The mind could consider them without cringing. Two-four-five-five-point-eight-seven; two-six-nine; one-one-one. . . . A clock chimed endlessly and then struck. She heard one stroke, and thought she heard another; for the life of her she could not be sure; it might

z

have been her imagination. Daniel she didn't think was asleep either. He lay very still, but people who were asleep moved a little naturally. He was lying still so as not to disturb her; he was often wakeful. Two-three-three-nought-point-three-nought— no, two-nought. Two-four-five-five . . . point . . . eight . . .

She snapped into full consciousness again. No, she didn't think she had really been asleep. It had been like a vision—half conscious. She lay in a tense glory of happiness. A new heaven and a new earth. . . . As she had relaxed and lain close to sleep the thoughts deep within her had combined themselves and taken form—yes, actual physical form—and suddenly possessed her conscious mind, snapping her out of the daze with a jerk.

She still saw the physical form they had taken. It was as plain as the brand on a steer's hip—and, in fact, it looked a good deal like a new brand.

There was a circle, and from five points on it short arrows pointed inward towards the centre. And she could name each arrow. One was the trouble about Jerry, and one her own discontent, and one the trouble about the ranch, and another the Ladies' Assistance Society, and the last was Mr Burke's ideas about a community. The circle and the arrows pointing at the centre meant that they should all be brought together into one.

She lay for a moment, almost trembling. A new heaven and a new earth. . . . Yes, heaven upon earth . . . She saw the old buildings at Rancho Amarillo transfigured . . . the beautiful valley glowing with a new beauty; the beloved line of the hills to the south now was more beloved than ever. And around the building and about the valley moved people—men, women, and children —with happy and healthy faces, working and playing, singing as they worked, coming home in the evening with beauty and love and happiness.

She must catch that vision—put it into words and plans before it died. "Daniel," she said softly, hoping that he was not asleep. He replied instantly. . . .

They put on their dressing-gowns and went into his study. They lit the fire that was laid there. And Daniel sneaked downstairs in his slippers to get a bottle of cognac. Daniel Melton, pretty close to sixty and maybe the richest man in San Francisco, sneaking downstairs in dressing-gown and slippers at two in the morning to get a bottle of cognac—like a youngster! She had known he would be with her. And when he came back it turned out that in the dark he had got rum instead of cognac. So they mixed it with water and drank it, anyway, laughing—like a couple of youngsters.

They were vague about how to do it, but they both saw the vision. Daniel was tired of making money, he said; he was no money-maker, anyway. He had made it to start with by an accident, and had made more just because anyone with any sense could make more money, once he had a lot to start on. He knew he was no financial wizard, even though people called him one. And spending it wasn't much fun either when you had more than you could possibly spend. What he had really been enjoying lately was his work with the Thomas Paine society, and his chess games—and, of course, his languages and his reading, just as he always had.

The circle with the pointing arrows didn't seem so important to him as it had to Judith, but when she explained about it he saw a little what it meant. They would discharge Mr Foster and take over Rancho Amarillo themselves again, and they would establish one of Mr Burke's co-operative communities upon it. Perhaps Mr Burke would help them. It would give them something new for an interest for themselves, and Judith would get away from this snobbish charity of the Ladies' Assistance Society. And it would be a constructive move, so that perhaps in the end the world would get better, and things could not happen as they had happened to Jerry Graham. They would not care whether it was successful financially or not, for they had plenty of money to make it go—so long as the people were happy.

They sat there before the fire, giddy with ideas rather than with rum. They kept laughing a great deal, and then telling each other that they must come down to earth and make some plans. Finally Daniel got out a piece of paper and sat at his desk looking very businesslike, and wrote at the top: "Plans for estab. Community." Then he wrote:

(1) See Burke again.
(2) Read books on idea by Cabet, Fourier, Greeley, *et al.*
(3) Visit community in Oregon, if possible.
(4) Give notice to Foster.

All these except the last were disappointingly vague, but they agreed in hoping that they might get the community actually started by spring.

By this time it was four o'clock, and the rum-and-water they had been drinking was making them sleepy. They went back to bed, and Judith lay for a little while feeling not quite so happy. Perhaps what she had seen was not a real vision, but only a sort of treacherous imagining. In the morning Daniel might grin at her, and both of them would be thinking—what a crazy night! And he would tear up the paper with the memoranda. But, anyway—whether it was rum or just reaction and weariness—she felt herself going to sleep.

MR DANIEL MELTON of SAN FRANCISCO felt himself very much indeed Mr Daniel Melton of San Francisco as he stood on the deck of the little steamer and looked out over the village of Portland, Oregon Territory Not, he considered, that he would have dared to call it a village—not at the present moment, when no less than four of its chief citizens were busy talking to him, trying to "interest" him in what they altruistically called "sound local investments." Mr Melton maintained what he knew to be the polite convention of a gentleman in a gentlemanly conference with other gentlemen, although he knew all the time that "sound local investments" meant merely that each of the chief citizens had something to sell—either something of his own or something of his friends' on which he could collect a commission.

Looking out at the village and not paying more attention to the citizens than was necessary for politeness, Mr Melton considered the view and was not much impressed. Practically everything was cheap wood construction; the place would probably all go up in smoke some time. But he was forgetting that Oregon had so much rain; it didn't dry out like California, and fires wouldn't be so dangerous. The forest on the edge of town had been burned, but that was probably by intention. It looked ugly—hundred- or two-hundred-foot trees burned to charred black spikes and leaning this way and that, about to fall. And then between the dead trunks the fir saplings were springing up in a jungle. That was another thing he didn't like; the trees seemed to be pressing in, strangling the town. After you lived a long time in California you got a feeling for space—wide valleys and grassy hills. The dank forest, working in raggedly at the edge of every clearing, seemed to say sinisterly, "Wait—I'll take the place over again." It made him feel creepy. Of course, Pennsylvania was woods country, but that was when he was a boy; he'd really come to feel like a Californian now.

"Yes, yes," he had to reply to a question, struggling to remember just what the man had said. "Yes, waterfront lots—always good."

It had come time for leave-taking, and Mr Melton shook hands all round. He felt himself being involuntarily a little lofty. Coming from San Francisco, everybody treated you as a metropolitan, and in a week or so you came to accept it.

"I'm sorry to disappoint you, gentlemen," he found himself saying, "but my—and Mrs Melton's—intention in visiting the north was to see the Aurora Community. The rumours that I was to buy a large tract of land or to invest in any way are completely unfounded."

Nevertheless, as the local citizens went ashore and stood on the wharf you could be pretty sure that they were saying what a shrewd close-mouthed old codger Melton was, and wondering what he really was up to. He wondered himself a little why he had not been more interested in Portland's possibilities. At present it was nothing better than a second-rate Californian mining town, Dutch Flat, say. But it was as good as San Francisco had been in '48, and that was the time to buy—not after the place had developed and looked good to any fool. Twenty or thirty lots, well scattered, bought now in Portland might make a man rich. He shrugged his shoulders—he was rich as it was. A good business-man would buy them, but he wasn't really a good business-man. Sentiment, Californian prejudice—yes. But he didn't like the way that forest, especially the ugly, burned part, came pressing in around the town; it gave him a choked feeling.

The steamer was casting off. Mr Melton looked forward, and saw Judith sitting in her deck-chair. It brought him a flood of recollections—more than twenty years ago it was now. He still remembered the way she had appeared when he had looked forward and seen her on the deck of the *Spanish Belle*. And even yet she appeared much the same—"whiteness and strength," you would say even now. She was better-looking, if anything—a certain girlish gangliness had disappeared into a mature poise. Not many women grew older so well.

She was his wife, and yet to look at her appraisingly that way gave him, as it had now and then ever since they were married, a certain little uncomfortable and uncertain feeling. He wasn't quite sure that it was right for an old fellow like himself, and never any very great person physically, to be married to a woman so much younger and so full of vitality. And there was the memory of Juan, who must have been so much more in that way than he himself was. In Boston you wouldn't admit that a woman—a lady—had any feelings of that kind, but in California you couldn't deny things so easily. And underneath her calm and her intellect Judith had that tumult of emotion, strange to him, which came cropping out sometimes—as when she lost her temper, or as when she had run off with Juan in the first place. And now this whole matter of organizing the Community at Rancho Amarillo—she had given herself up to it as passionately and as wholeheartedly as she had once given herself up to falling in love with Juan. Sometimes he had even thought that it might be a falling in love—that her enthusiasm for the Community was merely an expression of what she felt for Anthony Burke, perhaps unconsciously as yet. She and Burke had certainly seen a good deal of each other since Burke had undertaken to manage the organization of the Community. And he was a very attractive fellow, not much past thirty, with his wavy reddish hair and his shining blue eyes, and his contagious enthusiasms. And yet, he and Judith—it was really unlikely. And if it was going to happen, or had happened, Mr Melton didn't think that he should stand in her way. He had always felt a little humble with respect to her, perhaps more humble than a husband ought to feel, in spite of all his money

He walked forward towards Judith, still thinking. No, he didn't believe she was in love—with a man. Perhaps this enthusiasm for saving the world, so to speak, was the same thing that might have made her lose her head about Burke, only it had taken another direction. It had come on her suddenly, like love or like a conversion, like St Paul's vision on the road to Damascus. That crazy thing of the circle with the four or five arrows pointing inward— she had seen that, actually seen it, she said. Now her children were grown up, and yet she was not an old woman. Perhaps this new enthusiasm was supplying something which he himself as

her husband could not. " Without a dream the people perish "—
he had heard her say that; it was one of her favourite quotations.
A person like Judith, some one who really thought, couldn't go
on just from day to day eating and sleeping; she had to have a
dream. So did he too, for that matter; he was interested in the
Community as much as she was in a way, even if he couldn't ever
get that wild enthusiasm. That was the reason probably why he
couldn't focus on these Portland lots.

" Come and see the letters," she said, looking up at him.

There was a big pile of business letters sent on to Portland for
him, but Judith meant the personal ones.

" Lewis and Mrs Martin write that everything is all right at
home. This is Mr Burke about getting things started, with clippings from the papers—they're favourable enough, on the whole. I
think it was good to start things while we were away; it takes the
emphasis off our support.'

He looked at the clippings while she finished the letter. The
editors must know that he was behind the project, and so would
be careful not to offend him. He tried to read between the lines.
Several editors seemed to think of the Community as a charitable
enterprise for relieving the bad conditions in the lower parts of
San Francisco. He knew that Judith would resent this interpreta-
tion, but he himself felt that it was perhaps close to the truth.
Two clippings guardedly raised the issue of the strange marital
relations sometimes practised in such communities, but expressed
the belief that nothing of such a sort was indicated in the present
instance. Two others were pessimistic as to the outcome on the
grounds that community of property was inherently repugnant to
the American spirit. Most of the clippings cited the failures of
other communities, and then ended by expressing goodwill for the
career of this particular new and interesting social experiment.
This last, Mr Melton knew, meant nothing. Californian editors were
under the necessity of puffing new enterprises, and they had acquired
the habit. There was a story that a Marysville editor had once
wished " quick fulfilment of the promoter's desires and rapid expan-
sion," and had hoped for the co-operation of public-minded citizens
at the time of the arrival of a new ' madame ' with eight girls.

Mr Burke's letter was encouraging. A small office had been opened for Amarillo Community. More than five hundred people, most of them merely curious, had visited the office. About a hundred had registered, and to date fifty-two had been sufficiently interested to make out the papers of formal application. With their children this made a total of seventy-nine. Probably half of the applicants, however, were mere drifters who would never arrive at the sticking-point, and others were definitely undesirable. Applications were still coming in, however, and there seemed no doubt but that thirty good people—all who could be accommodated at the beginning—would be secured. One of the encouraging features was the large number of women, wives with their husbands and respectable widows, who had applied. This would seem to indicate that the prevalence of fast life in San Francisco had made the lot of the respectable poorer women very hard, and that the Community would profit accordingly. A mass meeting had been held with about two hundred present. Some of these had been antagonistic, but the police had co-operated by throwing out half a dozen hecklers. An opportunity had been had for the dissemination of information upon the coming social order. Speakers had expounded in turn the doctrines of Fourier, Owen, and Cabet. Finally Mr Burke himself had attempted to show the basic resemblances among the teachings of these prophets, and had spoken more concretely of the aims of the new community; he had also read a letter from Albert Brisbane expressing his hopes and good wishes. Then the letter requested advice on certain points.

A most enthusiastic applicant named Phineas Brown had written a song beginning:

> Amarillo, all for thee
> Thy walls I long to see;
> For thee I sigh. . .

It could be sung (approximately) to the tune of *God Save the King*, and had been so sung with great enthusiasm by Phineas Brown and others. They wished to adopt it as the official song. Mr Burke had doubts. What was to be done? Another applicant, Mrs Robert Firken, had started a movement to change the name to 'Amor-illo' to indicate that the Community was founded upon love of humanity. Mr Burke, rather surprisingly, seemed to take this suggestion as a good one, but he was afraid of it as possibly arousing the suspicions of the general public that the Community intended to practise 'free love.' Finally, what stand was to be taken on alcoholic beverages? About a dozen excellent applicants would like to join, but only on condition that alcoholic beverages should be completely banned.

On the whole, things seemed to be going as well as could be expected. During the afternoon Mr Melton and Judith sat in deck-chairs watching the great forested hills of the river-shore. At times they read—Mr Melton from Brisbane, Judith from the manuscript translation of *Voyage en Icarie* which they had had made for her; at other times they talked about their trip north.

The trip, they agreed, had been most successful—for pleasure, however, rather than for profit. Their visit to the Aurora Community, the excuse for the whole journey, had lasted only a few hours, and had not taught them much. Aurora was prosperous after the manner of a frontier village, and the people seemed happy under a benevolent despotism. But Dr Keil, their leader, had the shiny hard eyes of a religious fanatic, which Mr Melton with his deism could never abide. And Dr Keil had grown suspicious at once on finding that Amarillo was to be without religious requirements. So they had lapsed into unfruitful politeness on both sides.

But after all, as Mr Melton suggested and Judith was inclined to agree, the visit to Aurora had been something of a pretext. Judith particularly had been too close to San Francisco for too long, and especially the dragging illness of Jerry Graham and his death in February had worn her down. Now the sight of new places had brought her out like a renewal of youth. The very thought of the journey had made her insist on going north the hard way, overland.

They had taken the steamer to Sacramento with the greys and the carriage, and had driven to Red Bluff, through the wide Sacramento Valley, rich with the late spring flowers. At Red Bluff they found that Indian attacks had closed the Pit River road. So they sent back the horses and carriage, hired riding-horses, and went on by the new road that was being built over Trinity and Scott Mountains. Mount Shasta rose up on their right, white, imperturbable, unbelievably great. Ahead clattered two armed guards, for the narrow trails carried the threat of both Indians and bandits. Behind, came the pack-horses and the servant in charge of them, and Big Mike. The north of California was still primitive—almost like the central mining districts in '50 or '51, said Mr Melton. They rode through great forests of fir and pine, and came out suddenly upon the little mining towns. There, as they halted, their men would gossip, and in a few minutes the local politicians or editor would come up and introduce themselves and visibly bask in the warmth of being so close to the great Mr Melton of San Francisco. And the miners would begin to drift in; they were great bearded fellows with red or blue shirts and revolvers in their belts. At first glance they looked like cut-throats, and then when you looked closer you saw that the beards were often new and silky and that the cut-throats were really just youngsters who had run away from farms in Oregon or Missouri, and now were maybe home-sick and thinking about their mothers. They came to look at Judith. The way people came to look, she said, reminded her of that first long ride in California when she had gone north with Juan and he had nearly ridden her to death. But the old-time Californians had always looked hard with open admiration; these miners were bashful and turned away quickly if she happened to glance at them.

"Why are we so happy?" Judith had said once suddenly, as they were crossing the Siskiyous.

Mr Melton had wanted to say "because we are in love," but he had boggled, so he paused a moment.

"I think," he said, "because this new idea gives us something new to live for."

They were still happy as the little steamer, with much bumping of the engine, ploughed its way down-river. They quite ruthlessly snubbed various people who tried to start conversations.

They had both read their books before; so now they spent a good deal of their time comparing notes and reading aloud the marked passages, especially what they liked to term the "trumpet-calls." These were mostly from Brisbane, for as an American he seemed closer to them than did the Frenchman Cabet.

"The Earth," Mr Melton would read, "is the great theatre of action; the human race are the actors upon it. let the fertility and riches of the one and the genius and imagination of the other be the only limits to the happiness and greatness of man."

Once again he started, and then stopped. "Nobody," he said, "can read all these kinds of type out loud. The man's been carried away. Look." And he showed her the passage :

> We assert, and will prove, that Labour, which is now MONOTONOUS, REPUGNANT, and DEGRADING, can be ennobled, elevated, and made honourable—or, in other words, that INDUSTRY CAN BE RENDERED ATTRACTIVE !

That was the miracle—that a little, cheap, badly printed book such as this *Social Destiny of Man* could supply all the inspiration that it did. It was, they often said, like another Bible. Yet the paper was poor and the margins crooked; there were different sizes of type and the pages were full of misprints. It was not well written either, for the figures of speech got mixed You never could tell when Brisbane was using Fourier's ideas and when he was Brisbane himself. One of the two (Judith and Mr Melton laughed and argued which one) seemed to be particularly fond of pears, like Sir Gawain in Malory's book that Judith had read so often back on the ranch. He was always using as an illustration the growing or picking or consuming of pears, until you thought that pears must be the chief concern of a community.

But the man—was it Fourier or Brisbane?—was like a mad poet. You forgot his madness as you sensed the wild glory of his vision. Who but a madman would have put into that poor little book the frontispiece picturing the buildings of the ideal community. It was terrifying in its greatness, equalling or surpassing in size—and much resembling—the Palace of Versailles, as they remembered it from pictures. A parade-ground, so large as wholly to dwarf some small figures of people standing in it, stretched on three sides of the main building. This itself was three or four stories high (the artist had been a little vague on this point), and was on the whole approximately French in its architecture, except for the curious predilection shown for a kind of pointed pavilion placed on the roof at each angle. Beyond this enormous pile stretched a pleasant rolling countryside on both sides of a charmingly quiet little river. Groves alternated with well-cultivated fields. Here and there in the distance stood small buildings which one could easily recognize as the pavilions to which the workers were to repair for shelter, refreshment, and recreation. Judith and Mr Melton had difficulty in fitting the scheme into the treeless hills of Rancho Amarillo and its nondescript creek, bordered by slatternly sycamores. And, besides, the building was for the accommodation of hundreds and hundreds; it seemed as if the prophet was discouraging them before they really got started.

That afternoon on the boat was one of those rare times, Mr Melton thought, when two people's minds worked so closely in harmony that there scarcely seemed need for speech. Perhaps the reason was that they had already discussed most of these matters so that they merely came together again after having thought over the same topics separately. They agreed that they were not whole-hearted Fourierists, although they came closer to accepting Fourier's theories than any others. But when it was stated flatly that an association of more than two thousand or of fewer than eight hundred people would not be successful they were forced to consider that the master had spoken too much upon theory. Certainly no one had ever tried an association of more than two thousand, and, on the other hand, associations of less than a hundred had been going successfully for several years and were still alive.

" Besides," said Mr Melton, " it's practical knowledge that new things in this world start small. It's only in mythology that Minerva springs full grown into life. Real infants start little."

" The surprising thing is," said Judith, " the way theoretical and fantastic ideas are all mixed up with shrewd practical ones."

They agreed again, citing such practical ideas as the mingling of agriculture and manufacturing in a community, and its location near a large city to ensure having a market. It was a shrewd idea —and one upon which they had already acted—that people should be made to solicit admission so that they would be more likely to prize what they had been uncertain for a while of getting. The constant emphasis upon variety of occupation also seemed shrewd. In modern life labour seemed too monotonous. One man was always digging, another laying bricks, another herding cattle, when actually these occupations were not so difficult but that a man might learn all three and half a dozen more sufficiently well. No one had better reason than themselves to agree with the statement which Judith had marked: "The rich themselves find few occupations which unite pleasure and health."

The fanciful and impractical suggestions were even more fun to discuss—for example, the idea of domesticating more animals such as the beaver and the zebra and the quagga. Then there were the funny words which Brisbane coined, like ' civilizee,' which seemed to mean what ' civilized ' *man* ought to mean and didn't.

"Perhaps," said Mr Melton, "' civilizee ' is the opposite of ' chimpanzee.' "

There were all the amazing things (one hoped at least they would some day come true) which Milord Carisdell had witnessed in his journey through that mythical land of Icaria. Or, to shift back to Fourier, there was all the amusing mysticism—or foolishness, if you preferred—about 'pivots' and ' groups.' The sun was the pivot of the solar system, white of colours, mercury of metals, the lion of felines. " From these examples the reader will see what we understand by pivot." Judith and Mr Melton agreed that even had they understood to begin with the examples would have wholly confused them. And the symbol of a pivot, consisting of a capital X laid on one side, did not help any. As for the social groups, they were built up by an exercise in higher mathematics upon a theory of ' equilibration ' around a centre with ascending and descending wings. Finally, some twenty groups could be combined into a ' serie,' by which word Brisbane seemed to imagine the singular of ' series.' Quite characteristically the ' serie ' was presented as cultivating pears. It comprised a Centre of twelve groups devoted to juicy pears, an Ascending Wing of ten groups for hard pears, and a Descending Wing of eight groups for mealy pears. The thought of so many pears, especially of the hard and mealy ones, was enough to give anyone indigestion.

Then when you had laughed over such matters you would come

to some passage of noble humanitarianism, as when Brisbane stated the case of the downtrodden white workers of the northern states. In these days, when every one was weeping over Uncle Tom, it was good to find some one sympathizing with the factory slaves.

Fourier's sympathy did not stop at workers; cruelty to animals horrified him too. He even went to ridiculous lengths. His slaughter-houses were to be cleansed by a running stream and perfumed; animals were to be brought in by groups and struck down simultaneously so that they would be spared the sorrow of seeing their fellows die and the anguish of anticipated death. Judith and Mr Melton had seen too many cattle slaughtered to have any belief that death by anticipation bothered a steer, but they appreciated the general feeling for animals. Callousness towards animals had been one thing to which they had never got used in the old days, and the Americans were not much better than the Californians had been.

But, after all, the perfuming of a slaughter-house was at worst only the noble vagary of a great mind. Cabet, Brisbane, and Fourier—they were not mere practical men such as you could find by dozens on Montgomery Street. They were prophets, poets, blowers upon clarions and wavers of banners, divine madmen, preachers of crusades, builders of cities not built with hands. To their trumpet-calls and beneath their oriflammes might muster the practical people—people like themselves, reverently but firmly putting aside the oratorical and merely poetical, building cities which were laboriously built with hands. Brisbane himself had stated that the second step, the organization, must be undertaken either by governments or by wealthy people who could supply capital and direction. This was what they could do.

By and large, Mr Melton in his private thoughts didn't suppose that the Community would make any great difference in his life or in Judith's, in spite of the sudden lift which it had given to them now. Perhaps he was cynical. But still they would continue living in San Francisco, backing the Community with money and lending it direction from a distance. Its story would not be their story, and its success or failure would not be theirs. Tony Burke, enthusiastic, and brilliant with ideas, would see to getting things started; eventually the Community would have to become self-managing and self-sustaining.

As twilight was falling the little steamer was still ploughing down the broad, smooth river. The sky glowed bright behind the hill-crest with its dark forest. Mr Melton seemed to feel a benison come upon them. Stifling an antipathy to a show of feelings in such a public place, he stretched his arm across towards Judith's chair and laid his hand upon hers. He remembered that fear of uncertainty and insufficiency which he had had earlier; but it was a memory now, not a present feeling.

"WELL, WHO'S GOING TO CHURCH?" Lewis did not say the words, but he contemplated with amusement the prospect of saying them in a few minutes. It would be a bombshell for the placid breakfast party. All the family was here, even Guito.

Lewis cast his eyes around, considering how each of the persons would take the question. It would be especially surprising as coming from him. He never went to church any more. He had had his religious streak when he was about fifteen. He had gone to church twice a Sunday then, and Sunday School and mid-week service besides, and had thought of becoming a minister. But he had got over it, very decidedly.

When he put the question Guito would only laugh. Guito hadn't been inside a church for years. He had damn' near had to be, though, the time he got that girl into trouble—if he, Lewis, and Old Dan'l hadn't helped him out. Everybody stood by Guito in trouble; everybody liked him; he was probably the best of the family in spite of being wild.

Leticia would just smile in a superior way, and perhaps put a hand on the crucifix she was wearing. She had been to Mass already. Leticia was the only one of them that stuck by the old religion, or you might say any religion. That was what you would expect. She was the outsider; he and Guito had fought her ever since they could remember.

Henry was too little to count. You never could tell what he was thinking. Maybe he wasn't as bright as the rest of them were, even Leticia.

His mother would be surprised at his saying it, but might be ready enough to go. She went to church sometimes. As far as he could make her out, she started by being a half-hearted Congregationalist and became a half-hearted Catholic, and now was a kind of half-hearted atheist.

But Old Dan'l, he was the funniest. President of the Tom Paine Society, and yet he gave a hundred dollars a year to probably every church in town, Protestant and Catholic, and maybe the Chinese joss-house! He went to church too sometimes, said that he liked the singing, and the preachers were the best orators you could hear. Old Dan'l was the finest person in the world, thought Lewis. He would shoot the head off anybody who would be so disrespectful as to call him " Old Dan'l "; that was only a private way of thinking about him.

There came a lull in the conversation, and he said it :

" Well, who's going to church? "

It had just about the effect which he had expected. Guito looked at him as though he were crazy, and Leticia pulled in the corners of her nose and looked superior, and the rest were somewhat less definitely surprised. Then Lewis explained. You see, he had found out that the Reverend Doctor Jesson was going to preach about communities and interpret the Christian point of view towards them. Dr Jesson, in case any of them didn't know, was the kind of minister who didn't believe in just preaching about doctrines and general morality; he cultivated the reputation of reading widely and keeping abreast with current movements. Lewis made such a good case for going to church that before he knew it he had entrapped himself, although he had brought the matter up more as a joke than anything else.

An hour later Lewis was feeling entirely too conspicuous at being seated in a pew only half a dozen rows from the front of Dr Jesson's large church. That was what would happen naturally, for the usher was some kind of small business man, and when he saw Old Dan'l he bent double and led them down to the best seats in the house. Besides being conspicuous Lewis felt responsible, and vaguely worried. What *was* the Christian view on communities—that is to say, what was the view of Dr Jesson, who apparently thought himself capable of speaking for Christianity in general? If Dr Jesson had been going to say anything very adverse he might be considerably embarrassed at seeing them all in a front row. It might sour the poor man's whole sermon, for he certainly wouldn't want to attack the Meltons face to face.

There was an opening hymn and a short prayer and a selection rendered by the choir. Then Dr Jesson—a big, well-fed, smooth-faced man—read a chapter from Scripture. He read well, and Lewis enjoyed it thoroughly, although he wondered what connexion the chapter had with communities. It was Samuel something-or-other—about the battle of Mt Gilboa and the death of Saul. Lewis had always, like his mother. been fond of reading history, and he could sense its scenes with a reality that made him often feel tight-throated. Now he saw and heard the battle joined on the rough slopes of the mountain; the rattling of the chariots and the Children put to flight; the Philistine bowmen finding their mark at King Saul, the tall warrior; the King's command to his armour-bearer and the double death.

During the long prayer, his head bowed very comfortably upon the back of the pew in front, Lewis wondered still more about the significance of the chapter. He had heard of one old preacher who at his retirement boasted of having drawn at least one text for a sermon from every chapter in the Bible; perhaps Dr Jesson had the same ambition, and was to-day just working off a hard one.

Lewis was sure that the preacher was making what people would call " a fine prayer," but it had a tendency to put him to sleep; the language was too perfect and the voice too beautiful. He snapped to a kind of disgusted attention when he realized that Dr Jesson was praying for rain. You might know he had just come out from the East a couple of years ago. Of course it hadn't rained for three months, and things would look pretty dry and dusty to an Easterner and a city man like Dr Jesson, but that was the way they ought to be in California. Rain now would do more harm than good. This business of asking God for things was dangerous—that is, if you figured it worked at all. You couldn't run the insurance business that way. Probably the preachers down in San José were all praying for dry sunny weather. Lewis amused himself by thinking of God holding an audit on the prayers that came in on the subject, or counting them ' pro ' and ' con ' like ballots. The way to manage this prayer business rationally would be to hold a preliminary caucus of the

preachers, and decide just which Sunday they should start praying for rain, and then go at it with a bang so as to make some
impression.

Settling himself for the sermon, Lewis wondered what text
could come out of that chapter. " Then said Saul unto his
armour-bearer . . . " Of all things! What kind of sermon could
you preach from that?

But Dr Jesson seemed in no hurry to explain. He began talking about a ride which he had taken in the country that spring—
how beautiful it was and what fine thoughts it had inspired. There
was a delicate touch of humour at times too, not enough of course
to make people actually laugh. Suddenly Lewis thought that he
had it. Dr Jesson was an artist; he was developing his sermon as
that man Poe would develop a mystery story. The anecdote of
the ride in the country came to an end with something about a
coyote which he had seen ' skulking ' through a thicket. Then on
that narrow bridge of the single word ' skulking ' Dr Jesson took
himself quickly across and hit the main road of his discourse:
" A minister of God should act in the open; he should not be one
to *skulk* in thickets." And symbolically he moved out from behind his pulpit to the open platform.

He dropped his suave urbane oratory; his speech was faster and
his words more homely. He had visited this new community, and
he had read the books upon which it was founded. " He knew
whereof he spoke." And this new community was—he paused;
his eyes were somewhere upon the back wall; he had hushed his
audience: it was as if God's own voice were about to speak.
Then his words snapped out clean-cut—" Godless, un-Christian,
and vicious."

Lewis felt eyes turned upon the pew; he felt himself flushing
even to the back of his neck. He cursed himself violently for
having thoughtlessly brought this humiliation upon them all. He
could see Mr Melton's fingers working nervously. His mother
was looking straight to the front, head up; strangely, she was not
flushing, she looked pale. Lewis wondered if she would get up
and walk out. Or what? He wondered if the preacher had not
recognized them.

But the next words made that seem unlikely. "I speak," said the preacher, "not in hatred of anyone who may have been deluded into joining or into establishing that community; in my profession one must learn to hate the sin and love the sinner."

Lewis did not like to look at his mother much; he was sure anyway that she would understand he had not done this knowingly. And he had to admit that the preacher's discourse held him. Dr Jesson seemed to have read the books on the subject; he quoted Owen and Cabet, and Fourier and Brisbane.

First of all he took up Owen's idea of the importance of environment, and his famous saying, "Man s character is made for and not by him." With this conception, Dr Jesson declared, vanished man's personal responsibility, the conception of sin, and in fact all morality.

The idea of community of property he denounced as un-Biblical. The patriarchs had been admired for their possessions, and God had directly bestowed wealth upon Job. Dr Jesson quoted the amount of God's gifts to his servant Job down to the last camel and she-ass. He added New Testament citations, but, Lewis noticed, skipped the command to Onesimus, there being perhaps too many Abolitionists in the congregation.

He touched upon the breaking up of that sacred institution of the home. He denounced Fourier's advocacy of equal rights for women as being pernicious, citing especially St Paul. He quoted "spare the rod and spoil the child" as sufficient rebuke to Cabet's doctrine that loving solicitude and enlightened tenderness should take the place of restraint in the rearing and education of children.

On the question of sex-relations Dr Jesson remained well within the canons of good taste in his language, but perhaps by very reason of his having to speak guardedly he produced most striking suggestions. He implied that at Amarillo they might have to expect anything from polygamy, free love. and plain promiscuity to the equal debasement of complete celibacy. He denounced Fourier's foul attack upon matrimony without telling what it was, but managing to imply the worst.

In what seemed the peroration he touched the heights of elo-

quence in his scorn of " those deists—atheists, rather—who, denying God's own word as given in the Bible, pretend for their doctrines His own sanction."

But that was not the end. Lewis had forgotten. The preacher
had to solve his mystery story by connecting his sermon with his
Scripture-reading and text. It seemed a little flat. The Philistines
were Fourier, Cabet, and others. Saul—God's anointed, but gone
astray—stood for those who had succumbed to the Philistines and
were organizing the Community. The poor armour-bearer represented in some way the people who were joining the Community.
Lewis lost track; it took a man with the preacher's own love of
subtlety to put the thing together.

Instead of trying Lewis looked at his mother. But she was still
looking straight ahead—a little pale. She must be boiling within,
and he knew what his mother could be like when her anger
burst. What would she do when she met the preacher at the door,
shaking hands with the congregation as they went out? Slap his
face? Suddenly Lewis felt himself getting angry, as if a radia-
tion from her had spread out and touched him. By God, the
preacher deserved to have his face slapped! Standing behind his
pulpit and saying things like that to people when they couldn't
answer back—and to a woman too! Nobody but a preacher would
have dared do it. Anyone else would know that he would be
horsewhipped or challenged for saying such things. Lewis suddenly saw the smooth face across pistol-sights, and his hand closed
as if around the familiar grip of his favourite pistol. It was lucky,
he thought, Guito wasn't here. Guito would likely have gone up
and thrown the preacher out of his pulpit by the seat of his
pants. Guito was good at doing just what he wanted to.

As they got close to the door going out Lewis felt that he was
about ready to act as Guito might have. There was a throng of
people, and Dr Jesson shaking hands busily. Lewis got behind
some people so that he could pass out easily without speaking.
But he could see his mother right in the line that was coming up
to the preacher. By God, she was going to slap him! He felt his
muscles get tense. When she did he would let himself go and
knock some one down. It would be good.

Then his mother was bowing and saying something. Lewis did not catch it all, but what he heard was a mere politeness. Then they were out on the pavement waiting for Sam and the carriage, and saying not much of anything because of all the people close around them.

In the carriage Lewis burst out, " My God, mother, I admire you; you certainly are a civilized person, behaving so politely. I thought you would slap him."

He saw that she was almost in tears, and the tense bitterness in her voice appalled him :

" *Civilized*—I suppose it's *civilized* I *wanted* to slap him, but I had to lie and be hypocritical. I hate it! '

" Now, now," Mr Melton was saying, leaning over and patting her hand. " Now, now."

Tony Burke had come up from the ranch for Sunday dinner. His reports of the Community were good. About thirty people were there, and they had cleaned up everything around the buildings. The place had tumbled down a lot during the period of Foster's tenancy. They were digging a little irrigation ditch from the creek so as to put in a vegetable garden, and they were looking after the cattle.

When Tony heard of the sermon there were fireworks. He and Lewis were in the library alone, so that the presence of a lady didn't restrain Tony's language. Tony was Irish; as he said, the Irish were the most religious people in the world, and when they turned they became the most irreligious. Lewis began to realize that the Tom Paine Society represented a very polite by-your-leave dissent. It believed in God, and it thought that Christ, if not really God's son, was at least a good moralist and an admirable example of a human being. But Tony didn't believe in God at all, and he had a flaming hatred for Christianity. As for Christ, he quoted " the disciple Jesus loved ' in a way that made you think things you had never thought before. " ' Sell all that thou hast, and give to the poor,' " he quoted. " Was there ever a shallower, more unworkable social doctrine? "

As Tony talked Lewis began to see that after all the preacher had taken him in. He would like to hear a debate between the two of them, not just the preacher talking alone. As Tony showed, all Dr Jesson had done—if he had done that—was to show that the Community was un-Biblical or un-Christian. And then he had made the assumption that because it was un-Biblical or un-Christian it was evil. That was a big jump in the argument, said Tony. He himself was pretty nearly ready to put it the other way. Besides, what was Christian? Look at abolition—the ministers north of Mason-Dixon every day swinging more against slavery, and the ministers in the South pulling out more and more texts to show that the Bible, even the New Testament, was right behind them backing up the ' peculiar institution.'

Lewis had to calm Tony down a little before they could go to dinner. At the table Lewis asked Mr Melton how much money he had given that year to Dr Jesson's church.

" One hundred dollars, I believe."

" You can cut that off, anyway."

" Well, I'm not sure. The man was honest, when you come to think of it—honest and courageous to speak out that way when we were there. He knew he took a chance on his hundred dollars. I think I should keep on with it. We need honest, courageous men, even if they are opposed to us."

" Better make it two hundred," said Tony ironically. " To show him you admire his stand."

" Yes, but that would look as if I were trying to buy him off."

Lewis stared at his soup-plate, lost in amazement. He couldn't understand Dan'l. Seeing good in people even when they attacked you. . . . That sort of thing couldn't ever win. Between people like Dr Jesson and Tony—yes, and his mother too—Dan'l was going to be torn to pieces some day. He was too civilized, too liberal. Yet Dan'l was about the richest man in San Francisco, and Tony and Dr Jesson really amounted to pretty much nothing. Dan'l wasn't like the other rich men in San Francisco; Lewis knew them—hard men, fighters and drivers. Dan'l was rich just by accident—he was on the ground floor when lots went up in '49. It was a wonder he had ever held his money.

But, as they all agreed, the attack that Dr Jesson made on the Community was of no practical importance. Public sentiment might make or break the Community, but the preachers didn't make public sentiment. Look at the way they kept shouting for Sunday observance, and yet California went on horse-racing and whooping it up on Sunday just the same.

The usually silent little Henry seemed to sum the matter up: "Preachers don't count in California, do they?"

They laughed at his sudden contribution, and it led to the discussion that if preachers didn't count for much—who did? Before '56 it used to be the gamblers and saloon-keepers; now maybe it was the politicians like Gwin and Broderick.

"Yes," said Tony Burke, "and who runs the politicians? Men like our friend Judge Wingram—men who can afford to pay for franchises, and tax-favours, and Government contracts. We aren't in the hide-and-tallow era any more."

Tony was right, thought Lewis—but there wasn't any use letting a dinner conversation get too serious. "I give you a toast," he said: "Mr Daniel Melton, the richest man in San Francisco, therefore the most powerful, and therefore the most dangerous!"

They drank it as a joke, with Old Dan'l at the head of the table looking self-conscious and a little embarrassed.

JUDITH HAD NOT BEEN AT THE RANCH for a long time; she had thought it only right that while the Community was getting started she and Daniel should keep their fingers out of things. Now that Tony judged it time for her to make a visit and she was actually upon the old road up from the Mission she felt a distinct eagerness, not only to see the Community at work, but also to see the ranch itself. Now and then she realized that her feelings were centred upon the ranch much more than she usually admitted.

Sam was driving, and little Henry sat beside him. Only by habit did she still think of him as little Henry. He was sixteen now, taller than his mother, and giving evidence of going to be the tallest of the family. He had begged so hard to come along that she had let him leave school. She had never realized that Henry had—or seemed to have—so much affection for the old life. But then it was hard to know much about Henry—he was so quiet. It touched her that he should be the only one of her sons to share her feeling for the ranch. Luis was very happy in San Francisco building up his marine insurance. Guito was reading law now, but she was afraid that he was less well versed in law than in restaurants and races and the California Light Horse. He was like his father—too much perhaps. Everybody liked him, but she was sure that Daniel and Lewis must have got him out of scrapes and covered up his tracks more than once without letting her know anything.

› The road up from the Mission was more travelled now, and had fences along it in places. It had more bridges, and here and there were ditches to drain away the water in the winter. Otherwise it was worse than it used to be, for the greater number of wagons wore it down into ruts and made dust. The dust kept settling upon Judith's dark travelling dress in a visible powder, and getting into her nostrils so that she sneezed.

She sighted the down stage when it was a mile ahead. It came ploughing along, and leaving a cloud of dust resting over the road behind it, like a ship's wake. The four horses looked hot and dispirited, and seldom went faster than a walk. Judith thought of the lithograph she had recently seen. An Eastern artist had drawn it—*The California Stage-coach*. It showed six fine bay horses at a spanking trot; on the box were the driver, the express-messenger, and a spruce passenger. From within looked out a pretty and modishly gowned young lady. There was no dust.

But this driver was very dirty and looked sleepy. No guard was in evidence, for this stage probably carried nothing more valuable than a few dozen eggs. The only other person on the box was a Chinaman, and she knew that the reason why he was up there taking the full sun was that the other passengers had objected to having a Chinaman inside. They always did, on the grounds that Chinamen smelled. From the stage a woman with a baby—a farmer's wife probably—looked out; her face was dusty, and she looked tired and uncomfortable. A sweaty-faced man looked out too, a commercial traveller if there ever was one. Inside she saw another man asleep.

When they turned off the main road and approached the old Gómez place there was less dust. Dead brown grass was still standing between the wheel-marks. Neither the Gómez nor the García places had changed much in looks. The Johnsons had the first and the Brightmans the second. The American families lived in the old adobes, but the Johnsons had put up a small wooden barn. Mr Johnson was away, but Judith talked a little to Mrs Johnson, who was sallow-skinned and thin and had faded sandy hair; she had about as many children running around as there used to be in the Gómez days. Mrs Brightman looked much the same as Mrs Johnson, but her hair was black, flecked with grey. Mr Brightman had blond hair, and seemed very surly. He even got as far as starting to complain that the cattle from the Community wandered over and grazed on his land. Judith avoided argument; anyone knew that in unfenced country the herds got over the boundary lines sometimes—but it always worked both ways.

As she drove Judith felt a little dispirited over the Johnsons and the Brightmans. They all were sallow, and the smaller children had that pinched look which meant worms. There were too many hogs about; the two families must be half living on pork. The García and the Gómez stock had been pretty bad, but at least their half-Indian faces couldn't ever look sallow, and all the garlic and chile they ate kept the children clean of worms.

Neither García nor Gómez had ever bothered to get a decent title to his land; so probably they were down in San José now, living in hovels and doing day labour. Well, she couldn't waste much sympathy on them. But she had a twinge of feeling when she thought of Pablo—a good rider and a good fighter; and he had died as a good retainer should, with his master.

The only real improvements she could see in the two places were the outhouses which the Americans had put up, and even those might be far from sanitary. The Brightmans seemed almost as much trash as the Garcías. Yet one odd thing was that if it came to fighting one Brightman with his rifle was worth three Garcías, even if one of them was Pablo.

As when she had first ridden up this road with Juan so many years ago, she began to see cattle. She made Sam stop where a yearling was standing in good view. It had the new brand. The old Amarillo tied X, everybody had agreed, was too simple; it could be altered into almost anything now that so many artists with running-irons were around. So Judith had designed a new one. She had had to alter her original idea a little, so that the brand in the end was a circle with five lines—instead of arrows— extending part way in towards the centre. They called it the Broken Wheel. No one except Daniel and herself knew that it stood for the circle and arrows she had seen.

The road led over the little rise of the hill, just as it always had, and Judith called to Sam to stop again. The valley was in its late-summer austere yellows and browns, and, by and large, it looked much the same as it might have looked any September since she remembered. The main change was that over on the north side of the creek was a long line of fence, and inside it a different shade of yellow showed stubble from which wheat and barley had been harvested; a field of rather mangy-looking corn was still standing. Judith reflected that she should have warned Tony not to try corn;

the valley was too high and the nights too cold; they always used to buy their corn from San José.

Tony assigned a man to help Sam put the horses up and a boy to show Henry around. He apologized that Judith should have to sleep in the same room with one of the members, a widow named Mrs Barton. They were, he said, very crowded; he himself had to use the office as his bedroom.

After Judith had cleaned up Tony took her into the office, for she was eager to take a look at the books and discuss matters generally. The first thing she saw was the map; and, in fact, from its prominent position you could be sure that Tony wanted it to be seen.

" It isn't really accurate," he said deprecatingly. " We worked it out from the description in the grant, and that goes by landmarks and watersheds, except when it falls back on the old Spanish standby, ' more or less.' "

The map showed the ranch to be a crude rectangle with wavy rounded edges, especially on the north-east. It was about seven miles from north to south and five miles wide, and contained, according to estimate, a little less than nineteen thousand acres. The map showed the difference between hilly and level land, but the only big spot of level land was the main valley which lay a little south of the centre of the ranch. It was marked ' Amarillo Valley,' and far to the north was the inscription ' Quail-hole Valley.' She was puzzled.

" Oh," said Tony, " that's what people around here call it. It's a little valley, with good soil. It would take a lot of work to put it under the plough, though, for it would have to be cleared. The thicket is a regular jungle with new sprouts; it must have been burned over a few years ago."

Judith felt cold and sick—the dry, still day, her own treason to Juan, the shots, and the grey smoke rising above Ojuelo. . . . There was no use telling Tony, although he was looking at her, sensing something queer. No, not he nor any of these newcomers would understand.

" Oh, yes," she said, raising a wall of politeness between him and her feelings, " I remember the place. There are quail there, of course, and being such a deep little valley it is a kind of hole."

She was glad that Tony had quick enough tact not to ask questions. But 'Ojuelo,' that picturesque figure of speech, shifted to the ridiculous 'Quail-hole' by blundering Americans!

Tony's willingness to shift the subject was most likely a desire to get on with his own story. He was bursting with statistics and plans. Most of the ranch was hill-country suitable only for grazing; the arable land did not exceed four thousand acres. This was, however, much more than they could bring under the plough for some years. One of the immediate problems was fencing. The outer circuit would require about twenty miles of fence, and the separation of the plough land from the pasture about nine miles more. This was a stupendous problem, especially in a scantily wooded country.

Judith had the feeling about Tony that she had sometimes had before—that he was thinking in too big terms and not willing to work with the supplies in hand. Thirty miles of fence! . . .

She found that a compromise had actually been effected, although Tony did not quite like it. The thicket along the creek had been reinforced to serve as a fence for one side of a field. The ranch buildings themselves and the already fenced areas of the vineyard and the cemetery were on the map strung together with a line indicating fence. From the vineyard another curving mile of fence completed a field large enough for immediate needs.

Unfortunately, as further questioning brought out, neither end of the fence was completed, so that at times a man had to be placed at either end all night to keep the cattle out of the crops.

"But why didn't you build solidly from one end, so that there would be only one gap and only one man needed to watch?"

It was the first time she had ever seen Tony embarrassed, and his explanations were far from clear. The upshot seemed to be that the Community had come to loggerheads about the fence leading from the cemetery to the ranch buildings. This fence, Tony pointed out, did not fit into the general scheme, so that to construct it would be, eventually, lost labour. The question had been argued in meeting between those who believed in immediate and practical, even if makeshift, measures and those who believed in a long-reasoned scheme of development for ten or twenty years, or perpetuity. Judith felt herself torn two ways—she liked Tony's long view, but practical sense told her that the way to build a fence was not to start at the middle and work both ways.

Marked on the map in blue, just at the point where the creek flowed out from the hills, was the word 'Dam site.' Here was projected a mill to grind wheat, and to figure perhaps in other manufacturing projects. Judith objected that the creek was practically dry for half the year.

"Your objection would be well grounded," Tony explained "if we were considering an ordinary commercial establishment. But the very strength of a community lies in planning the work ahead and thus working efficiently. In the summer, when there is no water for the mill, we shall all be busy in the fields; after the crops have been harvested the rains will come and we shall all turn our energies towards utilizing the power which the mill can supply us only in the winter."

The sweet logicality of Tony's plans left her dazzled with a delight which survived even the examination of the ledgers. So far the Community had cost a lot of money—the materials for the new hall and barn, the renovation of the old buildings, the support of so many people during the months before they had harvested a crop. But she and Daniel had expected that, and the demands had not much exceeded expectations. The *personnel* book was more disturbing. In it were entered all the data concerning the members. The original entry recorded such dry facts as the name and age. Next came various notes—the kinds of work to which each individual had been assigned for such and such number of days, the days of illness, and so forth. Finally, in a surprising number of instances, came a date and the single word 'Withdrew.' Since it had first been well organized, about a year previously, the Community had generally had about thirty-five adults in residence, but the total number who had passed through must be twice that. Some had stayed for months, others had hardly lasted out a week. It troubled Judith that so many people were quick to be dissatisfied even in Paradise, and she pressed Tony for the reasons. From his point of view the blame naturally rested upon the renegades. Some had been cranks; they had entered apparently with the idea of regenerating the Community after the image of their own crankiness. They worked a while privately, and then, with the support of a few converts, sprang the idea in meeting —that the vineyard should be rooted up, or that everybody should turn vegetarian, or even that the whole direction of affairs should be turned over to the divinely inspired guidance of the agitator. Almost every current enthusiasm had raised its head—abolition, phrenology, celibacy, spiritualism, Swedenborgianism. But usually different cranks could be counted on to fight each other, so that the better-balanced people held the determining votes. No, he did not believe in trying to get rid of the cranks. Two of the best and most loyal members were the strictest vegetarians, and the only man who could do the essential work of blacksmith and veterinarian was ready any moment to talk you to death with some strange theory of the Lost Tribes.

But not all who had left had been cranks. Some had merely been lazy; they had joined for the sake of some meals to be gained without work, and on being discovered had been expelled as drones. Others, city-born, had simply got bored after being a few weeks in a place where they could not see at least the passing of an occasional fire-engine or a brewer's dray.

Judith was eager to see the new buildings. The barn offered little of interest. The new dining-hall, however, was imposing. It stood adjoining the old ranch-house on the east, and thus, she noted silently, almost fulfilled the dream of the Godoys of having a complete quadrilateral. But, far different from the thick-walled adobe tower which Juan's father had planned, the new hall had a highly unmilitary look, with its thin board walls and many windows. Tony proudly gave its inside dimensions as fifty by thirty-seven feet. At one end was a gallery which served as an extra men's dormitory, and was also useful as a choir-loft and an upper stage for dramatic performances.

Before dinner Tony introduced the members. It was less of an ordeal than Judith had expected. Several of the cranks, indeed, tried to get started with their special ideas. At the other extreme a few members were too unctuously servile, as if they were receiving a hand-out at the back door. But most of them seemed decent working people, embarrassed a little and hesitating for words, but maintaining their self-respect.

Most interesting were the few who, like Tony, represented the intellectual reaction against the modern world. There was old Hargrace, graduate of some New England college, who had been at Book Farm and was still ready to try again. With him was a younger man named Rappel, with a mystic's face. He was the kind, thought Judith, who in any age or place would have sought some way to retire from the world. Of this same group was a youngster named Conway, who spent all his spare time observing the birds of the neighbourhood, and was just now bubbling over with something which he had discovered about the habits of quail.

The meal was plentiful and tasty enough. The cooks were hired on a semi-permanent basis, but the assisting and serving was done by members, male and female, appointed in rotation. The conversation was varied, but Judith noticed an undercurrent of excitement about the 'meeting' which was to be held soon after dinner. Three times the long tables 'burst' into song. At least Judith supposed that one would be expected to say 'burst,' although the effect of spontaneity was not marked, and off-key singing, especially among the sopranos and tenors, was flagrant. The song-leader was Phineas Brown, and the first song was his *Amarillo All for Thee*, which he had finally succeeded in having voted in as the Community hymn. Perhaps some of the poor singing could be attributed to Mr Brown's choice of songs, for his second was *The Star-Spangled Banner*, which was patriotic, but very conducive to flatting, and his last was a sentimental, slow ditty which droned on with lifeless banality. The only genuine attempt at singing for enjoyment seemed to be a valiant effort by some young men to get going on *Sweet Betsy from Pike*, and Mr Brown quashed this; perhaps he thought it vulgar. Again Judith contrasted the old days with the new—how you would suddenly hear the guitars begin to twang out in the quarters and the vaqueros would start singing just as spontaneously and as naturally as the coyotes started yelping, and at just about the same time of dusk. Suddenly she jumped to find herself thinking that Americans were queer people—with all their running around to subdue the earth without stopping to enjoy it, and their funny idea that being a dependable rifleman was better than being a reliable baritone.

2 B

The meeting began with a minute of silence. This, Judith remembered, had been Tony's brilliant cutting of the Gordian knot after the discovery that no matter how simple a prayer was offered it offended some one's religion, or lack of religion. " But," as Tony explained gleefully, " even the atheists couldn't object to keeping silence for a minute's private contemplation of the complete absence of divinity."

Next came a five-minute talk. This, in its adoration of humanity, was obviously a sort of prayer-substitute. To-night the speaker took as his subject the recent linking of America and Europe by the submarine telegraph. He commented upon its significance for peace and international good-feeling, and even managed to make something out of the platitudes exchanged between Queen Victoria and President Buchanan.

Announcements followed—mostly routine assignments of various people to various duties. Then there was a hush, and Judith could see people drawing breath and looking around with a kind of satisfied expectation. Tony, as presiding officer, was on his feet. For the benefit of some new members, he said, it must be explained that the Community had been wisely established on a platform of only a few general principles, with the provision that more specific rules were to be adopted by vote in open meeting after the debate. The discussion of the first question for the evening would be limited to an hour, and the question need not be brought to vote at this meeting. The question was : " At what age shall members be retired from active service? "

The eagerness and vehemence of the debate amazed Judith. Old Hargrace, the oldest member, although grizzled, was probably not more than fifty-five, so that an actual case of retirement through age would hardly occur for ten years at least—and by that time any number of things might have happened. But this consideration failed to dim anyone's enthusiasm for stating his opinions. As usual in everything connected with communities, Judith found herself confused by the mingling of excellent arguments and sheer nonsense. Mr Hargrace himself spoke firmly for unconditional retirement at the age of seventy-three; he supported himself by ' medical science,' the Pythagorean theory of numbers, and some quotations—rather irrelevant—from Confucius. On his seventy-third birthday a man apparently went into complete mental and physical dissolution. Counter-arguments and examples ranging from Cato the Elder to the still flourishing Walter Savage Landor did not shake him into admitting more than that a man's powers might linger on for perhaps six months after the fatal date.

Other suggestions went all the way from sixty-five to no retirement age at all. Most speakers seemed to object strongly to any possible domination of the Community by the conservatism of old age, and many favoured Mr Hargrace's proposal of seventy-three as a practical, if not divinely appointed, year.

The hour ended, however, without a vote. The second subject—and one calling for a decision—was the report of the committee on manufacturing. The committee chairman, to Judith's surprise, was not one of the educated members, but a stocky middle-aged man, who used ' good ' for ' well.' Apart from grammatical errors and a fumbling for words, the report was excellent.

The committee, he said, had tried out the feelings of the Community and found almost unanimous opinion that the healthy life of a group should include manufacturing in the winter to balance farming in the summer. On its own initiative and through suggestions the committee had considered dozens of possibilities. The problem was difficult. Amarillo had no coal or metals, little wood, a small and uncertain source of water-power, and no assured market closer than San Francisco. Moreover, the conscientious feelings of the various members must be considered. Thus, even if mineral wealth was available, many were of the opinion that mining was unhealthy, and morally degrading since it was work carried on in the dark and removed from the sight of Heaven. Similarly, the preparation of wines and brandies, although it seemed practical, had been ruled out on the grounds of conscientious objections. From the stir in certain parts of the room at this announcement, Judith could see that the committee had acted wisely.

In the end the committee was going to present only two proposals. The first was the tanning and manufacture of leather. This seemed practical; they could make use of the hides of cattle slaughtered at the ranch and could buy others very cheaply from the surrounding ranches. By specialization in the finer grades of leather and in finished products, such as belts and horse-trappings, the bulk of the export could be kept small.

The other proposal was the establishment of a soap factory. In this they could make use of the animal fats supplied by their own and the near-by ranches. The caustics could be supplied partly from their own wood ashes, partly by purchase. Again, by specializing in expensive perfumed toilet soaps, they could keep the bulk of their export low and its value high.

As he closed Judith found herself thinking that either idea was good, and she was surprised at the fury of argument which immediately arose ' pro ' and ' con.' It was a tribute to the shrewdness of the committee that no serious attack was made upon the financial possibilities of either scheme. The fury raged over æsthetic matters.

A few objected that *both* tanning and soap-making were smelly, degrading occupations. One of the ' pro-leathers ' brought the immoral implications of perfumed soap to the fore. At best, was it not an encouragement to vanity, and at worst, was it not the prerogative of a certain class of woman? A ' pro-soap ' argued facetiously in return that one might just as validly attack the moral status of leather on the grounds that the chief duty of belts was in connexion with that article of clothing known as " unmentionables."

Finally the ' pro-soaps ' managed to put their own motion and carry it. There were threats of withdrawal from certain die-hard ' pro-leathers.' The meeting adjourned.

Judith's head was still much too active with the excitement to allow her to go to sleep; so she went again to the office with Tony, and they talked late. In private Tony confessed himself a ' pro-soap,' chiefly on the practical grounds that three of their members had some experience with soapmaking, while nobody really seemed to know much about tanning. . . .

Back in San Francisco a few days later, Judith talked the whole matter over with Daniel. On the whole, she reported herself well enough satisfied. The Community was not that ideal one which they had planned, but at least it was taking some thirty people, besides children, out of the slums of San Francisco, away from the chance of contracting disease and lying in some foul hole the way Jerry Graham had done.

Daniel asked a few questions. What about the man-woman problem? he inquired delicately. With women in the Community granted the same freedom as men, and with men well in the majority, it would be luck if there weren't some mix-up. And, in view of the Mormons and that other place, the general public was touchy about communities for that reason. So far, said Judith, there at least hadn't been any open scandal.

In general Daniel was very comforting. Naturally, he said, the Community hadn't attained the ideal; ideals were things you talked and dreamed about, but didn't actually expect to realize. The meeting must have been rather ridiculous with its great excitement over theoretical matters, but even so it showed that the people were training themselves in community living. Even those people who came and left must depart with some new conception of the human ideal of co-operation as opposed to what Tony liked to call "animal competition." And, besides, why worry about classifying people? Most of us would fall into more than one class. A man might be a faddist and yet a useful, hard worker—like the blacksmith-veterinarian who would talk your arm off about the Lost Tribes.

Then, not without showing her irritation, she told Daniel about 'Ojuelo' being made into 'Quail-hole.' He took it calmly.

"You know," he said, "I've wondered about that name, anyway. To mean 'little' eye in Californian Spanish it ought really to be 'ojito.' It may be just some Indian word that sounded like 'ojuelo' to the Spaniards, just the same as 'amarillo.'"

So it went in history, thought Judith—one race despoiling another, even to its names.

She lay awake for a while. Her head was full of ideas as she thought back over her visit and over her talk with Daniel. For her, middle-age was at least not proving the time of stagnation which it did for so many.

And, lying there beside Daniel, she thought how happy she had really been in both her husbands. For there was Juan, young and virile and handsome, rider and troubadour and fighter—he had taken her to heaven and dragged her down again, and given her children and the ranch that she loved, and let her know the bitterness of hardship and the sweet of victory. Those had been in the times of youth, when her body was so strong that it never seemed tired, and when things of the body meant so much.

Now she was older, and she got tired Sometimes she had pains in her side; they dated back, she knew, to that time when she had been carrying a child, but had ridden all that way to get the French doctor. And now that she was older she had Daniel—with his tenderness and his sympathy, his humanity and reasonableness, and his love of books that he shared with her. Yes, and his wealth too to protect her—a greater protection these times than all Juan's pistols and lances in the days far off.

JUDITH HAD JUST BEEN HAVING a hammer-and-tongs argument with Leticia. At eighteen Leticia was slender and Spanish-looking and pretty. She and Judith struck fire like flint and steel, especially about Leticia's Irishman. Having once eloped imprudently, Judith was at a disadvantage in arguing about marrying against your parents' judgment, but she did not like John Kelley, and she felt it her futile duty to tell Leticia why.

Then when she looked out from her bedroom window and saw Daniel and Lewis drive up to the house in a hired cab at three in the afternoon she knew that something must be the matter, and she had a pretty good idea that it was something about the Community. It was rather a faded dream now, the Community. Or you might say it was no longer the shiny birthday present it once was. It was a little rusty, and had mended places, and make-shift parts supplied where the resplendent original ones had broken down. It was the people, she thought, as she went downstairs. The idea was right, but you never seemed to get the right people to make it work; they bickered, and sulked, and went stale. They never seemed to realize, most of them, that they were living in a way which was best suited to the proper development of human beings.

Daniel and Lewis both looked so long-faced that they frightened her. When she read the letter that Daniel had got from Tony Burke she really felt relieved. Not that Tony seemed unconcerned. In fact, he sounded worse than Daniel and Lewis looked. But, after all, what did it amount to? Trouble with the neighbours, a couple of the Community members beaten up in a fist-fight, more squabbling about Jenny Dalton's baby, some anonymous letters which ought to be thrown in the fire and forgotten, and a couple of warning placards stuck up on the ranch-house doors at night. Some crazy boys playing at robbers might have done the letters and placards, or they might be a hoax.

But what sobered her was Lewis' attitude. Daniel, she knew, was likely to be jittery and untrustworthy in his judgment of matters like this which involved people. On books and even about real-estate and finance you could count on him—when people were not so important. But Lewis knew his way in the world; he spent his time with shipmasters and supercargoes and owners who were trying to collect more insurance than was due them. Judith had come to trust his judgment in most matters more than Daniel's.

Her first suggestion was that they reply to Tony's letter by writing him to stop being an old woman and get to work at the wheat-harvest. But it fell as flat as a stale joke. And before she knew it she herself was feeling frightened again, and agreeing with the others that some one ought to go down to reinforce Tony and settle affairs a little. If they were going at all they ought to go quickly. Who was to go? Lewis was tied up with his own business, and Daniel also was unusually involved. Judith felt herself flinch at the thought of an all-day ride through the hills; a few years before she would have enjoyed it, but now long riding brought out the pain in her side. They might take the steamer to Alviso, but that would be slow and would mean waiting. Lewis settled matters. He knew the waterfront, and he was sure he could charter some tug or river-steamer big enough to take the horses and carriage aboard, and yet small enough to put them ashore at the old Mission landing.

An hour later the little steamer was casting off. Daniel was aboard, having decided to take his secretary and dictate letters. They had taken Henry too, for he was always glad to go to the ranch. Lewis walked along the wharf, keeping pace with the steamer as its paddle-wheels began to churn up the water muddily. He was repeating things he had already said, in the way people always do at the last moment when seeing some one off.

"Sorry I couldn't go along, but this *Cambodia* business ties me up—criminal negligence almost, but we can't prove it. It's a scandal how they send out those cheaply built steamers to take their chances in the ocean. I'll see that the note gets to the sheriff all right. Daniel's probably right; Mike might just start trouble. Well, good-bye. Remember me to Tony."

The churning muddy water spread out behind in a wake. Lewis

stood on the end of the wharf waving for a moment, and then
went off about his business. Judith looked at the other figure that
still stood there. It was Big Mike, and under his coat she could
make out the bulge of the long-barrelled revolver; still hopeful of
being taken along, he had buckled it on before they drove down
to the wharf. He looked disconsolate now, the very image of a man
whose occupation was gone. Here was the first time in years that
there seemed to be any need for a bodyguard—and they had left
him behind. Judith was reminded of a big dog that had had its
feelings hurt.

Funny—she who did not think there was much prospect of
trouble had been the one to suggest taking Mike, and Daniel, who
was obviously worried, had vetoed the idea.

"This is '59, not '49," he said. "The time for gun-play and that
sort of thing is over in California. If we took Mike we'd just be
asking for violence. Instead, I'll send a letter to the sheriff asking—
demanding—protection."

The steamer changed course, and a pierhead cut Mike out of
view. Judith watched the pageant of the waterfront slide by. Ordinary brigs, schooners, barques, and ships. Now and then a tall, slim
clipper that, with luck, could run the Cape Horn voyage in under
a hundred days. Big river-steamers for Sacramento and Stockton;
little river-steamers that in time of high water went ploughing
through the mud clear to Red Bluff on the Sacramento and Fire-
baugh's on the San Joaquin. Big ocean-steamers for the Panama
run, each with great paddle-wheels, and a tall smoke-stack, and
short, stumpy masts rigged for enormous courses and skimpy top
sails, and nothing at all above the topgallants. On one of them
Judith made out the name *Cambodia*; that was the one Lewis had
spoken of. She had met heavy weather off the Mexican coast; her
engines had failed, and she had almost foundered. Finally she had
limped into harbour with only one paddle-wheel working, and sent
out a hurry call for insurance-adjusters. To the unprofessional eye
she seemed a fine ship, but Judith had heard enough of Lewis'
shop-talk to know that in too many of the liners the money went
into paint and deck-space, and not into engines and timbering.

As they got out from under the shelter of the docks the wind struck them, and their tiny steamer began to dip and bob. It was just the ocean breeze a little stronger than ordinary; it would be sweeping across the valley at Amarillo when they got there, making the yellow surface of the wheat-field dip in waves. It was a damp, chilly breeze here, but by the time it got across the sunny hills to Amarillo it would be drier and warmer and sweeter.

Daniel was already dictating. At Judith's request he had brought along from the office the big dossier of correspondence and reports and miscellaneous what-nots which covered the business affairs of the Community for the last year. She settled down to look it over, realizing that she had lost touch a little of late. Leticia's social launching and the foundation of a new hospital had been taking a lot of her time for the last half-year.

First came the quarterly reports. She had seen them before, and they were excellent. The Community was still absorbing money, but income was catching up with expenditure so rapidly that the next year could be expected to show a favourable balance. By writing off the improvements as capital charges, you could even show that the Community had already made money. The soapmaking particularly had proved profitable.

Next came a series of items relating to the display of soaps which the Community had presented at the California Exhibition, held in San Francisco that last February. Here was the official statement of award. In beautiful calligraphy and verbose English it stated that the " first and special award for quality of soap and soap products " had been granted to the Amarillo Community. Below this stood out an impressive gold seal and a cluster of flourished official signatures.

Judith doubted whether the award meant very much, for the judging committee had comprised four business men and a rather greasy-looking physician. Judith had never been much taken with feminist movements, but she thought women might at least have been asked to judge the soap. There had been a little fun in the award in that it had seemed to irk Alicia Wingram to have the Judge's Excelsior Soap Company beaten in open competition.

Not that the financial end mattered, for the Judge was richer than ever. The Wingrams had left Stockton Street for a magnificent house in the exclusive new South Park. The richer and more magnificent they got the thicker Alicia's Alabama accent grew: it had got past the creamy stage now, in Judith's opinion; it was practically butter.

Perhaps it was chagrin about the award which had made Alicia so catty about Jenny Dalton's illegitimate baby down at the Community. Alicia needn't be so pure; Judith could have told her some things about the Judge—for instance, that matter of Paquita and her friend down at the ranch. The Judge probably had enough illegitimates to start an orphan asylum. That sort of thing didn't bother Judith much; she had lived in Mexican California a long time and seen nature take its course very often.

Still, for the sake of the Community, she could have boxed Jenny Dalton's ears for getting involved with a fly-by-night lover when the Community could have got along just as well without giving anyone a chance to make comparisons with the Mormons and polygamy. People had written communications to the newspapers, and there had been editorials in the country weeklies. Jenny had played the martyr as the betrayed virgin, and had managed to throw the responsibility upon the way of life at the Community. This had made Tony furious, for he said the only reason she had not been in trouble before was luck rather than virtue. He wanted to send her packing, baby and all; but Judith and Daniel said that would be just plain inhumanity. Then the editorials and the communications to the editors—in the country weeklies again more especially—became more virulent against the Community. It was, thought Judith, a case of 'heads I win, tails you lose.' The Community was to blame for Jenny's going wrong in the first place, and was to blame again for not casting her out so that she could starve or go still further wrong. In the end—the publicity being so widespread—Jenny received and accepted by mail a proposal of marriage from a respectable and lonely, but probably very dull-witted, rancher in Tulare County.

There was a sheaf of clippings in the back of the dossier. It had been a point to save clippings, for they had all agreed that public opinion might determine the success or failure of the Community. At first there had been various editorials and accounts, most of them guardedly favourable. Then the Community had ceased to be news. Just lately there had been much more in the papers than there had ever been before, and it was all unfavourable. Judith had not seen many of the clippings, and she realized that Daniel had been keeping them at the office. She felt a little irritated with the suspicion that he had been trying to shelter her and keep her from worrying; she was a good deal younger and fitter to do the worrying than Daniel was.

Daniel's secretary had very neatly kept the clippings in chronological order. The time element raised some curious thoughts too. Here came February reports of the award of the prize at the Exhibition. Most of these merely included the award as one of the whole list, but one paper had taken the occasion for a special and very favourable comment upon the industry and progress of the Community. Then in a clipping dated a week later, *apropos* of nothing, there was an ugly attack upon the Community. The odd thing was that it was from the same paper which a week before had carried the favourable comment. Were there two different editors, or was the editor crazy, or had he simply been drunk when he wrote one or the other?

In March the Jenny Dalton affair had broken, and from then on there were plenty of clippings, and all bad. The big city papers like the *Alta* and the *Bulletin* kept out of it; since those were the papers that Judith read she had not half realized what was happening. There was one little San Francisco paper, the *Gazette*, which kept squealing as if the Community were going to seduce all the editor's daughters. Then in the country there were the *Farmer and Merchant*, the *Contra Costa Sentinel*, a Marysville paper, and two others back in the gold towns. These few papers supplied most of the clippings. Their articles started with Jenny Dalton, and then before you knew it they were throwing mud in general. Judith could not make it out, but she thought the editors might be prudish. or else they had really persuaded themselves that the Community had some connexion with Mormonism. Since the Mormon War in '57 you could always start a riot by calling out something about Brigham Young or polygamy. Even Alicia Wingram had tried to be facetious with something about "Muh-muhn-isuhm"—but it was hard to be facetious through a mush of cream cheese.

There were other charges—for instance, that certain people who had been members for a while and then left for one reason or another had been swindled out of money. One whole attack was built up around the idea that the Community was dangerously un-American, because in elections the members would be sure to vote as a unit, not individually. Besides being untrue, the charges seemed unimportant. Judith could not understand it; she had a feeling that there was something behind it all, but she didn't know what.

She looked across to where Daniel sat dictating. She was sorry that these additional worries came to him just now when he was having enough trouble, anyway. Since the financial panic and the failure of Sather and Church a year and a half before things had been getting worse and worse in San Francisco. Thousands had gone off with the Fraser River gold-rush, and people were saying that unless there was a new gold-strike in California San Francisco was done for. Daniel did not say so, even though prices of real-estate were slumping and far too many of his buildings lacked tenants. Daniel had seen San Francisco through a lot of ups and downs; Judith knew that he would have been buying more lots right now if he had had the money available.

Next morning on the drive up to the ranch they stopped for a minute at the little village which still clustered about the Mission. On the porch of the general store the inevitable loafers were carrying on the inevitable argument about the affairs of the world. They gave the carriage a good look, but they were newcomers to the country and did not recognize Judith. A moment later she was glad of it, for they were discussing the Community between spurts of tobacco juice. It sounded as if they had been reading the same editorials that she had been reading the day before. It was likely enough that they had, for everybody in these parts who read at all was likely to see either the *Farmer and Merchant* or the *Sentinel*. She could not hear everything, and they seemed to be saying little new, anyway. But once she caught the run of a whole speech:

"They're livin' up there all huddled in together like a lot o' Chinamen. No wonder they can sell cheaper than the rest of us. They ought to be run out o' the country."

For the first time Judith began to feel more than vaguely worried.

It was ridiculous for those men to be talking about being undersold; obviously they were nothing better than day-labourers. But in some way the idea had grown up in their minds that the Community was wronging them.

As they drove on Judith found that the familiar countryside had somehow grown sinister. In the old days it had always held a little risk of Indians, and for a few years after '49 a definite threat of bandits. But Indians and bandits seemed open foes whom people like Juan or Big Mike could fight. A misguided public opinion was an even uglier enemy, more likely to strike in the dark. Mike's long-barrelled revolver would be no good against it. She saw now that they had been right in not bringing him. She longed earnestly for Lewis. Henry was merely a youngster, and Daniel would be no use in an affair like this. Lewis might find a way out.

Daniel wanted to stop at the Brightmans', but Judith made him drive straight on. She was getting in a hurry to see how things were at the ranch, and, besides, she had a feeling that sullen Mr Brightman would be definitely among their enemies.

Henry was the first to see the horse. They were almost at the valley by that time. Sam pulled in the greys to a halt. It was a common-looking black horse, and they could all see the Broken Wheel brand. It must have been lying down when the noise of the carriage disturbed it. Now it was trying to get to its feet, but there was something wrong. It got up on its fore-legs all right, but the hindquarters seemed not to work. It rolled about help-lessly, half got up and then collapsed, wallowing as if frightened and in pain.

Daniel and Henry walked across to see, and then came back, looking pale. Both of them were fond of horses. They got clear back into the carriage before Daniel spoke; she could tell that he was trying to make his voice sound matter of fact:

" Hamstrung," he said.

" Accident? "

" No, knife-cuts."

There seemed nothing more to say, except that Daniel remarked a moment later that they would have to send some one to shoot the horse.

Judith felt relieved when a minute later the carriage came out of the narrow wooded ravine and over the rise into the valley. That meant coming out into open country where things could not creep up close without being seen—at least, not in the day-time. She was relieved to see that everything about the ranch buildings looked just the same, and that the good strong wind was making ripples in the yellow wheat-field just as she had known it would.

At the ranch-house they found the people practically in a panic. It was time to be cutting the wheat, but no one was at work. Tony met them; he was looking white. Judith could see that his nerve was shaken, and again she wished for Lewis. Two families were on the point of leaving.

The information about the horse did not make matters better. Judith, for her part, was horrified at the sight of one of the young men who had been beaten up. The other was still in bed. A gang of men had picked a fight with them down at the Mission, and without giving them a chance for defence had pounded them into insensibility.

Half the people of the Community were crowding about Judith and Daniel. They were like children frightened by the bullying of bigger boys, and expecting their parents to do something to pro-tect them. Two steers had been found killed and a horse wounded by rifle shots. Since the beating up of the two men they were all afraid to go to the Mission. Some one brought the latest placard which had been found stuck to one of the doors. It was a crudely drawn skull and cross-bones in red ink and the two words: GET OUT.

It was some minutes before Judith realized that she must take the lead; neither Tony nor Daniel seemed effective against the crowd. She made some quite unwarranted promises in order to restore confidence a little, and then managed to get the people to disperse. The thing to do was to call a meeting of the Council, which consisted of Tony and four other members, one of them a woman.

One member of the Council was the father of one of the families who were about to leave; he was badly frightened. Tony

was jumpy. Judith felt that he had failed her in the crisis. She had
thought him a leader and a fighter. Perhaps he was not exactly a
coward; few Irishmen were. He had too much imagination. In an
open fight he might, she still thought, be reliable, but he could
not stand things happening in the dark. The other three members
of the Council were in better state. Mrs Barton had her fighting
blood up. Judith sensed the pioneer strain; Mrs Barton came of
the stock which took it as a matter of course that the women stood
by to load rifles while the men fought. The other two members
were the blacksmith-veterinarian and old Hargrace. On her previous visits Judith had put these last two down as faddists; she
would have distrusted them in an emergency. But now there was
a martyr's enthusiasm about them both. She saw her error. In
times of danger the intellectuals and the common-sense people
looked ahead and counted consequences, but the enthusiasts and the
mystics and the faddists went up to die with a light in their eyes.

Things were not yet so bad that it was necessary to think of
dying. After the seven of them had talked matters over they got
rid of the panic and began to feel better. Tony even got as far as
saying :

"Well, after all, this is the nineteenth century, not the Middle
Ages; people don't go around killing their neighbours."

"Don't they?" said the blacksmith.

Every one looked at him blankly for explanation.

"I was at Hahn's Mill," he said, as if embarrassed. "Boggs'
men came up that morning suddenly and killed eighteen of us,
besides those they wounded."

Judith herself felt panic for a moment; she had not realized that
the blacksmith had ever been a Mormon. In the end they persuaded the father of the family to remain, chiefly on the grounds
of Daniel's letter to the sheriff. No sheriff, Mrs Barton pointed
out frankly, could refuse immediate help to a man with so much
money and power and influence as Mr Melton.

As another method of defence they decided to fight fire with
fire by stirring up some public opinion on their own side. Tony
would write letters to the editors of the *Alta* and the *Bulletin* defending the Community and stating the outrages which had been

perpetrated; Daniel would send a note to the editors along with Tony's letters. Judith would also write to Lewis telling him the situation, and asking him to help. All in all, they could probably get favourable editorials in both the *Alta* and the *Bulletin*, and that would counterweigh a hundred times over anything that the *Farmer and Merchant*, the *Sentinel*, and all the other little cow-county papers might accomplish.

They began to feel confident, and the more so when a man rode in with a letter from the sheriff. Daniel took the note, and Judith saw him get a little pale when he looked at it.

"The sheriff's sick," he said, "but he writes that he doesn't think there's anything dangerous, anyway."

They called the Council again. It had something to be indignant about this time, and indignation was better than panic. Judith found herself now more disturbed than the others. The wind was still coming in hard from the west, and steady wind had a tendency to get on her nerves, especially a dry wind. And she did not like the idea that the sun was getting close to the horizon. They had spent all the later part of the afternoon in what seemed useless bickering and discussion.

"Why sends he not his men?" she heard Daniel saying, and she thought that it was a quotation from Shakespeare. Every one agreed that the sheriff was most likely pretending to be sick. It was decided that the next move should be for Daniel to write to one of the leading lawyers at the county seat, explaining the case briefly and telling him to take immediately whatever measures seemed best. He might stir the sheriff into action, or he might get some kind of injunction from the court or bring charges against various suspected individuals so that they could be sworn to keep the peace. After all, there was a good deal of concrete evidence—two dead steers, two wounded horses, and two men pounded black and blue. No one was quite sure what a lawyer could do, but at least it seemed a definite move towards taking the offensive.

Writing this letter took still more time. The sun went behind the hills in a quick burst of gold. Henry had been ready for an hour, his horse saddled. He seemed matter of fact and almost stolid. But Judith knew that her youngest son was a hard one to judge. He had been too little to count for much back in the old days of the Indian fighting and the conquest. Lewis and Guito had always rather lorded it over him. Now she guessed that he was hot with concealed excitement at being about to ride alone through the night on an important errand and one which he could at least dramatize as dangerous.

It was dusk when Henry at last got started. Judith watched him gallop across the valley, lost sight of him in the gathering darkness, but finally had a dim glimpse as he went over the little rise and dropped out of sight. She felt worried, but it was mostly, she argued, that she was letting herself think back in terms of things as they had been ten or twenty years before. That time, for instance, when Lewis was a little fellow and had ridden out with old Tomás to watch for Sutter's raiders, and she had stayed with the other children, jumping at every sound, until in the dawn she had heard the rush of the Fuentes and their men galloping down from the north. She could smile, remembering how Don Diego had cursed Sutter.

Yes, things were changed. Old Tomás had been dead for years, and Lewis was a grown man; Sutter strutted around as a great hero, pretending he had won California for the United States; and the Fuentes had lost their land and were living proudly in poverty up at Martinez.

Probably Daniel was right. The time of violence and gun-play was all over in California. Things were getting civilized. You wrote a letter to a lawyer now, instead of riding out with your men behind you. Yet a hamstrung horse didn't fit in quite with your ideas of civilization.

But things were so vague and so senseless, and you couldn't quite reckon out why anything was happening at all. You had a feeling that there was something unknown working far behind the appearances, something intangible. And then you realized that that might be your nerves playing tricks, and remembered that you were maybe getting a little old.

RIDING DOWN THE RAVINE, Henry felt himself so happy that the half-darkness seemed almost to glow. After all those years of being a little brother and hearing what Lewis and Guito had done —and now here he was spurring like Paul Revere! Here he was at one with all of those—squires, couriers, and *aides-de-camp*— who went galloping through the night on perilous missions. Just a little imagination, and he could feel the stiffness of a leathern jerkin, and the weight of a loaded pistol in his belt, and hear the clinking jingle of a sabre. Well, at any rate, he had a good horse between his knees—the best on the ranch; and he would have to ride alone all the way through the night; and he had the dispatches (he could call them dispatches if he wanted to) safely buttoned into the breast-pocket of his jacket.

Probably it wouldn't make much difference how he rode past the Brightman place, but still it was fun to imagine that Brightman's might be a point of danger, and there was just the possibility that it really might be. He could walk the horse quietly and try to get by without being noticed, but ready to strike spur if a dog barked. Or he might tear through at full gallop so fast that he would leave the dogs with their mouths open, not sure whether there had really been anything to bark at. In the end he just went past at an easy canter, and the dogs barked listlessly, as if he were a farmhand instead of a courier.

There were sounds in the night. Most of them he knew—a coyote, an owl, the scraping of branches in the wind. Even when he could not tell what they were he could remember having heard them before; they were just part of the ordinary noises of the hills at night—nothing sinister. He knew that he remembered all these things from having lived on the ranch until he was nine; eight years in the city couldn't blot them all out.

But there was that light ahead. He didn't like it. Its flickering seemed to mean a big fire in the open. That would be dangerous with such a wind as there was to-night, even though the grass wasn't fully dry. As he came nearer he saw that the fire must be at the old Gómez place, where the Johnsons lived now. The blaze was not big enough to mean a shed burning. But why would they be having a bonfire?

He came to the top of a little rise. It *was* a bonfire. He drew rein sharply, and instinctively looked behind. Yes, the trees rose up high enough so that he was not on a skyline; the men he saw about the fire couldn't possibly see him. He was so far off that they were only small, dark figures about the fire; he could not make out what they were doing, except that once in a sharp silhouette he saw the unmistakable gesture of a head thrown back and a man drinking from a bottle. Dogs barked, and he realized that he was up-wind from the farmhouse. No matter—the dogs wouldn't much mind the scent of him at that distance, and the men would think they were barking at a coyote or wild-cat.

Henry wondered why he didn't just ride up and say good-evening to the men about the fire as he passed them, and ride on. Then he had a sudden memory of himself as a little boy perched on a horse out riding with his father and Miguel, and of the two men suddenly getting off their horses and down on their hands and knees to look at something which seemed very unimportant—a track or a fallen stone—just because it was unusual. The rule in those days was that what was out of the ordinary might be dangerous. And there was another old rule of the outer ranches that two or more unusual things close together were likely to be connected. Threats, a hamstrung horse, a bonfire where and when you would not expect it. He considered. He could go back a mile, cross the ravine, and get through the thickets by a side-trail. But that would bring him merely out on the grassy upper slopes of the hills, and steering blind across hill-country at night was no joke. At best it would mean losing an hour or two before he could circle back to the road; at worst it would mean getting badly lost, or laming the horse, or taking a fall into a gully. It would be better to investigate first.

He plucked a few grass-stalks, threw them into the air, and

watched which way the stiff breeze spun them off. By bearing to
the left he could easily creep up at an angle from which the dogs
could not scent him. He led the horse a little way off the road, and
tied him to a tree. He thought a moment, and then took off his
jacket containing the letters, rolled it up, and laid it under a bush.

A few minutes later he had got as close to the fire as he felt safe
to be. In fact, he was lying under the last little oak-tree on the
edge of the clearing, a hundred feet from the fire. He counted
fourteen men, and he was glad he hadn't ridden down among
them. He did not like the look of it; some of them had revolvers;
farther back the fire glinted on what must be the barrels of guns
leaning against the house. Again he saw the silhouette of a head
thrown back to drink. The man flung the empty bottle aimlessly
into the darkness. It splintered on a stone not twenty feet from
where Henry was lying; a fragment hit on the oak-leaves overhead.

" Have another! " Henry heard a voice call out; he wondered
where all the whisky was coming from.

It was hard to hear much of what they were saying. There was
a lot of aimless cursing and ribaldry, and of the senseless whooping noises of men beginning to feel their liquor Then a man stood
up to make a speech.

" Men," he began, " we're a bunch of good Americans. . . ."
The speaker kept right on, but everybody yelled and drowned out
his words, at least where Henry was lying. Henry decided that it
was about time for him to back out and take his *détour* over the
hills, and then he wondered if he hadn't better turn round and tell
them at the ranch what was happening. So he waited to hear just a
little more. Once he heard the man say: ". . . a bunch of goddam
Mormons and Com-myun-ists, taking the bread right out . . ."
And just then a dog barked, not ten feet away.

Henry lay still; no one around the fire paid any attention. The
wind had not shifted; so probably the dog was just wandering
around and had happened to scent him.

" Nice fellow," said Henry, and some more of the things that
people say to strange dogs. He had to speak very quietly of course,
and he was pretty sure that he made his voice sound matter of
fact and unafraid. But he was so scared that he was sweating, and

that made him more afraid, for he had heard that dogs could smell when a man was nervous. The dog did not seem much excited. He would bark four or five times, and then lower his head suspiciously, and then seem to start walking away. Henry reckoned that the dog had probably smelled a lot of strange people already this night, and before long would be satisfied. Henry did not dare start crawling away, for he knew that that would make the dog change his tone, and bring down some more dogs, if not men. But he was caught betwixt and between, for the men would soon notice the dog, anyway. The only thing to do was to lie still.

Henry was getting encouraged, for the men were making a lot of noise and the dog really seemed to be losing interest, but just then he saw the door of the house open into a dim oblong of yellow light with a shadow in the middle of it, and heard a woman's voice crying out :

"Hank, why don't ye go see what Buck's barkin' at? "

There was a sudden silence by the fire. Buck was delighted at hearing his own name and getting attention at last; he barked harder.

"Some goddam squirrel!" said some one at the fire, probably Hank. He spoke as if he didn't care about moving, but Henry knew that Hank must be enough of a backwoodsman not to neglect a dog's barking once he heard it, and that he would come, probably with a shot-gun.

There wasn't much choice of what to do. He wanted to break and run, taking his chance at fighting off Buck. But just then two other dogs came rushing up to get into the fun. Well, he couldn't run with a pack at his heels.

There was no use lying still and being pulled out by the scruff of the neck. So he got up, and yelled out lamely, "Don't shoot! " and walked up towards the muzzle of Hank's shot-gun.

The thing to do was to think fast and tell a long story about being lost, and make it sound funny. A glib talker like Guito could do it. But Henry in the confusion could not think of a word. They dragged him up to the fire, and stuck a lantern at his face. Nobody recognized him, but they took it for granted that he was a spy from Amarillo.

Now was the time to tell his story, but he knew that a poor story would be worse than none at all, and the way they jostled him he couldn't think of a good one. After all, he was a spy from Amarillo, just as circumstances showed.

"Are you from Amarillo?" some one asked.

"No," was all Henry could think of.

"You're a goddam liar!" The man drew his fist back, and Henry braced himself for a blow. Then he saw a smile break over the lower part of the man's face—an ugly smile. The lower part of the face was all that Henry could see, for the man had put a little black mask across his eyes.

"By God!" said the man. "How about a little rope's end?"

They're going to hang me, thought Henry. But they were holding him too fast for him to put up a fight. The woman gave a little squeal and ran into the house. By this time all the men either had masks on or had tied big handkerchiefs around the lower part of their faces.

They stripped off Henry's shirt, but the rope they brought up went around his wrists, not his neck. They flung an end of the rope over a projecting beam of the barn, and three men pulled until he swung from the wrists with his toes just touching. . . .

"That's enough," Henry dimly through his pain heard some one crying. "Hell, he ain't much more'n a youngster!"

The men on the other end of the rope must have let go suddenly, for Henry went all down in a heap. For a moment in the sudden relief of strain he felt as if he were going to sleep or faint. He hardly noticed that some one kicked him, contemptuously rather than vindictively. Then the searing shooting pain of his flogged back brought him again to consciousness. The men were moving off, leaving him where he lay. For the moment there was nothing better to do than to lie still.

All at once, worse than the pain, the humiliation swelled up. A Godoy triced up and flogged like an Indian or a negro slave or a sailor! . . . Men must die for this; he would tell Guito.

He heard horses. They were bringing horses up from where they had been tied; were mounting and starting off. Then he realized where they were going.

A new resolve stiffened him. He moved, in spite of the shooting pains it brought to his back. He sat up, and began working at the rope around his wrists. It was only a slip-knot, and he worked it loose in a few seconds. He stood up experimentally He felt stronger than he had expected. After all, he began to recollect they had not given him more than eighteen or twenty. He could feel a little blood flowing, but not enough to matter. The stiff wind was numbing his back; it deadened the pain, but he knew that the chill might be dangerous. He hunted for his shirt, shook the dust from it, and put it on. He listened a moment, but the sound of hoofs had died out. The three dogs walked about eyeing him suspiciously, but not bothering to bark. The fire was dying down already. A faint yellow light still shone from behind the shutters of the house. For a moment he had a diabolical thought of going in to take some wild vengeance on the woman and the children. Then he walked determinedly up the road

If they had found and taken his horse there was no hope. If not, he might still get to the ranch in time to give warning.

The horse was there. He fished out his jacket, being thankful again that he had had foresight enough to leave the letters behind when he had gone reconnoitring. Getting into the jacket made him wince, and he could feel the blood start oozing harder into his shirt. He set his teeth, mounted, and took the road back towards the ranch, looking for the place where the trail crossed the creek. In spite of his pain and in spite of the darkness he pressed his horse to a gallop.

To get warning to the ranch ahead of them he could count only on two circumstances. Being Americans and not feeling themselves in a hurry, they would trot or canter, not gallop. And they would probably stop at the Brightman place to palaver and drink and get Brightman worked up to joining them.

He had to feel his way slowly across the ravine, for the trail was bad in the pitch darkness and the branches were close at the sides and sometimes low overhead. At the bottom, where the growth was thickest, there was no wind, and in the lull the night seemed suddenly warm. He smelled the aromatic scent of some herb crushed by the horse's feet; with a sudden nostalgic rush the odour took him back to times when he was a little boy on the ranch. He tried to remember the plant's name, as if it mattered for the moment, and caught himself thinking in Spanish, although these days when he tried to talk Spanish he had a hard time.

The horse's neck rose as the trail pitched upward. In a minute they came out among scattered oak-trees, and the slope eased off. He took a quick glance at the sky to get his bearings, and swung off along the trail to the right, pressing the horse to a canter Back in the direction of the ranch he knew the lie of the land; the thing to do was to keep well up on the ridge. That way he would find fairly open going and miss the chaparral of the side-ravines. Once clear of the trees he set his teeth and spurred his horse to a gallop.

One way or the other it was a chance. There was no use getting there at all if he got there late. He trusted that the horse could see better than he could. Sometimes the ridge was wide-topped and he could gallop as if across open fields. Sometimes it grew narrow, and the horseshoes clicked on outcroppings and treacherous loose stones. And always there was the chance of a coyote-hole or a sudden gully that the horse would try to leap and couldn't. The stiff wind was at his left shoulder, and seemed to be lifting him along.

Straining his eyes ahead, alert to every quick shift of movement, he had little time to think The pain had changed to a dull, numbing ache; he didn't believe he was bleeding enough to weaken him. But he felt one resolve strengthening within him : he would keep his own troubles to himself; there was enough trouble at the ranch now. Why should he publish his own shame? At the thought self-pity came over him for the first time. Like a girl, he thought, caught by some man out on a dark road. She wouldn't tell—unless she had to. "And I'm better off. The girl wouldn't ever be quite the same again, but in a month I probably won't even have a scar. Nobody who did it knew me, and I'll go back to the city and won't come here again for a year—two years. By then I can start growing a beard, and nobody will remember what I looked like, anyway. If I tell Guito he'll kill somebody, and maybe get in trouble; and I don't know even who it is I want to be killed."

The horse pitched to his knees, and Henry went sprawling. He came up with nose and cheek skinned and bleeding; the horse had barked a knee, but didn't seem lamed. Henry's face stung worse than his back now, but he was glad it had happened. It gave an excuse for any smell of blood about him and any strange way he might look or act.

Five minutes later he was galloping down into the valley. The ranch buildings were only a dark blot, without a light showing. That was a sign that he was on time. He had feared many lights, or a fire.

He opened the gate and galloped straight across the field of ripe wheat. The dogs, down-wind, scented him and barked all together. Dogs!—they had caused a lot of trouble to-night, he thought bitterly. A light flared dimly in one of the windows as some one, scared by barking, jumped out of bed and lighted a candle. . . .

He was in the old outer room. His mother in a nightgown, wrapped in a big shawl . . . Mr Melton, and Mr Burke, and funny old Hargrace, and some one else with a shot-gun. . . . He cut them short about his face, and told them what to get ready for—as well as he knew.

There was a sudden burst of talk among the men, futile, confused talk, and people running about and a woman starting to scream. For himself, he was ready to drop, and he stood fighting a black dizziness, and wondering if somebody oughtn't to give him brandy. But his mother was looking at him, and she mustn't know. He fought the dizziness, and started to walk to a chair.

"Henry," he heard her saying, "are you hurt badly?"

He wished he could think of something to say quickly and brightly to cover things up—the kind of thing Guito could say. But all he could think of was a dull, heavy lie, which was almost worse than the truth.

"I guess," he said, with his tongue stumbling, "I guess—I'm just scared."

Then in a quick black dizziness the floor tipped, and he hit against it with a bang.

EVERYBODY MILLING AROUND—like a lot of cattle scared and ready to run. People in nightgowns and half-dressed. . . . The flutter of panic in yourself too. Steady; you're Mr Melton of San Francisco. . . . Not knowing quite how to go about things at such a time; listening with one ear for the rush of horsemen, and knowing something ought to be done—organization, orders—to stop people running about. Feeling the panic spread and deepen. . . . No time for a strong young fellow like Henry to topple over in a faint just because he scratched his face. If only Lewis were here, or even Guito. . . . Lewis . . . good at handling people . . . and Guito like his father, blossoming out in times like this.

One man was yelling out for them all to run for the hills, and another for some one to go out and keep watch. Some one had a shot-gun under his arm, and Mrs Barton was shouting that they could hold the old part of the house against any number of men. But Tony was saying that they'd no right to risk the lives of so many people; they'd better run for it.

Then some hysterical woman was clinging to Mr Melton's neck most embarrassingly and crying that he was a rich man and should offer the vigilantes money to go away. "There, now," said Mr Melton; "there, now." And he managed to get her arms loose, realizing that he was blushing, even as things were. Somehow he knew that what the woman was saying was no use; it was the old days again now; all the money in Montgomery Street wouldn't do a man much good in the next hour

And there was Judith, gone just as crazy as the rest of them; you wouldn't have expected it. She had come out first with her big shawl on, and *now* here she was, in front of everybody, pulling a dress on over her nightgown—one of her dark green dresses, of the shade she always liked to wear. When he tried to ask her what she thought they ought to do she snapped at him:

" Be quiet a minute till I get into my war-dress," as if she were a Sioux chief putting on his bonnet and feathers.

He couldn't see what difference clothes made at a time like this. But that Mrs Barton was fastening Judith up the back, and Judith was coiling her own hair into a great white roll at the back of her head and spearing it fast with pins. Then as she finished she stood for just a moment moving her body as if to settle the dress around her; then she drew herself up straight and shook her head quickly, and her voice, pitched low, cut in below the babble in the room :

" Get out, all of you! Take some blankets and coats and go up in the ravine on the trail to Quail-hole. Tony, you look after them ; I'll take care of things here."

It was amazing how people turned and ran once some one started to give orders. In a half-minute the room was almost clear. Henry still sat in a chair, looking pale except where the blood oozed from his cheek. Old Hargrace walked back and forth; he had his hands clasped and his fingers worked nervously, but there was a rapt look on his face. The blacksmith, with his shot-gun, crouched by the shutter, peering through a chink. Mrs Barton was on her knees. fastening Judith's shoes.

" Go on, the rest of you! " Judith said.

The three men swung around facing her, and stood silent a moment. Mr Melton was very uncomfortable, but couldn't think just what to say. It was the blacksmith who spoke :

· 'Tain't right, Mrs Melton, for a lot of men to go sheltering behind your skirts."

" Yes," said Mr Melton.

Old Hargrace nodded vigorously.

" That's nonsense,' said Judith. " I grant you could fight them off, even two or three of you. These rooms were built for a fortress; I know that better than you do. But what would it mean if you fought them off? Just more hamstrung horses and things going from bad to worse."

Old Hargrace spoke suddenly :

" That's right. We stand for an idea. You can't convert people by gunfire. ' Put up thy sword.' The only blood that converts is the blood of martyrs."

The blacksmith still held the shot-gun, but at Hargrace's words it slumped to a less belligerent angle.

"You're right," he said shortly. "All the blood at Hahn's Mill didn't settle anything. But, anyway, Mrs Melton, we'll stay and help you argue."

Judith merely looked at him, smiling a little. The others followed her look. The blacksmith was only half-dressed, and his bull neck and great arm-muscles stood out as a very challenge to violence. He grew suddenly self-conscious:

"Well, maybe I do look like the kind of a man who seeks for a fight. Maybe I wouldn't be a one to argue too long. I got a short temper sometimes."

Judith was quick to take advantage of the blacksmith's surrender to assume that they all surrendered.

"As soon as we know they are coming you can all go into the inner room."

Mr Melton felt very much disturbed. He knew Judith was right, and that she would handle the affair much better than he would, and yet his dignity as a man and husband was hurt. He stirred uneasily, thinking that he had in some way been subtly effaced. He thought of Juan Godoy; Juan was not the kind of husband to be thus put aside when a fight was looming. And yet hadn't Juan himself stayed in the inner room and let Judith handle things that time Judge Wingram and the raiders had come? He ventured a protest:

"This will be different from that other time, Judith. Just because you managed it that time doesn't mean you will this time. I'd better stay."

She shook her head, but if she had been going to say anything Mrs Barton's matter-of-fact remark cut her off:

"Probably they won't come, anyway. They'll see the lights and know we got warned."

From the way every one stirred suddenly you could tell that the likely enough suggestion brought a quick relief of hope. Then Hargrace spoke in his strangely rapt voice:

"Put out the lights. We want them to come. It's better to face it now than to have it eating at our hearts until it finally happens."

No one said anything, but Mr Melton knew suddenly that Hargrace was right. If the sinister thing was coming out into the open they had best face it now. He said so, and the others nodded agreement.

They blew out the candles, and sat silently in the dark. Henry went to bed in the inner room, and Mrs Barton bandaged his face. Mr Melton wondered again at how weak Henry seemed and the way he groaned sharply when some one put an arm around his shoulders.

It was glum work sitting in the darkness. There was no use trying to keep up a conversation. The blacksmith had gone outside where he could watch better. Mrs Barton kept a look-out from one of the windows. There was just enough light to let Mr Melton look at his watch occasionally; the hands slid round from one to half-past. Now and then came little noises, probably the stiff breeze moving branches or making a door rattle.

"They're coming!" It was the blacksmith; he slipped in through the door with amazing quietness for a man of his size. "I saw them in the middle of the valley; they'll be close to the ford by now."

He led the way into the inner room; Mrs Barton and Hargrace followed. Mr Melton looked at Judith, feeling that he ought to stay. But she waved him off; he went in, wishing that she had at least given him a smile.

In the inner room he joined the others in peeping out through the shutters. A group of horsemen had halted just where the road came up from the ford. Henry must have been right; there seemed to be about fifteen of them. Their halting gave Mr Melton a new hope. It was so easy, he remembered, to think that your enemies were resolute and courageous and terrible. But he would wager that most of the men out there were half-hearted about the whole affair, and had been argued and browbeaten into coming, and were now scared and wishing themselves well out of it, for all their masks and handkerchiefs. And if they had been drinking there was nothing like an hour's ride through a cool night to make the Dutch courage ooze out. At that moment they were probably all wondering what they would do next. It tickled Mr Melton to think how dark and sinister the house must look without a light showing, and without any dogs barking either. The dogs had gone along with Tony's party, and these horsemen out there would know that there was something funny about no dogs barking.

Then it was disconcerting to his ideas to hear some one give a sharp word like a military order, and to see the men dismount and tie up their horses and close in quickly upon the house. And the bang that came on the door made it rattle.

Mr Melton moved hurriedly, and half opened the door into the outer room as a last gesture of help for Judith. She was moving quickly, as if in a well-rehearsed part. She lighted a candle, and held it in her right hand so that it shone upon her face from the side and lighted up her hair. For a moment she patted her hair into place. She drew herself up very straight as the pounding on the door from the outside grew louder. She gave a last glance around the room, saw him looking from the inner room, and motioned to him to close the door. As he did so he saw her take a quick step forward with that sudden toss of her white hair which he had seen sometimes before; he knew that it was her last gesture as she went into battle.

Perhaps, thought Mr Melton, it was harder on the nerves for them in the inner room than for Judith outside doing the active fighting. They heard the *clump-clump* of men coming in. But the adobe walls were thick, and the door was heavy and close-fitting. And the sound of voices in the outer room kept low; that was a good sign, but it meant they could not make out the conversation. Henry stirred restlessly on the bed now and then; it seemed strange that he should be lying on his hurt face. Mrs Barton was praying. The blacksmith walked quietly from window to window, looking out to see whether anyone was sneaking around. Hargrace sat working his fingers with a peaceful, high look upon his face. Mr Melton glanced at his watch occasionally, and thought a great deal, but mostly the same thoughts over and over. He wished that Lewis were there, and he remembered what a fighting man Juan Godoy had been. He felt again the unpleasant sense of not being physically what Judith must remember Juan had been, and all that he knew he was and Juan never had been did not seem very important. Once he half got up to go into the other room and take up the fight, whatever it was, alongside Judith. Then reason told him that he would merely be making a foolish gesture, and that she could do much better without him. But thinking how futile he was did not make him feel any better.

Then finally the blacksmith gave a quick, low exclamation of delight. With his eye at a crack Mr Melton saw the men filing out towards their horses. He glanced at his watch; it was not yet quite two; Judith had settled things in twenty minutes. The men were mounting and riding off in silence down towards the ford. It seemed a foolishly commonplace gesture that one of them was making as he turned up his coat-collar to keep the wind out of his neck.

When Judith opened the door they all went into the outer room, except Henry. Even the victory did not seem to make him feel much better. Judith was jubilant, and so were the blacksmith and Mrs Barton. Hargrace seemed let down, as if it were an anti-climax. Mr Melton did not quite know how he felt. He realized that he ought to be proud of Judith, but for some reason he could suddenly remember a great many times when he had been fonder of her than he was at that moment.

It wasn't really so much that she had been successful and held the centre of things while he had been pushed aside. Maybe it was more that he never liked people very well when they were too prosperous and successful. It took a little of the humility which comes with failure to make a person really likeable.

And just then Judith was throwing off a very glow of power and success. She was telling about how she had met them at the door and startled them into the sudden respect of taking off their hats. Then she had asked them in politely, and insisted on their all sitting down—it had been just like the time before. She had ignored their masks, just as if they were ordinary articles of clothing. Then she had asked them politely, but point-blank, what they wanted and were going to do. That had embarrassed them, all except the leader, who had begun to bluster. But he had blustered too much, and she had managed to start a disagreement between him and some others. Before long she had ventured a remark about small boys wearing masks and playing robbers, and one man had snickered. Then she had asked them what complaints they had about the Community, and every point they brought up she had been able to show was false or else amounted to nothing. She had taken the offensive and flung at them the matter of the mutilated horses and cattle; that had been a good shot. And finally a man had begged her pardon and got up to leave, and then all of them had shuffled out, mostly saying they were sorry.

"The thing about a mob that's dangerous," she said, " is its motion. By showing myself at the door the way I did I stopped them in their tracks, and then it was easy to get them going the other way."

Mr Melton felt himself very small, but there was something in Judith's high confidence which he didn't like; it seemed to be shutting him out from her. The moment seemed more ominous than hopeful.

The others were all delighted, and even gay. They laughed about Tony and the other people out in the hills—it was a fine night, and in the ravine they would be protected from the wind; let them wait a few more minutes. Mrs Barton went to get out some brandy.

"For our stomachs' sake," said the blacksmith—" and the way mine felt an hour ago I surely need to take something for it."

It was just at that time, half an hour more or less after the men had left, that Mr Melton saw old Hargrace sniff once or twice. He too sniffed, and felt himself stiffen and grow cold at the faint acrid scent. Full of a sense of horror he sprang to the door and flung it open. Outside, a strange dancing glare lit up the fruit-trees.

By the time he could run around the corner of the house the great wave of flame was sweeping half-way across the field of ripe wheat.

Hargrace and the blacksmith ran to get the horses out of the stable. The rest of them rushed to save furniture and personal belongings. The air was full of smoke and blazing bits of wheat-straw.

The stable went first; its well-dried wooden planks seemed to burst into fire at a dozen points at once. Then the flames jumped to the newer part of the house. That was the section which Judith

2 D

had built, and she had had it roofed with wooden shingles instead of the native-made tiles, after the custom of those days. Tiles might have saved it now. The fire jumped the old part of the house, but the new hall, big and wooden and flimsy, went up like a bon-fire.

When the heat drove them away from the buildings they fought the fire along its northern edge as it burned through the grass. Tony and the rest of the people came down from the hills on the run. The air was thick with a heavy stench, for some of the horses had gone into a panic and refused to leave their stalls. In the high wind, without many tools, even the grass-fire was hard to turn, but they managed to pinch it off gradually and let it burn itself out along the creek-bottom.

By the time the sun was making a rim of light over the hills life was getting organized again. Two men were patrolling the fire-line, just for safety. Three more were drawing water from the well and sousing places around the buildings where fire looked as if it might still flare up. The rest of them gathered in the shade along the creek-bottom, and for breakfast the cooks broiled up pieces of a newly slaughtered calf.

Tony got the Council together, and Judith and Mr Melton sat in with it again. A young man whom Tony had set to watch was the only person who had seen the fire start, and he had been a good mile away from that edge of the wheat-field.

" It seemed to break out all of a sudden," he said, " in three or maybe four places—like——"

" Like what? " asked Tony.

" Like as if three or four men had been there and started the fires all at once."

Mr Melton put his arm around Judith; he felt she needed him. From the way her weight came against his arm he knew that some-thing in her had slumped. He did not look at her; it was not good, he thought, to look upon a loved one suffering and a gallant fighter beaten.

THEY STARTED EARLY IN THE MORNING, only twenty-four hours after the fire had died down. Sam had found the greys peacefully grazing just beyond the vineyard. The hay and barley had burned along with the new storehouse, but Sam had dug some half-roasted wheat out of the ruins somewhere, and the greys this morning were as lively as ever. The carriage, which had stood in the stable-yard, had some burns in the upholstery, and the varnish showed scorching. Fortunately they had saved their clothes. Only the makeshift harness gave indication that anything serious had happened.

At the top of the rise as they were leaving the valley Judith told Sam to stop, in spite of Mr Melton's half-voiced protest.

The fire had left a great black scar to the north of the creek. Along the edge of the wheat-field closest to her she could make out the scalloped edge of the burned part, the still-existing evidence that the fire had started from several points at once.

The ranch buildings stood almost in the centre of the burned part. The strange thought which struck her was the way in which the cluster of buildings seemed to have reverted to what she had seen when she first came there. Plans and solicitudes and labours of twenty years had flared in that sudden light and vanished. Of the hall and stable which the Community had built not a stick was left standing. Of the newer part of the house little remained. Judith first felt a lump gather in her throat when she thought of the gracious patio where her babies had played. But the wooden shingles had betrayed her; the roof and floors had burned, and parts of the walls had fallen. With the autumn rains the unprotected adobe would, she supposed, soak up into mud and collapse.

But the old quarters and storehouse were standing, and still intact, between the ruined newer house and the blackened site of the vanished hall, stood, squat and solid, the old house of Esteban Godoy. Built as a fortress, its two-foot adobe walls and thick tile roof had offered no hold to the flames.

"You can even see the flanker again," said Judith, after she had looked a long time. Daniel said nothing, but it was certainly true that you could see the flanker. For fifteen years it had been merely a passage-way from the old to the new house, and from the outside had been entirely concealed by the newer construction. Now it stood in almost full view again, architecturally as much a blot as ever, the same old flanker which Judith as a bride had wondered about. Tear down the crumbling walls of the dining-room, clean out the old loop-holes, and your musket-fire could enfilade an attack from south or west, just as in those first days when Juan's father had come up to hold his land by conquest and Rancho Amarillo was a far-flung outpost of California.

Only when they had left the hill and were going down through the ravine did Judith feel how tired she was. The pain in her side was bad; if she had realized how bad it was going to be she would not have set out on so long a drive. Henry worried her too—sitting there with a grey leaden face, as much of it as showed from under the bandages. She could see that he was stiff, and she was afraid that he might have sprained his back when his horse fell with him; but he kept saying that he had not.

Besides her pain and her worry about Henry, she knew that she was beaten, and she did not know quite how or why she had been beaten. Alone, she had met and outfaced those men, and yet after they left her they—or some of them—had treacherously sneaked through the darkness and fired the wheat. And this had been done by white men in a country supposed to be civilized. She had felt it before—most of all when she saw Jerry Graham dying—but now she felt it more strongly than ever: there was something base and sneaking about this way of life called civilization. Man still fought man, just as in the old days when white man fought Indian or Californian fought American. It was surprise and ambush and treachery then—and it still was. The Fourierists must be right when they talked of civilization as not the end-point, but as merely a stage which, with its 'man-eat-man' philosophy of the struggle for wealth, and even for food, would in future ages appear as horrible as any loathsome savagery.

The thoughts whirled round in her mind. So often, it seemed, law merely protected those who were unscrupulous enough to evade it against those who conscientiously sought to support it. The sheriff, she thought bitterly, had been ill. Behind it all there was something which she could not understand, and merely groped for —something perhaps working from far off, itself not deigning to wear a black mask or set fire to wheat. She would ask Lewis; he would know; he was part of this new world—this ' civilized ' world. There would be no use asking Daniel; he was an anachronism, just as she was, part of that old uncivilized world, in spite of all his money.

They went past Brightman's, and then past Johnson's. They did not stop. At each place Judith found the resolution to sit up straight and wear a look of what she hoped was haughty defiance. But each time after they had passed the house she felt herself slump down. She knew that if she could have looked in a mirror then she would have seen an old woman. She was not really old. Fifty-nine, take away sixteen, leaves forty-three. She was only forty-three. That was not old. But it wasn't the years. She had seen plenty of people get old, and they did not age year by year. Five years, ten years, or fifteen, they went along looking much the same, acting much the same, as strong as ever. Then something happened, sickness usually, a fever or dysentery, and they aged all those years in a week or a month.

Perhaps these two days at the ranch had done as much to her. It was not only the pain in the side or the defeat; it was also the sudden fiat of time.

She looked at Daniel as he sat beside her. He was fifty-eight. Years ago, as they rounded the Horn, she had pitied him as being weak. Now she thought that he would last better than she. He was grey-haired, but there was still vigour about the lean, stringy body; his thin, seamed face, clean-shaven in what was now the old-fashioned manner, was firm, not loose and fallen.

It seemed a long, long drive over the rutted roads. She was coming home defeated, with no more fight left in her. They had made no more plans about the Community. All she hoped was that Lewis would meet them at the Oakland Ferry; they had sent him word. In some way she counted upon Lewis. For the first time in her life she felt herself envying youth; she would like to be Lewis—twenty-one, not yet having known defeat, and at one with the age in which he was living, not a bewildered anachronism.

At dusk they turned down Broadway towards the ferry. Daniel with his eye for real-estate saw prospects in Oakland, and he pointed out two lots which he owned. But the village depressed Judith; the main street was so wide in proportion to the little flimsy buildings that it seemed not so much the prediction of a great thoroughfare as merely a field separating two halves of a town.

Lewis met them at the dock. There were reporters too, from the *Alta*, the *Bulletin*, and the *Gazette*. The Community had already been sufficiently in the public eye to enhance the news-value of the fire. Judith was glad that the reporters devoted themselves to Daniel, not to her. Henry went off to watch a man throwing bits of bread to the seagulls. She could sit down on a deck-bench alone with Lewis.

For some reason she felt a little uncomfortable with him at first. As she had expected, he did not apparently feel much personal loss in the burning of the ranch-house. He was too much a part of the present, too closely bound to the life in San Francisco to feel much sentiment for the things of his boyhood. And as for the Community, she knew that he had always regarded it with friendly tolerance as a sort of expensive plaything for the old people.

He asked questions now with some solicitude, but the horror and disgust which he expressed were polite rather than profound. Everything that had burned was dead loss, but with the professional interest of a man who dealt in insurance he figured an estimate of losses in his notebook.

She had hoped that he would offer some explanation of his own, but they were close to Goat Island by now and he had not. She blurted it forth:

"Lewis, I can't make it out. I'm getting to feel old; I don't belong to this present time. There doesn't seem to be enough reason for people feeling so strongly about the Community. We didn't hurt anybody. What's behind everything? I feel there's something, and maybe you would know."

To her surprise Lewis glanced around before replying.

" I know all right. Maybe I should have warned you before you went down there, but I hadn't taken the trouble to look into things then. And I didn't think the old devil would work so fast. Look here, mother, when you say you don't belong to this present time, you're—pardon me—but you're just right. And Daniel's the same as you. Nobody cared of course if you sent a few crazy men and women down there and raised some wheat and cattle. Wheat and cattle aren't a business that anyone worries about; there isn't enough money in them for the outlay and the labour; nobody but a lot of dull-witted ranchers bother about cattle and wheat. You were safe until you tried soap—there's real money there. Then you hit competition."

Something began to dawn upon Judith, but her mind rejected the idea :

" But how could anybody *do* such things? "

" That's the funny thing—I don't suppose any one person would. It's a lot of people in a system. I don't suppose now that "—he glanced around—" that our friend would actually go out and hamstring a horse any more than he'd jump a claim personally and kill a miner in doing it. My God! "—he was speaking with an intensity which he seldom showed—" getting the prize at the Exhibition didn't amount to much, but you were underselling the Excelsior soaps! They had to cut prices, and their books showed it; they skipped a dividend. Personally, I'd have felt safer setting out to make Canton in an open boat. You know who owns Excelsior Soap —a lot of it, anyway? "

" But," said Judith hesitating, " *he*—he's a friend; he's been to dinner."

" Yes, Judge Wingram "—she noticed that he dropped his voice a little—" he's Excelsior Soap; he's also the *Sentinel* and the *Farmer and Merchant* and the *Gazette*; so that proves the set-up. What's more he's the iron-works, and the brewery, and the Glorietta House, and a string of mines, and God knows what else! He keeps half a dozen state senators the way he used to keep a mistress before he married that pretty little Alicia, and there aren't half a dozen sheriffs in the state who wouldn't be sick abed before they would put down anything his newspapers stirred up."

Through her weariness Judith felt her self-respect and pride faintly rising up again. She could face down the masked mob in the outer room. But how could anyone have combated that absent and wholly unknown force which was driving the mob on? After they had left the house that other force had reasserted itself. And so some of them, perhaps against their individual wills, perhaps hating what they must do, had crawled around to fire the wheat. That, she thought blankly, was civilization, working in a system and by in-directions, not countenancing either honest love or good black hate, making the individual do what he didn't want to, smearing the surface with politeness—as when she had spoken the minister fair when she wanted to slap his face.

"You know, mother "—it was Lewis breaking out again—" you aren't in the 'hide-and-tallow' era any more. People are out to make money in San Francisco these days, and they don't mind some dirt on it. You'd be surprised how many frock coats in Montgomery Street have a little blood dabbled on them if you could work out the cause and effect of things all the way up and down."

He paused, and Judith felt a quick doubt of everything welling up around her

"What about Daniel?"

"Oh, don't worry about him. There's no blood on his coat. He's too good to live." The idea suddenly seemed to strike him another way. "Too good to live—that's just it! And it's a wonder they haven't got him before—the way they smashed the market two years ago and broke Dickenson, and the way they caught Baird short on his mortgages and squeezed him dry. But Old Dan'l doesn't give anybody much of a chance, with his real-estate and his leases. Besides, I'm old enough to keep a look-out for him from now on."

"But Judge Wingram——"

"Now don't take me wrong. He's no worse than the rest, and not even any more powerful than half a dozen or so others. I'd bet too that the Judge didn't order anything violent; he just said that your soapmaking was to be stopped, and let some underling do the figuring how. I'll grant you that arson, and hamstringing, and a mob—all that's spectacular. But it isn't any worse—any more cruel really—than things that happen in business every week right here in the city."

Probably Lewis was right. She was much too tired to argue. But she felt her mood changing. She had been despondent; now, somewhere deep, she felt the snarl of anger. The city was close ahead, its lights beginning to gleam yellowishly through the early darkness. It was Lewis' home; she could see him looking ahead with that deep satisfaction on his face that she might have had when looking at Rancho Amarillo—when there was a Rancho Amarillo. Lewis was still talking, but she hardly heard him. He was talking about the reporters; they knew how things stood all right; you could count on reporters to know everything and tell you nothing, much less write it. All that would get into the papers would be " Incendiarism is suspected," or at most, " There is evidence that the fire was the work of arsonists." My God, what chance would the historians ever have to write up this period, with everything important happening underground?

She was conscious that some men were standing before her on the deck. They were the three reporters. There was something about them that she liked; they were alert-looking young fellows, and polite. Then she remembered what Lewis had just been saying, and the thought of hypocrisy made her grow suddenly hot. These men knew so much and told so little that the upshot was practically a lie.

She felt an old-time anger rising within her, a white heat which she had not felt for a long time. It was good to ignore the pain in the side, to forget the years. As she rose the rage must have shown from her face. They were not short men, but she felt them as suddenly small before her. There was an alarmed, startled look on their faces as if they were little boys.

" Tell your papers," she said, and paused. Her voice was low-pitched and resonant, more forceful for its contrast to the scream which they might have expected.

" Tell your papers," she repeated, " we are not beaten yet—by terrorism and men hired to burn our fields and houses. We shall continue making soap. *The Community is going on.*"

She cut her words off short, and sat down. The three reporters seemed almost to slink away. The ferry-boat hit the dock with a little bump.

"Great heavens, mother," said Lewis, "that was magnificent! But you shouldn't have done it. That was Anderson of the *Gazette* there on the left; there'll be trouble. You shouldn't come out in the open for this kind of war."

She walked off the gangplank, and waited for Sam to drive the carriage off. She did not care what Lewis thought. She was still floating upon her own rage. "It is magnificent, but it is not war," that was what Lewis had been thinking of, what the Frenchman had said two or three years ago when he saw the English horsemen charging and being shot to pieces. Well, there was a time to be magnificent, even if you lost the battle. Men would remember the Light Brigade when they forgot the other one that charged according to the rules and won the battle. Lewis and this generation of business men wouldn't understand that, she thought, a little bitterly. A gap seemed to be opening between herself and Lewis. And Lewis was the son of Juan—Juan who had ridden back through the rifle-fire to pick up his hat just so no one could say that he had run away. Would Lewis ever understand that? Guito might—yes, but not Lewis.

Big Mike was waiting at the dock. She could see the big bulge of the long-barrelled revolver under his coat. He was another anachronism; she felt a sudden affection for him, ugly scarred face and all.

Magnificent—that was a battle-cry! Who cared for mere success?

Then as she settled herself upon the cushions of the carriage the accustomed position and surroundings brought back all at once the consciousness of the pain in her side, and the weariness and the hopelessness, and the years.

A BOUT TEN O'CLOCK THAT MORNING the secretary brought in some letters to be signed, and along with them four neat oblongs of newspaper print.

"Clippings about the fire down at Amarillo,' he said.

"Thank you," said Mr Melton, and began signing the letters. He had a slight feeling of embarrassment. Hoffman, of course, had presented the clippings as a mere bit of office routine, but his sombre expression of face seemed just a little too resigned to the misfortune, almost complaisant. Mr Melton did not feel resentment, for he had been wealthy long enough to realize that a rich man's misfortunes brought a little satisfaction to most of the underlings. The tears live in an onion, he found himself adapting a quotation, when a secretary cries over his boss's troubles. He had been re-reading his Shakespeare lately, and was surprised to find how much cynicism there was in some of the plays. The cynicism must have been there all the time; only, in more youthful days, he had not noticed it so much.

Hoffman took the letters out, and Mr Melton turned to the clippings. Those from the *Bulletin* and the *Alta* he had seen already; the news account from the *Gazette* was what he had expected, hostile and carping. But the *Gazette* had also run an editorial, and that was worse. Before he had finished the first paragraph he was not only surprised, but also a little alarmed. It was almost a personal attack, and that was rare. It seemed written in defiance of that strong Californian tradition that a gentleman who had been attacked in the public Press would challenge the editor, or else, more informally, appear at his office with a couple of friends and a blacksnake whip. The tradition induced a definite editorial restraint in adjectives, and thus, as Mr Melton had often remarked jokingly, furthered a more chaste and classic English style.

Perhaps the editor of the *Gazette* had been drunk. Mr Melton

427

stopped his reading for a minute to recollect who the editor of the *Gazette* was, anyway. With an effort he remembered that his name was Pennington—Alton J. Pennington. Not a very outstanding person, and likely enough fond of his bottle, a man of middle height and build, darkish. The only distinguishing feature which Mr Melton could remember was a kind of high bullet-shaped head. He read on :

> It is not too much to state that our greatest feeling of revulsion to communities in general and to that of Amarillo in particular springs from our abhorrence of their immorality in personal relations. That such practices have not been lacking at Amarillo the unfortunate case of the misguided young woman, whom we shall not name, makes only too lucid. Our great commonwealth must not allow to flourish in its bosom any such disguised Brighamism. Neither polygamy nor its reverse can be tolerated, no matter what the colour of the skin or the colour of the hair. .

Mr Melton felt himself actually blinking. He read again :
" . . . or the colour of the hair. . . . "
Well, just an accidental reference, perhaps :

> . . . or the colour of the hair. The indignation of the people must be aroused not only against the woman of low degree, but also against her of high station who cloaks her actions under the cover of such high-sounding names as Owenism and Fourierism.

Mr Melton was disturbed, but he kept a judicial attitude and read the paragraph again. " Polygamy or its reverse "—a foolish phrase, showing the editor's ignorance. What was the reverse of polygamy, if any? Monogamy, perhaps. . . . But the editor was surely not indicating that monogamy was not to be tolerated. No, he had merely used ' polygamy ' incorrectly for ' polygyny.' The reverse of polygyny would mean the having of two or more men by one woman. But very few people in San Francisco would know or care that the editor had used polygamy incorrectly; they would all know what he meant. The reference to the colour of the hair and " her of high station " made the implication clear enough, to say nothing of Judith's known patronage of the Community.

Mr Melton sat back and considered. He was not really very much disturbed. In the first place, he did not believe it. He could see how some malicious gossip-monger at the Community could have got the idea—Judith's visits without her husband, Tony's combined office and bedroom, and the evening conferences which they had held together. Judith's background was not such as made her bother about conventions. No, he didn't believe it at all.

Even if it were true, he had faced that possibility before, and could face it now with some equanimity. He was not, he feared, just the husband for Judith—too old. . . . He had had so much admiration for her, and for such a long time, that the admiration along with his own humility, he supposed, weakened the male possessive feeling. He had followed Tom Paine for too long to think of marriage sacrament. And, although he would have denied this in argument perhaps, the writings of Fourier and Cabet and the others by the very fact of their advocacy of woman's freedom must be taken as advocating some relaxation for women from the inflexible bonds of man-made monogamy. So even if it were true he would be sorrowful or humiliated, but he would not feel himself constrained to fall into the tragical passion of the conventional outraged husband. Besides, he did *not* believe it. He did not consider himself very quick or profound in his analysis of human relationships, but still he was no fool. And he did not believe that anything of that kind was happening, with Tony Burke or anyone else.

As for the fact of its publication, Mr Melton again considered that there was no need to give way to conventional rage. These people who shot and horse-whipped editors—their vehemence weakened their case. Protesting and storming suggested guilt. The innocent and falsely accused could afford to pass the slander by and go calmly on.

Yet when a friend came to see him a little later Mr Melton was not so sure. There was no reference, naturally, to the editorial in the morning's *Gazette;* but Mr Melton kept wondering if the other had seen it, or if gossip had already spread the word. He kept thinking that he saw strange expressions in the other's face—now amusement, now pity or disgust, now contempt. To be civilized, to disregard a bad convention, to renounce violence—it was not so easy. Mr Melton began to feel very uncomfortable. Deep within him something unpleasant was trying to rise to the surface; he could hardly call it memory, for he could not remember what it was, and having to talk to his visitor all the time he could not stop to recollect it. It was like the memory of a memory, for he knew that something bad had once happened, but he could not remember what.

That visitor left, and Hoffman stood again in the doorway:

"Mr Peleg Godoy to see you, sir."

Mr Melton motioned assent. He felt the immediate sense of pleasure that the nearness of his second stepson always gave him. Guito had so much of that charm of personality which Mr Melton felt was lacking in himself. He was as handsome as his father had been, and he seemed to have ready for every one that buoyant friendship which Juan had lavished only here and there. Juan had disliked many people and could be taciturn and even surly—that, Mr Melton thought, was because he had grown up and lived on a lonely ranch; Guito was like what Juan would have been if he had grown up in a city.

Hoffman was showing Guito in, before Mr Melton had his second and colder thought that Guito's visits usually meant that he was in trouble. The very least trouble would be that he was out of money; from there it would range up to a girl-involvement or the beating up of a policeman. Mr Melton tried to assume a suspicious-parental expression.

As it turned out three minutes later there was nothing more serious than lack of money, and Guito already had Mr Melton smiling. He stood easily in front of the desk, too vigorous to bother about sitting down. He had begun by saying that he had just come from his mother, and since that was about the most unlikely place anyone could have imagined him having come from Mr Melton was proportionately pleased. It was too bad, Guito went on, that his mother was ill, but the experience down at the ranch (Guito digressed a moment to indulge in some selected English and Spanish profanity) was enough to make anyone sick. And he didn't think that his mother was very bad; she seemed cheerful.

Mr Melton merely nodded. He wanted to say, "She would be cheerful at seeing you," but that would sound as if he were trying to reproach Guito for not seeing his mother oftener. Besides, anyone would feel better for seeing Guito; he radiated good cheer and health.

But as he stood in front of the desk talking Mr Melton noticed that the clipping of the *Gazette* editorial lay face upward on the desk and turned so that Guito might read it. Mr Melton looked from the clipping to Guito, and the two came together in his mind with the suddenness and the finality of a spark jumping in a Leyden jar. The pit of his stomach seemed to drop a foot, and a coldness ran along his spine. Guito kept on talking easily; he had probably noticed his stepfather's sudden start and shiver—Guito was quick to notice things about people; but he could not know the reason, and he probably thought it untactful to comment. He went on developing his needs for money in connexion with a fishing trip into Mendocino County. The return of that English sportsman Sir Robert Tyneman was the occasion of the party, and Guito was honoured by being invited. It would be a little expensive, for the Californians had decided to show Sir Robert that they understood luxurious sport as well as the English did. For instance, they had secretly planned a dinner among the Russian River redwoods with iced champagne and various other things as a surprise.

As Guito talked Mr Melton reached out towards the clippings. Casually, as if in a merely absent-minded way, he gathered them, withdrew his hand and dropped them safely into a drawer. He agreed readily to what Guito was saying. Yes, he had met Sir Robert several times, and even had had the honour of entertaining him at dinner. Was Sir Robert still planning that trip into the Crow country? Yes, said Guito, and probably to stay in the West for a couple of years.

"And by the way, Guito," Mr Melton went on, "I don't think that he'll be much impressed by iced champagne with trout. Get Fourchard to recommend something good—a Chablis perhaps; tell him to charge it to me."

Having thus established that he was quite nonchalant, Mr Melton began to write an order for Guido to present to the cashier in the outer office. Guito offered to withdraw, but Mr Melton hurriedly told him to wait. Mr Melton was jittery at the thought of the gossip that Guito might pick up during a few minutes in the outer office. He signed the order, rang for Hoffman, and told him to get the cash. Mr Melton drummed his fingers for a moment, thinking.

"By the way," he said, again in control of himself, "when is the party leaving?"

"This evening; we'll sleep in San Rafael."

That won't do, thought Mr Melton; some fool or troublemaker will be sure to blab. He thought fast.

"Oh, since you're going to San Rafael, anyway, do you suppose you could leave this morning, and do a little job for me over there? Could you take the day off from your law reading?"

It appeared that Guido could—quite easily.

"Well, then, wait in that chair while I write a note for you to deliver personally in San Rafael; it's important."

With poised pen and concentrated expression he sat for at least two minutes, as if trying to begin an unusually difficult letter. Really he was trying to think of the name of that lawyer whom he had once or twice employed in San Rafael. Finally he recollected and wrote:

MY DEAR MR MACK,

The bearer of this letter is my stepson, Mr Peleg Godoy. I have told him that this letter is important, and it is—to him. The fact is that the young gentleman has committed a boyish indiscretion, and his absence from the city is advisable until I can adjust matters. On account of his high sense of honour and quick temper I have had to keep some of the developments unknown to him; it will be better, therefore, not to refer to the matter and to let him assume this letter to be merely one of business. To keep him from becoming suspicious I suggest that you keep him busy this afternoon if possible—riding or rifle-practice are suggestions. You would thus confer a great favour upon,

Your obedient servant,

. . . . .

Mr Melton signed the letter with a steadier hand than he had had when he signed the order to the cashier. There were some advantages to being rich, after all. Say to a man, "Come, and he cometh; go, and he goeth." No, that wasn't Shakespeare either, but it stated the case. This way he could—at least there was good hope of it—get Guito out of the way.

Deliberately he addressed the envelope. He lighted a candle, heated sealing-wax, and fastened the flap with three good blobs of wax well pressed down. It really looked like a very important letter.

" When can you leave?"

" I can catch the noon boat."

" Good. I hate to rush you with your preparations for the trip
—but it's important. You're doing me a great favour."

Not quite knowing why he was doing so, he held out his hand.
Guito looked a little surprised at the formality. They shook hands
and said good-bye.

Once more alone, Mr Melton looked at his watch. Eleven-five.
If Guito was to make that boat in fifty-five minutes he would have
to spend every one of them rushing with his preparations—that
Chablis from Fourchard, for instance. There wouldn't be much
chance of his stopping to look at a newspaper or dropping into
any bar where he could overhear gossip. You couldn't be positively
sure, but it was fairly safe.

The secretary stood in the door again :

" Mr Angleman to see you, sir."

" Oh—make my excuses to Mr Angleman. I know he had an
appointment, but put him off till to-morrow, anyway. And, Hoffman, I can't see anyone more to-day. I'm going out."

Hoffman backed into the outer office, his methodical face showing bewilderment at the crotchety behaviour of his usually dependable employer. Hoffman was the one who would have to talk
blandishingly to Mr Angleman.

Mr Melton sat alone. The reaction struck him, and for a few
moments he fought physical sickness. Yes, he could ignore the
matter, but the boys wouldn't. That haunting memory had come
out into the open now. It was something that he had fought down
for more than twenty years, but of course he could never forget it.
He saw plainly the little Mexican restaurant in Los Angeles, and the
three men at the other table—the big truculent captain talking. Of
course it had been Judith he had been telling—lying—about. And
he, Daniel Melton, had walked out. It would have been better, he
thought bitterly for a moment, to have been lying dead these twenty
years in some forgotten grave. How many times had that act of
cowardice risen up between himself and Judith—even though she
knew nothing of it? What would Juan have done?

In spite of feeling sick he knew that he had resolved not to let

2 E

such another memory arise. Right or wrong—what was the difference? That was merely a mental reaction; the feelings that he had
were physical. Left to himself, he could probably have dismissed
the affair rationally. But the boys! . . . If he didn't do something
very quickly the boys would hear of the insult, and act. And if
anything happened to one of them!   . Thank God, he had—he
hoped—got Guito safely off for a few days! Lewis would not be
so bad; he could be argued into delay at least. Besides he didn't
read the *Gazette* usually and he didn't stand talking so much, the
way Guito did. Lewis might not even hear of the editorial for a
week.

Mr Melton got up and took his hat. There was a revolver, he
remembered, somewhere in the desk—a survival of the days when
revolvers were as much office equipment as desks themselves. But
he merely shrugged his shoulders and let himself out by his private
door.

As he walked down the street he was amazed at how fine he
felt. His step had a youthful jauntiness in it. He was delighted to
be actually doing something, and to be just about to wipe out the
twenty-year-old memory.

It was three blocks along Montgomery Street and then one over
to the left before he came to the office of the *Gazette*. It was delightful not to stop in the outer office, give his name and be shown in.
Instead, he merely walked to the door marked 'Editor,' opened it,
and stepped inside.

He had no idea what he was going to say or do. But he felt
strangely happy, and as confident as if he had prayed and had faith
that words and actions would be divinely supplied at the right
moment.

Mr Pennington sat behind a littered desk, not a remarkable-
looking man. Bullet-headed, with waistcoat cut low to show a stiff
white shirt-front, rather hard-faced as most editors were. As he
glanced up Mr Melton saw the flash of recognition. He saw also a
sudden line of tension across the forehead which showed that Mr
Pennington knew why his visitor had come The desk drawer was
half open, and Mr Melton knew that as a matter of course a revolver
lay in that drawer. An inner door opened, as pat as if the editor

might have rung a bell with his foot. Two printers appeared there in the time it took Mr Melton to close the door behind him and walk across to the desk. They looked villainous, but it was only printers' ink liberally smeared on their hands and clothes and faces. They stood in the doorway watching, but not looking as if they were about to interfere with anything.

Because of the rapidity with which his senses were working Mr Melton seemed to notice everything at once. He even noticed the monstrous big inkwell on the desk; it seemed as large as a beer-mug, and was nearly full of black, oily ink.

He stood before the desk and words came to him:

"Are you responsible, sir, for that editorial?"

"Yes——"

"Then, sir, you lie in your teeth!"

He saw the gaping faces of the two printers; he saw the editor's face change to a threatening scowl. But the hand did not move towards the drawer. In an instant, while time did not pass, Mr Melton saw the editor's mouth opening so that the dog-teeth showed. With a quick back-handed jerk Mr Melton seized the inkwell and slung round the ink into the snarling face. He saw the ink spattered upon the bullet-head; one eye seemed blotted out; the nose dripped liquid ebony; the mouth was spitting out blackness; a great blob spread upon the white shirt front. The two printers suddenly dissolved into uncontrollable laughter.

In a moment he felt himself floating upon a cloud of ecstasy. He was no longer afraid of anything. He had not only defied death; he had stepped up and tweaked death by the nose. He noticed that he had splattered some ink on his own fingers. With calculated deliberation, exposing all the while his breast within four feet of the half-opened drawer, he drew out a handkerchief, wiped his fingers, and then threw the handkerchief into a wastepaper-basket. Then he turned on his heel and walked out. Mr Pennington was spluttering and cursing as the two printers began to wipe him down, but his hand made no motion towards the drawer.

He is a coward, thought Mr Melton, as he carefully closed the door behind him. . . .

Out in the street the ecstasy ebbed a little, and yet not so much either. It was very pleasant to think of the scene reminiscently, to analyse it. Curious, for instance, it must have been the liberally inked printers that had suggested to his mind the throwing of the ink. And now that he recollected it he really believed that he had said, " You lie in your teeth!" It sounded like Mercutio.

Well, if a man read so much Shakespeare he was probably bound to revert to it. But he would wager that that was the first time in San Francisco, outside of the theatre, for any man to be given the lie direct in just those fine old words.

Mechanically he had taken the route back to his own office, but by the time he came to the door he had other plans. The matter would not, of course, stop where it was. He was by no means sure any longer that Mr Pennington was a coward—more likely just flabbergasted, not to mention being half strangled and blinded. There had been a lot of ink, and it had hit square.

In his mind Mr Melton checked off the names of his friends, and decided to hunt up Colonel Freisham. They were not close friends, but they were about the same age, and had known each other ever since the Colonel had come out from Maryland in '49. One should appeal to different friends upon different occasions, Mr Melton decided, and this kind of occasion called for Colonel Freisham.

At this time of the day the Colonel was more likely to be found in a bar-room than in his office, and Mr Melton began looking into the bars as he went along. By luck he found the Colonel in the third one he tried. After a few words the Colonel became interested, and decided that such intimate business could better be transacted in the privacy of his own office, just around the corner.

Mr Melton told what had happened; it was still necessary, he explained, that he should send a challenge to forestall Lewis and Guito.

" I've come to you," he concluded, " to ask you to act for me. You know the code. Can I still send a challenge?"

" By God, sir, you can! In some cases not, perhaps. But this one touches a lady's honour, and by the Galway or any other code ranks along with a blow. In my opinion you can throw a whole barrel of ink, and still remain the injured party. I'd be glad to carry the challenge for you, sir, but, to tell the truth, I'm not on good terms with Mr Pennington myself, and it never looks well to have a second with any personal feelings. Let's see "—the Colonel thought out loud—" Perkins, Van Deventer, Breckinridge, Poole—all good men; been out themselves. You know Poole?'

" Yes, he'd be satisfactory."

The Colonel sent out two boys to hunt up Mr Poole, and at that moment a general clamour marked the stroke of noon. Mr Melton gave a sigh of relief, hoping that Guito had caught the boat.

While they waited for Mr Poole the Colonel got out pen and paper and began to jot down the conditions. He was as businesslike as if he had been drawing up papers for a lease. Mr Melton's ecstasy had oozed away somewhat, but his resolution did not sag.

" Nothing complicated, of course," said the Colonel, his pen poised over the paper—" and naturally this is only a preliminary set of conditions subject to approval by the other party. But just as well to know our own mind." He jotted down a few words. "' Time of meeting '—to-morrow morning, I presume. No need for gentlemen to shilly-shally. Leave that to politicians."

Mr Melton started to laugh politely, but he saw that the Colonel had not been humorous.

" By God, sir, I mean it! When Dyer and Pendleton, the two Congressmen, fought they sent notes back and forth for two weeks until the dossier looked like the diplomatic correspondence leading up to the Crimean War. And Pendleton was a South Carolinian too. And after he was killed, shot through the liver at the second fire, didn't some scoundrel print the whole correspondence in a pamphlet for sale."

The Colonel was so indignant that he bacame red-faced, and got up to stride back and forth across the room. A little like a turkey-cock, thought Mr Melton; but he was very glad to have some one like the Colonel to arrange these matters.

" Place "—the Colonel was again making notes—" I know a nice spot over on the Contra Costa—conditions, light and so forth, good as you can expect. No likelihood of the sheriff interfering. King and Light, and I think a few others, Dawson and Lemon, I believe, have used it. And it's far enough off so that a lot of people don't just happen to turn up in time for the shots. By God, sir "—Mr

Melton wondered why the Colonel always introduced an anecdote by calling upon the Deity—" by God, sir when King and Jameson fought just across the city line in San Mateo County one hundred' and twenty-three people turned up—somebody counted 'em! As I said to Judge Pearson, ' Why didn't they set up a lemonade stand? ' "

The Colonel paused a moment, breathing heavily, as if in physical distress at the contemplation of such vulgarity. He began to write again, sounding out the words for Mr Melton's benefit :

' Dress—to be—ordinary—clothing—and—*must* be—examined for—pocket-testaments—and so forth. Better put it ' must '—' may ' is likely to cause hard feelings somewhere. Watches are allowable, being ordinary gentlemen's wear."

At this point Mr Poole came in, and Mr Melton had to go over the whole matter once more. Every time he told the story he felt his enthusiasm ebbing away some more, but he still felt very firm.

Mr Poole demurred at first upon a point of the code. Mr Melton being first wronged had taken satisfaction by throwing the ink, which was of course the equivalent of a blow. Was it not Mr Pennington therefore who now rested as the injured party? Should not the challenge come from him? But the Colonel ruled the contrary. True, Mr Pennington could now challenge if he wished. But the insult to the lady being a matter of such gravity Mr. Melton, in spite of the satisfaction which he had taken, still remained with a balance of injury on his side. Moreover, it was better for him to challenge, for in that case he, although injured, gave choice of weapons to the challenged. Otherwise people would certainly be found who would say that Mr Melton had deliberately thrown the ink so as to provoke a challenge, with the resultant advantage of having his own choice of weapons. " By God, sir . . ." And the Colonel cited two cases when that had been said, one in Maryland and one in North Carolina.

Mr Melton began to feel that a fine point at law was being discussed, but after all if you were going to do this sort of thing at all you might as well do it in proper fashion.

Mr Poole's scruples were satisfied, and he went to deliver the challenge. The Colonel and Mr Melton sent out for lunch, and ate in the office. The Colonel's flood of duelling reminiscences flowed

on. He himself had been out three times. He apparently thought it
bad taste to tell what had happened to his opponents, but he seemed
distinctly proud of the pistol-ball which he still carried in his thigh
—" within six inches, sir, of that Mexican musket-ball I got at
Molino del Rey." The Irish he declared to be the greatest of all
duellists. and their Galway Code to rank in its own field along with
the Constitution of the United States among political documents.
In Ireland there were cases of children being taken out and held on
the shoulder of a servant " to see papa fight. In Ireland the seconds
regularly used to fight along with the principals, standing at right
angles so that the lines of fire crossed. On Californian duels the
Colonel held mixed opinions. They were often most gallantly conducted, but there was too much tendency to the spectacular. The
Colonel rattled off summaries of duels as if he were reporting horse-
races " Hunt and Hubert, '54, pistols at ten paces, Hunt mortally
wounded at third fire. Smith and Scott, '53, pistols at eight paces,
Smith disabled at second fire. Woodlief and Kewen, '54, rifles,
forty yards, wheel and fire, Woodlief killed. Wethered and Captain
Schaffer, '51, guns, stopped by authorities. Dubert and Ellesler, '54,
broadswords—both skilled, sir—Ellesler wounded, but fought on
and killed Dubert in twenty minutes."

These were affairs which the Colonel—with more enthusiasm than
Latinity, thought Mr Melton—described as " *exempla classici* " of
Californian duelling. Still chewing on a bit of ham, he shifted to Mr
Melton's own case again :

" He'll take rifle or pistol, of course You don't know the sword,
I take it, and by all chances he doesn't either. Bowie-knives never
were a gentleman's weapon, and you can refuse em, just as you can
all this monkey business about sitting on a barrel of powder. What
kind of a shot are you? "

" Fair," said Mr Melton, trying to recollect whether he had fired
a rifle or pistol in the last ten years.

" I don't know anything about Pennington," said the Colonel.
" He's probably nothing much; comes from New York State, I
think "

A note came from Mr Poole; he had delivered the challenge, and
was in the Constitution Saloon awaiting momentarily the arrival of

Mr Pennington's second. Mr Melton had an idea now that he could go to his own office. He felt himself getting nervous at the long waiting about. But the Colonel would not hear of his leaving. " We'll have to get conditions fixed first," he said.

At about three o'clock Mr Poole himself came with a rough draft of conditions. Mr Pennington had chosen rifles; it was the challenger's prerogative to choose place and distance. Mr Melton deferred both to the Colonel. " The spot," dictated the Colonel, " previously used by Messrs King and Light, near the debouchment from the hills of the channel or branch known as Strawberry Creek, exact standing positions to be selected on the ground." As for distance, he advised forty yards. To Mr Melton this seemed a suicidal distance for rifles, but he kept quiet. Mr Poole voiced the same objection, but the Colonel stuck to his point.

" Every one hurries his shot when he's being shot at. By God, sir, Kearney and Imry, expert marksmen both, chose eighty yards, and then popped away three times with nobody even feeling the wind! "

The negotiations gave little trouble. Another conference of the seconds settled the various minor matters. Each principal was to be accompanied by his second, one other friend, and a surgeon. Mr Poole had urged a surgeon apiece in case of both principals being wounded; the Colonel, citing his lifetime experience, had scouted this possibility.

There was a matter-of-factness about the conditions which made Mr Melton a little shivery. " Rifles to be Mississippi jagers, of approximately same bore and length of barrel; bullets of size one hundred to the pound." The seconds were to procure weapons by arrangement with a gunsmith. Firing conditions had first called for a half-wheel fire, but the Colonel had objected, since within his sheaf of instances was one of a non-combatant having been winged by a confused principal who fired during instead of after his half-wheel. As the Colonel finally dictated : " The principals shall stand facing each other with the rifles held in the position known as ' port-arms.' "

With a shot-gun which happened to be handy the Colonel rehearsed Mr Melton in the manœuvre of bringing a piece from port-arms to the firing position. Mr Melton was a little awkward, but the

Colonel seemed well enough satisfied. " Take your time," he said.
" More duels have been lost by shooting too quick than too slow."

About five o'clock Mr Poole came in with the final conditions in
fair copy on a sheet of foolscap. They looked so much like a legal
document that Mr Melton was for a moment surprised to see that
they were unsigned; then he recollected that duelling was illegal, so
that naturally no one would put his name to the papers unless it were
really necessary. The Colonel read the conditions, cavilling a little at
the wording here and there, but, on the whole, satisfied.

Mr Melton went to his office, and spent about an hour there alone.
He found little that seemed to be of sufficient importance to do at
this particular moment. His will he considered to be in good shape.
He wrote two letters, more as a matter of courtesy than of business.
Finally he went out, called a cab, and drove home.

Dinner was ready, and he ate alone. Leticia was out somewhere.
Henry had been acting very queerly since that trouble at the Community; he seemed sicker than his scratched face would warrant;
he had asked to be excused from dinner. Judith had been in bed ever
since their return to the city.

There was roast lamb, and Mr Melton had a bottle of his favourite
Saint-Émilion brought up from the cellar He drank half the bottle,
and ate enough lamb to make the wine go down well. This, he considered, was just a reversal of things as they ought to be. But he
was not hungry. He sent the dessert away untasted, and sat drinking his coffee. He was very tired. The morning had been exciting
and glorious; the afternoon had been slow and dragging. But morning and afternoon together had in some way worn him down completely. That was a little strange too, for the only unusual exercise he had had during the day was the throwing of some ink. But
mental strain wore a man down—at least, a man of his age. He
would have imagined that a person dining alone on the evening
before a duel would have had some remarkable thoughts. Twirling
the stem of his wine-glass, he imagined himself proposing and drinking in solitary irony various toasts—heroical, Byronic, bitterly humorous. But no actual toast came to his mind. Not even a Shakespearean
quotation popped into his consciousness. He felt only the stupid
dullness of being very tired.

He went in to see Judith after dinner, and they talked for an hour, very companionably. They kept away from the subject of the Community. Mr Melton could not help admitting to himself that he was glad, under the circumstances, that Judith was ill. Otherwise the situation would have called for something magnificent— last embraces, noble words. Also in a purely practical way it was better so. Now he would merely sleep in the bed in his dressing-room; he would only tell her that he was leaving early—on business—and would probably not be back until the afternoon; he would not say how early or what business or how he might come back. Once or twice he thought that he ought to tell her, but he felt himself really too tired to go over the whole matter again. He argued to himself that additional nervous strain might unfit him for the morning. And, after all, he was not going out to certain death as if he were to face a firing-squad. Why put them both through a nerve-racking, tearful farewell? He had approximately a fifty-per-cent. chance of coming back unhurt, and only perhaps a twenty-to-a-hundred chance of being killed. Life was lived on chances, he kept thinking, as he answered Judith's questions about Guito's fishing trip; every morning when a man left the house there was a chance of being knocked over by a runaway horse, or of tripping at the top of some stairs, or falling dead with a heart-attack. A man of his age   Yes, he agreed with Judith in her opinion of Sir Robert as a very charming man; it would be a good thing for Guito to associate with him. Had Sir Robert been in the cavalry? she asked. No; Mr Melton thought infantry from the way he talked that night at the Condons'—the Indian army, apparently. That's funny, was Judith's opinion, there was a certain cavalry kind of look about him

AT FOUR IN THE MORNING Mr Melton was not just sure which one of the servants had knocked to wake him. He was surprised, considering what was about to happen, how well he had slept. He supposed that it showed how tired the excitement of the day had left him. But it might be something else too. If for a long time you had had some little gnawing pain like a growing tooth, then when it stopped you slept like the dead. So with him. For twenty years he had been perhaps a little restless under the feeling that he was not the man he ought to be—not a man like Juan Godoy. Now by the quick process of throwing some ink had he come to peace within himself? Who else was it who had thrown ink? Luther at the devil, wasn't it? But there was no record, he thought whimsically, that Luther had hit the devil, and probably the devil was so black that ink wouldn't show anyway. But quite likely Luther had slept better afterwards.

The room was neither dark nor light, but there was promise of a fine day. He dressed carefully, knowing that the tradition required it—his best broadcloth, the sort of costume one wore to a funeral or to church. He placed his watch in a waistcoat pocket, noting with grim cheerfulness that it was both large and thick—" watches allowed, being ordinary gentlemen's wear."

Breakfast was waiting, and he ate quickly; there was not much time. He knew that the servants must be wondering, even suspecting; but it was none of their business.

In the hall he slid into a light overcoat, partly to protect against the morning chill and partly to cover up the intense formality and sombreness of his early morning garb. A letter lay on the hall table; it must have come by special messenger—a large, important-looking envelope. He did not recognize the handwriting. He started to open it, and then laid it down. There was not much time now. If he came back there would be plenty of time; if he didn't come back the letter didn't matter Curiously, the thought elated him rather than otherwise. He had spent a large part of his life attending to business correspondence, and now for the first time to be able to thumb his nose at an important-looking letter made him feel carefree. The letter and his attitude reminded him of some quotation or other, but he couldn't place it—later he would remember perhaps.

In the drive Sam was waiting with the carriage and the greys. On the seat beside him Big Mike loomed up, revolver-bulge and all, looking defiant and immovable. Mr Melton felt a sudden flutter of uncertainty; it looked as if Big Mike were going along, whether or no.

"I'm going to drive myself this morning, Sam." Mr Melton tried to speak up boldly. "And, Mike, the carriage will be full; so you'll have to stay here."

They got down slowly, white and black, each displaying his own picture of disgust and reproach. Mr Melton gathered up the reins. What was the use, he thought, of pretending to drive away as if nothing were about to happen? He could see by their faces that they knew—or as good as knew.

"Good-bye, boys," he said, leaning down and holding out his hand. First Mike and then Sam shook hands. By George, in a moment Sam would be blubbering. Mr Melton felt a great surge of weakness swelling up within him. Careful—or he himself would be crying. He clicked to the greys and was off.

It was chilly on the deck of the ferry-boat—chillier than it had been in the drier air of the hill. Remnants of a fog were drifting about between the boat and the Contra Costa, sapping all the heat from the newly risen sun. Mr Melton shivered sometimes, but he honestly thought that it was from the cold. Why fight so early in the morning, anyway? What with the time of year and the distance to go there was no chance of fighting before sunrise. And once the sun was up making light conditions unequal you might as well fight late as early. 'Three-o'clock-in-the-morning' courage was the hardest, Napoleon or somebody had said. What was the quotation about the letter?

They talked a little among themselves—Mr Melton, Mr Poole

as second, the Colonel as the single other friend allowed under the conditions, and Dr Fries, the surgeon. They could see the four others, but each party kept formally at as much distance as the little ferry-boat permitted. There was nothing precisely to mark them as duellists. The rifles and the surgeon's bags were concealed in the carriage. Yet the glances which the crew and the few other early travellers bestowed upon the two groups were curious and knowing. After all, what else could it be? The formal dress so early in the morning, and two equal groups. You didn't go to a wedding or a funeral at this hour, and, in any case, San Francisco didn't hold their weddings and funerals at Oakland.

A two-seated buckboard met the other group on the Oakland side. Mr Melton saw them dismiss the livery-stable man, and drive away. It took a few minutes to get the greys and the carriage off the boat. Mr Melton would have liked to manage the reins to keep his mind a little busy, but Dr Fries offered to drive, and it seemed more polite, perhaps more dignified, to let him. Driving yourself to your own funeral. . . .

Everything was still. It was a fine sunlit morning now. The high brown hills rose on the right. Shadows lay heavy in the ravines, and the dark green of bay-trees emphasized the shadows. North across the littoral ran the road, merely a pair of dusty wheel-tracks. Half a mile ahead, the moving puff of dust indicated the other carriage.

Mr Poole was the only one who tried conversation, but he got little response. The doctor seemed busy enough with driving; Mr Melton felt no need of talk. The Colonel, curiously, did not seem to be reminded of a single anecdote. Glancing at him, Mr Melton had a new idea of his attitude towards duelling. Yesterday the Colonel had seemed to be thinking in terms of a sporting event like a horse-race. To-day he was silent, and you might even think exalted, as if he thought of the duel as a religious rite, a sacrament —baptism by fire. That was the way, Mr Melton had read, that Spaniards went to the bull-fight, their pageant of death. There should be a name for such people. Death-worshippers. Thanato-something-or-other, it would probably be.

"Yes," he said in response to Mr Poole's direct and repeated

liberty to bring your pieces into firing position and to fire. No fire
shall be made after the word 'Five.'"

They were the conditions already agreed upon; to repeat them
was a mere formality. Mr Melton had better thoughts, and he felt
the words of Hotspur singing in his mind; they steadied him:

> O gentlemen, the time of life is short!
> To spend that shortness basely were too long,
> If life did ride upon a dial's point,
> Still ending at the arrival of an hour. . . .

Mr Melton brought himself back to the business of the duel
sharply. But in some way the gentle slope of dried grass, and the
trees that ringed it about, and the tense faces of the men watching
seemed less real than the noble words resounding in his brain.

"Ready."

He pulled back the hammer, tense for the next word.

"One!"

He swung the rifle to his shoulder, saw the sights come true,
and fired. At the same moment he saw the blossom of flame from
the other's gun. "Four!—Five!" counted the second uselessly.

Mr Melton stood with his rifle still levelled; he had not heard or
felt his opponent's ball. He moved himself cautiously to feel whether
he was hit. Mr Pennington too was still standing. Mr Melton, as
his second came running towards him, lowered the rifle and raised
a hand in salutation to show that he was all right.

"Sit down a minute," said Mr Poole, "till I find how things
are at the other end."

Mr Melton sat down; at that moment he did not feel either elated
or depressed. He was waiting, and his feelings were in abeyance.
At the other end of the line Mr Pennington was lighting a cigar.
This must show that he was unhurt, but it would also indicate that
his nerves were shaken—lighting a cigar when he would probably
not have a chance to smoke half an inch of it!

The seconds consulted in the middle of the line, holding the
rifles. Then they began to reload. Mr Poole came back:

"Pennington demands another shot, and as the challenger that's
his right. I heard him talking; he seems bitter. Says if he kills a
millionaire like you he'll have to run for it, anyway, he supposes."

Mr Melton felt a sudden, and, he realized, dangerous, sympathy for his opponent. Standing at the opposite end of forty yards in some way gave you a curious sympathy for another man's point of view.

"Take your time," Mr Poole went on. "Pennington's nervous. You came close to him. I was watching him, and I think he felt the wind of your bullet."

"Which side?" asked Mr Melton in a cool professional way which made him a little surprised at himself.

"Left, I should say—yes, I'm pretty certain he jerked his head to the right; but of course he might not have been sure himself."

"'Trigger-pull,' probably," said Mr Melton. "I'll be more careful." He remembered that 'trigger-pull' had always been his fault.

Mr Poole was to give the words this time. Mr Pennington threw away his cigar. They both stood up again.

"Ready." Mr Poole looked from one to the other, waiting longer than seemed necessary.

"One!"

Mr Melton swung the muzzle down and the butt towards his shoulder. Fire on the down swing, don't try for the head. . . .

"Two!"

The sights swung diagonally across. Too far to the right; bring back to the left. . . . Steady.

"Three!"

Sights falling in line—his waistcoat. . . . Don't pull; squeeze it. Steady.

"Four!" . . .

He was lying on the ground. Something seemed to have knocked him down suddenly. He must have fainted without firing. Coward, after all!

Then consciousness dimmed in a mighty fit of coughing. "Through the lungs, close to . . . " he clearly heard some one saying, but he could not seem to see. Pain flared through his chest; he coughed, and something warm poured in and choked his mouth and nostrils. Darkness which seemed more than lack of light closed in around him.

LEWIS WAS DOWN IN THE HOLD of the *Costa de Oro*. He was in a seaman's dungarees, smeared with grease and smelly with bilge-water. He wanted to get things straight about her insurance, and the only way to be sure was to come and see for yourself. And he had found a crack in the drive-shaft to her starboard paddle-wheel—might be superficial, but looked bad enough to him. Wouldn't that be fine, to have it snap and your wheel go dead some night when you were trying to get around Concepcion in a gale, and a full load of passengers aboard. God, the narrow margin they ran these steamers on, with the cut-throat competition between Pacific Packets and Vandenburg! Well, he'd see that they'd fix that shaft before they got any insurance. Or would he now, either? It would be just like Brinton and Brinton to take it for a little extra premium, when no one else would. There was competition in insurance too. Well, let Brinton and Brinton do as they liked. They wouldn't last long if they kept that up. Insurance was one business you couldn't play fast and loose in—not for long, anyway. Might as well have a look forward as long as he was here.

He started forward, and then he heard the mate yelling to him from above. He couldn't hear what it was.

"Can't come up just now," he yelled back. "Be up in a few minutes."

But the mate bawled down again, and louder, so that this time his words were clear:

"Man here—says you'd better come up. Your stepfather—just been killed in a duel."

Lewis's first thought was to yell back foolishly asking the mate what he had said. But he didn't, for he really knew that he had heard exactly what the mate said. The only thing was that it was quite fantastic and impossible; it must be a hoax, or some one else killed—not Old Dan'l. It wasn't true.

But when he had swung himself up to the deck as fast as he could and got there all breathless—there was Hoffman the secretary, looking as pale as a sheet. And it was true.

Wasn't that a hell of a way to have it happen? As fine a man as Old Dan'l, and to hear about his death suddenly that way when you were in dungarees and greasy and smelling of bilge-water? And Old Dan'l shot through the lungs that morning, and dead.

He heard the story—as much of it as Hoffman could tell—while he changed his clothes in the mate's cabin.

" Has Mrs Melton been informed? " he asked.

" Colonel Freisham went on to tell her when we couldn't find you at your office. Somebody had to tell her right away; the news is running over the city like wildfire. Nobody could say where you were," Hoffman added apologetically. " I've been hunting you along the waterfront for an hour."

Lewis hailed a cab on the Embarcadero, gave the man the Stockton Street number, and told him to drive fast. Goddam, he kept saying to himself, an old man like that, and with rifles! He felt angry more than sorrowful as yet. Along with the anger he could feel a certain pride Goddam, Old Dan'l, close to sixty and he goes out and fights a duel, with rifles! There's the old-timer for you! These young fellows around here now won't be doing that when they're that old. Then the anger came back upon him. Pennington couldn't be a day over thirty-five. What did he mean, taking on an old man like that? And what the devil did Old Dan'l mean too—getting up suddenly on his hind-legs and throwing ink? And what was the editorial? Lewis hadn't even heard of it, as far as he could remember.

His mother's appearance shocked him. She lay in a darkened room, weeping on her pillow, quite gone to pieces. He could say little to her. Mrs Martin the housekeeper was doing what she could; the French maid flitted ineffectively in the background.

Lewis stayed only a few minutes, and slipped out, baffled. He had always counted on his mother as the strong one who would see them all through. Now she had crumpled. He conferred with Mrs Martin in the hall. He had not realized that his mother had been ill ever since coming back from the ranch—pains in the side and all that. It made him feel curiously a little better about her. With a physical illness first, and then this on top, it explained her going to pieces. And they hadn't even called a doctor. Well, he could do that, anyway, and the best in San Francisco. God, what people these old-timers were! Old Dan'l fighting a duel at sixty, and his mother so ill she could hardly move and not telling a doctor. She must still be thinking about things as if she were back on the ranch in the hide-and-tallow days.

It was on his way downstairs that he thought of Guito. The thought suddenly cleared everything else out of his mind for the moment. Guito? Come to think of it, where was Guito, anyway? At the thought all the hot, swirling emotions suddenly whiffed out of his mind. He was cold, and thinking hard. Guito, the younger brother, the happy-go-lucky, the quick-tempered, the beloved. He had looked after Guito since they were little boys on the ranch.

He turned in at the dining-room door looking for a decanter; he felt as if he needed a drink. But by the time he had got to the sideboard he had changed his mind. This was no time for drinking. He was turning the matter over rapidly and clearly in his mind. He thought that he began to see how it might all have appeared to Old Dan'l. He began to see that matters had not come to rest yet.

In the hall he came upon Mike. It was ridiculous to think that Big Mike had been crying, and yet there was a look about his eyes.

" He wouldn't take me along this morning," said Mike. " Me and Sam knew what was going to happen. But he wouldn't take me along."

Lewis felt more like crying than he had yet—Mike, the big old baboon, explaining how his master came to be killed without Mike's being there to know the reason why. . . .

" It wouldn't have done any good for you to be there, Mike. It was a duel."

" A duel, you call it! Him sixty and the other fellow young. And him not having shot a gun in ten years, maybe."

Mike paused; he was a man of few words. Lewis saw light as of grim satisfaction come into his eyes:

" Anyway, Mr Lewis, don't worry about one thing. I'll tend to that."

For a moment Lewis thought that it might be the best way out. After all, Mike had been a paid bodyguard for ten years without ever firing a shot. He had the fierce Irish loyalty. But no—it wouldn't do. To have Mike kill Pennington would be just about the same as hiring a thug to do it. And a jury would be sure to hang Mike. But there wouldn't be any use telling Mike not to. He temporized :

"Well, Mike, don't think of that just now. Wait till after the funeral. And look here—right now you go down to Dr Templeton's and tell him to come to see Mrs Melton."

Lewis left the house, and started for his own rooms. Then the professional thought struck him that he would not like to write a life-insurance policy for Mr Pennington now. First himself, then Mike, then Guito—no, even 95 per cent. would be a losing premium.

The affair which lay ahead seemed a little futile. Who was Pennington? Just a hired hand for Judge Wingram. And who even was Judge Wingram? Just a bit of a system, and you couldn't shoot a system. As a business man himself Lewis saw the matter dispassionately enough. If it hadn't been for Guito he would have stopped where he was. But Guito—Lewis was always ready to admit it—was really several kinds of a fool. He would be sure to do something, and do it in such a way as to end up being hanged. Neither of them of course could challenge Pennington again under any duelling code. But there was another code of even older standing in California.

Lewis went up to his rooms, and looked over his pistols. There was the funny little thing that had been in the old chest at the ranch, and had been his ever since he was old enough to hold it; a heavy Navy revolver, the curious over-and-under, two pepper-boxes, two derringers, a long-barrelled target-pistol. Lewis had always liked pistols, and he had quite a collection—as much museum as anything else. Certainly he would be a brave man who would ever try to shoot either of the pepper-boxes again.

The revolver was heavy and a little clumsy to bring into action quickly. The derringers would do, but they meant that you had only one shot, or else had to handle two weapons. Finally he took the over-and-under. It was English made, after the model of English sporting rifles, with one barrel under the other instead of the two being side by side. It must have been made to order, for Lewis had never seen another anything like it. He oiled the complicated hammers, which looked as if they would never work, and always did.

He was perfectly cool now, and everything he was going to do lay outlined clearly in his mind. He put on several coats one after the other, and practised drawing the pistol from the side-pocket, swinging it up and snapping it. The different coats made little difference in the draw, but he took one of them, and selected his other clothes to match it.

He had not been shooting much lately, and would have liked to go to a gallery for a few rounds. But he knew that it would not be a good idea for him to supply any evidence that he had been practising. He felt confident, anyway—close range and a big target. . . . Pistol-shooting seemed to come naturally to him; it was the one thing he had always been good at even when a boy. He could always outshoot Guito, although Guito could beat him at riding and roping and most other things. But Guito was too quick on the trigger for pistol-shooting.

He loaded both barrels of the pistol very carefully, dropped it into his side-pocket, and went out.

He hailed the first cab he saw. The news of Mr Melton's death would be all over the city now, and he did not want to be stopped for condolences at every street corner.

" Drive up Kearny and down Montgomery," he told the cabman.

He sat well back in the cab so as not to be easily recognized. The best thing to do would be to drive up and down the streets until he saw one of the men he wanted. It would probably not take long; San Franciscans spent an amazingly large part of their time in the streets. He ran over a list of three or four men who might serve. At first he was surprised to find that they were all much older than he, but on consideration he did not find it at all surprising. He was going to act by an older code, one which his own contemporaries hardly admitted; only the older men would serve his purposes.

On Montgomery Street he sighted " Doc " Peters. Lewis told the cabman to pull over and stop; Doc was as good a man as he could wish.

He cut short the condolences, and motioned Doc into the cab. Doc had been in California since '48, and it did not take much explaining to make him grasp the idea. He arranged to send a note to Lewis' office, and got out after a conversation lasting only the length of time which it had taken the cab-horse to walk two blocks. Lewis had himself driven to his office, paid off the cabman, and went in. Before he could get to his private room he had to talk with several people who wished to express their sorrow and sympathy. He disliked talking about the matter, but he realized that under the circumstances it was a good thing to have witnesses that he was continuing in a normal state and not overcome with passion.

In his office he answered some letters. He felt an almost deadly coolness. The only thing that worried him was a sort of hallucination that there might be dust or lint in his pocket which would get into the muzzles of the pistol-barrels. He took the pistol out twice for inspection; and turned his pocket inside out to clean it. Satisfied at last, he began to reckon out the rate on a projected policy. The figures clicked contentedly through his mind; he did not make mistakes.

He had given orders that he was positively not to be disturbed unless a letter came by special messenger. It was more than an hour before the letter came ·

Our friend is at the Brooklyn alone—inside corner table, next bar, facing out. Drinking beer, not corned. Not many others here now. We're at inside corner table away from bar. Burn this.

It was unsigned, lacked a salutation, and was apparently scrawled with the left hand. Doc was taking no chances.

Lewis read it again carefully all the essential information was there. He recalled to himself the interior of the Brooklyn. You entered, and looked down the length of a bar with two or three bartenders. In front of the bar were some small tables, three rows of them as he remembered, and three or four tables to the row—not a large place. Pennington would be sitting at the inside corner next the bar; Doc and whatever friends he had collected would be at the other inside corner.

He scratched a match, and watched it as the sulphur fumed and finally broke into blue flame. He touched it to the corner of the note; kept his hold until the paper had burned up close to his fingers, and then let it fall and burn out on the bare wooden floor. He ground the charred paper to bits beneath his feet.

At the window he looked out until he saw an empty cab approaching. He went out quickly, hailed it, and got in.

"Brooklyn Saloon," he said.

It would not be five minutes' drive. He examined the pistol again. Perhaps he should have left a note; it might be a nasty business for his mother. He would have to draw fire first. No, he didn't feel any conscience. Where the hell was Guito, anyway? Well, here they were.

Some men were just coming out of the Brooklyn. Lewis pretended to be fumbling with his change until they had got clear of the door. The fewer people around the better

Firmly, but not hurriedly, he stepped in. His eyes swept the room —bar-tenders, three men standing before the bar, some others at a front table, Pennington as expected, and Doc with two men. He didn't recognize the men with Doc; it was clever of Doc to choose strangers.

He strode to the middle table as a sudden hush fell over the room. Funny, how quickly people knew.

Pennington glanced up; he looked startled, and his hand went to his side.

Lewis spoke quickly and low:

"You shot an old man this morning; defend yourself, you bastard!"

Lewis dodged sideways and down and felt the wind of the bullet. His own pistol was out, and he fired by feel without sighting. The two reports were blurred together. Through the smoke he saw Pennington's head jerk, and his body slump down. Lewis did not need to look, but he was sure that his bullet had struck just above the left eye.

Doc was on his feet.

"Gentlemen, gentlemen," he was crying above the sudden clamour of the room. "A most unfortunate affair, but you must give me your names. In the cause of justice we must all be witnesses that the gentleman who has been killed shot first; Mr Godoy drew and fired in self-defence."

DEFINITELY JUDITH DREADED seeing the ranch again. But Sam sat on the seat ahead of her as stolidly driving onward as if he were the very coachman of Time's chariot, and every plunk of the greys' feet in the dusty road · signalled the passing of the moments.

Henry sat beside Sam, and on the seat beside Judith was the young man, bleating on. It was hardly fair, either, to think of him as bleating; most people would certainly have thought of him as a very intelligent and lively talker. He was really an extraordinary young man. It was remarkable how quickly he observed things as they drove along, picking out anything unusual or colourful that he might use in his writings. Judith had read many of the pieces that he had written for the *Golden Era* in the last two years over his pen-name " Zutano," and there was no denying that they showed a remarkable talent. He had a gift for words and sentences and the quick sketching of characters. People in San Francisco were beginning to point him out and say that he would go far. That was why the children had all urged, even insisted, that she should bring him down and show him Rancho Amarillo. He was a newcomer to California, but he wanted to learn something about the old times so that he could write about them. And where, all the children had said, could he learn about the old times better than at Rancho Amarillo, and who was better fitted to tell him about them than Judith Melton, who had been Judith Godoy and known as Señora Blanca, the White Lady? As a duty to the development of Californian literature she should take Zutano to the ranch.

Guito's and Henry's sudden apparent concern for the advance of letters was not at all convincing. What they wanted, of course, was to get their mother interested again in something—anything. She had been ill for three months, and through the winter and spring had convalesced slowly. She herself knew well enough that what she needed was some new impulse to get her life started again. During the last months she had kept thinking of that great talk they had had that night at the ranch when Uncle Enrique had taken just a glass too many and begun expatiating upon the course of human life being like the course of a river. But Uncle Enrique had not suggested that a stream could enter a morass and stand stagnant among reeds and mud.

Well, she had come to like the young man well enough during their long drive together. And probably people were right in saying that he was destined to be, as they put it, " an ornament to literature." He had not published any books, but his pieces in the *Era* showed fine workmanship in their sense of phrase and rhythm. Judith realized a little sadly that she had never had much power of fine workmanship herself; her skill ran to handling people, not things. But she had always recognized and admired that kind of skill, whether it was a novel by Thackeray, or her father handling the *Spanish Belle*, or even Ramón and Miguel roping cattle. Zutano had the gift of fine workmanship in words, but it took more than that to make a great writer. A writer must have subject-matter, not merely—as Zutano usually did—put into good prose something which to begin with was essentially nothing. Lewis was very fond of Zutano personally, but he must have realized this fault; he and Leticia, Judith knew, were the children who had inherited her own love of good reading. "Right now," Lewis had said, "he's just like a spider, spinning things out of his own insides. But he realizes he needs knowledge and experience. Take him down and show him the ranch."

They would come to the hill-crest and see the valley in a few minutes now. She dreaded it, but she hoped that it would be like any kind of a cold plunge—once she was in she would feel revived and stronger than before. And the young man had been an interesting companion, with his trick of picking out the colourful and unusual sights and incidents.

They topped the rise, and the valley lay spread before them. Sam drew in the horses. All but Sam got out and stood looking. They had happened to arrive, Judith explained, just at the time—the moment, one might almost say—when spring was passing over into summer. A few days ago the hills must have been green; in a few more days they would be brown. She tried to make Zutano see the curious shade of darkness, blackness—she struggled ineffectively for a word—which the grass displayed in the sunlight. It had, she ventured finally, a dull sheen, like lead. The young man obviously could not understand; he had been in California only a few years, and had lived mostly in the city She was relieved when Henry called him to look at something else.

She herself was glad to stand and look her fill. The deep grass and the cup of the valley, the creek with its sycamores, Brushy Peak rising up beyond. . . . She felt a lump in her throat. This was her home; she would come back to live here. She would bring Henry with her; he had always wanted to return.

The vision faded. Her mind was too keen and honest to accept it. The grass and the hills and the house might be much, but they were not all. Most of what she remembered and loved of those days was what she herself had been and enjoyed then—youth, vigour, children, love. Those she could not bring back, any more than the stream could lift itself from the swamp to return to the hills.

She was even more depressed as they drew near the house. Some peach- and plum-trees in the orchard, neglected last year, had cracked and split beneath the weight of the unpicked fruit. In the winter rains the unprotected adobe walls of the fire-gutted new house had crumpled and fallen in great pieces; blank windows stared. The wreck stood gaping and ugly—the office where as mistress of the ranch she had presided proudly over her account books, the pleasant upper room where Lewis and Guito had slept when they were little boys, the sunny patio.

" Picturesque old ruin! " she heard the young man saying. At that instant she hated him. This was no Greek temple or medieval abbey. This was her home. She had seen the adobe clay for the brick dug from the hillside, and the timbers brought in by slow-pacing ox-teams; she had worked over the plans, and seen the walls rise surely.

Judith talked with the married couple who were the only people still remaining—a last remnant of the Community. They were scarcely more than caretakers for the buildings, for the herd had been leased to a neighbouring rancher on the north, who, as far as they could learn, had not been involved in the raid and burning.

The caretakers told a very cheerless tale. Everything was going to decay. Even the old house had suffered by the falling on it of parts of the second-story walls of the new house. They seemed remarkably loyal to the Community, and asked timidly if it were to be re-established. Judith could give them no encouragement. With the fire, Daniel's death, and her own long illness everything had been in abeyance, and with the uncertainty and the fear of more outrages the people had oozed away. Old Hargrace had died of a bad heart. Mrs Barton had remarried and gone to Oregon. The blacksmith, Tony Burke, and several more had joined the rush to Washoe. Lewis had found jobs for others. Like Brook Farm and New Harmony and so many others, the Amarillo Community was a memory.

At the inquiries of these simple people who still sought Utopia Judith felt the lump in her throat again. She had reflected many times already that her bravado in defying the reporters and saying that the Community would go on had probably led to the editorial and to all that had happened later. She had bearded fate, and fate had struck her down.

In spite of what she had said, the Community would not go on. The people were scattered; the buildings were in ruins; her own forces seemed to have left her. And there was no money.

Daniel had died at a bad time. Gold-production was falling off, and San Francisco was panicky. Daniel, never doubting in his city's future, had put his name on notes to bolster up the credit of others. In his will he had left what seemed moderate specified amounts to charity, and to servants, employees, and old friends, like Uncle Enrique Godoy and Williamson the hide-trader, who had lost his money and was having a hard time of it. The payment of these fixed sums with the bottom knocked out of the real-estate market had left Judith as residuary legatee just about enough to live on modestly. Lewis, indeed, was making money, and she and the children still owned the ranch, but she could not attempt the Community again. As she replied to the caretaker and his wife that there was no chance of a new establishment of the Community it seemed to her that she had tasted a final humiliation.

She turned to her duty of showing Zutano about the house. Much which she had thought would interest him seemed to make no impression. The planning and construction of the house, even the flanker, he passed by with only a polite attention. She explained how they had made the adobe bricks, how they had built the walls of the first story and then laid a wooden stringer as foundation for the cross-beams of the upper floor, spiking each beam into place with one precious nail. Both wood and nails, she explained, had been scarce. She thought that she should tell about such essential matters as the food-supply—what they had got from the ranch, what came from San José, and what from the Boston ships. But for these solid foundations of living Zutano seemed to care little. His questions indicated other interests. Had they held fandangos often? Where would a man stand when he serenaded? Were there any stories about ghosts? Or legends—such as buried treasure?

The young man, Judith thought, had read his Scott, his Poe, and his Irving. He was doing his best to see at Rancho Amarillo what they had seen elsewhere.

In the patio a coping-stone had fallen from the well-curb, and grass had found foothold in the cracks of the pavement. A little lizard scuttled out of view. The young man quoted some poetry, very patly, about lizards and ruins. But it was silly, thought Judith. There was no more homely little animal than a lizard. Never had she known a summer when lizards did not scuttle through the sunshine in the patio and climb up the adobe walls. Alert, shy little creatures, looking as if they wanted to be friendly. Sometimes the cat would catch one, and, eating it, get sick. Poets were fools to couple them with ruins. Lizards were as domestic as mice.

Finally she stopped trying. It was obvious that the young man would never feel about Rancho Amarillo in any way as she did. He was walking about looking for nuggets as if it were a mine to be exploited; only flashes of colour interested him. She loved the dull texture of the rock itself. He thought of fandangos and serenades. She thought of children playing and fighting, of Lupe patting tortillas, of the tortillas between the teeth, of so many hides and so many pounds of tallow. It was like the chocolate that Lupe used to make and beat up for them in the old Mexican way. She was thinking of the rich chocolate itself; he was thinking of the showy bubbly foam floating on top.

She began wearily telling him what she knew he wanted to know. She even elaborated a bit. He was a very clever young man and would go far, she was sure. People would like what he wrote, and the way he wrote it. But she felt a little weary to think of the mould inevitably forming, to think that because this young man could handle his participles well and tuck his prepositions in neatly all those people of the old days who had lived with the hills and the grass and the cattle, chewing tortillas and lustily smelling of garlic, might go down through the ages insipidly treading jarabes to the ceaseless twanging of guitars.

It was a little while before she grasped a new trend in his questions, for the young man was not crass, and seemed to believe in surrounding his art with a little mystery. Finally she decided that he must be looking for a villain to the piece. The setting might be Arcadian, but the story needed a villain.

The she thought of Julio—fat, pudgy Julio. He had been major-domo at the ranch for six years, and had served them well enough in his lazy fashion until he began drinking too much. True, he was thought to have fathered an illegitimate child or two out in the quarters; Judith had rather doubted it, for she could scarcely imagine Julio going to so much trouble; but even if it were so it was hardly held against a man in those days, perhaps the contrary. Then that night when Daniel had come in hurt Julio had been drunk or crazy, and she herself had half accidentally shot his hat-brim with the pistol.

She made a very good case for Julio as a villain—repulsively fat and pudgy. She thought of Hamlet's uncle, and added that Julio smiled, and thus covered his villainies. The young man was delighted.

Well, she had perhaps immortalized Julio. She could imagine the major-domo going down through the ages as the villain. He might be called Julio, or Ignacio, or Antonio; but it was all the same. This young man was shaping the wet clay; according to the form which he gave it in his books it would harden. Others who came after would see not the shapeless wet clay, but the firm shape which he had given it.

Yet she could not blame the young man. It was not to his discredit that he had a caressing way with adjectives. Probably he knew his own business. Those long years at the ranch which meant so much to her—what would they mean to others? Year after year— the spring round-up for the gelding and branding, the summer round-up for the killing; the daily ride of inspection; the foamy chocolate, the steaming beans, the tough, stringy beef from a new-killed range steer, the tortillas and peppers and onions; the children; the fruit-trees in bloom; and year after year the grass, nobly growing. Yes, the young man was right in hunting for fandangos and ghosts and villainous major-domos.

Towards sunset she turned him over to Henry, and went out to the porch. The posts were charred a little from the scorching they had taken when the hall burned. She sat down on a bench which had stood there for a long time; but it was not there when she had come to the ranch; she could remember when it was made. She was tired and spiritless. The stream of life, she thought again, was still languishing in the morass, not knowing where to issue forth. That was not the way for a life to do—at least, not hers. She would rather the stream went surely, even swiftly, down to the ocean where it lost itself for ever.

The pain in her side was not bothering her much now, but the doctor thought that it had been the cause of her illness. She had told him about her long ride, and the miscarriage which had followed. But he was not even sure that that had caused the trouble. People, he said, tended to blame their troubles on one particular event, when the connexion might be only coincidental. On the other hand, that might have been the cause; he was not certain. He would not say much, but he thought secretly, she was sure, that the trouble was serious. He said, however, that she might live for a long time. He gave her no hope that the pain would ever really disappear. It might be worse, and then become almost unnoticeable for a while, and then be still worse—until the end came. Probably, she had decided privately, the only way she could fool it was to die of something else before it made up its mind, so to speak, to finish her off. She did not relish the idea of just waiting around on its pleasure.

Yet she felt too stagnant to live actively. Probably she would just live on, sleeping in soft beds and watching against colds, until finally the pain finished its work. Others would effectively take charge of the world—young Zutano, for instance. It did not seem to her fitting for her thus to fade from the scene, she who had always wrestled the world. But the pain was a subtle worker; perhaps the pain itself was changing her, making her thus stagnant, unable to struggle.

She looked out, as she had done a thousand times before, towards the southern hills. The sunset was bright on the ridges; in the ravines it had stretched out the shadows. She let her eyes follow upwards until the lines blended together and reached the far-stretching skyline. The familiarity made her feel a little comforted.

REALLY TO BE GOING EAST AGAIN after all these years was a startling thought. Judith had never been given to fluttering, but she could feel herself beginning to flutter as she waited for the carriage, walking back and forth in her room, wondering at the last moment whether she had forgotten anything.

She was almost in a panic and ready—even with her trunks on the steamer—to say she would not go. It was obvious that the children were merely trying to shove her off so that she would see something new, and get some change, and shake off the lethargy and depression which had held her so long. At this last moment she resented their attitude. If she wished to remain stagnant it was her own business. She would rather be allowed to stay quietly at home, and nurse her illness. The pain in the side was still lurking there; twice in the past year she had had to go to bed. If she were going to die she would rather stay at home to do it.

Yet there were some real reasons for going East. She would like to see Cousin Carrie after so many years—gentle Cousin Carrie, who had written letters and sent books for so long and had never realized that life in California wasn't just the same as life was in Boston. And Judith had decided that she would go up to Appleby and see her mother. It was foolish for her mother to have been estranged all this time on account of such a bit of ancient history as Judith's elopement with Juan—and Juan himself dead these ten years. On the whole Judith had expended little thought upon her mother, but in the last year she had thought of her more often. It was as if they had at length become old ladies together—contemporary widows who should be friends. Yet in the years between Judith had lived through so much—and in all those years her mother had merely retired to Appleby and been sitting in an old lady's cap. And Appleby itself had probably not changed a jot; perhaps they had put new heating-pipes into the church.

Then there was Guito too; that was another real reason for going. Guito was a soldier like his father. At the first sound of guns he had gone; he was a captain already. in a cavalry regiment. The Federals, she thought proudly, would not have many such cavalrymen as he—men who had ridden and shot since childhood, and who came of a line of soldiers as far back as you could find the records. She would go to Washington, and in the winter Guito could get leave and come to see her.

Lewis came to carry down her last satchels; she would see the other children at the steamer, but it was naturally Lewis who came to tend to things. It made her sorrowful to ride behind Sam and the greys for perhaps the last time. The carriage had been the one luxury to which she had clung when she had had to economize elsewhere.

On board it was like a reception. Leticia, Mrs Kelly now, was there with her husband and baby, and Henry behind the immature little beard he was cultivating so carefully as if he wished to disguise himself. He was going back in a few months to take charge at the ranch, as he had wished for so long. Big Mike was there, saying good-bye in some embarrassment and confusion. She saw that there was no bulge under his coat any more; it made her feel a little sad to think of him now, merely a janitor.

There were other friends too—Hoffman, Mr and Mrs Buxton, and some of the ladies from the Assistance Society. Judith was touched that so many had come to see her off. She was embarrassed more than angered when she saw Judge Wingram At least she was relieved that Alicia was not hanging on his arm. It would have been worse somehow facing Alicia than the Judge. He had gambled with Juan, he had wrecked the Community, he had as good as murdered Daniel. Yet when he came and held out his hand and cried " *Bon voyage!* " in his great booming voice Judith accepted his good wishes. One couldn't make a scene. And civilization was too complicated. However much he had pulled the strings it seemed hardly real to think of him as having committed arson or murder. As Lewis had said, it was the system.

The real surprise was to see suddenly, as in a dream, three faces out of the far-off time. Lewis of course was the one who had thought of it and arranged their coming. There was Antonia, bent and shrivelled and leather-faced, but still with sharp, quick-glancing eyes. There was Don Diego Fuente, a little man always and now seeming smaller than ever, but looking wiry and fit enough even yet to ride as far in a day as he ever had and to fight some Indians at the end of the day. There too was Uncle Enrique, only a little more dried up than he had been twenty-five years before. Those were about all that were left to come, for Catalina had been dead these two years and Don Alonzo was bedridden with a broken hip.

It was good to see them for a few minutes, to feel yourself swept off in a swirl of memories, and to talk Spanish, even though from lack of practice you blundered a little. Don Diego was wearing his old Californian clothes, with a big hat and a long dark-blue cloak; it was threadbare, and Judith knew that he was too poor to buy anything new. Uncle Enrique, who had had a legacy from Mr Melton, was wearing American clothes. He was still living in the same house, he said; Monterey didn't change much Judith calculated quickly to herself that he must by now be just about seventy, but he had passed himself for an old man for so long that he seemed to be a hundred. The reporters who had come to pick up news at the steamer-sailing descended upon him eagerly. . . .

By early afternoon the *Magdalena* had passed the Golden Gate, and was steaming down the coast. Judith sat in her deck-chair; she had a book beside her, but was not reading. Already she was beginning to feel that the children had been right. She had left something behind in San Francisco; she had a new faint stirring of interest in life, in the future. The day was sunny, and she could see the coast clearly. It was a bold, hard coast—the high, wooded hills falling away to yellow-brown cliffs, and below the cliffs the great rollers hitting and going up into the quick whiteness of spray as suddenly as if they had exploded. She could not see a village, or a house, or a field. Strangely enough, in spite of all the ranches and towns farther inland, this mountainous coast still looked as deserted as it had on that first day when the *Spanish Belle* had poked her nose in through the fog around the dark forest of Point Pinos.

The *Spanish Belle*—she thought of the long Cape Horn voyage and of all those years when she had been Captain Peleg's daughter and had lived always with the thought of the sea. Sometimes she had felt almost like a traitor to the family—the first one who had gone inland to live among the hills. It was good to get back to the sea. For the first time since Daniel's death she began to feel strong and calm again—strong and calm enough even to think back, step by step, over what had happened.

What struck her was the seeming inevitability of it all. From the time when she had visited poor Jerry Graham and found him dying each step had merely led on to the next step. There seemed to have been little choice, only a few points at which she had made conscious decisions, except in minor matters. And what proved it was that the end had been so different from anything which she had planned or wished. She had started things, and then the forces which she released had taken charge, and hurried and hurled her along with them. It was the same when she looked farther back. During the years of revolution and conquest and gold-rush she, like other people, had been merely thrown about by powers outside of her. But even earlier it had been the same, if more subtly. The most momentous action of her life had certainly been her elopement with Juan, and she could hardly even say that she had made that decision. Apart from the fact that her emotions had seemed to have control of her as if they were external forces, she could remember that she had actually gone down the ladder with the feeling of still being able to change her mind and return if she wished.

Perhaps, she thought, all this was because she had lived in California, where everything happened largely and violently and marvellously, where one could imagine without much difficulty that just beyond the horizon-line the Flying Island menaced from the sky and the Giants of Brobdingnag walked with a tread more than elephantine.

She had thought of the geography of *Gulliver's Travels* so often that at times it became real for her. After all, it was only a fantasy. Yet a fantasy too might be real; a symbol might be truer than actuality. If so, the analogy would hold not only for California. It must mean that somewhere just over the horizon of all human experience lurked an unknown region of gigantic and hovering forces, distorting and misdirecting the projects of the human will. . . .

A gentleman was apologizing and saying the proper things for taking the chair beside her. She saw that it was Sir Robert Tyneman, the English sportsman, returning now to England from his second expedition after grizzly bears and bighorn. She had met him some dozen times perhaps, and had known that he was to be on the *Magdalena*; now she felt definitely glad to see him again. That must be another sign that she was already renewing her interest in life; since the time of her troubles she had always felt a tendency to shrink from people.

It was remarkable how soon they were talking as if they were old friends. Partly, she supposed, it was the comparative isolation of being shipmates. There was just the suggestion of a common danger. Sea-voyages always had a touch of hazard, and now rumour ran that a Confederate cruiser, masked under Mexican colours, was going to put out from Mazatlán, intercept them, and make off with the million dollars in Californian gold which the *Magdalena* was reputed to be carrying.

And Sir Robert remembered Guito; spoke very highly of what a good companion he had been on the fishing trip into Mendocino County, and predicted that he would make an excellent cavalry officer. Judith felt herself warming as he praised her son.

Sir Robert was still tall and ruddy and hawk-nosed, just as she remembered him; but his temples were definitely greyer. He must be fifty years old, she supposed. She noticed again his left hand with the two fingers missing, and she thought how he had eased himself gently into the deck-chair to keep from hurting his stiff right leg, which made him walk with a limp. All at once she recognized a certain wistfulness about his face, and she knew why he had come to sit beside her and why she could talk to him so easily. He too had suffered, and was lonely and uncertain of life. Why else indeed, she thought, should a man of his age, half crippled, go off into the wilderness to face charging grizzlies and stalk mountain-sheep? She felt a renewed sense of human companionship.

For a long time her illness and her sorrow had turned her inward upon herself. Now she felt that here was some one else who needed sympathy, and strangely enough, of all persons, this seemingly self-sufficient Englishman. She began to ask questions, to draw him out;

and by the way he responded she knew that she must have been right.

He had been born, he told her, second son of a baronet, and had taken a commission in the Indian army. He began to tell of a campaign; now and then he paused, as if afraid of boring her, but she nodded him on. She knew little of the geography, and the place-names were a mere rattle of unintelligible syllables. But she had a sense of vast hot plains and of a little army of British and sepoys moving up against a greater and well-appointed army of tall, bearded men who could outfight the sepoys and almost outfight the British. The cannon sounded and the battle joined.

"I started that day." he said, 'a young hearty man and a captain and a younger son; and by evening I was a major and a baronet and an old man and a cripple. For both our majors were killed; and, as it happened, that same day my older brother broke his neck at a fence in Yorkshire.

"They rolled back our first attack, and my sepoys almost broke. My fingers were smashed, but I tied up the hand and kept on, for we had lost so many officers that it was touch and go that the whole centre would cave in. Then they fought on the flanks all afternoon while we lay in a nullah—'gulch,' you would call it—and their guns pounded us, and I bit my lips for the pain of my fingers. At evening two companies of British moved in to stiffen us, and we went at them again and broke their centre, and I got the grape-shot in my knee.

"So I got back to England an old man and a cripple fifteen years ago, and my younger brother's wife has worried ever since for fear I should marry and my children should cut hers out of the inheritance."

Then she told him something of herself. And, as had happened many times before, she swung round to the old problem·

"During all those years we lived with the Indians I thought how fine it would be when civilization came. And then when it came it was worse, more dangerous and brutal, than what we had before."

"But, my dear lady," he said, "you haven't ever really seen civilization; California isn't civilized, or even America. You ought to come to England."

It was the first time he had assumed that patronizing air which she so hated in the English; she bristled sharply, recalling something of what she had read:

"What about the London slums, and the Lancashire mill-towns?"

It should have been a hit, but it rolled off harmlessly from his self-assurance.

"Oh," he said, "but those fellows that run factories aren't civilized either"

Civilization! She made a gesture of despair. What was the use of civilization if it was such a delicate flower as only to root in a few English country-houses? And could civilization itself, even, escape the giants and the Flying Island?

"But that idea of coming to England, you know—not bad," he went on, becoming friendly again as he dropped his air of assurance. "You could come to Tonby; we have big parties and my sisters keep house for me."

They sat there talking until it began to grow dusk. Once as he looked at her she had a quick feeling of self-consciousness such as she had not known in years. Before she thought she had put up her hand and fluffed her hair a little. In this dusk, she remembered, against the darkness of her mourning costume it must be showing up almost like a light; it had always been her best point.

She went below to get ready for dinner. In the tiny mirror in her cabin she was surprised to see that in some way she looked younger; there was a new touch of colour and life in her cheeks. Sea air, she thought, and then laughed. Why had he said that his younger brother had three sons, so that the family needed no more heirs? She remembered herself in the little cabin of the *Spanish Belle*. But she shook her head sharply; that was twenty-five years ago.

She liked Sir Robert. It was not interest in his position or his wealth. She who had ruled Rancho Amarillo from the midst of its spreading leagues! She who had been the wife of Mr Melton of San Francisco! What by comparison would it be to displace the Misses Tyneman at Tonby and be a mere baronet's lady in a countryside that swarmed, so to speak, with countesses? Well, imagination

would run on, just as if one were not a grandmother, with a pain in the side.

There was no need to think so far ahead. At least it was pleasant to have him on the steamer. It was good to have a new interest, even though it might be nothing more than the amiable philandering of two congenial people well advanced in middle age.

◆───◆

SIR ROBERT WOKE UP WITH A SNAP, knowing that something had happened. It was a soldier's habit. This time he could not tell for a moment what it was that had waked him. Then he realized that the engines had stopped. Well, it was the business of those engineer fellows to get them going again; they had stopped once yesterday too, and only one wheel had been working since that time.

The *Magdalena* gave a wallowing roll, and slowly came up again. Naturally, with the engines stopped, she had turned broadside to the waves and was rolling in the troughs. In a minute they would get a sail or two up, and bring her back to her course. He heard men running about the deck. The next roll was as bad as the one before; and in spite of having been several days at sea he felt a twinge of sickness. He was a good sailor, as landsmen went, but he couldn't stand much of this. It was dawn already, he realized; he might as well get dressed and go on deck, out of the stuffy cabin. The steamer must be off the Lower Californian coast now— a very good distance off, he hoped, with this wind and the engines temperamental.

It was only when he got on deck that he suddenly knew that there was danger. Not a mile away, perhaps, surf was spouting. Towards the south-west, where there should have been open ocean, he followed with his eyes a long rocky headland. The ship was embayed. With this stiff north-wester driving them dead ashore and the engines stopped it might be nasty. He was too much of a landlubber to know how they had got into such a fix, but there were still wisps of fog floating about, and he could imagine that in the misty night, with an inshore wind and possibly a current, the steamer had simply got off her course. It could happen that way, he knew. One of the Atlantic liners had piled up not so long ago, somewhere on the Newfoundland coast, or Nova Scotia perhaps. The papers had been full of it; quite a few passengers had been drowned.

How they came to be here was not very important. It mattered more how they were going to get out of the fix. The *Magdalena* had sail up now on all her three stumpy masts, and the captain was obviously trying to head her up enough into the wind to clear the point and get into open sea again. Probably that was all there was to it, and the captain had gone back to bed; and any moment the engineers might get the engines started, so that the *Magdalena* could steer in any direction they wanted.

There were almost no other passengers on deck. Sir Robert went as far forward as he was allowed, and watched with interest the course of the *Magdalena* with respect to the point of land. Before long his interest changed to anxiety. He didn't have to be a seaman to tell that the ship was losing. They were getting closer to the headland, and they seemed closer to shore on the beam as well as ahead. She would have to try the other tack.

He was right in his prediction, but he was a little appalled to notice how much the ship lost before she could put about and head off in the other direction, right for the mainland of Lower California. He looked towards land, across the starboard rail this time. Far off were low dome-like hills, barren and uninhabited-looking. Closer to shore were what looked like sand-dunes. There was a beach, but whether sand or shingle he couldn't tell. A little off-shore there seemed to be a broken reef or line of rocks, some few above water, but most of them showing merely as the waves smashed upon them. When the rollers hit these rocks the spray rose in great spouts; and where the rollers went up the beach they died in a long turmoil of white water. Beautiful under some conditions, he thought, but definitely ugly just now.

More passengers had come on deck; the confusion of the ship's going about must have roused them. Sir Robert decided that he would call Mrs Melton; he didn't like the look of things.

As he went down the companion-way, a woman came rushing up, half-clothed and screaming.

" Damn' fool! " he thought. " I suppose it's starting."

He waited outside the cabin while she dressed. It seemed a very intimate thing to do, but he was afraid that the confusion might grow so great that he would not be able to find her. Stewards and pursers were hurrying about, saying that there was no danger, and by their own excitement and pale faces only adding to the sense of emergency. Men—there were not many women aboard—came scurrying along in various stages of dressing and in various stages of panic.

He was glad that Mrs Melton did not take long to dress. She came out all in black, of course; the black only serving to set off her hair more magnificently. He couldn't resist giving her an admiring glance. By Jove, there wasn't any panic about her, and she had high colour in her cheeks! She looked like the kind of person she was—one who had looked death in the face before. No nonsense about her clothes either; she hadn't put on a ridiculous big hoop-skirt, and she had a long serviceble-looking cloak about her shoulders. She did not break out like some silly young thing either, saying, "How completely exciting! Are we going to have a shipwreck?"

In fact, she did not say anything at all She held out her hand to him, as if they might have been old comrades going into battle together. But as he took the hand he was very conscious that it was a woman's, smaller and softer.

"There may be some trouble," he said. "We'd better go on deck."

It was a ridiculous understatement, he realized, especially when at that very moment a frightened man came hurrying by in nothing but his nightgown.

All she said was "Yes." But he saw a quick light spring up in her eyes, and she gave a curious little toss of her head so that the loose wisps of her white hair shook about.

He led the way towards the deck. By Jove, she was a woman! She blossomed out more now in the moment of danger than she ever had before. All the time he had talked to her in the last few days he had felt a certain dullness about her mood, as if she were a person who had lived her life and was merely waiting for the end. Sometimes he knew she was in physical pain. Now he had a sudden vision of her framed in the old arched doorway at Tonby, greeting visitors.

On deck he felt immediately that the game was up. The spouting rollers were closer; the mainland was ahead. The ship was just on the point of putting about once more. The deck was in confusion; passengers were running everywhere, and mates and seamen were pushing them out of the way roughly. Some people were already crawling into the boats. He fished some life-preservers from under a bench; there were both cork and tin ones. He took the cork ones, remembering now very clearly that in the wreck of the *Iona* many people had been lost because the tin life-preservers leaked and became dead weights to drag a person down.

As he came back he was surprised at the look of scorn on her face.

" The old tub! " she said. " I wish I had the *Spanish Belle* and a dozen good men from Boston and Salem and Marblehead. You should have seen the *Spanish Belle* work up to windward."

" You know the sea? " he asked in surprise.

" Generations back. I was the first Hingham who ever went out into the cow-country. This old thing is built for a steamer; her masts are too short, and she's too long for her beam to handle with sail. In this wind she loses more when she goes about than she gains on the tack."

Sir Robert felt a little chagrined; after all, as a man and an Englishman he had naturally assumed that he would know more than she about ships.

" Well, what are our chances then? "

" They may get the engines going, or the wind may fall. Or an anchor may hold, although this doesn't look like a place for good holding-ground."

" There are the boats."

" Yes, but a couple of them will be swamped, trying to launch them in this sea. Besides, they never have enough boats for all the passengers and crew. Lewis—he's in marine insurance, you know— says it's criminal the way they run these steamers, on account of the competition." She paused. " We have a chance too, I suppose, that the ship may strike and hold together, at least for a while, and then in the end we have the life-preservers. What chance has a person in a life-preserver, do you think, among those rocks there? "

" Just about even I should say. You might hit a gap between

them and be rolled up the sand. Or a big wave might lift you right over the rocks—or it might smash you right against them."

There was a new lot of men on deck now, their clothing and faces dark with grease and coal-dust—stokers and engine-room men. Perhaps the engineers were still at work, but it looked as if there would be little hope from that source.

The deck-hands were taking sail off her now; probably the captain was going to try the anchors. Forward, they were getting a boat over the side amid a wild milling of passengers.

" You ought to get into that boat," he said. " There aren't many women aboard; you'll have first chance."

" I don't like the look of that sea," she said. Then she shrugged her shoulders a little. " Or, to tell the truth, I'd just as soon stay here with you for company. It's a matter of chances anyway—like all life and death. I might get drowned if I went in the boat, and I may go through the breakers safe in my life-preserver."

The boat had got away safely; they could see it bucking the heavy sea precariously, but well handled and making progress towards a break in the reef. But the next boat was swamped in the launching, and the water was full of screaming people, some floating in life-preservers, some swimming, and some clinging desperately to the boat.

" You see! " she said, looking at him as if in justification of herself.

They were standing in a little corner of the deck which no one seemed to want. The ship's stern was towards the rocks now; he supposed that this was because there was an anchor out. But it was probably dragging. Certainly the rocks seemed closer. The ship was pitching horribly, and they had to cling to a railing. He had a feeling that things were going to happen fast. He put his arm around her shoulders as if to steady her, but really because he felt that they were two human beings very much alone in perhaps their last hour and much in need of each other's sympathy. Yet although she was not so much shorter than he, by a certain feeling of slightness about her shoulders he was again very conscious that she was a woman.

" You don't seem to care much," he said, " one way or the other."

" No, I suppose not. There were plenty of times when I would have seen to it that I was sitting in that first boat. But now the children are grown, and Juan and Daniel are both gone—and there's my pain in the side. It's hurting me this minute; not that that matters. I should rather enjoy fooling it. But I'll still keep on my life-preserver, even though I won't fight for a place in the boat."

They were so close in now that as he looked aft he thought they might strike any moment. Would it be smashed, he wondered, or would the ship settle gently in sand and then lift with the next wave to strike again?

" I feel it would be a good way to go," she spoke again. " My father and any number of Hinghams before him went down in salt water."

" Frankly, it doesn't appeal to me. The Tynemans run to breaking their necks at hunting, or having their heads shot off at Fontenoy and Talavera and Lord knows where else."

They exchanged messages just in case one of them got through and the other didn't. On account of the inheritance it would be a good thing for every one to be sure that he was out of the way. They agreed to try to keep together in the water.

For a few seconds the pitching and the confusion was worse than ever. They held on, without being able to talk, but once he heard her saying :

" It's ripe, not dead."

He knew that she must be thinking of something which had happened far off and a long time ago.

As the ship struck it heeled suddenly to starboard. A great wave swept the deck, and Sir Robert felt himself lifted and hurled off irresistibly in a whirl of wreckage. When he came to the surface he could not see her. . . .

Sir Robert had volunteered to watch over the line of dead which the sailors were gathering in from the surf and laying side by side in a hollow of the sand-dunes above the beach. The sun was breaking through the clouds now, and the worst of the storm seemed to be over; but his wet clothes still clung to him, chillingly. He had to grit his teeth, but he managed to keep his feet. He had hit a rock somewhere coming in, and from the way it felt his arm might be broken; it was worse than the time he had been shot in the hand, and he was an older man now.

The Americans were handling things well, he thought—apart, that is, from their letting the disaster happen in the first place. They had a fire burning, and people were drying themselves about it. Others were gathering wreckage, food or fuel or whatever might be useful. The ship's surgeon was at work in an improvised hospital. Runners had been sent inland to find some ranch from which a rider could spur northward for help. And it was not more than an hour from the time the ship had struck.

There were not as many dead as he would have expected, but now and then sailors came bearing some one whom they had picked out of the boil of the surf. He was standing at the other end of the line when they brought Judith's body.

He walked over, just as he did with each body, to be sure that it was laid out properly and decently. He tried to tell himself that after all he had hardly known her for more than a few days.

The sailors had laid her on her right side. If she had suffered any wounds among the rocks they did not show in that position. She looked pale and peaceful. The sunlight glinted on her white hair.

At that moment half a dozen horsemen came galloping down through the sand-dunes. Most of them went on towards the beach, but three dismounted, took off their big hats, crossed themselves, and stood looking in awe at the line of dead lying between the sand-dunes. They were dark men, like Indians, with long knives in their boots—vaqueros from some ranch, Sir Robert supposed.

They talked in Spanish, speaking with hushed voices. He could not understand much of it. Only, when they looked at the white hair a new touch of awe seemed to come upon them, and he caught the words:

" *Señora ... blanca.*"

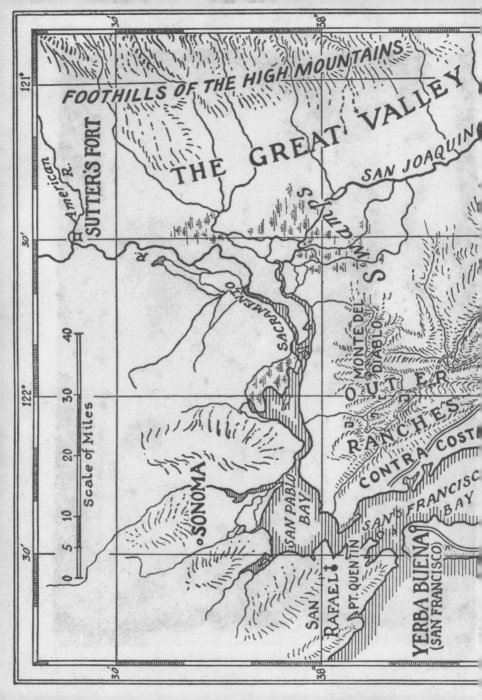